In a world of privilege, where the heart's every desire can be bought, Claire discovered the price of loving a man who both attracted and frightened her....

"You'll stay with me tonight," Quentin said when they were alone. His arms were around her, one hand caressing the back of her neck. "I don't like your leaving. And driving back alone."

"Which is it? You don't like my leaving because you want me next to you when you wake up, or you're worried about my safety?"

"Both." He kissed her, slipping her short silver jacket off her shoulders. In an instant, Claire was open and longing, straining toward him. He could always arouse her to a tumult of desire simply by wrapping her within his arms and holding her as if she were fastened to him, a vessel he could enter and leave at will. He knew it; he felt her desire, and Claire saw him smile as he led her to his bedroom.

"But I can't stay," she said, forcing the words through the fog of her desire. "I want to be home when Emma wakes up."

He shook his head. "Not tonight." He began to unbutton her dress....

Books by Judith Michael

Deceptions
Possessions
Private Affairs
Inheritance
A Ruling Passion
Sleeping Beauty
Pot of Gold

Published by POCKET BOOKS

> Most Pocket Books are available at special quantity discounts for bulk purchases for sales promotions, premiums or fund raising. Special books or book excerpts can also be created to fit specific needs.
>
> For details write the office of the Vice President of Special Markets, Pocket Books, 1230 Avenue of the Americas, New York, New York 10020.

JUDITH MICHAEL

POT OF GOLD

POCKET BOOKS
New York   London   Toronto   Sydney   Tokyo   Singapore

The sale of this book without its cover is unauthorized. If you purchased this book without a cover, you should be aware that it was reported to the publisher as "unsold and destroyed." Neither the author nor the publisher has received payment for the sale of this "stripped book."

This book is a work of fiction. Names, characters, places and incidents are either products of the author's imagination or are used fictitiously. Any resemblance to actual events or locales or persons, living or dead, is entirely coincidental.

POCKET BOOKS, a division of Simon & Schuster Inc.
1230 Avenue of the Americas, New York, NY 10020

Copyright © 1993 by JM Productions, Ltd.

All rights reserved, including the right to reproduce this book or portions thereof in any form whatsoever. For information address Pocket Books, 1230 Avenue of the Americas, New York, NY 10020

ISBN: 0-671-88600-2

Pocket Books Export Edition Printing May 1994

POCKET and colophon are registered trademarks of Simon & Schuster Inc.

Printed in the U.S.A.

for our fellow travelers and researchers—
David and Judy Schramm
Alan and Leila Marcus
Larry and Carolyn Zaroff

POT OF GOLD

1

CLAIRE won the lottery on a Wednesday afternoon in May, the same afternoon that Emma graduated from high school, the dog ran away, and the landlord raised the rent.

They had returned to the apartment after the graduation ceremony, Emma beautiful and glowing in the buttercup-yellow dress Claire had finished sewing just the night before, and Claire was glancing through the mail while Emma looked for the dog. "Toby!" she called, looking into the two small bedrooms and the tiny, windowless kitchen. "Mother, Toby isn't here."

"Didn't we let him out before we left this morning?" Claire asked absently. She was opening an envelope with the landlord's name rubber-stamped in the corner. "He's probably in the yard; he never goes very far without you. Fifty dollars a month!" she exclaimed, reading the landlord's letter. "We can't pay that much more; he knows we can't."

"Toby!" Emma called through the window. She went outside, to the street and the small side yard, calling as she went. "He's gone," she told Claire when she came back. "He's never done that, he's never run off, ever since I found him in the alley that day. Maybe he found a girlfriend; I saw him with another dog last week. I guess he doesn't need me

1

anymore." She stood in the middle of the cramped living room, her eyes wide. "Everything's changing at once."

"We'll have to move," Claire murmured. A smaller apartment, a different neighborhood, maybe a little closer to her job. But perhaps not as safe ... She brushed it aside. She'd gotten around Danbury by herself for seventeen years; she wouldn't start worrying about it now. And she could make do with fewer rooms now that Emma had her scholarship and would begin college in the fall. But I'll still need a place for her, Claire thought; she'll come home all the time. She belongs here; she needs me. We need each other.

And then the doorbell rang.

"Someone found Toby," Emma said happily. "I knew he couldn't be gone for—"

But the door was flung open and Gina flew into the room, waving a piece of paper. "Look at this! I think this is it, Claire; I think you did it; I think you won. Look!"

"Won?" Claire repeated.

"Where's your ticket?" Gina demanded. She was tall, with black hair combed close to her head in a gleaming cap, strong features, and large hands that gestured extravagantly when she spoke, especially when she was excited. "The one you bought yesterday when we were at the drugstore. Come on, Claire, wake up. Where's your ticket?"

"What ticket?" Emma asked.

"The lottery," Claire said. She was standing still, transfixed, staring at Gina. "You really think—"

"Where is it?" Gina repeated.

"Mother, are you still buying those things?" Emma asked. "They're such a rip-off; I thought you'd stopped a long time ago."

Claire opened her purse. For years, it had been a game she played with herself, buying one lottery ticket a week, on the same day at the same time: the only time she let herself drift into fantasies. "It's in here somewhere," she murmured.

Gina snatched the bag from her and with the familiarity of fifteen years of friendship riffled through it until she found a

POT OF GOLD

small blue ticket. "This is it, I remember the first number was twenty and I thought I remembered the rest—oh, God, I can't stand the tension—twenty," she read, looking from the ticket to the paper in her hand. "It was on the afternoon news and I wrote them down, just in case . . . and it sounded right . . . three, ninety-eight, nine, two, zero." She looked up, a grin breaking over her face. "Bingo." Her voice rose. "Bingo, bingo, bingo. Claire, do you know what you've done?"

"She won?" Emma burst out.

"She won!" Gina held out the ticket. "She won the lottery! Your wonderful, marvelous, magical mother won the whole goddamn thing!"

"How much?" Emma asked, looking from Gina to Claire.

Stunned, Claire opened her mouth to speak, but nothing came out.

"Tell her! Tell her!" Gina said, almost dancing in her excitement.

There was a pause. "Sixty million dollars," Claire said, forcing out the impossible words.

Emma gave a shriek and sat down hard on a small hassock.

"Say it again," Gina urged. "I love the sound of it. Sixty. Million. Dollars. Can you believe it? God, Claire, I didn't even want to stop at the drugstore and you insisted; you said you'd just be a minute, just long enough to buy a ticket. Good Lord, what if you'd listened to me? I could have ruined your life. Thank God you didn't pay any attention. I can't believe it. *Sixty million.* . . . Of course they don't give it to you all at once, do they? They've got all kinds of rules."

"They pay it over twenty years," Claire said. Her voice sounded as if it were coming from someone else, and she felt numb. These things happened to other people, not to her; nothing ever happened to her. So how could this be real?

Emma's eyes widened, as if making the numbers smaller made them more real. "We get three million dollars a year for twenty years?"

Claire met her eyes and both of them burst into nervous

laughter. And in that moment it began to seem real. "Wait, I have to think," Claire said. "No, I'm sure we don't get that much; I'm pretty sure they take out the taxes first. I guess that's about a third. But still . . ."

"Still not too shabby," Gina said mockingly. "A couple million a year for twenty years? I wouldn't sneeze at that. And, hey, that's only a start, you know? I mean, if you wanted to, you could probably borrow the moon right now; who'd turn you down when they know you'll be getting that check every year from the State of Connecticut? Claire, you can do anything you want!"

"We're rich," Emma said softly. Her eyes were shining. "Rich, rich, rich. I never even dreamed of anything like this."

"So, what's next?" Gina asked. "How do you get it, Claire?"

Claire was listening to the echo of Emma's voice caressing the word *rich*. "What?" she asked.

"How do you get the money? Do they mail you a check for two million dollars, or give it to you with their hot little hand?"

"I don't know. I can't even imagine . . ." The sense of reality faded in and out; one minute a wild excitement filled her, and the next a sinking feeling that this was about someone else: Gina had made a mistake, the television announcer had made a mistake, someone else had won the lottery, not Claire, never Claire, because Claire never won anything.

"Maybe they mail it," Gina said.

"How can they?" Emma asked. "Do they know Mother's won?"

"Oh, God, of course not," Gina groaned. "We're standing around talking . . . Claire, you've got to call them."

"Call who?" Emma asked.

"There should be a number," Claire said. "Probably on the ticket. If I could see it . . ."

Gina gave her the ticket, and while Claire found the number and made the call, she pulled Emma to her feet and

POT OF GOLD

hugged her. "Your whole life is going to change. Every single thing you do ... *everything* is going to change. Can you believe it? Can you wait for it all to start? You'll never be the same again."

"Sure we will," said Claire, hanging up the telephone. Her face was bright; excitement bubbled within her. She had won; it was real. An anonymous voice on the telephone had confirmed her winning number and told her she was the only winner. She would get it all. Claire Goddard had just won sixty million dollars. She smiled at Emma and Gina, loving them, loving everyone, loving the whole world. "We'll have a lot of money but that won't change the way we are. We'll be the same people we've always been, and we'll have the same best friends."

"*Nothing's* going to be the same for you. It's going to be ..." Gina frowned, then sighed. "Well, maybe. Why not? Stranger things have happened. We've been through a lot together, maybe we can survive sixty million dollars. So, okay, what are you going to do first?"

"Pay all my bills," Claire said promptly. "Pay off the loan on the car—"

"Oh, Mother," Emma groaned. "What are we going to do that's *exciting?*"

The telephone rang and Emma picked it up.

"Claire Goddard?" said a woman at top speed. "This is Myrna Hess of the *Danbury Times* and I want to interview you about winning the lottery; I can be there in ten minutes, less, actually; I'd just like to be sure you don't talk to anybody else before I—"

"This isn't Claire Goddard," Emma finally managed to say. "I'll let you talk to her—"

"No, wait—are you a friend? A relative?"

"I'm her daughter."

"Oh, terrific, there's a family. Tell your mother I'll be right over. Remember: Myrna Hess, *Danbury Times*, don't talk to anybody else." She hung up.

"There's a reporter coming here," Emma said to Claire. "How did they find out so fast?"

"There are probably reporters who hang around waiting to see who wins these things," Gina said. "There's no such thing as privacy anymore. Anyway, this is probably the biggest thing to hit this town since the Revolutionary War."

The doorbell rang and Claire answered it.

"Hi, Parker Webb, Mrs. Goddard, from the *Danbury Times*." Behind him, a photographer's flash went off, and when the blinding light faded, both men were inside the apartment. "How does it feel to be one of the richest women in America?"

"I don't know," Claire said. "Someone else called from your paper, some woman. She said she was on her way over here. Are you together?"

"Myrna called already?" he asked. "Sharp girl, Myrna. But not sharp enough to beat Parker Webb. This is really going to tick her off."

"Mrs. Goddard," said a tall, dark-haired woman at the open door, "I'm Barbara Mayfair from WCDC television; I'm so excited to meet you, it's absolutely fantastic that you won the whole thing. Our viewers are going to be so thrilled to see you in the flesh."

"In the flesh?" Claire repeated.

"You know, in person; viewers see famous people on television, they think they're seeing them in person. It's the closest they'll ever get, after all. Now we want to tape an interview for tonight's news, but it's awfully crowded in here. If we could clear it out a little bit . . ."

"She wants us gone," said Parker Webb amiably to Claire. "Barbie, sweetie, wait your turn; we were here first. Mrs. Goddard, how did you feel when you heard you'd won six-ty mill-ion dollars?"

"I didn't believe it," Claire said.

"But now you do." Webb saw the blue ticket that Emma had picked up and he swooped down on her hand. "Sid, get a shot of this. . . . Hey, Sid, you with me?"

POT OF GOLD

The photographer had discovered Emma's glowing beauty and was circling the room, taking pictures of her while she watched her mother. She did not acknowledge his presence, but she was leaning slightly toward him, a small smile on her perfect lips.

"Right," said the photographer when Webb nudged him with his foot. "The ticket. Would you hold it up, Miss . . . uh . . . Miss?"

Emma held up the ticket but was silent.

"So have you decided what you're going to buy first?" Webb asked Claire.

"A butler to answer the door," said Claire.

Barbara Mayfair laughed. Emma smiled with her, and the photographer took another picture.

"Why would you do that?" asked Webb.

"So I don't get surprised by people wanting interviews."

"You mean I should have called first. Right, right, but we've been through that. I mean, if I'd called first, Myrna would have beaten me, and Barbie, too, and I'd never live that down. So, come on, Mrs. Goddard, could we do an interview? This is crucial; I mean, it's pretty dry country around here, Danbury, for a reporter; there's not a lot that you could call spectacular, you know. But this is a terrific story; this is history in the making. Fifteen minutes, I promise, and then Barbie can have her turn."

A small, round woman burst into the room. "For God's sake, Parker, you could have checked with me!"

"Hi, Myrna," Webb said. "Next time somebody in town wins the lottery, it's yours, word of honor."

Myrna looked from Claire to Gina and then locked onto Emma. "You're the daughter? You said you wouldn't talk to anybody else."

"I didn't promise anything," Emma protested.

"She didn't," said Gina, speaking up for the first time.

"You a relative?" Myrna asked Gina.

The telephone rang and Claire answered it. She looked at Webb. "Do you know Mick Wales?"

7

JUDITH MICHAEL

"The *Norwalk Crier*. They've got it already? Listen, we've got to get moving."

"Here's the *New York Post*," Barbara Mayfair said. She leaned against the wall, making room for her cameraman beside her, while a short, gray-haired man with thick, black-rimmed glasses sidled past them. "Skip Farley," he said to Claire, though she still held the telephone to her ear. "Are you giving out numbers?"

"Just get in line," said Webb testily. "I'm outa here as soon as I get my interview."

"I can't see you today," Claire said into the telephone to Mick Wales. "Call tomorrow morning." She hung up and gestured toward a small dining table surrounded by four hardback chairs in a corner of the room. "You sit there," she said to Skip Farley and Myrna Hess and Barbara Mayfair and her cameraman, "while I talk to . . . I'm sorry; I've forgotten—"

"Parker Webb." He looked at the others, considering whether to demand that they leave, but Claire, understanding him, shook her head. "If you all hear what I say, I won't have to keep repeating it. That should speed things up. Emma and I haven't had a minute to be alone and think about all this."

Myrna cornered Gina. "I can talk to you, right? You're a relative? Or a friend? How did you find out she'd won? What did she say?"

Gina shook her head. "Whatever Claire wants in the paper, she'll tell you."

Reluctantly, Webb had taken a seat in a corner of the couch. Claire took a chair opposite him. She looked at Emma, gazing dreamily out the window, and suddenly realized her daughter was posing, subtly changing her body position and her smile while pretending to ignore the photographer who was stalking her, coming in close, then moving back, silent, totally absorbed in her beauty. It was like a dance, Claire thought; in a strange way, the young girl and the man and his camera were locked together, almost merging, almost one. It made Claire nervous and inexplicably fearful. "That's enough," she said sharply to the photographer. Then, more quietly, she said, "I think you have enough."

"Jesus, Sid, get with it," muttered Webb. "A couple shots of the apartment—outside, too—and then get Mrs. Goddard. Talking, holding the ticket, you know, the whole bit. So let's start at the beginning," he said to Claire. "You and your daughter have lived here for . . ."

"Seventeen years," Claire said.

"Just the two of you? You're divorced? Widowed?"

"Divorced."

"Recently?"

"A long time ago."

"How long?"

"That has nothing to do with your story."

"Just a round number. It would help a lot. Five years? Ten?" He paused. "Seventeen?"

"It has nothing to do with your story," she said again. She was uncomfortable. She had never been interviewed by anyone except for a job. But this was the press. Strangers reading about her, looking at her picture, and Emma's, too. She ought to be witty and clever and in control of the interview. She had no idea how people did that. "What else do you want to know?"

"Human interest, Mrs. Goddard; readers want to know all about you. How old are you?"

"Thirty-five."

"And Emma is . . . ?"

"Seventeen."

"Uh-huh. How many lottery tickets did you buy?"

"One."

"*One?* You won with *one* ticket?"

"It only takes one," Claire said, smiling.

"Yeah, but to increase your odds . . ."

"I didn't think of winning. I only thought of playing."

"Didn't think of winning," he muttered, writing it down. "So why keep buying them?"

JUDITH MICHAEL

"I told you: it was a game. It was a way to dream. I like to dream."

The door opened and a thin, gray-haired woman scanned the room and picked out Claire. "Mrs. Goddard? Blanche Eagle; I write for the *New York Times*. They asked me—"

"Over there," Webb said, waving toward the group in the corner. "Shoulda sold tickets," he muttered.

"Mrs. Goddard, the *New York Times*," said Blanche Eagle, emphasizing it. "Surely you'd rather talk to us than a local paper."

"I promised Mr. Webb," said Claire. "He was here first. If you don't want to wait—"

"For a short while," she said briefly, and joined the others at the table.

"Likes to dream," Webb murmured, writing. "So, okay, Mrs. Goddard, what do you like to dream about? I mean, what's going to change now that you've won this pile of money?"

"I told you. I haven't decided."

"Yeah, but give me a break, Mrs. Goddard; there's no story in haven't decided. Okay, then, let's talk about . . . well, what do you eat for breakfast, and is *that* going to change?"

"I eat toast with raspberry jam, and coffee, and I may try scrambled eggs with truffles," Claire said, surprising herself. She remembered reading about that in a magazine a long time ago; had she really been pining for it all these years?

"Great," Webb said cheerfully. He wrote swiftly. "What about your work? You work here in town?"

"At Danbury Graphics."

"Doing?"

"I'm an assistant to a design team."

"Designing what?"

"Everything from books to cereal boxes."

"No kidding. You study that in college?"

"Yes."

"Where?"

"Western Connecticut State University."

"And you got your degree when?"

"I didn't graduate. I had to go to work."

He nodded. "So are you going to quit?"

"Quit my job? I don't know. I haven't thought about it."

"Well, could you now? I mean, just *having* sixty million bucks means your life is different, right?"

"Yes, but . . ." Claire sighed. "I guess I'd like to own a house, and my car is ten years old, so I'll probably get a new one."

"Mercedes? BMW? Porsche?"

"I don't know. I haven't—"

"You haven't thought about it. How about a plane?"

"A *plane?*"

"You going to buy one? A little jet?"

"No, I can't imagine why I would."

"So you can get where you're going on your schedule, not theirs. You are going to be doing some traveling, right?"

"Oh. Of course we will."

"Haven't done much up to now, right?"

"We haven't done any; we never had the money."

"Better and better. So, travel. And then clothes for all the travel. What kind of clothes do you dream about?"

Abruptly, Claire stood up. "I'm sorry, Mr. Webb, I'm not very good at this. These are all too personal. I never talk about myself; I don't like to do it. I can't do it. And I'm not going to start now."

Webb turned to Emma. "How do you feel about your mother winning the lottery?"

"Rich and happy," Emma said.

"You going to ask your mother for lots of new clothes, your own car, jewelry, furs, whatever?"

"I don't know. I guess we'll talk about all those things. Mother has always bought me more than she's bought herself."

"Nice," murmured Webb, writing. "You still planning to go to college?"

Surprised, Emma said, "Why wouldn't I?"

JUDITH MICHAEL

"Well, you don't need to learn a profession now; you could just play."

"I'm not going to college for a profession. I'm going so I can learn about the world and meet wonderful people and ... grow up."

"Nice," Webb murmured again. Nice girl, he thought; stunningly beautiful but not aware of the impact she made, or at least not arrogant about it. Nice voice, low and soft; she probably never shouted. And all that red-gold hair, long, uncombed looking, like the girls did these days, probably took a lot of time to get it that way, and an incredible smile. And great eyes, huge, with the longest lashes Webb had ever seen. And she liked her mother. In fact, Webb thought suddenly, she looked like her mother, too.

He glanced at Claire, who was watching Emma. Hard to tell exactly, because the daughter had all that youth and bubbly kind of energy, and that gorgeous hair, while her mother looked more withdrawn, subdued, sort of ... pinched. And her hair was dark brown, though it had glints of red whenever the camera flash went off, and she wore it straight to her shoulders, not good with her narrow face. But the face was good, Webb thought; she and Emma both had the same terrific, wide mouth; they both had eyes like brown velvet beneath level brows; and, though Emma was taller—tall for a girl—they both were slender. And if the mother would straighten up, get rid of that slouch, she could have the same easy grace Emma had, almost like a dancer.

"I want some shots of the two of you," Webb said. "Okay? Sid, let's do it."

"One or two," said Claire, "and then we'll be done."

Webb nodded. "I've got enough to put something together. You'll have to go through it again for Barbie, you know, and her cameraman."

Claire glanced behind her. "I think we should wait ..."

"No, there's really nothing to it," Barbara Mayfair said, standing up in alarm. "You'll talk to me just the way you talked to Parker, just the two of us, chatting. Or three of us;

I'd like Emma, too. You won't even notice the camera. It's just a conversation."

"And I only have a few questions," said Blanche Eagle. "I do have a cameraman who should be here any minute, but we won't take long. We'll be gone before you know it."

"So will I," said the man from the *New York Post*. "I take my own photos; we'll talk a little and then I'll be out of here."

Claire looked at their intent faces. They seemed to fill every corner of her small living room. There had never been this many people here at once; even when she entertained friends, she only invited two or three at a time; she didn't like crowds. Emma seemed perfectly comfortable; she liked the attention and the excitement of a crowded room. But Claire felt hemmed in and pressured; she felt the familiar outlines of her life sliding away; and, for just a moment, she wished none of this was happening. But she couldn't wish for that; this was the most exciting thing that had ever happened to her. And these people had a job to do. She knew all about that: a job that had to be done, a deadline that had to be met. She understood their urgency.

"You want some help?" Gina asked.

Gratefully, Claire smiled. "I'm fine, Gina, thanks." She turned to the others. "Let's get started. As long as it doesn't take too long."

She posed with Emma at the side of the room, then sat at the dining room table and waited for the reporters to begin their questions. How odd it seemed; she sat in her own home, talking about herself to strangers. She remembered Emma's wide eyes when she realized Toby was gone. *Everything's changing at once.* Not everything, she reflected. Money doesn't make such a huge difference in people's lives, not if they don't let it. There are lots of things Emma and I won't change, like love and caring and trusting each other, and being closer to each other than to anyone else, and loving our friends. It's just that everything will be so much easier from now on. We can handle whatever happens; we can handle anything. That's what money does: we can handle anything.

And pretty soon everyone will be gone and this whole circus will be over, and no one will pay any attention to us anymore. Why should they? No one ever noticed us before, and there won't be any reason for anyone to notice us later on, as soon as a more interesting story comes along. We'll just fade into the background.

The telephone rang, there was a knock at the door, and beyond the living room window another television truck pulled up and men and women jumped out.

"Welcome to fame and fortune," said Parker Webb, grinning, and he gave a smart salute.

2

THE car was a white Mercedes with white leather upholstery. Emma said it looked like an ambulance. "Well, pick another color, then," Claire said. And when Emma put an admiring hand on the hood of a cherry red, two-seat Mercedes sports car with black leather upholstery, Claire nodded casually to the salesman. "We'll take that one, too."

Emma gasped. "Two cars?"

"I thought you might like to have one at college."

"I *might* like—? Oh, Mother!" Emma threw her arms around Claire. "You're incredible. Everything's incredible. Isn't everything totally off-the-wall incredible?"

"Off-the-wall," Claire echoed with a smile. Whatever it meant, it sounded weird enough to describe the way she felt: not quite awake, not quite real, not quite firm on her feet. It was as if a river of excitement was always flowing inside her, beneath everything she did. At first, six days ago, when she won the money, it had been a trickle; now, one minute it was like a rushing river, so powerful she wanted to fling her arms out and embrace the whole, wonderful world that lay before her, the next minute subsiding as she began to wonder if someone would soon call to tell her it was a mistake after all. But then her elation flared up again and she felt as if she and

Emma were on a merry-go-round, reaching out to grab all the possibilities that spun by, close enough to touch.

Close enough to touch. So close, so close; it was like a giddy kind of dream. Because, for the first time, the whole world—not just her narrow corner of it but all of it—had been flung open to her, its doors and pathways beckoning, no longer closed. If she needed proof, she had only to look around, at the paneled walls of the Mercedes salesman's office, at her checkbook open on the desk in front of her and her pen beside it, and at the salesman himself, figuring the total cost, being very quiet, fearing that if he said one wrong word he would lose his sale: two luxury cars in twenty minutes, without any more effort than opening the door for two women to get in and take a test drive.

Claire picked up her pen. She had bought it that morning because her two Bic pens were both dry and she wanted something a little nicer. When the clerk showed her this one, she had tried not to gasp at the price; she had lowered her head as she tried it out on his white pad of paper and told herself that it would last at least ten years and that would only be thirty-five dollars a year, and that was nothing. Oh, no, that's the old way of thinking, a voice inside her said. You don't have to amortize anything anymore; you're rich enough to buy whatever you want, whatever it costs and however long it lasts. And so she had lifted her head and told the clerk she would take it. It was heavy and black, with a white star on the end, and it filled from an ink bottle. She liked the old-fashioned feel of it, and the smooth flow from its pure gold tip. It nestled snugly in her purse, her new purse, sewn of leather so soft she marveled each time she opened it. She had bought the purse right after buying the pen, and it had taken her a much shorter time than with the pen: she was getting used to high prices.

And now these things were hers, these things that had been behind all the doors closed to her when she had had barely enough money to support herself and Emma. And so now she began to believe that the treasures of the world really could be hers, the myriad treasures she had thought were only for other people. The river of excitement cascaded through her and she shivered with wonder and anticipation. There was so much she hadn't discovered yet; she and Emma were just getting started.

She had quit her job three days before. She had driven to work on Monday morning as usual, but instead of taking her seat at her drawing table, she had gone to the office of Sal Hefner, the head of her group, and told him she was leaving.

"Well, I can't say I'm surprised," he said. "And it's better all around; you wouldn't be happy here, plugging away, when you could be out somewhere playing. That's what I'd do if I'd won that pile. You figured out where you're going to do your playing yet?"

"No," Claire said. "There are more things I haven't done than things I have. I'm not sure where to start."

"Well, you'll figure it out," he said, his attention wandering. Claire no longer worked for him; she was no longer of interest to him. He held out his hand. "If you ever want to come back—you know, something could go wrong—let us know. You've always done good work here. Well, now, you have yourself a great time and spend up a storm; we'll miss you, but you'll be too busy to give us a thought."

"No, I won't," Claire said. She felt a sense of loss. "I'll miss all of you." They shook hands formally, as if they had not been working together for fourteen years. "I'll come back and say hello," she said.

"You'll be too busy," he said again. "No time for your old life." He turned back to his drawing table. "Bye, now, Claire; you have yourself a ball."

"He's jealous," Gina said that night at dinner. Emma was out with her friends, and Gina and Claire sat a long time over coffee. "He sees you going off to have a whole new life, and he's just where he was last week and where he'll be next week, and that doesn't exactly make him ecstatic."

"I suppose," Claire said. "But he seemed to go out of his

way to make it seem that he was pushing me out, not the other way around."

"Well, I guess that was what he wanted." There was a pause. "And, you know, you really will be too busy to think about them, or go back and say hello. You really will be having a ball and they won't seem so important to you as they do right now."

Claire shook her head. "Everybody thinks I'm going to change. I'm not, Gina."

"Well, that's good enough for me." Gina raised her wineglass. "To not changing."

"Or, at least, to keeping the good things," Claire said. "I don't ever want to lose those."

"You don't ever have to lose anything again," Gina said. "Maybe that's a new definition of being rich. Unless you lose the money. You won't, will you? Have you got it out there making more money for you?"

"I've got a money manager doing that." Claire shook her head. "Can you imagine me talking about a money manager?"

"Who is he?"

"She. Olivia d'Oro. I asked at my bank, and they gave me a few names and I chose the one woman on the list. She's only twenty-nine, which I found scary at first, but she really knows a lot and I like her."

"In New York?"

"She's with an investment firm in New York and she has an office in Greenwich."

"So what's she doing with your money?"

"Well, nothing risky; I told her I'm not looking for risk. She'll do the standard things—invest in stocks and bonds and treasury notes—and she's already set up an interest-bearing checking account with a minimum balance of a hundred thousand dollars."

Gina tilted her head. "So what happens if you spend more than that? Your checks bounce?"

"No. Well, I haven't done it—I can't imagine spending

that much at one time—but Olivia said she's set up an automatic transfer system, so that if I do, more money goes into the checking account to cover what I've spent."

"Good God, it's a perpetual-motion machine. Or the fountain of youth, only in this case, of course, it's money."

Claire flushed. "I know it sounds incredible. It is incredible. I don't even really believe it. Except that I keep spending and my checks don't bounce."

"Well, that's a paradise if I ever heard of one." Gina walked around the table to put her arms around Claire and hug her. "I think it's fantastic and nobody deserves it more; you've waited a long time for good things to happen. Enjoy, enjoy; I love being part of your paradise."

Paradise, Claire thought a few days later as she lay in bed after the alarm went off. She had set it the night before, as usual, forgetting that she would not need it, and now she stretched luxuriously, listening to the music softly filling her room and thinking of being free to do whatever she wanted. This is me, she thought. She still had to keep saying it. This is me, lying in bed, not going to work, thinking of all the things I can do with my day. This is me, with money, and time. Both of them. Money and time.

She slipped out of bed and stood at the window, looking at the clear sky. A good day to go shopping, she thought. But then she looked down and saw the people, sitting, standing, waiting in their cars. They had appeared soon after the first newspaper story came out about the lottery, and each day it seemed there were more. They knocked on her door and rang her doorbell, or they just sat and watched her windows and waited. Claire shivered. It was a little like being haunted. She looked up again, at the sky. "I can't think about it," she said aloud. "I can't do anything about it." And she turned away and went to dress for breakfast. She and Emma were going shopping.

"Clothes," she said, and once again she felt a shiver of anticipation: shopping for clothes was still a rare treat; she had always sewn most of their clothes. "I thought we'd go to Simone's."

"I've never even been inside there," Emma said. "I was afraid of being tempted."

"I want you to be tempted," Claire said. "I think we'd better park a block away until our new cars are delivered; I can't imagine Simone being impressed with what we're driving now."

Simone was short and stout, with gray hair pulled into a tight knot high on her head, and a French accent she had worked very hard not to lose in her fifty years in America. She took the measure of Claire and Emma with one swift, cold glance, head to toe, and looked just past Claire as she spoke. "If Madame pleases, she and Mademoiselle would be altogether happier in the shops in the mall, a short distance away; my small shop is not to her style."

Or budget, is what you mean, thought Claire angrily. No one was more snobbish, she thought, than the people who served the wealthy, and how did these snobs know, in an instant, who was wealthy and who was not? She would have turned and left, but she saw Emma flush with embarrassment, and she knew she could not let her daughter be defeated by this woman. "My daughter needs clothes for college," she said, her voice as cold as Simone's. "And I need a number of things for a cruise." *A cruise? Am I going on a cruise? When did I decide that?* "If you have nothing that pleases us, then of course we'll go elsewhere, probably to Lisbeth's in Norwalk, but we do prefer to support local establishments whenever possible, and as long as we're here, we'll look at what you can show us."

Emma looked at her mother in amazement, and Claire felt a rush of pride. She never spoke up that way; she always backed away from confrontation, fearing she might hurt someone's feelings or be made to feel inadequate. But as she watched Simone become flustered and confused, she thought, this could get to be fun, and added severely, "We don't have much time."

POT OF GOLD

Simone gave her a second appraising look and slowly nodded. "As Madame wishes." She took in Emma's figure, and Claire's, gauging size, height, weight. "If you will wait in here," she said, sweeping aside a curtain to reveal a boudoirlike dressing room lined on three sides with mirrors and furnished with a love seat and two armchairs, and a small desk in a corner. She beckoned to an assistant. "Do Madame and Mademoiselle wish tea? Or coffee? Or perhaps wine?"

"Tea," Claire said, surprising herself again; she seldom drank tea. "Jasmine." She saw Emma's quick look, but she waited until Simone and her assistant had left to break into a low laugh. "I don't know where I got that," she said. "It just appeared."

"Like the cruise?" Emma asked.

"Like the cruise."

"To where?"

"I have no idea." Another assistant appeared with a tea service and a covered silver tray and set them on the desk. Emma lifted the damask napkin to reveal petits fours and tiny cucumber sandwiches. She bit into one and looked around as she chewed. The room was as large as the living room in their apartment; the furniture was velvet, with fringes, the carpet was deep and smooth, and the wall that was not mirrored was hung with silk lit by soft lights in gold and silver sconces. The air was fragrant with flowers, and the rippling notes of a harpsichord floated to a high ceiling painted pale blue, like a summer sky. "Let's move in," Emma whispered, and they laughed softly together, afraid of seeming unsophisticated, but reveling in Simone's luxury, hugging to themselves the feeling that they were really here and could afford to be. This is me, Claire thought again. This is us.

Simone and her assistant appeared carrying clothing, which they spread on the armchairs and hung on a rod along one of the mirrored walls. Then they stood back, letting Claire and Emma gaze at the brilliant fabrics and colors flung with seeming carelessness before them. Claire felt as if she had walked into a kaleidoscope. She was surrounded by swirls of color and texture, the frail scent of silk and linen and wool, the deep shadows of velvet and satin, the gleam of buttons, the delicate curves of ruffles, and the sharp edges of perfectly pressed collars and cuffs. She had done their sewing for so many years that she knew fabrics, and she knew, without even touching them, how fine were the wools and chiffons, the silks with their slight nubby accents, and the crisp linens, woven of the finest threads. A soft sigh broke from her. She had often picked up bolts of fabrics such as these, but she had always set them down again, gently, reluctantly, never able to afford them. She put out her hand and lifted the sleeve of a blouse, as soft as a cloud.

"Ah, Madame appreciates fine fabric," said Simone. "Now, if Madame and Mademoiselle will care to try on those which please them, there is a second dressing room next to this one."

Claire and Emma exchanged a quick, startled glance. Was that what wealthy women did, go off into their own dressing rooms so that no one would see them undress? Didn't they like to share with their daughters? Oh, the hell with it, Claire thought; I can't help it if Simone doesn't approve of everything we do. "We'll stay here," she said casually. "We like to try on clothes together."

Emma drew a sharp, astonished breath at the prices, but Claire forced herself to ignore them. She tried on dresses and suits, blouses, sweaters, skirts and pants, and never looked at a price tag. It doesn't matter, she told herself; I can afford whatever I want. But once, when Simone was out of the room looking for a particular belt for a particular pair of pants, she could not help herself; trying on a midnight blue dress with a beaded jacket, she took a quick glance at the price tag and saw that the number was over five thousand dollars. She felt faint. What am I doing? she thought wildly. I can't buy this; it takes me two months to earn that much at work.

But she did not work anymore. And every year for twenty years she would receive a check for four hundred times the price of this dress. She turned in place, looking at her many reflections. The beaded jacket sparkled as she turned. She looked different; there seemed to be a new lift to her head. The dress set off her shoulders and long, narrow waist and showed off her legs. Her eyes were bright. And she was smiling. "I'll take it," she murmured to herself.

"Mother, how about this?" Emma posed before the mirror, swirling a short chiffon skirt topped by a gold metallic sweater. Her red-gold hair fell in long waves down her back, tendrils curled over her forehead, and her face was flushed with excitement. She was tall and slim and vibrantly beautiful. "You look like a model," Claire said.

"I feel like one. Oh, this is fantastic; what a fantastic day. Shall we buy this?"

"Yes, of course." The words came easily. *Yes, of course.* It was so simple; after years of saying *We can't afford it,* everything was possible. Exhilaration leaped within her: she could do whatever she wanted for Emma, for herself, for their friends, for anyone and anything she pleased. "And all the other things you tried on; they were all perfect on you."

"You, too," Emma said. "You look so incredible. Are you buying everything?"

"I don't think so." Claire looked around. "There were a few things I didn't like. Not many, though; I can't believe how good most things looked on me."

"Do you think she's psychic?" Emma asked. "How does she know what's going to be right for us?"

"It's her job. And she's very good at it."

Simone came back, carrying the belt and also cashmere sweaters and matching scarves in a spectrum of colors. "Madame wanted something like this?"

"Yes, that's exactly what I wanted." Claire ran her hand over the soft, silky sweaters. "I'll take the black and the red and the white. Can you put them in gift boxes?"

"Of course," said Simone, faintly reproving.

Flushing slightly, Claire said, "And necklaces and earrings; we'll need those, too."

"I have only a few," Simone said. "For the rest, I will

send you to a friend; you know Elfin Elias, in Westport? My favorite jeweler in the country. Now I bring the little bit I have."

When she was gone, Emma stroked the sweaters Simone had left on a chair. "The blue is stunning, isn't it?"

"Yes, and it's a good color for you," Claire said. "Add it to your other things."

"Really? Oh, sensational. I'll wear it with that necklace we found at the flea market, remember?"

"We'll buy a new necklace. I like that name, don't you? Elfin Elias. It sounds like someone who lives in the woods and chants all day. Do you think Gina will like these? The red and black are for her; I thought the white would look good on Molly."

"They'll love them, you know they will. I guess they don't have a lot of cashmere. If any."

"Probably not. I can't wait to see their faces when they open the boxes. Oh, we ought to take a few of these scarves, too. There are some people at work who've been so nice to me; I'd like to give them something. And maybe a couple of extras, just to have." Claire wished she had more people to buy presents for. But she couldn't exactly pass silk scarves out to the grocery and pharmacy clerks who always waited on her, or the mailman or the newspaper delivery boy or the friendly crossing guard near her office who always wanted to chat as she held back traffic for the children on their way to school. "I guess I have everything," she said reluctantly.

When the seamstress had finished pinning the clothes that needed altering, and the assistant had hung everything else in garment bags printed with Simone's name in bold calligraphy, Claire took out her checkbook. Simone, apologizing and waving her hands as if trying to brush away all regulations, had to call Claire's bank, to verify her account for the total sum. In a blissful three hours, Claire had spent on herself and Emma what it would have taken her two years to earn at Danbury Graphics. "Mother, we can't carry all this," Emma whispered.

POT OF GOLD

"No, no!" Simone cried. "Mademoiselle does not carry from Simone's! All will be delivered to your home by late afternoon, even those which need alterations. You need not worry; I will see to it myself."

When there was proven wealth, Claire thought, Simone handled a young woman's ignorance gently. Had there been no money, she would have treated Emma's naïveté with contempt, if she would have deigned to respond to it at all. Emma's beauty and sweetness made no impression on Simone: all her ideas about the world were based on who had money and how much they had.

"She kind of oozes, doesn't she?" Emma asked as they walked to their car a block away. "Like her voice is coated in honey and it sort of slithers all over you. She's got a weird smile, too, like she practices in front of a mirror. But she's got the most incredible clothes; I can't believe what we bought. It must have cost a fortune."

"Not quite; we still have a little bit left," said Claire, and they laughed, because in this unreal world they knew they could never run out of money again.

They stopped for lunch in a restaurant famous for its escargot and starched waiters, and then they met the realtor Claire had called and drove with him to look at three houses. "No, no, no," Claire said as they stood in front of the third house. "I told you on the telephone: it has to be light and bright, with big rooms and at least two fireplaces—I want one in my bedroom—and lots of closets and a big yard; I've never had a garden."

"You didn't give me a price range, you know," the realtor said, "and I thought . . . something modest . . ."

"I don't want anything modest," said Claire. "I told you what I wanted when I called you: something large and bright and absolutely wonderful."

The realtor contemplated her, trying to figure out what she was worth and how seriously he should treat her. "Perhaps you'd like to build a house, to get exactly what you want," he said.

"I don't have time," Claire replied. "I want it now. All of it. Now that—"

"Claire Goddard," the realtor burst out, suddenly making the connection with the story he had read in the *Danbury Times*. "That *was* your picture, wasn't it? You should have told me . . . I would have . . . my goodness, there are so many houses that are perfect for . . . this is very exciting for me, just to meet you . . . you should have told me who you were!"

"And then you would have taken me seriously?" Claire asked coldly. She got in her car. "Never mind; I'll find someone else to show us some houses." And with Emma staring, she started the car.

"Mrs. Goddard, please!" the realtor cried. He put his hands on Claire's open window. "I have a house in Wilton to show you, right now. Please take a few minutes; it's exactly what you want. I didn't fully understand . . . I apologize for that . . . but I promise you'll be delighted with this house; if you'll let me drive you there, I even have the key, from an earlier showing. Please, please let me show it to you and your daughter."

For the first time, Claire knew what it was to have financial power over another person. He shouldn't plead, she thought; it makes him seem weak. But she could remember herself, in past years, pleading for a chance to prove herself in a new job. He is weak, she reflected; and so was I. It's money that makes us strong. She inclined her head. "We'll look at it. But we'll drive our own car; you can show us the way."

The house was at the end of a long driveway that curved through a dense forest of towering oak and sycamore trees. It was pure white, with a steeply pitched roof and a high front door recessed behind a porch with a welcoming lantern. Large paned windows looked across a wide lawn bordered by a low stone wall, beyond which the trees stood tall, their branches entwined, keeping out the intruding world. Gardens bordered the front walk and spread in flowing beds around the sides of the house and to the back, where a small brook flowed.

POT OF GOLD

Inside, oak floors reflected the streaming sunlight, and pure white spindles supported a maple banister that swept up to the second floor, where four bedrooms, one of them with a fireplace, led off a broad landing. In a corner bedroom, Emma looked through the windows at the trees and the clear blue sky and the bubbling stream flowing through the early-summer gardens, filled with lilies, late irises, and the first roses, and sighed. "This is the most beautiful place in the world."

The realtor led Claire through the house. "There's a lot of house here for a million and a quarter, a lot of house, Mrs. Goddard. A brand-new kitchen, as you see, granite and wood, a nice combination of modern and traditional, and all of it very efficient; and in here you see how the fireplace opens to both the library and the living room, and the library doors open to make one large space; you and your daughter can entertain in grand style. And now the lower level: family room, laundry room, wine cellar, exercise room, cedar closets and storage areas, and the terrace off the kitchen and dining room, all in flagstones, of course, so very Wilton, you know; this is definitely a New England house but with all the special warmth of a—"

"Yes," Claire said. "You were right; I like it very much. I'll take it."

The realtor stared at her. "You mean you're making an offer?"

"No, I don't want to bother with that. I'll take it. I want to move in as soon as possible."

He cleared his throat. "The price is one million two hundred fifty thousand dollars."

"Yes, I heard you say that."

"Well, of course it's a perfect house for you and your daughter, a truly extraordinary house . . ."

Claire did not hear him go on; she was thinking about paying for the house. She had thought she would simply write a check, as she had for the cars, but she realized she could not do that. She had bought two very expensive cars and a great many clothes, and now she had to furnish this house. And she only had two million dollars, or a little less after her recent purchases, to get her through the next eleven months and twenty-four days. *Only* two million dollars, she thought suddenly; *only, only, only.* What in heaven's name has happened to me that I'm talking about *only* two million dollars?

She closed her eyes. This was crazy. One minute she had thought she would never be able to spend it all, and now she could not afford to write a check and was thinking *only.* A rueful laugh broke from her. She had a lot of sorting out to do.

The realtor was talking about the title search and a mortgage—"unless," he added delicately, "you're thinking of using cash."

"No, I'll want a mortgage," she said. "We can speed that up, and I'm sure the title search won't take too long. Unless there's a problem . . . ?" The realtor shook his head. "Then, if you'll call my money manager"—she took Olivia d'Oro's card from her purse and gave it to him—"she'll arrange for the deposit and everything else."

"Earnest money," the realtor said. He beamed at her. "You're buying a very special house, Mrs. Goddard. I know you'll be very happy here."

"Yes," Claire said. "We will be." She found Emma still upstairs. "Where would you like your bed?" She was so excited by what she had done, and amazed at herself, that her voice trembled.

Emma swung around. "You *bought* it? Already?"

"Yes, why not? Isn't it wonderful? I've always dreamt about a house just like this. You do like it, don't you?"

"*Like* it? Oh, Mother!"

"Well, then . . ."

"But . . . oh, I don't know . . . I guess I just thought . . . you know, a *house* . . . it's so *big.* I thought you talked to lots of people before you bought anything so . . . well, but, you didn't, with the cars, so . . ."

Terror struck Claire. From the heights of exhilaration she plunged into doubt. Of course she should have talked to someone. Gina or her money manager or someone from work who knew about buying houses. She should have gotten good advice and thought it over carefully and then, if it all seemed all right, gone ahead.

But I don't want to be careful, she said to herself. I've been careful. I know all about that. Things are different now; everything is different now. And so am I and so is the way I do things, and I want this house.

"Anyway, it is wonderful," Emma said dreamily, turning in place. "This incredible room. I can have friends over; there's plenty of room for two beds. And I can have parties in the family room—we could dance there, too—oh, wouldn't it be fantastic to have a jukebox? No, they probably cost a fortune."

"Of course we'll buy one," Claire said. "What a good idea."

"Really? We really can get one? Mother, you're unbelievable. Every time I say *I want* you say it's all right." Emma whirled around the empty room. "I'll have lots of parties. I hate the way everybody hangs out at the mall all the time; they just vegetate and make out. It's so boring and stupid. But I could have everybody here, and we could do anything we want. That whole family room . . . it's like a private little club; it has a bar and everything."

"Of course," said Claire again. She listened to Emma's bubbling voice and thought she sounded young and happy and innocent, but, often, in the past year, she had wondered just how innocent Emma really was. So many times she had wanted to ask her if she was still a virgin, but there never seemed to be a good time for it, or for the leisurely, probing kind of conversation between a mother and daughter that could lead to revelations about sex, drugs, alcohol, all the things that made news on television, but seemed to have nothing to do with them. Emma had told her once, almost casually, that she and her friends did not use drugs—in fact, that she had never even tried them—and Claire believed her, but she knew that could change; there were always experiments for young people to indulge in that never made it to conversations at home. Emma never seemed to be anxious for advice, so she did not ask the questions that would give Claire a chance to offer thoughtful, wise answers and in so doing perhaps find out how experienced her daughter was. She could not imagine Emma in bed with a man, but now she wondered what Emma meant by saying she and her friends could do anything they wanted in their private little club. What did they want to do?

"We'll have to see about the private club," she said. "We'll probably make some rules for it."

Emma's mouth turned down at the corners. "You mean you don't trust me?"

"Of course I trust you." Instantly, Claire backed away from any possible confrontation. Emma's willfulness flared up and disappeared as swiftly as the sweep of a searchlight against the sky, but Claire always pretended it was not there. "We won't have any rules you can't be happy with, Emma. I'm not trying to make you unhappy, you know."

"I know, I know, it's just that everything's sort of ... wild, isn't it? I can't believe we'll be living here, moving out of ... oh." Her face clouded over. "What about Toby? What if he comes home and we're gone?"

"I don't know. I guess I haven't thought much about Toby the last few days."

"Neither have I, isn't that awful? I've been so busy.... Could we leave a note on the door with our new address? Then if anybody finds him, they could call us."

"Of course," Claire said. "But you know, Emma, it doesn't seem likely that he'll come back. What do you think about buying another dog?"

Emma nodded. "I guess. I mean, sure. He's probably found a new family, anyway. At least I hope he has." She stood for a moment, and then her brief melancholy was gone; too much was happening for her to be anything but exuberant. She turned and hugged her mother. "I'm so excited about all

POT OF GOLD

this . . . this room, this house, the cars, the clothes . . . can you imagine life being any more incredibly spectacular?"

Claire watched Emma walk around the room, appraising spaces as if calculating them for furniture. How had she had such a daughter? Emma had all the energy and volatility and strong will that Claire lacked. If someone painted Emma's portrait, it would be in vivid oils, while Claire's would be in watercolors. Well, maybe at my age that's all I can expect, Claire reflected, but she was not really sure she felt that way, not nearly as sure as she would have been a week ago. The thought came to her, still unformed but taking root for the first time, that maybe she had settled too easily for the life she had; maybe she should have gone after more.

"This is so cool," Emma said, "being able to do whatever we want. We're really good at it, aren't we? Even though we haven't had any practice."

"We're fast learners," Claire said. "Come on, now, we have a lot to do."

"Like what? Where are we going?"

"I don't know. I'm so restless, I just want to keep moving, keep doing things." They left the house and watched the realtor lock the door behind them. Next time I'll do it myself, Claire thought, with my own key. She and Emma got into their car. "Shall we go to Joseph's? We both need shoes."

"Could we just go home?" Emma asked. "I thought I'd call Marie and Lorna and have them come over and look at my new clothes, and then take them for a drive when my car comes. He said it might be this afternoon, late. Oh, I can't wait to see Lorna and Marie's faces; they'll die. This has been the most wonderful day. Everything was wonderful, but you're the best; you're spectacular. Are you really going on a cruise?"

"I might. Why not? I've been reading about them for years, and they always sound wonderful; I guess it's been in my mind for a long time. Why don't we go together? Wouldn't it be a good thing to do before you go off to school?"

"Oh." Emma looked blank for a moment, and Claire knew she was thinking of the new house, and parties and barbecues with friends for this last summer before college, the last time they would be together before they went separate ways.

"If you'd rather not—"

"No, it might be fun," Emma said. "They're pretty short, aren't they? I mean, it wouldn't be for all summer."

"Oh, no, we'd find one that was just for a week or two. It depends on what we want, how we feel about it." Claire turned into their street and parked at the curb. The people were still there, scattered about, waiting; she could not tell if they were the same ones she had seen in the morning, or if new ones had come during the day. But she was not looking at them; she was looking at the house where she had lived for so many years. Once, probably, it had been grand—a three-story frame house on a corner near the center of Danbury—but now Claire was shocked at how shabby it was. She had stopped looking at it long ago, but now she saw that the window frames were peeling; the paint on the outside walls was faded and flaking; the narrow strip of land at the side and front was hard-packed dirt, with a few scraggly blades of grass that still struggled to grow each spring. How did we stay here so long? she wondered.

She opened the car door, absently watching a stooped man with a gray beard and long curling hair who was loping across the street toward them. "Mrs. Goddard?" he said. "You are Mrs. Goddard, aren't you, I recognized you from your picture in the paper. If you could give me just a minute . . ." He pulled a thick wad of paper from his jacket pocket. "I won't take much of your time, but this is so important—it could be the most important thing you do with your money—it's a way of revolutionizing the way automobiles are built, and I only need . . . Mrs. Goddard!"

"I'm sorry," Claire said over her shoulder as she fled up the front walk with Emma just behind her. "I can't help you."

POT OF GOLD

"But I need the money and you have it!" the man cried, following them. "You could make millions more; you'd be the major stockholder!"

"The only stockholder," Claire murmured. He was close behind her, and she walked faster, glancing over her shoulder. The others were watching, getting ready to follow him: all those who sat on the curbing or in their parked cars with the doors open, all of them waiting. She felt besieged, and guilty. They all seemed so needy.

The van from Simone's pulled up, and the driver began piling garment bags on his arm. "Oh, I'll help with those," Emma said, and ran back to the van.

"Claire Goddard, I'm so *pleased* to meet you," said a young woman with owl-like rimless glasses and sandy hair flying in all directions. She planted herself in Claire's path, her hand outstretched. "My name is Heredity Semple, you've probably heard of me, maybe you've even seen me, I do performance art at the Dollhouse Club downtown, I've never been able to get to Broadway or even off-Broadway, it takes connections, you know, but you can't get them unless you live in New York for a year or two and meet people, I think if I had fifty thousand dollars I could do it . . . oh, wait," she said as Claire dodged around her outstretched hand. "I could do it for forty, or even thirty, but . . . listen, I've got to do this!"

"Please go away," Claire said helplessly. "I can't help you." The man who had been following her stood close by, listening.

"You can help!" Heredity cried. "You've got to! I mean, it's my destiny, and you can help! You've got all that money!"

Claire ran up the stairs as Emma came up the walk. "Excuse me," she said, and slid past Heredity Semple to hold the door for the man from Simone's, almost invisible beneath his load of garment bags. While he walked up the stairs, with Heredity Semple on his heels, Emma opened the mailbox and pried out the envelopes that were jammed inside; she had never seen so much mail in their small box. "Mother, look," she said, climbing the stairs to their open door. The telephone rang and she heard Claire answer it.

"No, I don't," Claire said. "No, I have a money manager and I don't need a stockbroker. . . . No, I'm quite satisfied with the arrangement I have. . . . No, I am not interested in changing anything."

Heredity Semple was wandering around the living room. "Please go home," Claire said, and then the telephone rang again. "Yes," she said. " . . . What? You're not serious. No, I don't want to buy two plots in Fairfield Cemetery for me and my daughter. No!" She slammed down the telephone. "Go away or I'll call the police," she said angrily to Heredity Semple as the telephone rang again. "Yes," she said sharply. ". . . No, I don't want anything . . . oh. Well, I don't know. The Danbury Society of Firemen's Wives? I guess I might give money if I knew something about it. Send me some material and I'll look it over. . . . No, I'm not going to make a pledge. . . . No, really, I don't want to until I . . . look, it doesn't do any good to keep pushing; I want to read about it first."

She hung up, frustrated because she should have been more forceful. "We have to get an unlisted number," she said to the room at large.

"I put everything on the bed," said the man from Simone's, coming out of the bedroom. "There wasn't much room," he added disapprovingly, making them understand that Simone's clients did not usually live in such places. He stood still for a minute, then stalked out. Claire wondered if she should have tipped him. No, of course not, she thought, but she was not completely sure. There was so much she did not know.

The telephone rang beneath her hand, and without thinking, she picked it up.

"Mrs. Goddard, this is Morgan McAndrew of Silver and Gold in Darien; I just wanted to alert you to a delivery we're having made to your house, a selection of jewelry you can examine at your leisure and send back only that which you don't—"

"You're *sending* me jewelry? Why?"

"Our most valued customers prefer it," McAndrew said gently, as if giving a lesson. "You can try the various pieces with your own garments in the privacy of your home, think about what you want without interruptions or distractions. It eliminates the mundane aspect of shopping. I'll call you later today, to see if you have any questions or if you need other pieces from which to choose; our deliveryman will be waiting—"

"No!" Claire exclaimed. She cast a look around her small apartment, her bed and Emma's piled high with garment bags and boxes, the dining table covered with mail. What would she do with jewels and a deliveryman, waiting in the background? "I don't want any of it. Call him; tell him to turn around; I don't want it."

"But, Mrs. Goddard, we've put together a very special collection; we've even named a necklace the Lottery Necklace; it could be known as the Goddard Necklace if you decide you want it. Believe me, you won't see another collection like—"

Claire hung up.

"Mother," Emma said, standing at the door, "there's someone here from Braithwaite's, it's a fur store? They have a bunch of coats they thought you'd like to see."

"No," Claire said. In her mind she saw herself, and Emma, too, swept away by a tidal wave of people, each of them reaching out to tear off a piece of her winnings, and her life. "I don't want a fur coat. Not today, anyway. Just tell him no."

"But you should see the coats," Emma said. "They're unbelievable."

"Not here!" Claire cried. She saw the tidal wave flooding her apartment, drowning her. "Tell him no!"

"No," Emma said at the door. "Maybe we'll come in to your shop sometime. Not today. Today isn't a good time."

Claire saw Heredity Semple still hovering near the doorway. She picked up the telephone. "I'm calling the police."

"You wouldn't really do it," the young woman said. "I mean, I came in peace and love; all I want is money."

Claire pushed the numbered buttons slowly and deliberately.

"God, what a selfish bitch," Heredity Semple said, and left.

"Look at this," Emma said. She was sitting at the round dining table, opening letters. The table was covered with them. "Everybody wants money. Some guy wants you to pay his way to Africa so he can photograph some kind of rare snake, and there's a woman who says she needs half a million dollars to develop the perfect sugarless cake, and ... oh, listen, I love this one: somebody who says he's ninety-three and he wants to die in the house where he was born, but that's in Ireland, so he needs airfare and then he has to buy the house, he says, so he'll have a place to live, because he may not die right away; he might live to be a hundred like his father."

Claire laughed. "Maybe we should give all our mail to writers who are looking for plots." It was easier dealing with mail than with the people who pleaded with her on her doorstep. The telephone rang and, automatically, she answered it. "Yes, it is.... No, I'm not ... oh, well, yes, in fact I am interested in cruises. You can send me all the brochures you have. Particularly for any trips that don't include a telephone."

The doorbell rang. Claire did not move. "Aren't you going to answer it?" Emma asked.

"I don't think so. We shouldn't have talked to those reporters; we just should have kept quiet. I don't know what to say to people."

"Oh, Mother, if you just keep saying no, they'll get the idea after a while. I mean, they won't be hanging around forever. There must be other rich people they can haunt. You just have to be firm. I'll do it, if you want. You'd think they'd

POT OF GOLD

figure out that if we said yes to all of them, we wouldn't have any money left. But I guess they don't think of that." The doorbell rang again, firmly and persistently. "I'm going to answer it; I can't stand not knowing who's there."

Emma opened the door and looked down at the small woman who stood there, thin and frail-looking, but with her feet apart and firmly planted, as if she had rooted herself to the doorsill. Her face was a web of fine wrinkles and her eyes were as bright as marbles, peering up at Emma with instant approval. "Very nice," she said. "Very lovely." She held out a small hand speckled with brown spots and ridged with veins. "How do you do, my dear. We're related, though I'm not sure exactly how."

"I don't think so," Emma said cheerfully. "I don't have any relatives."

"Not true, not at all true; you have me. Hannah Goddard, my dear." Her hand was still outstretched, and Emma took it. "It's a pleasure to see you. You're a lovely girl, and I congratulate you on your great good fortune. I'm an aunt several times removed, or perhaps a cousin, it's so hard to keep track, you know. But I do know the connection is there. When I read about your mother in the newspaper, I knew without question the connection was there. I'd heard of her, you see, but I never knew where she was. One moment, my dear." She walked a few steps down the hall and came back, pushing before her a large suitcase that had been out of sight. "I lost my apartment in Philadelphia, my dear; they turned it into a condominium and told me I could buy it, but that was a joke; old women with small pensions don't buy condominiums. I'd planned to stay there forever, the rent was quite reasonable, perfect for an old woman who doesn't need much, but then everything changed, just about overnight. And then—such a stroke of luck—I read about your mother. I do congratulate you both; I rejoice at your good fortune. And of course I came as soon as I could."

She pushed the suitcase into the living room as Emma jumped out of the way. "Pleasant," she said, giving a swift look around, her glance pausing at the two bedrooms, visible through their open doors. "Very . . . cozy. But certainly not appropriate for someone with your assets. You'll be wanting something bigger now, much bigger, more bedrooms, larger rooms, probably some land, too, gardens and so on. And of course much brighter. I'm quite sure you won't be living here very much longer; you'll be anxious to move. And with three of us working at it, that won't be a chore at all."

Her bright eyes came to rest on Claire, who was standing beside the round dining table. "My dear Claire," Hannah said, extending her hand again as she walked across the room. "I'm Hannah. I've come to live with you."

3

THERE was no stopping her; she was like an ocean wave, sweeping everything before her, changing everything in her wake. "Good heavens, I never saw so much mail," she marveled, and began to collect the letters Emma had scattered over the dining table. "Money," she murmured, skimming one and then another and then a third. "Money and money and money. Do any of them congratulate you on your good fortune?"

"No," Claire said shortly. She was angry; she felt her house had been invaded, but when she thought about ordering Hannah to leave, the words would not come out. And it occurred to her that Hannah *was* the only stranger who had congratulated them on winning the lottery. A point in her favor, but not enough, she thought, and forced herself to speak. "I think you'd better—"

"You may want to save some of them," Hannah said, "as a souvenir. Of course you don't have much room, but just for a while.... I'm sure you have some grocery bags." She bustled into the tiny kitchen and opened the doors beneath the sink. "One. But that's all we need." She was sweeping the mail off the edge of the table into the paper bag when the doorbell rang.

Claire sighed and began to stand up. "I'll do it," Emma said. "I know how to say no."

"To what?" Hannah asked.

"The same thing as all the letters," Emma said. "Everybody wants money. Everybody thinks we can give them everything they want—" She stopped, her face flushed. "I don't mean you; I mean—"

"Of course you don't mean me," Hannah said brightly. "How could you, when I'm family? But you shouldn't have to be bothered by all this; let me take care of it. I was a bouncer, once." She was on her feet, already on her way to the door. "Yes?" she asked, beaming up at the man and woman standing there.

"Mrs. Goddard?" the man asked. "Wow, you don't look anything like your picture in the paper. Listen, we have to talk to you." He tried to edge his way into the room, but Hannah, her small, thin body amazingly firm, blocked him. "If we could come in . . ."

"No," said Hannah simply.

"Just for a few minutes . . ." He shoved his way past Hannah, pulling the young woman with him.

"Young *man!*" Hannah exclaimed.

"No, see, this is really urgent. Oh," he said, looking past Hannah. "*You're* Claire Goddard; I recognize you now. Look, Claire, this is the thing. I'm a painter and Liza's a photographer and we want to go to Paris to live a real artistic life and get ourselves launched, and we could do that if you'd be our patron. You know, like in the old days? I mean, if there hadn't been patrons, there wouldn't be a Beethoven or Mozart or Goya or, you know, all of them. We brought photos and slides for you to look at, and you can see what we do and then you could discover us, the same way people discovered Picasso and Monet."

"I'm sorry—" Claire began.

"No, look, it's not a lot of money, you know, just for a few years, and we'd pay you back when we got famous—"

"No," Claire said.

"Hey, listen, you've got this *fortune* and—"

"Young man." Hannah's chin was almost touching his chest as she edged him back toward the door. "Picasso and Monet and all their friends worked for their living and paid their bills with their paintings when they ran out of money. That is a kind of dedication you would do well to emulate; history demonstrates that it spurs the flowering of genius." She propelled him steadily backward, into the hallway. "You, too," she said to the young woman and swept her through the doorway with both hands. "I wish you both much success in Paris."

She closed the door and came back to the table.

"My goodness," said Emma.

Claire was gazing at her. How useful, she thought. And amusing. But who asked her to take over our lives? "Thank you," she said. "You did that very well, but Emma and I can manage—"

"He should not have gotten past me," Hannah said. There was a faint thread of desperation in her voice. "That will not happen again."

"You were a *bouncer*?" Emma asked.

"Oh, very briefly. Mostly I was a teacher; I taught—"

"But whom did you bounce?"

"A group of people who wanted to crash some meetings we were having. But there's nothing mysterious about being a bouncer, you know. You just have to believe in what you want more than the other person believes in what he wants. It's not muscle; it's strategy. I used that in teaching, too."

"Did you teach college?" Emma asked.

"Oh, no, my dear, I taught third grade, for forty years."

"Forty years!" Emma exclaimed. "You must have been bored out of your mind."

"Oh, no," Hannah said again, and smiled gently. "I loved third grade; the children have such curiosity and humor and love. Later they worry about being like everyone else and they lose so much of their spontaneity and creativity, but in third grade they're still quite simply themselves, and I loved helping them discover the world. Once in a while some of us would trade places and try other grades, all the way through high school, but I never liked any of them; I couldn't handle all those adolescent agonies and sexual tensions. When my third-grade children came to me for advice and comfort, I could always help them, even in groups. I miss that," she added, her voice falling away. "I miss helping people."

"Don't you have children of your own?" asked Emma.

"I never married, you see."

"Because you didn't want to?"

"Because it didn't happen," Hannah said quietly. "But I taught, and that gave me a chance to be useful, to be a part of other people's lives. I like that; I do like helping people; it really is what I do best."

Claire met Emma's eyes and saw that Emma would be no help in sending Hannah away. The three of them sat at the table, and the silence stretched out.

"I could help you move," Hannah said when the silence became unbearable. "You will be moving, won't you? To a larger apartment? Or a house?"

"We just bought a house," Emma said. "The most beautiful house in the world."

"Oh, wonderful," Hannah said. "A large house?"

"Huge," said Emma.

Hannah looked at her and then at Claire. Her eyes were bright, but her mouth trembled a little. She squared her shoulders. "Well, then, there's a lot of work to be done. I can't wait to see it; it's so exciting to take an empty house and make it your very own. I did that once, for a while, interior design, you know, making houses beautiful and livable, not just four walls and a bare floor. And I want to help shop for kitchen supplies, Claire; I'm considered a very good cook."

"Really?" Emma said. "Mother never liked to cook."

"How could she, after working all day?" Hannah asked. "Good cooking takes time and energy and creativity; it's too much to ask anyone to do it after a long day at work; to do it well is definitely a full-time job."

POT OF GOLD

What a kind way to put it, Claire thought, and her anger and irritation faded a little. But she isn't going to live with us, she thought; that's impossible. We're fine by ourselves, and we'll furnish our house by ourselves and live there by ourselves.

She glanced at Emma, who was listening to Hannah talk about a kitchen she had once designed. Emma's face was absorbed, like that of a child listening to a storyteller. She likes her, Claire thought. Both of us like her. She's a stranger who walked in here like all the other strangers . . .

But she wasn't like all the other strangers. Emma liked her. And there was something more: Emma trusted her. And so do I, Claire thought.

But that doesn't mean we have to take her in.

No, but she has no other place to live.

That isn't our problem.

But wasn't it a relief when she got rid of those people who stampeded their way in here?

Yes, and I believe she would do that again and again, and as many times as she had to. She would take care of us.

Claire thought of that with surprise. *She would take care of us.* There was something about Hannah that made her sure of that.

"Is that what you did in Philadelphia?" Emma asked. "You were a cook?"

Hannah stole a glance at her suitcase, still standing just inside the front door, unopened. She had been glancing at it frequently, hoping Claire and Emma would get the point and let her take it into the bedroom. She longed to unpack. One was never sure of staying until one had unpacked. But they kept her talking. "No, I only cooked for friends," she said. "They're all gone now: moved to warmer places or died. Sometimes both."

"And you designed their houses, too?" Emma asked.

Claire watched Hannah answer. She was beginning to seem interesting. She had an odd, formal way of speaking, her words as precise as small stepping-stones marching to the end of each sentence, and there was a kind of cadence to her speech, too, that was almost mesmerizing, as if she were telling a story. And she seemed to have a great many useful skills.

The door opened. "Oh, now, really," Hannah said in exasperation, and jumped up.

"Good afternoon, the door was open," said a bearded man. Two women and a young boy followed him in. "My name is Carter Morton, and I need to talk to Claire Goddard about a story in the *Norwalk Crier*."

"That's enough," Hannah said. She grasped the man's arm and began to turn him toward the door. "You're well-dressed and well-spoken; you ought to know enough not to barge in on a family—"

"One minute!" he said desperately. "That's all I ask." His gaze settled on Claire, he planted his feet and began to speak so rapidly they could barely make out his words. "I thought, with your good fortune, you might help us. You see, my boy needs medical treatment—this is my boy, Alan, and my wife, Pat, and my sister, Beth—and I lost my job a few months ago and my insurance went with it. The doctors say Alan has a good chance if he starts treatment right away, but it's very specialized and very expensive, and we thought we had no chance at all until we read about you, and so we came here because—"

"We didn't want to ask," Pat Morton said, her voice low and strained, her words tumbling out as rapidly as her husband's. "We don't beg, we've never had to, but he's only nine, and no one will loan us money and our savings are almost gone, and"—her voice broke—"we don't know what to do."

"What's wrong with him?" Hannah asked.

"He has leukemia. But childhood leukemia has a high cure rate, if you get it early and treat it properly."

"Where would you go?" Claire asked.

"Boston. That's where our doctor sent us. And the doctors there said we have a good chance; they told us that Alan has a life ahead of him. We all believe that. We do believe it. And we'll do whatever it takes to give that to him. We'll give him a life!"

Claire met Hannah's eyes. Hannah gave a tiny nod. "How much do you need?" Claire asked.

"We don't know," Carter Morton replied. "The doctors say, with all the treatments, it could be a hundred thousand dollars. Maybe more. Of course it would only be a loan, until I get another job and get back on my feet again, but I can't say how long it would take to pay it back. I haven't even got collateral or anything. Nothing but my word that I'd do my damnedest to pay back every penny, with whatever interest you set, however much it costs."

"We won't worry about collateral," Claire said, feeling confident because of Hannah's nod. "Or when you pay it back. Have the hospital send the bills to me."

Morton stared at her. "You'll do it?"

"Of course we'll do it," Hannah said energetically. "Now you write down your name and address and telephone number for us, and then you be off. You've done what you came for. Anyway, you have to get ready to go to Boston."

Claire and Emma exchanged a glance as Hannah took over. Emma started to say something, but Claire shook her head. Something had changed in the room; Hannah had become a part of them. It no longer seemed outrageous to Claire that she would live with them. Why not? Claire thought. A relative who cares about us, who seems to want to take care of us . . . why not? And I relied on her; when she nodded, she gave me approval to say yes this time, instead of no.

The young boy walked up to Claire. "Thank you very much," he said solemnly. "I'll do everything the doctors tell me, so maybe it won't take so long and cost so much. And I'll try to make you proud of me."

"Oh, my," said Hannah.

Tears pricked Claire's eyes. She had so much, and they had so little. And Emma had never been seriously ill; Claire had never known a moment of fear for her life or her well-being. *I'm remaking my whole life with everything I could possibly want, and they're just trying to save what they have.* She put her arms around the boy and held his wiry body close. "We're proud of you already," she said. "I hope you'll call once in a while and let us know how you're doing."

"Sure. It'll probably be awfully boring, but if that's what you want . . . sure." He rejoined his family and stood straight and silent while his father wrote on the back of an envelope.

"I don't know how to thank you," Pat Morton said. "You've given us a life, too."

"Hi, I've come to greet the famous Claire Goddard . . . oh, sorry, I'm interrupting."

"Come on in, Gina," said Emma. "It's the thing to do."

"Thank you," said Carter Morton. "We can't ever thank you enough. I'll let you know when I get a new job and I'll make sure my boy calls; we won't forget. I promise, you won't ever regret—"

"Be off!" said Hannah, shooing them out. "We'll pray for you. And you can write to us, you know, instead of calling; it's a lot cheaper." She watched them leave, then closed the door behind them.

"It's amazing how crowded this room gets with a few people in it," Gina said. She hugged Claire and Emma and dropped her jacket on a chair. "We haven't met," she said, holding out her hand to Hannah. "Gina Sawyer."

"Hannah Goddard. I'm glad to meet you. You're a good friend of Claire's?"

"The best." Gina paused. "Have we met before?"

"No, but I hope we'll be friends." Hannah smiled.

"Okay," Gina said, amused. She always believed in letting people make their own introductions and give their own explanations. She turned to Emma. "What's the thing to do?"

"Oh, wander in and out of our living room," Emma said. "Mother bought you the most beautiful presents."

"Really? You made me part of your shopping spree?"

Claire brought two gold boxes embossed with *Simone's* from the bedroom.

"Simone's," Gina said in wonder. "How about that. There's a reason to win the lottery; you get to go to Simone's. And I get Simone presents; just as good." She opened the two boxes and drew in her breath. "Hey," she said softly. She held up the deep red cashmere sweater and matching fringed scarf. "Spectacular. My color. And my first ever cashmere sweater. Claire, I love you. Oh, it is spectacular." In one swift movement she pulled off the sweatshirt she wore, then, more slowly, she pulled on the sweater. She flung the scarf over her shoulder and turned in place. "What do you think?"

"Very, very good," said Hannah. "You look very dramatic, very Shakespearean. I hope you wear it to a dramatic event."

Gina looked at her consideringly. "Do you live around here?"

"I will," said Hannah with a bright smile. "I'm Claire's aunt."

"Aunt?" asked Claire. "I thought you said you were either my aunt or my cousin."

"I believe I'd rather be an aunt. It sounds better for someone who's about to be seventy-five years old, especially someone who tends to meddle in other people's business. Anyway, I like being an aunt. Unless you have an objection."

"Of course not. You can be anything you want."

"Well, what *I* am right now," said Gina, "is unemployed."

"Did you quit?" Emma asked. "I thought you liked it."

"I did like it, and I didn't quit. I went down with the ship. They went out of business, just like that; in the morning everything was fine, and then about two o'clock they called us all in and said they couldn't make a go of it and they were closing down. That's happening to so many small companies these days." She gave a short laugh. "All the ones I'd be going to, to find another job. It's not like a secretary, you know; they always find work. But lab technicians need a lab and there aren't so many of those around right now."

"So what will you do?" Emma asked.

"Oh, scrape along for a while. With unemployment and what I've got put away, I can go for a few months, while I send out a few hundred résumés. After that, who knows?"

"Well, you don't have to worry about money," Claire said. "That's another good thing about winning the lottery; there's plenty for everybody. Are you sure you don't need any right now?" She saw a strange look, almost of distaste, sweep across Gina's face. "What's wrong?"

"I think I ought to see if I can get along on my own before I start sponging," Gina said lightly.

"*Sponging?* Gina, it's not sponging to take money when you need it from somebody who's practically family."

"Maybe not, but I just want to wait awhile and see what I can come up with on my own. But you're lovely to offer, Claire, and if things get really bad, I'll take you up on it."

"It wasn't meant as an insult," Claire said stubbornly, refusing to let it go.

"I know that. You're too nice to insult anybody. But, it's odd, you know, Claire, all of a sudden you've gotten awfully casual about money. Like you've already forgotten what it's like not to have any. I'm not a big expert in this, but I've sort of noticed that people who have plenty of money are the only ones who are casual about it; the rest of us are always sort of zeroed in on it, thinking about it, worrying about it, you know, and we get prickly when somebody pulls that laidback, 'Oh, take a few hundred or thousand or whatever and don't give it a thought.' Do you know what I mean?"

Claire was frowning. "You think I've changed."

"Well, not basically; you're still the Claire we know and love. You're just starting to have different ideas about money, is all."

"But I don't feel that I'm better than anyone else, because I have money."

"No, of course you don't; you wouldn't, though a lot of rich people do. It's just that you . . . oh, what the hell, I don't know how to say it."

"It's a way of thinking," Hannah said. "When you don't

POT OF GOLD

have much, you think about yourself in a certain way, working, earning, saving if you can. But as soon as you have money, you start thinking about yourself as someone who spends, and that makes a huge difference. It means that you feel differently about who you are. It's much more than the things you can buy; it's how you walk through the world and feel you belong everywhere, instead of just perched in a small corner of it."

"I like that," Gina said. "That's very good. Is that from experience?"

"Oh, I know a little about money." Hannah stood up and started to walk toward her suitcase, afraid the moment might never come for her to unpack and settle in. But just then the telephone rang and she detoured to answer it. "Oh, no," she said sadly after a moment. "I never invest in oil wells I haven't personally inspected. That may sound eccentric, but, then, I'm a very eccentric person." She hung up and turned to Claire. "I thought you wouldn't mind a little meddling there, or my pretending to be you."

"That wasn't meddling; that was coming to the rescue," said Claire. "I don't know the first thing about investing in oil wells. Thank you."

"Very smooth," Gina said admiringly. "Is that from experience, too?"

The telephone rang again and once again Hannah swooped down on it. "Yes. . . . No, our telephone is working just fine. Well, it's been busy because people keep calling and . . . oh, wait, I just had a thought. We should have an unlisted number. Could you set that up right away?"

"Hannah, just a minute," Claire said sharply.

Hannah looked up. "Don't you think it's a good idea? Why should all these strangers know where you live and be able to invade your house, in person or on the phone, and you don't even know who they are?"

"It sounds good to me," Gina said.

"But when our friends want to call, they won't know our number," Emma said.

"You have little cards printed and you send them to your friends," Hannah said. "And call up your special friends and tell them. People do it all the time, especially people in the public eye. Claire? What do you think?"

Claire and Emma exchanged another glance. *She keeps taking over.* But then Claire nodded. She had had the idea herself, a while ago, but she hadn't done anything about it. What was the harm in letting Hannah do it now? "Fine," she said. "Thank you, Hannah."

Hannah beamed and turned back to the telephone.

"She's a tiger," Gina said. "Do you think she'll need a leash after a while?"

Claire laughed. "She might. But then again, I could get used to having someone take care of all the little details. I just hope there aren't a lot of other relatives running around who decide to descend on us."

"Are we going to have servants in our new house?" Emma asked.

"Servants!" Gina exclaimed. "Didn't they go out with the last century?"

Emma flushed. "I mean, maids and cooks and things."

"I don't know," Claire said. "I haven't thought about it."

"Not a bad idea," Gina said. "Why shouldn't you take it easy?"

"That's done," Hannah said, rejoining them. "They wouldn't give me the new numbers until we do all the paperwork, but I did tell them we wanted two lines; it's so much more convenient." She gazed at the bemused look on Claire's face. "I'm going to unpack; it won't take long, but I should get it out of the way. And then we should think about tomorrow. We have furniture to buy, and the kitchen to plan. . . . I have so many ideas for a really professional kitchen. And then"—she tilted her head and contemplated Claire—"I think, my dear, you need a haircut."

"Mother cuts her own hair," Emma said.

"And very nicely, too," Hannah said. "But I think the time has come to make some changes."

Again, Claire felt a flash of annoyance. She had not had a mother since she was in high school, when her parents had died within a year of each other, and she had long ago stopped wishing for one. Now here was Hannah, moving in, taking over, by turns irritating, useful, and overwhelming. "Where do you think I should go for a haircut?" she asked coolly.

Hannah raised her eyebrows. "I have no idea; I'm a stranger to Danbury. Why don't we ask someone for a recommendation?"

"Simone!" Gina cried. "Claire, it's a great idea; I think you should do it. Ask Simone; she'll know the perfect place. It's time you had something dramatic done to you."

"You don't think sixty million dollars is dramatic enough?" Claire asked wryly.

"It's only a beginning," Hannah said. "Of course it's an excellent beginning, but by itself money doesn't do a thing; it's how cleverly you use it. You could bank it all, but then you'd have nothing but security. And security is wonderful, I'm an ardent believer in security, but you and Emma must have adventures, Claire. And we're going to start with a haircut. The first step to bigger and better adventures, whatever they may be. But right now I am going to unpack my suitcase. The question is . . ."

In the silence, Emma and Claire exchanged a long look. "Take my bedroom," Emma said. "I can sleep on the couch."

"Oh, no, my dear," said Hannah. "I'm the one who should sleep there; I'm really quite small."

"It's only until we move," Emma said. "Go ahead. It's fine. I want you to do it."

"Well. Well, that is lovely of you." Hannah stood and kissed Emma's cheek. "You are a lovely girl and I thank you." And pushing the suitcase before her, as she had when she brought it in earlier that day, she went into Emma's bedroom and closed the door.

"I guess she's terrific," Gina said, "as long as you don't mind being run over."

"I mostly like her," Emma said. She saw Claire put a finger to her lips with a quick glance at the closed bedroom door only a few feet away, and lowered her voice to a whisper. "I mean, I guess I wouldn't like it if she tried to take over my whole life and tell me everything I had to do, but she's very efficient, isn't she? Anyway, I like her."

"So do I," Claire said. "I think she's a lot lonelier and more frightened than she makes out. She's been desperate to unpack her suitcase for the past couple of hours, as if we might kick her out if she didn't get settled in a hurry."

"Do you suppose she'll really stay with us forever?" Emma asked.

"I'll bet she would, if you let her," Gina said. "It's not bad, you know," she added almost wistfully, "having somebody run interference the way she does, and worry about your hair and plan your kitchen . . . she must cook, if she wants a professional kitchen."

"She says she does," said Emma. "She's like a little wizard, isn't she? All wrinkled up, with little magic tricks, and she's done thousands of things, at least that's what it sounds like. I think she can do anything."

"Well, I guess we've got her for now," Claire said. "But if she pushes too hard, we may have to ask her to leave."

"How would you do that?" Gina asked.

Claire laughed. "I don't know. It was probably easier to win the lottery than it would be to get rid of Hannah. I'll figure it out, if it ever comes to that. I don't even want to think about it now. I have so many other things to think about; so many things are going on. Life used to be a lot slower."

"And duller," Emma said.

More manageable, Claire thought. She had always liked things to happen gradually, so she could get used to them. For seventeen years she and Emma had lived such a quiet life, in a routine that seldom changed. She had gone out with men now and then and she had had affairs with some of them, but

POT OF GOLD

even the affairs seemed to follow a pattern that matched the calm rhythm of her life, with little passion, and no upheavals. Whatever was part of her life was there because things happened to her; she did not make them happen. She did not want anything startling.

But now everything seemed startling. Amazing things were happening at headlong speed, and Claire was right in the middle of them. Gina's right, Claire thought; I really am changing. How else could I have practically bought out Simone's and bought a house in less than an hour and be planning to move in a few weeks?

And so when Hannah announced the next day that she had made an appointment in New York for Claire to have her hair cut, Claire went along. Left to herself, she would have put it off. But since Hannah had taken care of it, she let it happen.

She sat in the chair, watching herself in the mirror as Gregory snipped and combed and snipped some more, and Hannah hovered nearby, keeping a close eye on his swiftly moving hands. "It's the shape of the face," Hannah said, wary of intruding on his concentration, but unable to keep silent.

"Of course, madame," Gregory said shortly. "It is always the shape of the face that is crucial to the haircut. But without the genius of the hairstylist, the shape of the face is meaningless."

"True," nodded Hannah. "But sometimes geniuses get carried away with the thrill of their own innovation and expertise and violate the principles of harmony in nature."

Gregory met her eyes in the mirror. "Very wise," he said, and turned back to his snipping.

"Just follow the line of my hair," Claire said, uncomfortable at being discussed, and worried about what Gregory might do to her, with or without Hannah egging him on. "It has a curl when it's left alone."

Gregory and Hannah shared a swift, shocked glance. "Left alone, madame?" Gregory repeated. "Then why are you here?"

"To have someone more experienced follow the line of my hair," she said, hoping that was an adequate answer. She did not add that she thought that anyone who charged three hundred dollars for a haircut, and stayed in business, must be doing something right.

Gregory worked in silence, and Hannah, too, was silent, watching him snip one hair at a time for almost two hours. And when he was finished, she sighed. "Perfect," she said. "My compliments."

Claire was looking at her image in surprise. Her hair swept back from her face, freeing her high cheekbones and framing the long, elegant shape of her head. Her mouth looked fuller, her eyes larger; she looked younger and more like Emma.

"Madame would like to talk to Margo?" Gregory asked. "She is an expert in the art of makeup."

"Yes," said Hannah.

"Yes," echoed Claire, and they moved to a room hung with velvet curtains where a dressing table stood in a flood of lights. Margo held Claire's chin in her hand and studied her features. "A good face," she pronounced. "Superb cheekbones, excellent eyes, a fine mouth. A good chin. The face is a little too thin, but Gregory has alleviated that with his perfect haircut." Her hands fluttered and stroked like butterfly wings over the left half of Claire's face; then she watched and gave instructions as Claire used the same creams and powders on the right half. "You do not want a transformation," Margo said. "Makeup is supposed to make more wonderful what is already wonderful in you. Anything more and it becomes a mask and you are no longer you."

Once again, Claire sat back and looked at herself in the mirror. It was not a transformation, but she was not the same. Everything that had been quiet and a little fuzzy in her face was enhanced, made vivid, and it startled her and made her oddly uncomfortable. "You are a beautiful woman, madame," said Margo, and Claire, who had never thought of herself as even pretty, knew it was true and that she would have to think about herself differently from now on. *I'm remaking my life and I'm even remaking me.* And then she wondered what Emma would say when they got home and she saw her mother suddenly looking younger and more dramatic; looking, in fact, like her daughter.

Emma stared. "You look nice," she said. "He did a nice job."

"Emma," Hannah scolded. "You could be more enthusiastic for your mother."

"No, it's all right," Claire said. "She's surprised. So am I. We'll both have to get used to me. But I like it. At least I think I do." She heard the plea in her voice, asking them if it was all right for her to look like this; whether she should style her hair this way tomorrow after she washed it; whether, tomorrow morning, she should put on the makeup she had bought, in just this way, after she had scrubbed it off when she went to bed tonight.

"You must never be ashamed of pushing yourself to be the most you can be," Hannah said. "If you are, then you will be even more ashamed when one day you are seventy-five years old and you realize you let your life slip through your fingers and never tried . . . so many things."

"Like what?" Emma said.

"All the adventures that let us stretch ourselves in new ways and make us bigger and better and wiser people."

"Yes, but, like what?" Emma insisted. "Do you mean lovers? Or drugs? Or what?"

"I don't think lovers and drugs make you bigger or better or wiser; do you?" Hannah asked. Emma frowned and did not answer. "I was thinking of how we see ourselves, the pride we take in ourselves, our experiences that we make a part of us, the ways we learn from other people, and the things we teach them, too. I was thinking of how we use the world, how much we manage to squeeze out of it, and how much we give back to it before we die."

"Yes, but what *exactly*—" Emma began, and Claire interrupted.

"I think what we should be doing now is deciding how we're going to move in a few weeks."

"We must buy furniture," Hannah said promptly.

"And everything else," Claire said. "I'm not taking anything from this apartment except our clothes and books. We'd better start making lists; it's been so long since I moved, I'm not sure I remember how."

But by the time they moved, everything was under control, and that was because Hannah was there. "I've done this so many times, I'm an expert," she said, and she organized everything.

She began with furnishing the house. Calling Simone and Gregory and Margo for names of shops their clients used, she made a list. "At most stores, there is a wait of six months to a year for furniture," she told Claire. "These shops carry antiques and one-of-a-kind pieces, and of course they're quite expensive, but if you don't mind that . . ."

"I don't mind," Claire said. "I don't want to wait."

They found deep couches in dark red, textured fabrics, soft armchairs in subtle patterns, an Italian coffee table made of painted plaster and mosaic that somehow fit harmoniously with antique French drum tables and a fringed Victorian ottoman. For the dining room they found a square, antique mahogany table with twelve Queen Anne chairs; they found nineteenth-century Danish pine armoires for the bedrooms, and an eighteenth-century pine hutch from Scotland for the kitchen. Hannah ran a loving hand over its surface, smooth and deep golden brown from centuries of use. "It makes a homey kitchen to have some old wood with all those modern cabinets," she said, and so they bought an early-American pine table with six ladder-back chairs to go with the hutch. They bought antique Oriental rugs, their colors softened by time, their texture like velvet, to lie on the gleaming plank floors in all the other rooms, and drapes and curtains and lamps.

This time, as they shopped, Claire looked at prices, but her alarm over high numbers was fading. Oh, she thought, so a triple French armoire for my bedroom costs thirty thousand dollars. How interesting. And three thousand for a pair of antique English andirons. They're probably worth it.

They took a day to buy television sets and video recorders, and a stereo system for the library. Then they went to an enormous music store and wandered up and down the aisles, plucking discs and videotapes from the racks, choosing every movie and piece of music they had ever wanted. Claire could not stop; the bright packages were so alluring, and she had never before been able to afford more than one disc every few months, and now, as she picked each one up, she thought, of course I can buy this; why shouldn't I? and tossed it into her basket.

"Mother," said Emma, awed, "we've got about four hundred discs."

"Yes," Claire said, and felt a momentary twinge of an old fear. It was too much; she was being insanely extravagant. But as she took her credit card from her wallet, it faded. Of course she could buy all this. Why was it taking her so long to get used to that?

Then Hannah led them on shopping trips for the kitchen, and whatever else took their fancy. The days blurred into each other as they went from store to store, checking off items on their lists and wandering into other departments to find treasures they had never thought of. For Claire, everything was like a dream: wherever she looked, objects of beauty glistened before her. She reached out and curved her fingers around vases and bowls, the frames of paintings, a set of silver goblets, the sleeve of a fur coat ... everything was within her reach, and everything was desirable. She could not stop buying. She had never known how many wonderful things there were in the world because she had never looked; she had never known how many artists were at work all over the world, making the most intricate glass sculptures, knitting the softest cashmere throws, weaving tapestries of the richest hues, painting china in scrolls and fruits and flowers edged with gold. Now she discovered bed linens of such fine cotton they felt like silk, and towels so large and thick they seemed to wrap her in a warm cocoon, and down comforters in subtle patterns that shimmered in the light. She discovered the beautiful things of the world, and she picked them up and pointed and nodded and could not stop in her rush to make them hers.

Then Hannah took a day to put away what they had bought for the kitchen and dining room. Humming with pleasure, her eyes bright with excitement, she filled the dining room sideboard with china and cut crystal and silverware; then, in the kitchen, she moved purposefully from cabinet to cabinet, sliding out the smooth drawers and shelves and arranging in them every tool and gadget she had been able to find. And she stored a supply of food in the cupboards and refrigerator and freezer that Emma said would last them through three hurricanes and tornadoes or any other disasters that might strike their part of the country.

"It makes me feel secure," Hannah said. "After all, one really never knows what might happen, and this way, whatever comes along, at least we can eat. There is one thing, though, Claire . . ."

"Yes," Claire said. They were back in the old apartment and Claire was sitting on the floor, packing books, thinking of all the empty shelves that awaited them.

"I want to do my part," Hannah began, and then stopped, waiting for Claire to look up.

"Yes," Claire said again, putting down the books in her hand and looking at Hannah.

"I don't mind doing the cooking; for me that's pure pleasure. But I'm not sure what else you think I should be doing. I could run the house, of course, I've done it so often, but if I do all the laundry and cleaning and running errands *and* cooking, I would feel very much like a servant, earning my bed and board. A poor relation, here on sufferance. And I would wonder—worry about—what would happen if I got ill and couldn't do everything. You see, if we could avoid that . . . if I could believe that I'm here because you want me . . .

Also, of course, at my age, even in full health, which I am, I might not be as efficient as someone younger."

"No, of course we don't expect you to do all that," Claire said. "And of course you're here because we want you. I can't even imagine how Emma and I would have furnished the house, or moved into it and got settled so quickly, without you."

"Well." Hannah's smile creased her small, lined face. "Of course that is what I had hoped. You're very generous, Claire, to tell me; it makes me feel more at ease."

Claire nodded absently, wondering, to herself, how it was that, in just a little more than two weeks, Hannah had become so much a part of their lives, as fixed and purposeful as if she had been there always. "We'll find someone to come in once a week to clean," she said.

"Perhaps," Hannah said gently, "with a house that size, two or three times a week would be better."

"Oh, well, of course. Of course you're right."

"And someone to do the laundry. Unless you send everything out, but it's always better to have it done at home; it's not as hard on the clothes. And I don't know about you, but I'm not good around the house with repairs and such; I think a maintenance man would be valuable, don't you? A house needs so much upkeep, painting and patching and repairing broken wires and leaky plumbing and the washer and dryer when they go out ... it's a very big job."

"It sounds daunting," said Claire, who had never owned a house. She wondered when Hannah had. "Well, we'll find a maintenance man. Is there anything else?"

"A landscaper. Those gardens didn't get to look like that without a professional being in charge. And I don't know about you, but I'm not good in the garden, though I do have a flair for flower arranging."

"A cleaning person, a laundry person, a maintenance man, and a landscaper," Claire recited. She glanced at the cartons of books. Everything had seemed so simple when she bought the house: those bright, lovely rooms with so many closets, so many shelves and cabinets, so much space in which to move around and feel free. Now she felt as if her new house were swelling, ballooning, engulfing her.

"But you don't have to worry about any of that," Hannah said. "I'll be happy to supervise them for you; I know a lot about it. And you'll be busy with all your new activities; you won't want to fret about whether the work is being done or whether it's on time or whether it's the way you want it. I'll be very happy to take care of all that."

Now it was Hannah who seemed to get bigger, sweeping into her embrace the new house, and Claire's life. But she seemed to know what needed doing, and Claire did not. And it would take a while to learn. *And you'll be busy with all your new activities.* What activities? Claire wondered. What am I going to be doing with my time, once we're settled, now that I don't have to go to work every day?

Well, I did think about a cruise. That's something to do, for a start.

"Thank you, Hannah," she said. "I'd be very grateful if you would take care of all that." She found the telephone directory in one of the cartons and turned to the classified section on travel agents. She had never used one, and so she chose the one with the largest advertisement and, still sitting on the floor, dialed the number. "I'm interested in cruises," she said. "I read a while ago about one to Alaska."

"We have a great many, and they're all magnificent," said the agent. "And very popular. In fact, I just finished planning one for the owner of Eiger Labs—you know, in Norwalk?—and his son. And another couple from this area; we get an impressive group of people on our Alaska cruises."

"Is there one soon?" Claire asked.

"The end of June; that's not far off, but we do have room on it; it's a little early in the season for the big crowds."

"Fine," said Claire. "I'll take that one."

"Is it just yourself?" the agent asked.

"And my daughter." Claire gave the agent her credit card information, and the address of her new house, so brochures

POT OF GOLD

and tickets could be mailed to her. When she hung up, she was smiling. *Another adventure.* She looked up and saw Hannah watching her. "I've always wanted to do this," she said. "I don't know why; it's just that it sounds different. Different from everything."

"Cruises can be wonderful," Hannah said. "I think it's very good that you're going. Shall I finish packing these books?"

"Thank you." Claire leaned against the wall and watched Hannah pack and thought about the cruise, with an impressive group of people on it, and the airplane she and Emma would take to Vancouver. Neither of them had ever flown. A new life, she thought. Everything, everything was new.

And then, finally, they moved. Trucks carrying furniture and rugs all converged on their new house on the same morning from a dozen places in New York and Connecticut; the moving van arrived with their clothes and books and Claire's drawing materials; and Claire drove her white Mercedes, and Emma, with Hannah beside her, followed in her red one, up the long gentle rise that led to their gleaming house, serene and safe in its oak and sycamore forest.

They walked from room to room, directing where the rugs and furniture would go. "So beautiful," Hannah whispered to herself, and her long sigh was like a prayer of thanksgiving. Claire heard it and, for the first time, felt proud of what she had done in taking Hannah in. She had given Hannah a new life; she had made her happy and no longer fearful. I can do good things, she thought. I have to find more of them to do.

All the deliverymen were gone, but still Claire roamed through the rooms of the house. This is mine, she told herself, this is mine, this is mine. She loved the brilliant reds and blacks and blues of the Oriental rugs against the shining floors; she loved the red couches and soft taupe armchairs and curtainless windows that looked out onto the gardens; she loved the dark green walls of the library with its white couches and walnut shelves, empty now but, by tomorrow, she thought, with the three of them working, filled with all their books. She loved the sound of the front door closing, the whisper of the windows opening to the evening breeze, the fluttering moths against the screens, the faint click of Emma's and Hannah's shoes from other rooms, the sound of her own breathing in the silence of her bedroom, a spacious, high-ceilinged room with a fireplace at one end, furnished in apricot and white, with lace curtains at the high windows. My room, she thought, my home. I cannot believe all this is mine.

"Where shall we go for dinner?" she asked, but Hannah shook her head.

"You're not going to take me away from this kitchen. I can't wait to try it out. You two sit down and watch."

So Claire and Emma sat at the pine table with a bottle of wine and a plate of Scandinavian bread and smoked salmon and watched Hannah move about the kitchen as if she had known it all her life. She hummed and talked to herself as she worked. "Who would believe it? Six weeks ago I thought I was on my way to being a street person. I had visions of me with all my belongings in a grocery cart, trundling along looking for an empty park bench. Oh, was I terrified of that. I thought I'd used up my lifetime supply of happy times and from then on everything would be dark and wretched. But I was wrong. Everything changed and the darkness is gone. And here I am. Love, warmth, comfort. Heaven. Now where might I have put the soufflé dishes? I thought, a lemon soufflé for dessert. So festive, a perfect way to celebrate so many lovely things . . ."

Claire and Emma exchanged a long look. "What would you think," Claire asked softly, "if we take Hannah along when we go on our cruise?"

"I think she'd love it," Emma said.

"But would you love it?"

"I don't know. I guess she'd spend more time with you than with me. So if you're thinking of meeting some men and having a good time, she might be a problem."

POT OF GOLD

Claire's eyebrows rose. "Are you thinking of meeting some men and having a good time?"

"Sure. I mean, isn't that what cruises are for? Lorna and Marie and some of the other kids have been on them, and they say that's what they're all about. Nobody goes for the scenery. That's what they say, anyway."

"I guess I was thinking of the scenery," Claire murmured. But then she remembered what the travel agent had said. *An impressive group of people.* Why not think about meeting new people? If you're making a new life, she thought, everything opens up. All kinds of people went on these cruises: young and old, executives, professionals, artists, retired people. And they'd all be together for a week. Long enough to get acquainted and to find out which ones would become friends after they got back.

She looked again at Hannah, who was concentrating on whipping egg whites in a copper bowl. I can do something good for Hannah by taking her on this cruise, she thought, but she could help me, too. She could keep an eye on Emma. Just in case. "Hannah," she said, "when we go on our cruise to Alaska in a couple of weeks, we'd be very pleased if you'd come along."

4

THE ship gleamed white in the sun, trim and sleek on the softly slapping gray waves of the harbor. It was a floating small city with shops and a swimming pool, a nightclub, two restaurants, even a gambling casino. Emma and Claire had adjoining staterooms on the boat deck, and Hannah was in a room on the other side. "I love it; it's huge," Emma said. "I could live here forever, except I love our new house, too. Am I dressed all right for dinner?"

She was wearing a very short red chiffon dress with a skirt that swirled as she walked, and high heels. Her legs were long and elegant, her hair gleamed red-gold against the red dress, and teardrop crystal earrings sparkled at her ears. "You're beautiful," Claire said. "You'll be the star of the dining room." But when they walked in together and the maître d' led them to a table in the center of the room, both of them attracted attention.

"Isn't this a blast?" Emma whispered as they made their way between the tables and heads swiveled to watch them pass. "I feel like the queen of the world. I love the way you look, too; you're really great. Don't you think we make a great team?"

Claire felt a rush of love and gratitude. How wonderful, to

have a daughter's approval. Emma had been withdrawn the past few days, getting ready for the trip, as if, Claire thought, she had suddenly realized she would have two chaperones on her very first trip anywhere. But then she would become cheerful and talk happily about all the things they were going to do.

And now she seemed happy to be sitting with Claire in the center of the large room, looking at the women in satin dresses and silk pantsuits, the men in suits and ties, and waiters in tuxedos pouring wine and passing small trays of hors d'oeuvres. Music from a piano and flute wove lightly through the talk and laughter and clatter of dishes, and the ship's captain went from table to table, greeting all his guests.

Claire tried to take it all in. She couldn't believe it. Ever since she won the lottery, she had felt like this: like a young girl just launched into a strange and fabulous world. It was almost as if she and Emma suddenly were the same age, stepping out into a land of wonder, filled with more than she had ever imagined in her fantasies—because how could she fantasize about things she didn't even know existed?

Even now, six weeks after winning the lottery, she could not stop herself; still, wherever she went, she bought and bought and bought, accumulating treasures that she knew she did not need—but what did need have to do with it?—that piled up in her rooms and closets, her drawers and shelves and cabinets, even her garage. And she moved through her house and watched the staff clean it and manicure its lawns and fix whatever needed fixing, and she hugged it to herself—*I own this; this is mine*—but even then somehow she could not feel absolutely certain that it was truly and forever hers.

Now she caught a glimpse of herself and Emma in an oval mirror and marveled at the way they looked, her black silk dress contrasting with Emma's red one, their jewels glinting in the bright lights, their smiles as casual and their heads as high as any in the room, as if they, too, took all of this for granted. But of course they didn't, because everything about the ship seemed magical to them: their spacious staterooms with sitting room and bedroom and large picture windows framed in heavy draperies; the wide deck of polished wood that circled the ship, lined with smoothly curved deck chairs, their arms touching like close friends telling secrets to each other; the echoes in the tiled room where the swimming pool rippled with the motion of the ship; the cozy library with walls lined with books on Alaska. Claire had a brief memory of herself sitting at Danbury Graphics, working at her drawing board, frustrated because she was working on someone else's idea, not her own, feeling locked in but believing there were no other options for her, nor would there be, ever. Less than two months ago. Long enough for her to remake her life.

"How very pleasant," Hannah said, taking an empty chair at Claire and Emma's table. "What a place to find myself, when just a little while ago I was thinking I'd never again go farther afield than my own apartment." She smiled at Claire, who smiled back, wondering why she could not talk about her feelings the way Hannah did. But she had never been able to talk about herself; she always felt no one would be interested, and she was afraid of putting herself forward because others might grow bored or impatient. She'd always felt it was better to keep quiet and fit in everywhere and not make waves.

"Perfect," Hannah sighed as the waiter put an iced glass of vodka in front of her. She saw Emma looking across the room and followed her gaze. "Oh, isn't he handsome. And he certainly seems aware of *you*."

Emma turned away, her color high. "I only noticed them because they're alone, like us. Everybody else has their own private party."

"I guess people travel with their friends," Claire said, and turned in her chair. "Where were you looking?"

"At those two men," Hannah said, "near the piano."

Claire located them. One of them, the younger, was looking fixedly at Emma. Hannah was right: he was extraordinarily handsome, his face dark, almost brooding, his hair thick and black, falling over his forehead. He had a full mouth and heavy brows and a restlessness in the way he shifted in his chair, as if it were too small for him. The man with him was clearly his father, with the same full mouth and black brows that almost met, though his hair was a steel gray and his eyelids were hooded, making him look more remote and secretive than his son. He met Claire's eyes and smiled and nodded a brief greeting.

"They're both quite handsome," Hannah said reflectively. "And how interesting to see a father and son traveling together. I wonder if they're American. They look foreign to me. Italian, perhaps."

"I didn't notice," said Emma, and they all laughed.

The waiter came to take their order, and then their dinners came, and while the ship left the lights of Vancouver behind and moved smoothly northward through ice blue waters, they ate in a leisurely way, barely aware that they were moving but somehow feeling, already, the sense of being cut off from land. "It's kind of eerie, isn't it?" Emma asked as they sat back with their coffee. The dining room was emptying as others left for the nightclub or the casino or the cocktail lounge, and it became easier to hear the music and the murmur of a few other voices. "Isn't it eerie?" she said again. "I mean, here we are in the middle of nowhere, going off into the unknown with five or six hundred people we don't know."

"In the middle of nowhere," Hannah smiled, "with fax machines and telephones and television and movies and—"

"Well, but it feels odd," Emma insisted. "We're *not on land;* not even close enough to touch it. It's like we've lost what makes us *us.* I mean, we couldn't live here; if the boat sank or we fell overboard, we couldn't live in the water; *we're in the wrong place.* It was the same on the plane, when we flew to Vancouver; didn't you feel it? We weren't connected, we were just floating, you know, cut off, sort of *out there* where everything is endless and so . . . mysterious; it's like there's nothing to protect us if something goes wrong. I don't know, it just seems pretty eerie to me."

"That's the romantic way of thinking; I like it," said a

deep voice. They looked up quickly, at the two men they had been looking at earlier. "Forgive us for interrupting," said the older one, who had just spoken, "but we'd be very pleased if you would join us for an after-dinner drink. I'm Quentin Eiger." He held out his hand to Claire, and she took it. "And my son, Brix."

"An unusual name," said Hannah. "A family name?"

"My mother's," said the young man, his voice as deep as his father's. "Brixton."

"Well," Hannah said, "ours are not as exotic. I'm Hannah Goddard, and this is Claire and Emma Goddard." She looked at Claire, her eyebrows raised.

"Yes," Claire said into the silence, "we'd be glad to join you." She tried to sound casual, but these two tall, powerful-looking men looming over their table made her nervous and worried about what they would all talk about. Like a young girl, she thought again; Emma and I, there's so much we don't know. Everyone was standing now, and she stood with them. This is what it means to have money, she thought: to learn how to deal with other worlds.

As for making conversation, Hannah would be there. And Hannah always seemed able to think of something to say.

They were all moving toward the lounge, led by Quentin Eiger and his son. Like sheep, Claire thought, but when they were seated in deep armchairs grouped around a low cocktail table, and she met Quentin's eyes, she saw only admiration in them. She glanced at Emma, absorbed in listening to Brix, and then at Hannah, who was gazing around the cocktail lounge, deliberately letting Emma and Claire make their own way. Quentin leaned toward Claire. "I admire you and your daughter. You're both extraordinarily beautiful, and you seem to be good friends."

"Thank you," Claire said. "We are good friends. At least, most of the time."

He chuckled. "Well, that's honest. Brix and I don't even do that well."

Surprised, Claire said, "You seemed so close at dinner."

POT OF GOLD

"We look alike. That always makes people think we're close. But we've never managed it, from the time he was born." Claire was amazed at his instant, intimate revelations. They made her wary, but Quentin did not seem to notice. "I suppose part of the problem now," he went on, "is that we work together; that often adds to the tensions between generations. It's unlikely that you and Emma have that problem."

"Working together? No, Emma just graduated from high school."

It was his turn to be surprised. "She looks older." His face was thoughtful as he watched Brix and Emma.

"She's seventeen," Claire said, her voice casual, but it was clearly a warning, a message for Quentin to give to his son. Claire had watched Emma and Brix as they moved ahead of her into the lounge, aware of what a striking couple they made, Emma tall and willowy in her red froth of a dress with her flaming red-gold hair catching the light, and Brix, darkly handsome, half a head taller, broad shouldered, walking with a slight swagger that Claire did not trust.

"Then she'll be going to college?" Quentin asked.

Claire nodded. "This September."

"And you? Where is your home?"

"Wilton, Connecticut. We just bought a house there."

"What a wonderful surprise," he said, smiling broadly. "We're neighbors. I live in Darien; I have a company in Norwalk."

"Norwalk," Claire repeated, recalling what the travel agent had said. "Some laboratory, is that right? I don't recall the name . . ."

"Eiger Labs. How would you know that?"

"The travel agent told me about some of the prestigious people she'd booked on this cruise."

He frowned. "She's a stupid woman. I wonder how many other people she's advertised my travels to."

"I'm sorry. I didn't—"

"It's not your fault; it's hers. And in this case I should be grateful, because it seems she brought us together. But I won't use her again, and if you value your privacy, I'd advise you not to either. You said you just bought a house. Is it just you and Emma living there?"

"And Hannah." The waiter brought their drinks and fussed with them, arranging them precisely in front of each person, and organizing baskets of nuts and after-dinner mints in the center of the table.

"Fine," Quentin said, and the waiter recognized the word as an order to leave, and did. "Just Hannah?" he asked.

"Yes," Claire said.

"You're widowed? Divorced?"

"Divorced." She picked up her cognac and sat back. She was more relaxed now, though part of her, watching Emma, was alert and surprised to see that Emma had ordered cognac; Emma never drank anything but a glass of wine now and then, and Claire had only let her do that when she became a senior in high school. Cognac and Brix Eiger in one evening, Claire thought; powerful stuff. At that moment, Emma glanced up and met Claire's eyes. She gave a quick, startled smile and then looked down, at her clasped hands. We'll have to talk, Claire thought, tonight or tomorrow morning.

But now she turned back to Quentin. She knew very well the ritual that men and women go through in getting to know each other; usually she dreaded it because she hated the predictable litany of questions about job and home and previous spouses and likes and dislikes that turn the first date, and often the second, into an interview more than a conversation. But Quentin was smooth and easygoing; perfectly at ease and completely in command, and he did not push; he moved the conversation along as unobtrusively as he had shepherded them from the dining room into the lounge.

How comfortable, Claire thought, to let a strong person take charge.

She saw Emma look up again, stealing a quick glance at her, and she wondered what her daughter saw. She sat straighter in her chair, putting herself a little distance from

POT OF GOLD

Quentin, and lowered her eyes. I mustn't show too much interest in a man in front of my daughter; it might shock her.

"Brix and I lived together, off and on," Quentin was saying. "We always seemed to rub each other the wrong way, but we kept trying, until he went to boarding school, and then college. Now, of course, he has his own place. He's done all right, I think; most kids somehow land on their feet even with a rough childhood, but Brix has probably done better than most."

"Rough childhood?" Claire repeated.

"Oh, the usual: parents too busy with their own problems, that sort of thing." There was a pause. "No, I'll bet that wouldn't be usual for you, would it? You probably made Emma the center of your life and gave her everything she wanted."

Claire smiled and shook her head. "I couldn't; we never had enough money. But I paid a lot of attention to her."

"Most of your attention."

"Well, yes, when we were together."

"And you never remarried?"

"No." She paused. "And you?"

"Oh, a number of times. Three, after Brix's mother and I were divorced. She tried it twice more. Brix hated it, of course; I think he felt like some kind of mascot that we handed back and forth from one new family to another. And I wasn't there a lot; I was at work most of the time. But then, you were, too, weren't you?"

"Not most of the time. I took Emma with me when she was a baby; they let me do that. And the first few years she was at school, when she was still so young, I worked a short day and brought work home. Did your wife work?"

"No." He smiled. "She made a career of shopping. She was the sublime shopper."

"What does that mean?" Claire asked curiously.

Quentin's eyebrows rose. "It means a passionate lifetime study of the best the world's craftsmen have to offer, where to find it, and how to get it at the best price." He smiled. "I thought all women are born knowing that."

"Why would they be?"

He shrugged. "Sorry; it was a poor joke. The women I know seem to be experts from the time they can walk, but they may not be typical. You do shop, of course; you must have had shopping sprees now and then with your daughter." He looked at her silk dress. "You have excellent taste."

Claire flushed with pleasure. "We've done a lot of shopping lately, but we're not experts." She felt a strong reluctance to talk about money, and how she came to have it. "When you were at work while Brix was growing up, was it at Eiger Labs?"

"No, I was a bond trader in New York. I made a great deal of money—it wasn't hard to do in the eighties—and then I got bored and went looking for something else, something that had nothing to do with Wall Street." He looked across the table at Brix. "I didn't feel in control of anything except making money; nothing else was going exactly the way I wanted it. So I found two other investors and we bought Eiger Labs, called Norwalk Labs, then. It was a good move."

"For you or for your family?"

"For me and for the company."

"And Brix?"

"He lived with his mother in New York, and with me and my wife in Norwalk in the summers. We always had a governess for him; so did his mother; but he never got along with any of them. Of course he wasn't easy to take care of; he had a slow-burning temper that could take the roof off when it was full-blown, but still, no one we hired seemed willing to try to become his friend."

Claire was watching him, puzzled at the pride in his voice when he talked about his son's temper. "But weren't his parents his friends?" she asked, surprising herself with her boldness.

There was a silence. "I tried to talk to him as an equal, to explain to him that it was hard on me, too, all those years, with one marriage after another that didn't work, but of course he never believed me; he thought I was doing whatever I wanted, at his expense, while he had to tag along behind."

"He was right," Claire said, surprising herself again.

"Partly," Quentin said shortly. "You were more successful, it seems, in making Emma feel secure."

"Well, I've only had one husband, so I've had plenty of time." Claire wondered what was happening to her: she never was so forward, especially with strangers.

He frowned. "You mean we give more of ourselves to marriages than to our young. That's a decision we all make; I don't believe in diminishing my own life to give children whatever some experts say they need. You seem to look at it differently. When were you divorced?"

"Before Emma was born."

His eyebrows rose. "A brief marriage."

"Yes. He didn't want to be a father, so he left." There was a pause and Claire wondered if he wanted her to talk about herself as openly as he had talked about his own life. But I can't, she thought; I have almost nothing to talk about except Emma. She caught a glimpse of a nearby oval mirror in an elaborate frame—the ship seemed to be filled with mirrors; evidently people on cruises liked to look at themselves all the time—and saw her reflection with Quentin's profile just behind her. Here I am, she thought in amazement. How could I have guessed I would be here, on this wonderful ship, moving through strange waters to a strange land, with this very handsome man who seems to enjoy my company? A small shiver gripped her, as if there were something to be afraid of. No, no, no, she thought, that's crazy. This is everything I ever longed for; I'm having the most perfect evening of my life. Just because things are wonderful does not mean something dangerous is waiting around the corner. Adventures are waiting; not dangers. Because we have money. Money makes all the difference; money makes everything an adventure.

She felt a flurry of movement and turned to her left to see

Hannah standing beside her chair. "I'll say good-night," she said to Claire, and nodded briefly to Quentin.

Claire looked beyond her and saw a tall man with flowing blond hair and a full, blond beard. His eyes were a brilliant blue, and his mouth, partly hidden, had an unexpected sweetness as he met Claire's eyes and smiled. He wore a corduroy jacket and an extravagantly patterned tie. "Forrest Exeter," Hannah said, following Claire's look. "We're both from Philadelphia, almost the same block. We're going to the library to look at some books he thinks I would enjoy."

Claire stared at her. Hannah was self-conscious, almost embarrassed—probably because her new friend was very young, Claire thought—but she wouldn't be embarrassed unless this might be a romance, and that couldn't happen. It couldn't, could it? Claire wondered.

"I'll see you in the morning," Hannah said, leaving no room for comments. Her back straight, she took Forrest Exeter's arm and they left the lounge.

"How odd," Claire murmured. Slowly, she turned back to Quentin and tried to remember what they had been talking about. Oh, yes, he had asked her about her marriage. Well, that didn't bear talking about. "Tell me about Brix," she said. "Is he your only child?"

"No, there are two other boys, but their mothers didn't want me to be part of their upbringing and I let that happen; I've always known that other men do a better job of parenting than I do. I'm impatient with children; I assume you've gathered that. It's not that I don't like them, it's just that I don't enjoy the effort it takes to fill the gaps in their knowledge and experience so we can communicate. I find Brix interesting now; I never did, before. Were you and Emma always close?"

"Always. It was just the two of us, and we had so little money that we depended on each other for everything. And I had such a good time introducing her to the world and sharing her excitement at every new discovery; it was as if I were seeing it, too, for the first time."

"Well, your fortunes seem to have changed," he said.

POT OF GOLD

The waiter hovered at his side and he nodded. "The same all around."

"Not for—" Claire started to say, but stopped. Emma's glass was still almost full; she was barely drinking, and it would be better to have another drink in front of her than for her mother to make decisions for her in front of the others.

Quentin was quiet, and she thought he must be waiting for her to say something about the change in her fortunes. She was suddenly embarrassed by the word *lottery*. She hadn't earned her sixty million dollars; she hadn't done anything but buy a ticket. She was not a success; she had just had a stroke of luck. That was the way it always was with her: she didn't make things happen; they happened to her.

I could say I inherited it, she thought. Or borrowed to take this trip or saved up for it.

Or she could be silent. What business was it of anyone how she and Emma came to be wearing these clothes and jewels, and sailing on this ship?

But Quentin had openly confided in her about his son and his marriages, and she felt she would fail some crucial test if she lied now or was silent.

"I won the state lottery," she said abruptly.

He was amused. "Good for you. I gather it was a big one."

Claire nodded. "It changed everything for us."

"And before you won. What did you do then?"

Obviously he had not read about her in any newspaper, and just as obviously he was not especially interested. He did not even ask how much she had won. She gazed at him in silence, wondering what it was about her that did interest him. "I was a graphics designer," she said at last. "Assistant, really, with a team at Danbury Graphics."

"I know them. They bid on a job for us once. We finally gave it to someone else, but I remember one design, for the packaging of a new shampoo; it was very good." Claire was silent, and he looked closely at her. "Did you work on that?"

"My group did."

"And whose concept was it?"

Claire hesitated. "That one was mine, but we worked as a team."

"You mean they were a team and you had no choice."

"No, I meant what I said. I was part of the team and I did my share of the work."

"Including not getting credit for your own ideas."

"We all pooled our ideas."

"And no one in your group ever took credit for them?"

She felt a flicker of anger. Why couldn't he leave it alone? She had made her peace with the fact that others took credit for her ideas; it went with the job. "It didn't matter," she said briefly.

"I don't believe that. You're a proud, beautiful woman; why wouldn't you take pride in everything you do? You have a right to be proud, and to be recognized and rewarded; you have a right to demand full control over whatever you do, from start to finish. I wouldn't tolerate anyone trying to take that away from me."

Claire saw Emma look up again, but this time she was too absorbed to worry about what her daughter saw. "How would you stop it?" she asked Quentin with a smile.

He shrugged. "There are ways. Once you let others stand in your path, or cross you successfully, they'll see you as a victim and treat you like one. No one will ever do that to me."

Claire's smile had faded. She felt a chill at the careless assurance of his voice. "No one has ever stood in your path? Or crossed you?"

"Not for long or more than once. That was a lesson I learned from being passed around from one set of foster parents to another until I cut loose when I was about fourteen. You learn to take care of yourself, Claire, when no one is around to do it for you, and you learn that everything rests on having the power to control the things that happen to you, instead of being swept away by them. After that, the only thing that matters is having influence. There's a difference between influence and power on a broad stage, a nation or across international lines: a handful of people have real power, and guard it, but influence is available to others if they know how to achieve it. Those are the people—most of them invisible—who really run the machinery of the world."

"And are you one of them?" For the first time Claire found his talk distasteful, and she wondered if it showed in her voice. But if it did, he ignored it.

"Not yet. I will be. You've done well at controlling your own life; you've done well for yourself and for Emma, and you did it on your own. Or did you have parents to run to?"

"No. I had no one."

"Well, then, you know what I mean. In a harsh world, we're often forced to behave harshly, and no one can fault us for it. In fact, others probably envy us because we know how to do it. You said you *were* a graphics designer. What does that mean?"

"I left that job a while ago."

"When you won the lottery."

"Yes."

"Good for you. I can never understand why people say their lives won't change when they come into sudden wealth. Most people's lives should change; they're banal and stultified. What will you do after this trip?"

Claire was silent, frozen with the fear that whatever she said would sound banal or stultified.

"Because if you haven't filled your schedule," Quentin went on, "I hope to see you when we get home. I have some favorite places I'd like to show you, and I'd like you to meet my friends."

Claire felt herself relax. Whatever test he had set for her, she had passed. "I haven't decided just what I'll be doing," she said. "My schedule isn't full."

Across the table, Emma and Brix stood up. "We're going for a walk on the deck," Emma said to Claire. "I don't know what time I'll be back." *Don't wait up* hung in the air, unspoken.

"I think midnight is a good time," Quentin said to Brix. He glanced at his watch. "That gives you enough time to get to know the deck very well."

"Sure," Brix said. But his mouth grew heavy and Claire saw how easily it could become sullen, and how his whole face could follow, heading for a temper tantrum that could take the roof off. She was not sure why she could imagine it so clearly. He was extraordinarily handsome, stockier than his father but with his father's broad shoulders, square chin, and short, strong fingers. Like his father, too, he was wearing a perfectly cut suit and a tie that was not too bold and not too restrained. In fact, there seemed to be absolutely nothing in Brix to worry anyone, even the mother of a seventeen-year-old girl. But Claire worried.

"Mother's worried," Emma said to Brix as they made their way through the crowded lounge. He held one of the double doors open for her and they went out onto the deck. "Oh, it's cold. I didn't think of that."

"No, it's fine," he said, and took off his jacket, draping it around her shoulders. "It gives me a chance to be gallant."

"That's a strange word," Emma said. "Nobody uses it anymore."

"My dad does. He likes words like that. Sort of old-fashioned."

"Is he old-fashioned?"

"Not really; he likes everything modern, you know, furniture and paintings and things; and he can be a real bastard—oh, sorry—but he is, you know, in business. He just likes people to think he's old-fashioned, buying flowers and holding doors open, you know, things like that."

Emma nodded. "He's very handsome. He and my mother seemed pretty close, pretty fast."

"So what's she worried about?" They were strolling along the deck in the diffuse light from overhead ship's lanterns. On one side of them were the slatted deck chairs in a long, unbroken row; on their other side, beyond the ship's railing, a white ribbon of moonlight stretched across the slow,

POT OF GOLD

dark waves of the Inner Passage. A few stars could be seen, and Emma fastened her gaze on the brightest one, suspended low in the sky. For me, she thought; it's shining just for me. Brix's jacket was warm on her shoulders. It's shining for the most wonderful night of my life.

"She can't be worried about me," Brix went on. "She doesn't know anything about me."

"I don't know. Mothers worry, and half the time you don't know why. I suppose it's different for boys."

"Well, nobody ever worried about me. My mother wasn't around much, and then there was this parade of stepmothers I told you about, and they hardly noticed me; they were too busy trying to figure out how to hold on to my dad. They didn't, though; they all lost. The only people who cared what I did were all those governesses my mother kept hiring, and they only cared because they were afraid of losing their job. Between wives, my dad would have me come and live with him, and then *he'd* hire a governess, but then he'd find some woman and I'd go back to my mother until he got tired of whoever he had. Lots of times they weren't married, they were just living together, and he'd decide he was finished and ready to move on. He's always been that way; he does what he wants. He doesn't give any hints up front, he just makes his move, and if something's in his way, he gets rid of it."

His voice was almost flat, but Emma heard the pride in it more than she heard his words. Why would Brix be proud of a father who didn't pay attention to him? But she did not want to criticize Quentin until she knew whether Brix really was proud of him or not. "He's very impressive," she said.

"Right." They walked in silence for a moment. "He needs things to be happening, you know, something always happening; it kills him to stand still. Every year he's got to be richer than before, and more important, more powerful, you know, bigger and better. Otherwise it's like he's dead. He said that; he told me that. It's like he's always running a race with somebody."

Emma had a swift moment of clarity in which she knew

that Brix was talking about himself as well as his father, that they were identical in this, and that Brix was proud of his father and would want to be like him in other ways as well, maybe ways that weren't so nice. But she let the thought fall away; she felt too slow and lazy to hold on to it. The deep murmur of Brix's voice, so close to her, the hum of the ship's engines that seemed to vibrate within her, the lingering fire of the cognac she had sipped, all made her want to open up to the soft night, to stop thinking and just feel.

"You're amazing, the way you listen," Brix said. He took Emma's hand and brought it through the crook of his arm so that the long side of his body pressed against hers. "You know, I told you about Eiger Labs in there. It's usually not the greatest, working for your old man, but we really work together, I mean, he trusts me, you know, and it's getting better; I'm a vice president and I'll take over in a few years when he retires or buys some other companies." There was a silence. "You can learn a lot from him; he's so far ahead of everybody, he's outthinking people and outdoing them all the time."

"You look like him," Emma said.

"I know. You should see pictures of him at my age; it's like twins. Sometimes, it's sort of scary, like I'm not really me, I'm just him repeating himself." He stopped and turned Emma to him. "I like talking to you. I like your name, too. Emma." He said it softly, caressing it with his voice. "Emmmmma. It's like humming; you can sort of hum it under your breath even while you're talking about something else. And you're so beautiful. I'll just look at you and say your name; how would that be? My God, you're blushing. I didn't know girls did that anymore. You don't have to blush; I'm very sincere. Sincere and gallant."

Emma searched his face for mockery, but could see none. In the dim light, shadows marked the hollows of his cheeks, the prominent bones at the sides of his forehead, the sharp ridge of his nose. She liked looking at him; she liked watching him talk. She loved his mouth, full and sensual, seeming to promise mysterious pleasures, and his eyes, as black as the sea, as black as mirrors that gave nothing away.

He began walking again, turning Emma with him. Taken by surprise, she stumbled a little and his grip tightened. "Stay close; I don't want to lose you."

Emma floated beside him, step for step. *This is what it means to be rich; it means meeting people like Brix and his father and living the kind of life they do.*

"The thing is," said Brix, "when you grow up more or less by yourself, with nobody paying much attention, you learn to do whatever you have to do to get along. I figured that out a long time ago and now I don't need anybody; that way I don't get kicked around; I'm in charge of me."

I could make you need me, Emma thought. I could make you happy.

For a minute it struck her that what Brix had said was very odd. Why would he say he didn't want to lose her and then, right away, say he didn't need anyone? She started to ask him, but then bit back the words. Someday she would, she thought, but not now; she did not want to break the spell.

He was so beautiful, and he knew so much, and when he said her name, holding it in his mouth as if it were fine wine, it sounded so different to her that she thought it must mean she, too, was different, a new person, just for Brix. He was twenty-four years old and knew more than any boy she had ever known. He knew about scuba diving in the Cayman Islands, and motorcycling across the Welsh countryside; he knew about skiing at Gstaad and hang gliding above Aspen; he knew about bicycling through the vineyards of Spain and ballooning over Burgundy and racing a motorboat off Monaco and horseback riding through the Tuscan hills. It seemed there was nothing he had not done, and Emma listened to him with a sinking feeling that she could never catch up, because however much she could do, Brix would always be far ahead, more knowledgeable and expert and sophisticated than she could ever hope to be.

Her hand was warm and steady within his firm grasp; their

bodies brushed together as they walked, and Emma felt open and ready for anything, and so happy she could barely contain it, but underneath the happiness was a thread of worry that she would bore him because she didn't know enough. She tried to think of something that would show him she was special, something that would impress him enough to make him want her more than the other women she was sure were lying in wait for him all over the world.

"My mother won the lottery," she blurted out.

"No kidding!" He stopped again. "How much did she get?"

A wave of embarrassment swept over Emma. It was too much; it would sound like a lie.

"How much?" he repeated.

"Sixty million dollars," she said, and added, in a rush, "but of course we don't get all that; they pay it out over twenty years and they take out taxes—"

"Sixty million! God damn; *sixty million?* That's more than a lottery; that's the pot of gold! Hey, that's the greatest thing I ever heard! So what are you going to do with it?"

"Everything," Emma said.

He laughed; he was tremendously excited. "Like what? What's a for instance?"

"Oh, seeing places I've never seen—that's the whole world, practically—and learning things like scuba diving and horseback riding and skiing and riding in balloons and . . . everything."

He laughed again. "When are you going to do all that?"

"I don't know. I'm starting college this fall, but I could do some things in the summers—"

"You could put off college. You could start right away. Emma, this could be terrific; I could help you. You know, teach you. I'll take you anywhere you want to go; we'll go around the world; we'll go—"

"But you work. And I have to go to college. My mother absolutely wants me to go to college."

"Hey, you're old enough—"

POT OF GOLD

"It's her money," Emma said coolly.

Brix caught himself. "Right. I didn't mean to get carried away. You know best, you and your mother; I'm not about to push in there. But maybe, when you decide what you're going to do, you could let me know? I'd like to be part of it, Emma, help out any way I can. Emma. God, I do love your name." He turned her to him and put his arms around her. He was four inches taller than she was; just right, Emma thought. "God, what luck that you're here. Emma. Emma."

He kissed her lightly, then tightened his arms around her and opened her mouth with his. Emma's fingers were in his hair; she wanted to melt into him. *Luck. Such luck. My lucky star. My lucky night.* Don't let it stop, she prayed; don't let it end. I'll never ask for anything else; I just want this to go on forever.

"Getting close to midnight." Brix's voice was thick. "Next time we'll figure out a better way to do this. Come on, Cinderella; I'll deliver you to your doorstep. Will you have breakfast with me tomorrow? And lunch? And dinner?"

Emma opened her eyes. She swayed a little within Brix's arms. "Yes," she said. "Yes to everything."

5

BREAKFAST was very quiet. Emma did not eat. She had wanted to eat with Brix, but Claire had said no, and so, pouting, she slouched at the table, turning her coffee cup around and around, stubbornly silent. Claire and Hannah made conversation about the small, forested islands through which the ship wended its way, and the glimpses of life on the shore: puffins with curved red-and-yellow beaks, seals sunning themselves on slick rocks, shore birds picking their way daintily through the surf. The forest reached the water's edge, so dense it seemed almost black beneath the morning sun. "The light," Hannah mused. "This is the strangest light."

Claire, too, had been gazing out the window, her artist's eye caught by the effects of the slanting rays. "We're so far north," she murmured. "The sun is always at an angle. Much more of an angle than at home." She was fascinated by it: those steeply angled shafts of light that cast long, thin shadows, and the clarity of the light that brought out the tiniest details of land and trees, wildlife and waterfalls, and the towering, jagged mountains, their peaks cloaked with snow. Beneath the overarching, cloudless sky, it was a land of exaggerations, and for the first time in weeks, Claire wished for a sketching pad. I'll have to buy one, she thought, and suddenly was swept up in a feeling of perfect well-being. Everything was beautiful and new and bursting with the promise of more, always more, because now she was rich and she was still young, with health and energy and good looks, enough to impress her daughter, anyway, and Quentin Eiger. She felt capable of anything; she wanted to hug the world that waited for her, none of it closed to her, ever again.

But Emma was sitting across the table, pouting, casting a cloud on Claire's bright day, and Emma was more important than anything else. They were almost alone in the dining room as the other passengers left for the deck, and Claire poured more coffee and sat back, hoping she looked casual, hoping Hannah would help. She almost always gave in when Emma got angry and unhappy, but this time she wanted to be firm. "Okay, sweetheart," she said, "let's talk about what we're going to do."

"I just want to be with Brix," Emma said. "What's so terrible about that?"

Claire shook her head. "No one said it was terrible. All I said was that I wanted you to be with us for breakfast. And I said I didn't want you to spend all of your time with him."

"Why not?" Emma demanded.

"Because you're with us," Hannah said crisply, but at Claire's exasperated sigh she knew it was not the time to step in, and she subsided.

"It's too fast, when it's all concentrated in one week and one place," Claire said, "when everything around you is unfamiliar. It's not . . . real." She saw the waiters cast impatient glances at them, waiting to clear the table and set it for lunch. "Sometimes we cling to people when we're cut off from our regular life and we know it's for a short time. Everything gets exaggerated and speeded up; we elevate people to something special, something they may not be, and our own feelings, that ought to take months to develop, seem wonderful and terribly important, even when they're not."

"How do you know?" Emma cried. "You've never been on a cruise; you don't know anything about it."

"I know how this can happen—" Claire began.

"Anyway," Emma went on, her voice rising, "we don't *have* a familiar life! It's all changed, it's all new. We're doing all these things we've never done before, and you think it's okay as long as *you* decide what new things we do, but if I want to do something new, be with somebody new, you say I can't. Why shouldn't I? *You're* with somebody new; if you can do it, so can I!"

"I didn't say you couldn't see him," Claire said. "I said you should slow down. I told myself the same thing; it's too easy to get caught up in something that seems special but doesn't really mean anything. Emma, please, we've come to this wonderful place; let's see everything we can, and share it with new friends, but with each other, too. I'm just asking for a little restraint."

"Restraint is for old people," Emma said coldly.

"Dear me," said Hannah. "That sounds like an epitaph." She watched Emma blush. "I think you should apologize."

Emma threw an exasperated look at the ceiling. "I'm *sorry*. I'm sorry for what I said, but, you know, it's hard."

"Yes, I remember," Hannah said. Emma looked at her in surprise. "Well, of course I went through the same thing when I was your age; did you think you were the only one? Or that it's new? I fought with my mother all the time, over one thing or another; I suppose I would have fought with my daughter, if she'd lived."

Emma's head jerked up. "*If she'd lived?* You had a daughter who *died?*"

"I'll tell you about it sometime, but not today," Hannah said, and stood up. "We should be on deck; your mother was right: that's what we're here for."

Claire was staring at her. "You never told us you had a child. You said you'd never married. Were you married?"

"No, that didn't happen, which almost broke my heart. We'll talk about it sometime, when I'm ready. I'm sorry I brought it up now."

No, you're not, Claire thought. You brought it up deliberately to distract Emma and get us out of our quarrel. *What a clever woman you are. I wonder how many other bombshells you have stored up, ready to set off whenever you think we need one.* "I hope you will tell us," she said to Hannah. "We'd like to know all about you."

"Well, I don't know about *all*," Hannah said lightly. "Now, one more thing. What are we doing for dinner?"

Claire hesitated, then let it go. If Hannah liked being mysterious, they'd have to get used to it. "Emma," she said, "did you make plans with Brix for dinner?"

"Breakfast, lunch, and dinner," Emma muttered.

"Well, we've settled that; it's too much. But I think dinner would be all right. Quentin and I are having dinner; Hannah, will you join us?"

"No, no, my dear, good heavens, what a nuisance for you, and not exactly fascinating for me. No, I've made my own arrangements with Forrest. He's an astonishing young man, a college professor, and an expert in every one of my favorite poets; such an amazing discovery for me. Every one! We'll find a quiet corner by ourselves. So, we're all taken care of; how satisfactory. Now shall we go on deck?"

"A college professor," Claire said, smiling. "Maybe I should be telling you to take it easy, too."

"Take it easy? Oh, you mean a romance. No, no, it's nothing like that. He wants to start a poetry center somewhere and I want to hear about it; it does sound exciting. Now, then, let's go look at the scenery."

"Can I go now?" Emma asked, sounding like a child kept after school.

"Yes," Claire said. She could not fight Emma for the entire trip, and so she watched her dash away and told herself that somehow it would all work out.

The ship glided silently along the coast, weaving through the small islands dense with cedar, fir, and hemlock, the silence broken by passengers calling out as they saw a killer whale or porpoise, a salmon leaping up a waterfall, or the long swooping turn of an eagle. Unexpectedly and without an explanation, Emma came back and spent the day with Claire and Hannah, smiling at the porpoises and talking about the mysteries of the forests. A heavy cloud covered the sun and everyone pulled on sweaters and jackets. Someone caught a glimpse, through the trees, of a magnificent pair of antlers, and a hush fell over the ship as the elk moved into the open, and then came the sound of hundreds of clicking cameras. Impervious to it all, waiters served drinks and snacks, cleared glasses away, and returned with more. The day slid by as easily as the ship moved through the channel, a lovely day of countless wonders.

And then it was evening and Quentin knocked on Claire's stateroom door. He took in with one glance her hair, loosely pinned back, her pearl earrings, and her white silk suit, the collar and cuffs sewn with tiny pearls. "Very lovely," he said, and took her hand as they went to dinner.

"I want you to meet some of my friends," he said as they were shown to a round table with six upholstered chairs. "They'll be here in a few minutes. Did you have a pleasant day?"

"Yes." Claire masked her disappointment; she had looked forward to a quiet dinner. "I didn't see you; you weren't on deck? Everything was so beautiful."

"We were one deck down; our friends have a suite there. I kept Brix with me; I thought a little separation would be good for the young people."

Claire was silent, wondering if he always took other people's affairs so thoroughly into his own hands. That was why Emma came back, she thought; either she never found Brix, or she found him in his father's orbit.

"We even did a little work," Quentin went on. "One of my friends is a lawyer for Eiger Labs, and we had some papers to go over. And here they are." He stood, putting his arm around a short, stocky man with a blond crew cut, and leaning down to kiss the cheek of the petite redhead at his side. "Lorraine and Ozzie Thurman; Claire Goddard."

As they all shook hands, Lorraine tilted her head, her

mouth pursed. "I know you. No, I don't; but I've seen your picture. Where was it? And I read about you. Lots. Oh! The lottery! You won the lottery! Quentin, for heaven's sake, why didn't you tell us? She's a famous lady. Well, congratulations, what a super thing to happen. I hope you're having a ball with your money, buying up the world. What's money for, if not to buy everything you've ever fancied, is what I always say. Can we sit down? I'd love a drink. Claire, you sit next to me so we can get acquainted."

"Where are Ina and Zeke?" Quentin asked.

"Late, as usual," Lorraine said serenely. "They're fighting, and you know they never socialize when they're yelling at each other. Which is fine with me; I absolutely cannot stand it when couples make snide remarks and snap at each other in front of the rest of us; what do they expect us to do, choose sides and cheer them on, or lay bets on who wins or just pretend nothing's happening? Anyway, good for them, they do it behind closed doors and they'll be here as soon as they cool off. What's a marriage for, if you can't blow off steam now and then, is what I always say. Martini," she said to the waiter. "Very dry, with a twist. That gorgeous daughter is yours, isn't she?" she asked Claire. "We saw you in the dining room last night; what a joy she must be to you. Ozzie and I have four sons, so I'm waiting for a granddaughter; that ought to be enough fun to make up for the shock of being a grandmother. And it will be nice to have someone need me again. I do like to be needed. And what about you? You're from Connecticut, I know that much from the paper, and what else?"

"And I'm having a ball with the money," Claire said with a smile.

Lorraine laughed. Her little face with its pointed chin wrinkled up like a monkey's. She was amazingly homely, Claire thought, but somehow it was forgotten in the rush of her chatter and the brightness of her eyes, which beamed rays of good cheer to everyone around her. She wore a blue satin pantsuit that overwhelmed her tiny figure, and a necklace and earrings too heavy for her, but none of that mattered because she looked happy with herself. "What else?" she asked Claire. Her glance dropped to Claire's left hand. "You're a widow? Divorced?"

"Divorced," Claire said.

"For long?"

"Long enough to be used to it."

"And?" she pressed. "And, and, and?"

"And it doesn't seem fair that you've read about me but I don't know anything about you."

"I don't believe this. A woman who doesn't want to talk about herself. Come on, Claire, I'm giving you the stage. You're more interesting than I am; I've never won anything, unless you count Ozzie, and that was a humdinger, but it was thirty years ago and since then I never needed to win anything, he's always taken such good care of me. I don't work, I don't have a single skill, except for friendship; I'm a truly good friend. And traveler; we've been all over the world a dozen or so times and I'm really good at that, shopping, you know, and finding the best nightspots and museums and châteaux and great churches, you know. What's a wife for, if not to be a walking guidebook, is what I always say. The article in the paper said something about you being an artist? Is that right?"

"A designer," Claire said.

"Quentin told me you bought a house in Wilton," Ozzie said, breaking in. "I've been thinking of buying a couple of farms north of there, for development. Have you lived there long?"

"I've lived in Danbury all my life."

"Well, good. I'd like to talk to you sometime; get your feeling about the area. Where people are moving and shopping, the way it's growing, you know, that sort of thing."

"I'm sure there are realtors—" Claire began helplessly.

He shook his head. "It's always better to talk to people in a town, especially people with money. They have a feel for

POT OF GOLD

what's going on before anybody else does." He looked at Claire as if waiting for her to make pronouncements.

"I absolutely cannot believe you're talking business," Lorraine said. "Claire, who was the other person at your table last night?"

"Hannah Goddard," Claire replied.

"Oh, a relative. Your grandmother?"

Claire smiled. "I think she's my fairy godmother."

"Fairy godmother." Lorraine stretched out the words. "I like it. I want one. What does she do?"

"She knows when I need her. I never ask; she just knows. She showed up on a day when everything seemed to be too much, and she took over, and since then, somehow she's known when to step in and organize things."

"And you allow that?" Quentin asked. "Someone organizing your life?"

"Not such a bad idea, now and then, when things get crazy," Ozzie said. "If I could wave a wand and have somebody come in and make everything smooth and sweet-smelling, would I take it? You're damn right I would."

"I would, too, whatever it is," said a man coming up behind Ozzie, and the men stood up.

"Ina and Zeke Roditis; Claire Goddard," Quentin said, and when they were all seated, Lorraine said, "We were talking about Claire's fairy godmother."

"How quaint," said Ina. Tall, large-boned, with straight black hair falling to her shoulders and prominent eyes, she was not beautiful but striking, and in her black dress, red silk shawl, and ruby necklace and earrings, she looked, Claire thought, like a dancer, or perhaps one of the eagles they had seen that afternoon, surveying the scene, prepared to swoop. "Does she grant all your wishes? Or just convince you you didn't want whatever it was in the first place?"

"Oh, Ina, that's so cynical," said Lorraine. "Why not believe in fairy godmothers? I'll bet you'd be a lot happier if you did."

"Easier to live with, too, no doubt," said Zeke. He was an

91

JUDITH MICHAEL

enormous man with a hooked nose, bushy eyebrows, and a paunch that hung over his hand-tooled leather belt. He put an arm around his wife. "You should give it a try. Claire, how did you come by a fairy godmother to guide you through the minefields and pitfalls and so forth of life?"

"She came to me," Claire said evenly, "and I'm sorry there aren't enough of them to go around."

"What does she do, other than organize?" Lorraine asked.

"Organize?" Ina echoed. "You mean, like closets?"

"Bad joke, Ina," Ozzie said.

"Oh, Lorraine, that reminds me," Ina said. "Dolly wants you and Ozzie at her birthday thing at Cap Ferrat; she rented a villa. She said she sent you an invitation but it came back with 'Unknown' stamped on it."

"Wrong address, probably," Lorraine said.

"Well, of course. She's really not all there."

"Did you ever try to have a real conversation with her?" Zeke asked. "She mostly talks about money, which let me tell you is very boring after a while, but all the time she's coming at you with her significant boobs out in front like an advancing tank. And I'm backing up, you know, just to keep a little distance, space, air, and so forth, but she keeps coming until I'm in a corner and she's still moving. I mean, we're at a party with two hundred people; what does she want me to do, start fondling?"

"How about the time she talked for an hour about why she likes giraffes?" Ozzie asked.

"Well, you men were all listening," Lorraine said. "Ears erect, and I'll bet other parts, too."

"I was watching Earl," Ozzie said. "The husband sitting there with a weird smile on his face while his wife performs."

"He bragged about it when she did that nude series for Lord Snowden," Ina said.

"That was a performance, too," said Zeke. "Some people just have to be in the spotlight all the time. And he gets it through her."

POT OF GOLD

"People with money don't usually do that," Lorraine said.

Zeke shrugged. "We do whatever makes us feel good. Dolly and Earl like to act the fool. They're tiresome, but unimportant."

"So we'll see you at their party at Cap Ferrat next week?" Ina asked.

"Why not?" Lorraine said. "Ozzie, just this one party, and then we'll go home, I promise."

"She's always promising me we can go home," Ozzie said. "And then another party comes along. Ina, you're a bad influence."

"Not bad, just powerful," said Zeke. "Like that goddess who makes the wind blow or whatever. Tough to live with, let me tell you."

"Oh, Zeke, lighten up," said Lorraine.

"That was a god," Ina said.

"Who was?" Zeke asked.

"Aeolus, king of the wind. A god, not a goddess. You can't blame the wind on women."

Zeke shrugged.

"Anyway," Lorraine said to Ozzie, "you like these parties, too."

Ozzie nodded. "You're right; I confess. Most of them are okay; I like having people to talk to. The best are Quentin's, though. Those I wouldn't miss."

"Because Quentin gives people what they want," Ina said. "Or talks them into wanting what he wants to give." She put a casual, faintly possessive hand on Quentin's arm. "Isn't that what you do with your cosmetics? Convince all of us they're what we want?"

"Exactly," Quentin said lazily.

Ina looked beyond Quentin, to Claire. "You'll have to watch him; he's a magician. He mesmerizes all his friends and we become his happy little camp followers; no will of our own at all."

"Oh, Ina," said Lorraine, exasperated. "Claire, don't listen to her. She's not in a good mood tonight."

"It's my fault," Zeke said. "I dragged her out here before she was ready. I was anxious to meet Claire. And we've barely talked to her."

"You're right," said Lorraine. "We've been terribly rude. Claire, I'm sorry; you're not seeing us at our best. I think we get a little snappish when we travel; maybe it's something in the water. You'll see the difference when we're home and we're all close by."

"Close?" Ina looked at Claire again. "I don't remember seeing you."

"We haven't been at the same parties," Claire said.

"But you would have read about her if you ever picked up a newspaper," said Lorraine. "Claire won the lottery a little while back; she's a celebrity."

"The lottery," Ina said, as if it were a foreign word. "The lottery. But how sweet. So now you have a little extra money; how nice for you."

"I heard about that," Zeke said. "There was a lot of hoopla, TV, newspapers, and so on and so forth. Sorry, Claire, I didn't make the connection. But it wasn't little, I remember that; it was megabucks."

"Was it," Ina said. There was a silence. "Well, how big was it?"

The silence went on. "Isn't that like asking somebody's salary?" Ozzie asked.

"It's hardly private information if it was in the newspapers and on television," Ina retorted.

"But I'd rather not talk about it," Claire said.

"Well, I know how much it was, because I remember what I read," said Lorraine, "but I won't give it away. Let's just say it was more than a pound of caviar and less than the national debt."

"But it's part of the story, isn't it?" Ina asked. "Not just winning, but how much you won. I'd really like to know how much you won."

"But Claire doesn't want to talk about it," Quentin said flatly.

There was another silence. "Well, but how exciting for you," Ina said to Claire, leaning forward to speak across Quentin. "Did you go on a shopping spree?" Her glance swept Claire's white suit. "But of course you did; that's from Simone's, isn't it? I come up from New York sometimes to shop there; such a dear little collection." She stole a quick glance at Quentin, to see if she was redeeming herself in his eyes. "And then you came to Alaska; isn't it an amazing place? So different from Europe and Africa."

"Well, we can't argue with that," Zeke said.

"Aren't you enjoying it?" Lorraine asked.

"There are a few too many icebergs," Ina said. "And forests. And not a single Bergdorf's. Oh, what the hell, I'm sorry." She put out her hands. "You're right; I'm just not in a good mood. I think it must be the altitude."

"We're at sea level," Zeke said.

"It's just that we had one of our fights." Ina looked at the others. "But you knew that, didn't you? So I'm a little wound up." She looked at Claire. "Anyway, congratulations. I'm sorry you thought I was rude; I was curious, and why wouldn't you be proud of winning a lot of money? I would be. I'd tell everyone. So we should propose a toast, shouldn't we? To Claire."

"To Claire," said Ozzie.

They all raised their glasses. "Thank you," Claire said. She was uncomfortable. It was the kind of occasion she would share with Gina and a few other friends in Danbury, but not with these strangers, caught up in their own relationships and not really interested in her.

"And if you need investment advice," Ina said, "you should come to Zeke; he's really the best."

"Lighten up, Ina," Zeke said. "This is dinner, this is a cruise. But I certainly do humbly offer my services and advice and guidance, Claire." He handed her a card. "I'm in New York and I have an office in Norwalk. Call on me anytime. That's my home phone number there, in the right-hand corner."

"This is dinner, this is a cruise," muttered Ozzie. "Come on, Zeke, you're doing business here, for Christ's sake."

"Just getting acquainted," said Zeke.

"Not really," Lorraine said. "We've been talking about ourselves and people Claire doesn't even know."

"Who?" Zeke asked. "Oh, you mean Dolly and Earl. Well, but she wouldn't want to be acquainted with them."

"But I don't know why you're going to their party," Claire said.

"Damned if I know," Ozzie sighed. "Ask my social secretary."

Lorraine shrugged. "People just go. What are parties for, if not to go to, is what I always say. It doesn't seem to matter whether you like someone or not; you go to their parties and you invite them to yours. You know what it's like, it's like those pinball machines where the little ball bounces around in a maze, but instead of rolling out, it just keeps going around in the maze, forever. That's us; we don't know the way out."

"That's clever," Ozzie said with surprise in his voice. "A maze. You don't usually say things like that."

"It must be Claire," Lorraine said. "She makes me think of new things."

Claire looked up and met Quentin's eyes. These were his friends, and she could see he was amused by them, but there was also a flicker of boredom in his eyes, and she wondered if he made a point of surrounding himself with people he considered inferior to him; people who thought him superior. *Happy little camp followers; no will of our own at all.* Certainly, tonight, he dominated their table; he had hardly spoken at all, but the others were always aware of him and often spoke to him even when someone else had asked a question. There was a quality to his stillness—watchful, coiled, implacable—that sent a message of power, and Claire could see that many would be drawn to it, even as others would stiffen in opposition. Like the land they had come to, she thought,

POT OF GOLD

Quentin Eiger was a man of exaggeration, nothing subdued or pale about him. And when he turned to her, to hear what she had to say, or to watch her with approval or admiration, and she felt herself respond, sitting straighter, proud that she had impressed him, she felt she had become someone else, someone she did not yet understand.

Later, when the others had gone to the theater for a movie, the two of them went out to the deck and he asked her what she thought of his friends. They were standing at the railing in the long, fading twilight that cast a pale glow over the ship and the narrow passage through which they sailed. Claire had wrapped a black and silver cashmere shawl around her, and Quentin was looking at her while she gazed at the dense forests that opened up now and then to reveal sudden glints of waterfalls and small villages tucked among the inlets and bays. A breeze blew steadily, the birds had fallen silent as twilight deepened, only a few passengers were on deck, and Claire felt happy and keyed up because Quentin wanted to be with her alone.

"I liked Lorraine and Ozzie, as you thought I would," she said. "And I wasn't fond of Ina and Zeke, just as you expected."

He contemplated her. "How did you know what I expected?"

"The way you introduced them, the way you looked at them when they were talking, the way you said goodnight after dinner."

"You make me sound transparent."

Claire shook her head. "You give away much less than most people; I think you're very guarded. But I couldn't be a good designer if I weren't a good observer. I'd think I'd lost my touch if I hadn't seen something as simple as how you felt about your friends."

He smiled slightly. "When do you relax and stop being a good observer?"

"I don't. Why would I?"

"Perhaps so the rest of us can relax." He was still smiling, but Claire saw that he was serious. "What was it about Ina and Zeke that you didn't like?"

"They take themselves too seriously and they don't take other people seriously enough."

"And do you take people seriously?"

She looked at him in surprise. "I hope so. I like people, and I usually believe what they say, and I don't make fun of them or the way they feel about the world."

"But you don't have many friends."

"What an odd thing to say. I have one very close friend and a few friends I see now and then. Emma and I are quiet people; we don't look for crowds."

"And your husband? Did he feel the same way?"

Claire sighed. "Why does everyone ask about my husband? Isn't it enough that I obviously don't have one?"

He smiled. "Evidently not. Most people want the whole story; don't you?"

"As much as anyone wants to tell; I don't pry." Claire looked away from him, at the shadows on the shore. It was after eleven, and finally, the twilight was melting into darkness. The moon skimmed the tops of the trees, a crescent that grew brighter with the coming of night. She thought of the night before, when she had believed Quentin was being completely open about his marriages and about Brix. But of course he had not been completely open; she had watched him tonight, sitting coiled and watchful, and she had wondered if he was ever completely honest with anyone. But, still, she felt she owed him an answer. "My husband liked lots of people around him, all the time. He liked to believe that something more exciting was always about to happen."

"And was it?"

"I guess so." She hesitated. "He followed it, whatever it was, and I never saw him again."

Quentin took her hands and held them in both of his. "That was hard for you to say." Claire was silent. "He didn't stay in touch? He just—"

"He just wasn't there anymore."

POT OF GOLD

"And he didn't leave you any money. Or send any."

"No."

"Or try to see his daughter."

"I don't think he gave her a thought. She wasn't a person when he left."

"This was before she was born?"

"Yes."

"How old were you?"

"Seventeen. Almost eighteen."

"You were in high school?"

"I'd just started college, but I had to drop out and go to work when he left. We were married the day after we graduated from high school. He left when I was four months pregnant with Emma."

"Because you were pregnant?"

She shook her head slightly. "I'm sure he didn't want to be a father, but I think he just couldn't stay very long with one woman, and having a baby on the way made him face the fact that that's the basic definition of marriage. My friends had warned me about him, but I didn't believe them, and anyway, I thought I could change him. Of course I was wrong; it isn't easy to change anyone, and love isn't enough to do it."

Quentin put his arms around her and kissed her. It was a strange kiss, without passion or excitement. As cool as a handshake, Claire thought; or testing the waters. "You're very lovely, and very wise," he said, his lips close to hers, and Claire pulled back. She was confused and vaguely disappointed, as if they had taken a wrong turn in a journey she had been enjoying.

"Good night," she said, and because she could not think of anything else to say, she turned and walked away, through the door into the lounge and up the stairs to the boat deck and her stateroom. She took with her the memory of Quentin's face as she walked off: thoughtful, but also amused, as it had been when he watched his friends at dinner. Maybe he thinks I'm inferior, she thought, just like his other friends.

"It wasn't a pleasant evening?" Hannah asked the next

day. She and Claire were walking slowly down Creek Street in Ketchikan, waiting for Emma, who was browsing in the shops. Once, in the early part of the century, the street had been the town's red-light district, but now the tiny houses, perched on stilts over the creek, had been converted to boutiques, craft shops, and art galleries. The town was nestled at the edge of a mountainous island, its climate so rainy the forests were emerald green. But today the sun shone, and passengers from two cruise ships crowded the streets. Claire and Hannah had visited the totem parks early, before Emma was awake, and now, walking through the town, Claire suggested they climb Deer Mountain.

"It's three thousand feet high, and the trail is three miles long," Hannah said mildly. "I read about it last night. If you want to go, I'll find a tearoom and wait. Are you looking for something strenuous to work off last night? It wasn't a pleasant evening?"

"It was very strange. I didn't like a lot of it, but I can't stop thinking about it." She paused, waiting for Hannah to say something, but Hannah was silent, and finally Claire added, "Or Quentin. I can't stop thinking about him, either."

"Why not?"

"Because he's the kind of man people like to impress, and please; they feel good about themselves when they've done it."

"And did you please him?"

"I think so. He made me think I did."

"Well then?"

"I don't know." Claire stopped walking. "He makes me feel . . . young. Inexperienced. As if I'm on my first date. Something like that, anyway. I've been through all this; I've gone out with men and had affairs and I ought to be used to it and at least know what I'm doing. But I don't, with Quentin, and I hate it and it's exciting, all at the same time. He's scary, in an odd way: I can't tell whether he's really honest or what he thinks of me or what he expects of me. He seems to get his power over people partly by keeping them at a distance, so maybe I'll never really get to know him. And what difference does it make? I gave such good advice to Emma; I ought to follow it myself. It's crazy: I'm on my first trip ever, the first time I've been more than a few miles from Connecticut, and all I'm thinking about is a man I met two days ago."

"And what is wrong with that?" Hannah asked gently.

"I just told you. Everything in my life has changed and I ought to be paying attention to all the new things I'm doing, all the things I'm able to do."

"Well, I don't know about that. I used to think about men all the time; I thought they were more interesting and fun, and more important, than schoolwork or my job or all my women friends put together."

Diverted, Claire said, "When did you think about men all the time?"

"Oh, when I was young and ignorant. Because I was wrong, of course, as I soon found out; generally speaking, women are a lot more interesting and important in our lives than men, and much more reliable. But that doesn't mean we shouldn't think about men, even when we're traveling to new places. Just keep everything in balance and you'll be fine."

"It's hard to keep everything in balance." Claire stopped and made a gesture of annoyance. "That's what I mean about sounding young. I worry about Emma keeping things balanced, but I sound like I'm about her age."

"Well, maybe you ought to feel young. Maybe you missed being young when your husband disappeared and you had to be mother and father to Emma, and breadwinner, and everything else at seventeen. Right now you ought to be paying attention to how you feel and what you're going to do with yourself with all the changes in your life. You've had a great fortune come to you; how do you know whether things will be better or worse because of it? Maybe lots of good things will happen, but maybe bad things will, too. Give yourself some time, Claire; you'll figure things out as you go along."

"Bad things?" Claire repeated.

"Well, it's a possibility."

"I never thought of that. Everything's been so wonderful. It never occurred to me. And what does that have to do with Quentin?"

"Probably nothing. What do *I* know? Now. Tell me about the people at dinner."

Claire hesitated, then shrugged it off. She looked back to make sure Emma was still in sight, and then they started walking again. She glanced at the women's names on the front of each house: small signs that identified and advertised each of them. Ahead was "Dolly's," supposedly the most famous madam of them all. Claire smiled slightly. "They talked about someone named Dolly last night. They don't like her but they go to all her parties, and I guess she goes to theirs. Well, I liked Lorraine and Ozzie; they probably get along with everyone. He's a lawyer and she says she's good at friendship and traveling. I think she'd like to do something with her life but she doesn't know what. They're not unhappy, so they don't try to needle others into unhappiness to spread their misery around; and they don't seem to be terribly greedy or insecure, so they don't put down people who have more than they have. Ina and Zeke fight a lot and I don't know whether that means they don't like each other or they're just so worried about other things they can't be content with each other."

"Worried about what?" Hannah asked.

"Oh, I guess keeping their place in society, whatever that is. They all seem to worry about that, not missing parties, that sort of thing. Oh, and I think Ina wants to go to bed with Quentin."

"And will she?"

"I doubt it."

"Why not? Does he dislike her?"

"I don't think he thinks about her one way or the other."

"But he invited her to dinner."

"Probably because of Zeke. He has an investment company and he may handle Quentin's money. That may be one of the things he worries about: keeping Quentin as a client. He made a pitch to get my business, which was peculiar, at a dinner party."

"Well, people have been trying to get your money since you won the lottery."

"But he chose an odd time. In fact, the whole evening was odd: none of them really liked each other, but all four of them wanted to be close to Quentin. Like puppies, all squeezing against the stomach of the largest dog." She paused and added in a low voice, "I don't want to be one of the puppies."

"I don't see you doing that," Hannah said briskly. "You're too smart. And besides, when a woman starts to remake her life, she isn't looking to stretch her neck out so somebody can put a leash around it."

Claire smiled. "I like that."

"So you weren't fond of the friends."

"I wouldn't choose them for my friends, if that's what you're asking. Well, maybe Lorraine. But I can't imagine spending a lot of time with any of them."

"And Quentin? Will you see him again?"

"I can't really help it; it's a small ship, you know, not like those huge ones with over a thousand people."

"That's not what I meant."

"I know. Oh, I guess I will. I guess I want to. I liked being with him and I keep thinking about being with him again. If he wants to, of course. He may not." She smiled at Hannah. "You're wonderful to talk to. I told the others last night that you're my fairy godmother."

"Good heavens, what do I do to live up to that?"

"Just what you're doing; I love having you around."

"Well, I love being around, and I thank you for it. Now why don't you go climb your mountain? I'll walk with Emma."

"Oh, would you?" Claire turned to look for Emma. "Oh, damn," she sighed. "Now what should I do?"

JUDITH MICHAEL

Hannah turned with her. Brix and Emma were standing in the middle of the narrow sidewalk, deep in conversation, oblivious to the crowds. "They do make a handsome couple," Hannah said. "So tall, both of them, and so beautiful to look at. Oh, all that youth and energy and everything ahead of them! That's how I always wanted to look, and I never did."

"But what shall I do about them?" Claire murmured.

"Right now, nothing, wouldn't you say? I can't imagine us dragging Emma down the streets of Ketchikan, or even having an argument right here, in the middle of town. And why would you want to? What's wrong with him?"

"I don't know," Claire said slowly. "I just don't trust him."

"Because you don't understand his father?"

Claire gave a small, embarrassed laugh. "That makes it sound absurd. I don't know. I wish I did."

"Well, it's going to be hard to keep them apart, you know: as far as I can tell, they're the only young people on the ship, and that does throw them together."

Claire nodded. "And it's only a week."

Hannah squinted in the sunlight, watching Brix put his arm around Emma. "And we do trust Emma."

"It's just that she's never known anyone like him before," Claire said, and then thought, and I've never known anyone like Quentin. That's probably why he makes me feel so inexperienced. I'm not nearly as ignorant as those people at dinner thought I was; in fact, I think I'm a lot smarter than they are, but I'm not worldly, and that makes all the difference.

"You're sure about what you saw last night," she said to Hannah.

"I told you: they went to a movie and then they sat in the upper-deck lounge until Emma went to bed. They're being very good children; I wouldn't worry about them."

"They're not children, and you know it."

Hannah contemplated them through the shifting crowds. "I could think of them as my children."

Claire looked at Hannah. "Your children? Did you have more than one?"

"No, only one."

"And you were going to tell us about her."

"And I will; there's plenty of time. Now, why don't I walk with Emma and Brix? They can keep me company. And if you want to climb that mountain, you'd better get started; the ship leaves at four."

"You'll keep an eye on her? Thank you." Claire leaned down and kissed Hannah's cheek, then walked swiftly in the direction of the trail up Deer Mountain while Hannah made her way along the crowded sidewalk to Emma's side. "Your mother is climbing a mountain, so I'll spend some time with you," she said cheerfully, ignoring the look of dismay in both Emma's and Brix's eyes. "And, Brix, Emma is dining with us tonight; you're certainly welcome if you'd like to join us. There's a lecture after dinner on Glacier Bay and we're going to that, too. We have so much to learn and to see; after all, who knows if we'll ever get back here?"

"Mrs. Goddard," Brix began.

"Miss," Hannah corrected gently.

He looked surprised. "Emma said you had a daughter. Who died?"

"True. But I haven't been married. I thought I told Emma that, too."

"Doesn't matter," Brix said. "Look, Miss Goddard, Emma and I really want to be alone. I was just telling her I love her and that's just for us."

Hannah was stymied. Few people had ever stopped her cold when she put her mind to something, but Brix had done it, leaving her nothing to stand on.

"We'll see you later," Emma said. "We can talk then." There may have been a small note of apology in her voice, but it was drowned out by exultation. Her eyes were shining. Brix was beside her and he loved her, and she was not about to worry if an old woman had been shoved aside.

"I'll knock on your door later," Hannah said, still cheerful. "Your mother will want to talk to you, too, don't you think?"

"I guess." Emma looked at Brix and he put his arm around her and turned her with him to walk away. Hannah watched them go: tall, confident, beautiful. That is a very sly young man, she thought. Someone to be reckoned with. And so, perhaps, is his father. This could be a very complicated vacation. How fortunate that I'm here, to keep an eye on things.

6

THE helicopter lifted off its pad early in the morning and in an instant was over the glacier that lay in Juneau's backyard. Under a brilliant sun, it flew low over the long river of blue-white, roiling, choppy ice that cut ever deeper the valley through which it had scraped and carved its way for centuries. The pilot flew lower and settled the helicopter slowly onto the ice. The guide opened the door. "Don't go too far, and only walk where it's packed down; there are thin spots all around."

Emma was the first one out, taking long steps in the boots the guide had given them. She moved away from the helicopter until she stood alone, turning in place. Claire and Hannah followed, and the three of them gazed at the massive river of ice that seemed to tremble as they stood on it. On each side was a solid, dark wall of larches and hemlocks, and rising above them were brooding mountains of gray rock, stark against the cloudless sky.

Even Emma, who had so far seen Alaska through a romantic haze, was struck by it, and for the first time, she really saw the landscape. "It's fantastic," she said. "Isn't it? It's totally unbelievable. Everything is so huge, and . . . pure. It's so odd; it makes me feel really small but like I'm part of something really enormous." She shivered. "I like that, being part of something so big. I mean, it doesn't have anything to do with us, nobody built it and nobody can tear it down, and it couldn't care less whether we're here or not; it'll be here forever. So if I'm part of it, I will be, too. In a way."

"That's very poetic," Hannah said.

Claire put her arm around Emma. "It's the way I feel, too, but I couldn't have said it so well."

Emma flushed, for the moment in perfect harmony with her mother.

"Well, of course it's always good to find things that last," Hannah said.

"Lots of things last," Emma said. "Love lasts."

"Oh, dear, not always. That's probably what makes it so wonderful, knowing that it's fragile. Oh, look at that eagle, riding the air currents; he's barely moving his wings. He looks like he owns the sky."

Emma looked dreamily at the eagle. "Brix saw eagles in Africa."

"Is that so," said Hannah.

"He was on an animal safari. He was ten feet from a lion; he said you could hear it breathing."

Hannah nodded. "I did that once."

Emma stared at her. "*You* were in Africa?"

"A long time ago. Before the hordes of tourists came."

"And Brix climbed Kilimanjaro." She looked challengingly at Hannah.

"Well, no," Hannah said amiably. "I certainly did not climb Kilimanjaro."

"Brix said it was really tough, but worth it." Emma walked back to the helicopter, not wanting to hear anything more that might chip away at Brix's uniqueness.

She stayed with Claire and Hannah for the rest of their time in Juneau, walking the winding streets left over from its days as a mining camp, past modern buildings dwarfed by the forests and the glacier they had just flown over and, always, everywhere, the mountains. All of Alaska gave Claire the feeling that she was on the edge of the world. The towns were

POT OF GOLD

wedged between mountains, forests, and water, and most of them, with worn wooden buildings, many on stilts, had a frail look, as if a strong wind could topple them. Even the state capital in Juneau, with its marble pillars, looked to her like a mirage in the midst of the wilderness.

She loved the vastness of the land, its serenity and silence, and the exuberant abundance of its wildlife. Nothing could be further from the tamed landscapes of Connecticut. Now I know why I wanted to come here, she thought. I wanted something wild and free, more dramatic than anything I've ever known.

But as the ship moved north and seemed to be swallowed up by the wilderness, she began to feel a sense of loss. Everywhere she looked, couples stood at the rail or ate together or danced or played in the casino at night. Claire knew there were other single people on board, but she stopped seeing them after a while; she saw only couples. She wanted to be part of one. She wanted to see this gargantuan land with a man she loved.

Emma was doing that. She had told Claire she was in love, the night after Claire's climb up Deer Mountain. "I love him and he loves me," she said. Her eyes were wide with the wonder of Brix and her own feelings. "And we want to be together, and why shouldn't we? What's so terrible about it? I wouldn't be normal if I wanted to be with you and Hannah all the time, instead of Brix."

"Well, that's true," Claire said with a smile. She contemplated her beautiful daughter, wearing a pale blue chiffon blouse and short skirt, her hair curly and windblown from walking on the deck with Brix until midnight. "What is he like?" she asked.

"Oh, he's so wonderful. He's very smart, and sweet, and he's been everywhere and done everything, but in a lot of ways he's still like a little boy, and he needs so much love . . . he never really had a mother, there were just all those women that his father married. Brix never had a real family, ever."

"He has a father who cares for him."

JUDITH MICHAEL

Emma shook her head. "I don't think Quentin really cares for him at all, not from some of the things Brix says. And Brix is really confused about him. I mean, of course he loves him, but he's awfully angry, too, because he feels like he was cheated out of a lot when he was growing up; his father wasn't around much and there were all those wives, and Brix was never sure where he belonged. But then, you know, underneath all his anger—and his sort of swaggering—I think he's really dying for his father to be proud of him, and I think he wants to be just like his father. He didn't tell me any of that; I just think it. Did Quentin talk about him to you?"

"A little. And I think you're very perceptive."

Emma's eyes widened again. "Really?"

"Perceptive and smart. But I think you should be careful and not get in too deep with him. I know you think you love him, but—"

"I do love him!" Emma cried.

"Well, then you do. But a young man with a lot of anger may not be able to love fully, or even commit to you the way you want. The way you deserve. Anger doesn't leave much room for love."

"I could change that. I could make him not so angry; I could make him happy."

Claire heard echoes of herself at Emma's age. "It isn't easy to change people; I wouldn't count on it. Just use a little caution so it doesn't get so heavy it drowns out everything else. You don't have to spend every waking minute with him, and you don't have to go to bed with him."

"I haven't."

"Good."

"But what if I did? What would be so terrible about it? We're two grown-up people; we're not children and we're not dumb; we can take care of ourselves."

"Emma, we've had so many talks about this—"

"We wouldn't do anything stupid; I'm not going to get AIDS or anything."

"That isn't the only thing I worry about; I worry about your getting hurt, and I think—"

"You're always worrying! You're always talking about being careful and . . . *using caution*. You're so busy worrying you never *live!* I mean, you've been great, working and taking care of me all alone, but that was all you did. You never went anywhere or made new friends or had exciting lovers or anything; you just sort of got through every day, and you never *lived*. Now you can do anything you want, because you're rich, but now you're old—" She saw Claire's eyebrows go up. "Well, not really *old,* I didn't mean that, but not young, either—I mean, I suppose you're *middle-aged*—and I'm not going to wait till I'm middle-aged or old or anything; I'm going to do everything now while I'm young. I don't want to be like you, I want to be me, and do everything, and *live!*"

Claire sat still, looking at her clasped hands. Emma's words settled within her like small lumps of lead. Emma had never talked to her that way; she had always been quiet and obedient and sweet-tempered. Oh, now and then she was willful and stubborn, but even then Claire felt they were more like sisters than anything else. Other mothers had trouble with their daughters, but Claire had never had any problems at all. Until now. She took a long breath. "I'm not telling you not to live. I think you've had a pretty good life so far, and you can have a wonderful life without Brix Eiger being at the center of it. Emma, I think it would be a mistake for you to get deeply involved with him; I just have that feeling."

"But that's your feeling, not mine! You think just because my father left you, men are going to leave me."

"No, that's not what I think. A lot of things happen besides desertion, Emma; there are lots of ways of being hurt. I don't want you to make a mistake that hurts you—"

"You can't stop me from making every mistake in the world; you can't do it. Let me make my own mistakes! You did what you wanted; you were lucky, you didn't have parents to tell you—"

"*Lucky?*"

"Oh, I'm sorry, I'm sorry, I didn't mean that. I just meant, nobody tried to stop you from getting married."

"My friends did; I didn't listen. I can't say I'm sorry I married Ted, because I have you, but if my parents had been alive they might have helped me make other decisions—"

"You wouldn't have listened," Emma said boldly. "You would have done just what you wanted, just—" She stopped.

"Just like you?"

"You've got to trust me!" Emma cried.

"I do. But we all can use help once in a while, somebody to talk to, somebody to point us in a different direction or just make a suggestion. . . . When Hannah does that for me, I'm grateful."

"Hannah meddles," said Emma with the scorn of youth. "I really like her, but she ought to know when to mind her own business."

"She lives with us. We're a family. And if Hannah is concerned about us and thinks we're her business, we should be grateful. There's a big world out there and only a few people are really going to care about you."

"I'm not her business," Emma said stubbornly. "I just want her to leave me alone."

Claire knew that meant her, too, and as always with Emma, in the end she backed off. "We'll both leave you alone, if that's what you really want. But I would like to see you once in a while on this trip; I thought it would be nice if we could share some of it."

"Sure." Then, suddenly alarmed by how careless she was being with her mother's feelings, she said, "That's what I want, too. I love to do things with you; you know that. Remember Simone's? We had so much fun. I love to do things with you."

And so Emma joined Claire and Hannah in Juneau and dutifully spent the day with them. But the next day, their fifth in Alaska, she and Brix were together from the moment the ship entered Glacier Bay at six in the morning. Claire caught glimpses of them all that long day; they were always touching, their shoulders brushing, their hands clasped, Brix's arm around Emma. For the first time, Claire envied her daughter. She remembered the sparkling clarity of the world when love and sexual excitement heightened every perception, and once again she wished for someone to put his arm around her. And that made her think of Quentin. But they had not spoken since she walked away from him on the deck, and Claire could not push herself forward with him. Perhaps Emma was right, she thought; after so many static years, she probably didn't know how to live, didn't even know how to begin.

The ship sailed through water as smooth as glass, mirroring a clear, azure sky as they moved deeper into the bay, past old forests of spruce and hemlock to newer forests of alders, and then, at the far end, fields of plants and lichen. Park Service naturalists who had come aboard at Bartlett Cove walked around the ship explaining everything, and helping passengers spot black bears, mountain goats, and whales. Everyone was on deck, cameras ready, and the ship's engines and the murmur of a few hundred voices had a hollow sound, as if they were bottled up, surrounded by huge glaciers whose rough-hewn walls were a hundred or more feet high. Suddenly, with a sound like a cannon shot, a chunk of ice the size of a building broke off one of the glaciers and fell, almost in slow motion, into the bay. Sprays of water and chunks of ice flew hundreds of feet up and splashed thunderously down, making long waves that rolled across the bay and rocked the ship.

Claire felt apart from all of it. She heard the excited voices around her, the snapping of cameras, the clink of china as waiters brought orange juice and coffee to the deck, and Hannah's murmurs about how grand everything was, but Emma's sharp words were still with her and she was thinking about where she was in her life. They had been in Alaska more than half of the week-long cruise, and suddenly she could not figure out why she was there, or why she would be anywhere. Her life seemed so random, without rhyme or rea-

JUDITH MICHAEL

son: she had bought a lottery ticket, a small piece of paper, and then nothing was the same, or would be, ever again. If she had earned a lot of money with her own clients, or if she had inherited a fortune, everything would make more sense. But now, she felt adrift.

She never had to work again, or watch over Emma, who would be in college. She had a staff of people who did all the housework she had once done, and Hannah did the rest. How did a person fill the days when there was no work to do? Would she take one trip after another, just like this one? Would she keep meeting people she did not care for, but who seemed to know the secret of a kind of life that Claire had never before tried to understand?

That made her think, again, of Quentin. They had not spoken for three days. She had seen him with others in the dining room and lounges, but their eyes had not met. She had seen Ina and Zeke dancing one night on the small dance floor in the bar, Ina striking in green silk and Zeke with his tie loose and gold cuff links gleaming, and they had looked intimate and happy. Ina had waved to Claire as if they were old friends, but they had not come to her table. Lorraine had stopped to chat one morning at breakfast, saying they should get together on one of the shore excursions, but that had come to nothing. It was as if their life were closed to Claire unless Quentin brought her into it, and as the days went by and it seemed unlikely that he would, that life began to seem more desirable to Claire: exciting and busy and exotic, even with its squabbles and animosities and backstabbings.

So the scenery in Glacier Bay slid past her as she thought her thoughts and looked for Quentin, but did not see him, and watched Emma and Brix from a distance, all that long day.

"You've been very quiet; are you worried about Emma?" Hannah asked. They were having drinks in the lounge, before going to change for dinner.

Claire smiled faintly. "She says I worry too much. She says I'm old and haven't lived. She thinks I don't have the courage, or maybe the know-how, to really live, as opposed to just getting through each day."

"Oh, dear. Well, she's young and full of opinions, many of them wrong."

"Which ones?"

"You could answer that yourself, my dear. Your courage, for one; you know you're not a coward. And know-how, for another. You've done a lot, all on your own; you built a life, for goodness' sake, by yourself. You have friends, you have a profession, and you're going to do a lot more." Claire was silent. "Well, what's the problem? Just Emma? Or is it Quentin? You haven't talked to him at all?"

"No. But it's not important."

"Well, of course it is. You liked him, you were intrigued by him, and you wanted to see more of him. It does have a bright side, I suppose; there's something so trite about shipboard romances, you might have been embarrassed to find yourself in one."

"I said something like that to Emma, and she ignored me."

"She'll find out for herself. Cruises are tricky; I know that for a fact. They make nice fairy tales, but how do you sort out what's true and important and worthwhile in a relationship when you're in this artificial atmosphere? Here we are, floating past glaciers that are breaking apart while we sit in velvet armchairs, drinking French wine and eating caviar on toast points. How real is that?"

"How do you know for a fact that cruises are tricky?"

"Well, as it happens, I was on one once. They're all alike, you know, whatever part of the world they're in: luxurious hothouses that have nothing to do with what we were doing last week or what's ahead when we get home."

"And did you have a shipboard romance?"

"Yes, indeed. Hot and heavy. I was eighteen and he was fifty, a thoroughly married Italian industrialist with seven children; oh, a respectable, settled man if there ever was one. I was a lovely girl in those days and he made me feel I was a princess in a fairy tale, a nymph floating through paradise. We were in the Mediterranean, and I didn't see anything on that whole cruise but him. I can still feel his hands on my waist, lifting me into bed."

Claire watched Hannah in amazement. "Where was his wife?"

"On the ship, with three of their children. They were on another deck and they stayed there. I'm sure he and she had made their arrangements a long time ago; that was why the marriage lasted. I didn't ask. At the time I was sure he would leave her as soon as we docked. How could anyone say those things and touch me that way and look at me the way he did—good Lord, those Italian eyes, like melting chocolate— and then go back to his wife? In any just and reliable world, he couldn't. But of course that was exactly what he did. Without a backward glance or a single romantic sigh of regret."

There was a silence. Claire finished her wine and set it down. She was seeing herself, eighteen years ago, standing at the telephone, her throat dry with fear, frantically calling everyone she knew who might have an idea where Ted had gone, who might have seen him in the last twenty-four hours, who might be willing to tell him to go back to his wife and the child she was carrying. No one had known where he was. As far as Claire knew, he had left without a backward glance or a single romantic sigh of regret. And she never saw him again.

"Did you ever see him again?" she asked Hannah.

"Never. It's such an old, trite story, and for a long time, after I recovered from him, I was too embarrassed to tell it. But by now I think of it as one of Grimm's fairy tales: the young princess and the horny bull who didn't turn into a handsome prince at the end. Married men without a conscience are like wild bulls outside their pen: you can't stop them with reason; they run amok, crushing anything in their way, and they never look back to see what damage they might have done."

POT OF GOLD

Claire gave a small laugh. She had long since recovered from Ted, but still, it was not pleasant to remember. "How long did it take you to recover?"

"Oh, months. Close to a year. I was sure I would die. Quite literally. I thought it must have been my fault—I'd done something or not done something to make him change his mind about us—and I felt I was smothering under such despair, such a sense of loss and deadly emptiness, that I really thought my body could not sustain it and it would simply stop. It wasn't that I would kill myself; I didn't have the will to do that. It was just that I didn't see how a human organism could function so full of grief and self-hatred."

Yes, yes, yes, that's how it was. And it went on and on, past the time Emma was born. I think it must be the reason I stayed so close to home all these years. No adventures; nothing I couldn't be sure of. Even the affairs I had were tepid dead ends, and I always knew that, too.

"But my organism kept going," Hannah said. "Isn't it amazing how tough we really are? And eventually I got over it and started taking trips again. I did a lot of traveling in those days." The waiter appeared and she looked up. "I'll have a vodka this time. And another glass of wine for my friend." She turned back to Claire. "Why am I going on as if this is new to you? You had it even worse; you had Emma on the way. My little affair seems puny by comparison."

"Unhappiness isn't ever puny. It's always bigger than we are, at least until we can look back on it and turn it into a Grimm's fairy tale."

Hannah smiled broadly. "I like that. It's nice to hear you give words of wisdom."

"Oh." How strange, Claire thought; I never do that. It was not that she lacked ideas about what people did and why they did it; she had a lot of ideas. But she always kept them to herself because she could not believe anyone would find them sensible or interesting. But Hannah was smiling. Maybe I can do this sort of thing as well as anyone, Claire thought.

"Well, it must be contagious," she said lightly to Hannah. "I must have caught it from you."

Their drinks arrived and Hannah raised hers. "To your health and happiness and words of wisdom. I want you to know what a good time I'm having. And how grateful I am. And I hope you're having a good time, too."

"Of course I am."

"But"—Hannah contemplated her—"it isn't enough."

"It's more than I've ever had. I'm very satisfied."

"Well, you shouldn't be. You should always want more out of life, Claire; why are you in such a hurry to declare yourself satisfied? You know what you do? You treat yourself like a painting; you put yourself in a frame—a cruise ship, Alaska, Hannah for a companion—and you hang it on the wall and there it is, fixed, permanent, finished. Absolutely no place for surprises. You're too young for that; that's for people my age. I'm very touched and pleased that you like my company, and I hope you feel that way for a long time, but if you want to get to know other people—Quentin Eiger, for instance—why don't you invite him for drinks after dinner tonight? He invited you, once; maybe it's your turn."

"I can't do that. Anyway, didn't you tell me a few minutes ago how trite shipboard romances are?"

"Does it have to be a romance? I said, if you want to get to know him."

Claire flushed. "It won't be a romance."

Hannah let it go. She did not comment when Quentin came into the lounge with Lorraine and Ozzie Thurman after dinner and nodded a greeting to her and Claire, or when they saw him at breakfast the next morning with a woman they had not seen before. And by the time they reached Valdez that afternoon, the last port before Anchorage and the end of the cruise, Hannah was talking about what they would do in the new house when they returned to Wilton, and other trips that might be interesting in the fall, after Emma left for college, as if she already was finished with Alaska and thought Claire should be, too.

POT OF GOLD

At Valdez, the passengers went in different directions, to glaciers and canyons, and a waterfall named Bridal Veil Falls, while Emma and Brix went on a raft trip, with a guide, and to dinner in town. Hannah went to explore Valdez and Claire went with her, feeling melancholy. The cruise was almost over and she felt disappointed. She was not sure what she had expected—probably excitement and glamour and romance—but then she should have chosen a more exotic place than Alaska. Maybe I'm not made for glamour and romance, she thought, or excitement either. But then, what good is all this money? It was supposed to change my life, it was supposed to change me. It's got to change me; that's what money is for: to turn us into people we can't be when we're poor. As she followed Hannah around Valdez, as far from the glittering capitals of Europe as she could be, her melancholy deepened. Maybe I'm just one of those people who never have anything dramatic happen to them, she reflected, no matter what they do. That is a very depressing thought.

"I've never spent so much time thinking about myself," she said to Hannah later, at dinner. "It feels incredibly selfish. It must be because of the money. I used to think about basic things, like food and rent, and now I think about all the things I ought to be doing. And wondering why I'm not doing them. Where do you suppose Emma is? I told her to be back at eight-thirty."

"I haven't seen her." Hannah met Claire's eyes. "But of course they're on the ship; they knew it was leaving at nine. They're probably on deck somewhere; you know how everyone likes to watch the crew cast off."

"I suppose." Claire was beginning to feel a familiar sinking inside her, the same sinking fear she had every time Emma was late coming home from a date. "But you'd think she would have found us, at least to let us know she's back."

"She's a little self-absorbed right now," Hannah said gently.

"But maybe they're not here at all. Maybe something

happened to them." Claire looked up to see Quentin coming toward them.

"I'm looking for Brix," he said. "Have you seen him?"

"No. We were just wondering where they are." She pushed back her chair. "I'll take a walk around the deck . . ."

"I've looked there. And in all the other obvious places." Without being asked, he pulled out a chair and sat down.

Claire's fear ballooned; her heart began to pound. "Something's happened to them."

"There isn't a lot that can happen in Valdez."

"But they were on a raft."

"Brix told me they were going with a guide. There's no way a guide would take them anywhere dangerous, or bring them back late."

"Weren't they planning to eat dinner in Valdez?" Hannah asked.

Quentin glanced briefly in her direction. "Yes. Brix didn't tell me where they were going."

"There can't be too many places," Claire said. "It's such a small town. Couldn't we call the restaurants to find out where they were, and when they left?"

"Mr. Eiger?" The ship's captain stood beside the table. "We have had a telephone call for you. From Mr. Brix Eiger."

"Where is he?"

"And also one from Emma Goddard for Mrs. Goddard, if you know who she is—"

"Yes," said Claire. "That's my daughter." *She's all right. She's all right. Not drowned or kidnapped or murdered in some forest, not lost. She's all right.*

"Where are they?" Quentin asked again.

"In Valdez. The young man said they missed the ship and they are at the Westmark Valdez Hotel. You understand, Mr. Eiger, and Mrs. Goddard—"

"You could have brought us the telephone," Quentin snapped.

"Your son said we should not bother you. You under-

POT OF GOLD

stand, Mr. Eiger and Mrs. Goddard, this is a grave matter. We of course make clear to our passengers that we cast off exactly on time and it is their responsibility to be on the ship, not ours to go hunting for them, but I understand the young lady is underage, and this poses a serious problem for us."

"I'll take care of it; there won't be any problem." Quentin stood. "I'm going to call Brix," he told Claire. "Do you want to come with me?"

"Yes. I'll come to your cabin later," she said to Hannah, and then she walked with Quentin to his cabin.

"Damn fool," Quentin muttered. "Damn fool; he knows better."

"So does Emma," said Claire.

"Brix is older. He was in charge."

Claire was silent. Of course Brix was in charge. And Emma, willful with her mother and with Hannah, would probably follow Brix Eiger wherever he led, because Emma thought he was perfect.

In his sitting room, Quentin sat at the desk and called the hotel in Valdez and asked for Brix. "Sit down," he said to Claire, who was standing in the middle of the room.

"I want to talk to Emma," she said.

"Hi, Dad," Brix said, from Valdez. His voice had a quaver and he spoke loudly to try to mask it. "I'm sorry, I kind of fucked up—"

"What the hell are you up to?" Quentin demanded.

"Nothing, Dad, we missed the boat, that's all. I don't know how it happened; we were at dinner and I guess we lost track of the time. It's not a big deal, though; we'll get a plane tomorrow morning and catch up with you in Anchorage."

"How?"

"I'll take care of it, Dad. Either a plane or a helicopter. They're all over the place; that's how people get around. Enough money, somebody'll fly us to Anchorage. It's only about a hundred miles; I checked. It's no problem, Dad, don't worry about us."

"You're responsible for that young woman. Do you understand that?"

"Christ, Dad, of course I do. She's fine. Everything's fine. You don't have to worry. We'll meet you at the airport tomorrow."

"I'll expect you early. I don't intend to miss my flight home because of you. Is that clear? You get in to Anchorage before nine."

"Dad, listen, I'll get us there as soon as—"

"Before nine. That's not an option. Where is Emma?"

"In her room."

Quentin's eyebrows rose. He started to say something, then checked himself. He looked at Claire. "Emma is in her own room; shall I have the operator ring her?"

Claire met his eyes. "Yes, thank you." She took the telephone Quentin handed her and sat at his desk, listening to the repeated ringing in Emma's room.

"Hi, did it ring a long time?" Emma said. "I was in the shower."

Claire listened to her daughter's voice, slow, sensual, a little sleepy. It was a voice for a lover. She barely recognized it. "Emma," she said.

"Mother? Oh, you got our message. I was going to call you as soon as I got out of the shower. I couldn't talk to you earlier because Brix didn't want to talk to his father so he just left a message for both of you. But at least you knew where I was."

Don't scold her; this isn't the time. "You had us worried," Claire said, trying to keep her voice light.

"I know, I know, I'm sorry. I knew you'd be worried. I'm really sorry. I don't know what happened; we were at that Totem Inn place—there was a fire in the fireplace and it was so warm and cozy and we were starved, and cold, too, after being out on the raft, and one minute it was seven-thirty and then all of a sudden it was after nine. It wasn't Brix's fault, you can't blame him; it was just an accident. Brix says we'll meet you in Anchorage tomorrow; he's taking care of everything. I'm really sorry, I know how much you worry, but I'm fine; there's nothing to worry about. We were just late getting back and the ship was gone. I mean, we could see it—isn't it absolutely unbelievable the way the sun stays up so long? I mean, it was after nine and it was like noon—so we saw you sailing off, but there wasn't anything we could do about it. We knew the captain wouldn't turn around and come back for us. I was really worried until Brix said he could get a plane or a helicopter and we'd meet you tomorrow. So everything is fine, and I'm fine, and there isn't anything to worry about. I'm sorry you were worried, but we didn't mean for it to happen, and anyway, it's not a tragedy, you know. It could happen to anybody. It probably happens a lot."

Five hundred and ninety-eight other people got back on time, Claire thought, but she kept it to herself. She was listening to Emma's nervous babbling and wondering what secrets Emma had to guard. She wanted to know if Emma's door was locked and if it would stay locked. But there was no way she could ask her that.

"I'll be waiting at the airport tomorrow," she said. "I'm glad you're fine. Good night, sweetheart."

Quentin was at the bar. "A glass of wine? Or something stronger?"

"Wine, thank you."

He poured Scotch for himself and brought her a glass of wine, then sat on the couch. "I'm glad to see you; I've missed being with you."

Claire was not listening. "Would Brix have planned anything like this?"

"He might. But only if he was with a willing girl. Would Emma go along?"

"I don't think so. Emma likes her own way, but she's not particularly adventurous. I don't think she'd do anything like this. Will Brix get them to Anchorage in the morning?"

"Yes. I'd bet on that. Is Emma's mother adventurous?"

Claire looked at him for a long moment. "I don't know."

"We could find out." He went to her and took her hand,

bringing her out of the chair to stand with him. "I've thought about you this whole trip, Claire; I've missed you. I told you once you're a lovely woman and a wise one and you walked away from me, so I'm not sure what you want to hear." His face was close to hers and Claire tried to fathom what was in his eyes, but they were as smooth and glasslike as the water in Glacier Bay, mirroring her image, giving nothing back. "So lovely," he murmured, and he took her face between his hands and kissed her, his mouth opening hers.

This time his kiss was warm, with an urgency that had not been there before. Old hungers stirred within Claire. She put her arms around Quentin, and he pulled her to him, one hand on her breast, his tongue insistent on hers. Claire was dizzy with wanting him. It was a long time since she had been with a man, but there was more to it than that; she wanted Quentin, with all his complexities, all that she could not understand about him, even all that she did not like about him. She was drawn to him just as his friends were, and she had not realized how aroused she had been when she was with him, and how bereft she had felt when he ignored her for the rest of the week. All the time she thought she had been concentrating on the wild grandeur of Alaska, it seemed she had been wanting him, keyed up, on edge, ready for him. And he knew it; his kiss was confident, even in its passion.

And that's why he stayed away for four days; that's how he operates with insecure women. He makes them hungry for him before he makes a move.

She slipped out of his embrace and backed up until she was against the desk. She wanted to be in bed with him so much that she was trembling, but she was angry, too, and she knew, through the turmoil of her desire, that if he set this first pattern, all those that followed would be made by him and she might not like them any better than she liked this one.

"Now what the hell." Quentin was annoyed, more puzzled than angry, and Claire knew, with a sudden flash of delight, that he did not understand her and that it bothered him that he did not.

"I don't believe in shipboard romances," she said. "They make nice fairy tales, but it's really impossible to figure out what's true and important when everything around you is artificial." Thank you, Hannah, she said silently. "That's one of the reasons I'm worried about Emma."

There was a silence. Quentin went to the bar and made himself another drink. "More wine?" he asked.

"No, thank you."

Once again he sat on the couch. He stretched his arms to either side along the back of the couch and stretched out his legs, crossed at the ankles. He was relaxed, but he dominated the room with his size and the force of his energy. "What's true and important about us, Claire, is that we like each other, we're attracted to each other, and we want each other. And if you are even slightly adventurous, there are no impediments to our doing whatever we want to do. What could be more important? What other truths do you need?"

"I'd like to know how much the glaciers have to do with it," Claire said lightly.

"The glaciers," he repeated.

His flat voice made her feel foolish, but she had gone this far and so she went on, wanting him to understand. "This is so new for me, everything about this trip, that I can't make sense of it all at once. Maybe that means I'm not adventurous, but maybe it's just that I don't know whether all this incredible beauty has spilled over and made us seem more beautiful or exciting or desirable to each other than we really are."

"Does Ina look beautiful to you after you look at glaciers all day?"

She smiled. "No."

"Does Zeke seem desirable?"

A laugh broke from her. "No."

"But I do."

"Yes."

"Well, that's honest. So something else is going on."

"I guess. I guess it's just me. There's a lot I don't understand about myself right now. And I guess I think it would be better to wait until I know what's important and what isn't."

He let out his breath in a long sigh. "If you don't know what's important, let me decide. If this is really so new to you—you haven't traveled? At all?"

"No."

"Incredible, these days; everyone travels. Well, so you've lived in one small town all your life and raised your daughter, and I suppose you read a lot of books. You don't know a damn thing about the world; how can you know anything about yourself, or what you could be with me? You could come with me, wherever I take you, and discover a world you've never imagined and become a woman you've never dreamed of. Even with all your money you can't do it by yourself. One of us is going to have to take control of our friendship, Claire, and it can't be you because you don't know how. I think you do know that."

Of course I know it. I just don't know how to deal with it.

"I just have to think about it," she said, wishing she sounded stronger and more sure of herself.

"And if you miss the chance, with me?"

She looked at him steadily. "Then I'll never know."

"You may not." He went to the door and opened it. "Good night, Claire."

Her anger rose again. Without a word she walked past him and down the corridor to cross to the other side of the ship, and her cabin. Damn it, she thought, what was I afraid of? Why can't I be lighter about things, less serious; why can't I let go and just have a good time? *You should always want more out of life, Claire; why are you in such a hurry to declare yourself satisfied?*

Well, I'm not satisfied, she answered Hannah in silence as she went into her cabin. And I don't know when I will be, at this rate. She looked at the closed door leading to Emma's cabin. Maybe I did what I did because that was what I was hoping Emma was doing. Maybe I'll ask her tomorrow. *I stayed out of Quentin's bed; did you stay out of his son's?*

POT OF GOLD

* * *

"Mother called," Emma said when she opened her door and Brix came into her room.

"So did my dad." He put his arms around her. "Everything's fine. I found a pilot; he's picking us up at seven. God, I missed you. I haven't seen you for two hours." Emma put her face up, like a child, and he kissed her. "You're so beautiful. What's that thing you're wearing?"

"The bedspread. I took a shower and washed out some of my clothes and they're drying."

"Oh." He looked down at himself. "I guess I'm not presentable."

She laughed, loving the worried frown between his eyes, the sheepish sound of his voice. "Of course you are. We're not going out, are we?"

"Christ, no, I want to stay here. But I want to impress you."

"You do," Emma said, her voice low.

"Good." He pulled her close again. "God, you are so beautiful. My most beautiful baby doll."

Emma felt a jolt. She wasn't a baby, or a doll. And she wasn't his. But his arms were strong around her and she felt warm and safe in them, and he was kissing her with little kisses all over her face, and she closed her eyes, feeling as if she were dissolving, as if she had become a small, clear stream merging with the powerful river that was Brix. Because Brix loved her. Brix took care of her when they were stranded in a strange town. Nothing else was important.

Brix put his hand inside the spread Emma had wrapped around her and began to push it open. Without thinking, Emma's hands came up and covered his, stopping him. "Hey," he said softly. "This is me, Brix, remember?"

Emma looked at him.

"Listen, doll, how many times does something like this happen? It was meant to be, right? The two of us at the end of the world, all alone. It's just us, all by ourselves. We can't let it be like every other night." When Emma was silent, he frowned at her. "What is it? Your mother? Did she say something on the phone? Like, 'Don't let him take advantage of you?' God, *take advantage*. That's old-fashioned enough for my dad. Did she say something like that?"

"No," Emma whispered.

"But she was thinking it, right? And you knew it. And you want to be just like her."

"Oh, no, that's not—"

"What?"

"I don't want to be like her. I mean, she's wonderful, but she's shy and doesn't do very much; she doesn't look for new things to do. I always wanted to be different, but I didn't know exactly how. I mean, I kept thinking, *I want, I want,* but I didn't know what I meant . . ."

Brix ran his fingers down her face and neck and kissed her lightly. "You're not like her at all. You're an exciting woman. And you're not afraid of anything."

Emma knew that was not true. But she wanted it to be true. She wanted Brix to think it was true. And he had called her a woman, not a baby doll, so she had to act like one and talk like one. She looked at him, trying to think of something to say.

"I'll help," he said. "You're not afraid, but maybe you need help sometimes. Right?"

Emma let out her breath. Brix always said the right thing. "Yes," she said. "I'd like that."

"Well, just follow along," he crooned. "And relax." Once again he slipped his hands into the opening in the spread. This time she did not stop him and he pushed the fabric off her shoulders, to the floor. Emma tried to stop herself but she could not: she folded her arms across her breasts. "No, you don't," Brix said cheerfully. He took her hands and held them wide. "Look at you, look at you, what a bod. You are a gorgeous woman."

Emma's face was flaming. "Don't," she whispered.

"Don't what?" Brix stared at her. "Emma, for Christ's sake, hasn't anybody ever looked at you?"

POT OF GOLD

She shook her head.

"Christ," he muttered. "What have I got here? I must be living right." He held Emma's hands outstretched, and then, without warning, he leaned down and kissed one nipple and then the other, and ran his tongue over them, slowly, like a cat in a warm and sunlit place.

Emma gave a low moan. She was dizzy, she was embarrassed, she was afraid, but somehow she was excited, too; her body seemed completely separate from her mind. She didn't like standing naked before Brix, but after the first shock, it was not really terrible; she did not like his holding her hands out so that she was helpless, but she liked his strength; and she loved the look in his eyes before he bent down to kiss her breasts. *I have a good body. Brix said so. He likes to look at me. He has so much experience; if he says I'm gorgeous, I must be.*

Brix let go of Emma's hands and swiftly pulled off his clothes. Emma looked away. She was wet and heavy and terrified.

Brix took her in his arms, and she felt the warmth of skin on skin, the hard ridges of his muscles, the curves of hip and stomach against hers. It felt so good she pressed closer, crushing her nipples against the black, curly hair on his chest. "That's my baby," he said hoarsely. He put his hands on her buttocks, kneading them as he pulled her even tighter. "My beautiful baby doll."

Emma felt his hot, rigid penis against her wetness and she tried to pull away, but Brix kept her close. He kissed her again, holding her mouth open until she gasped for breath, and then he turned her and pulled her with him onto the bed.

Emma closed her eyes. She didn't especially want to do this, but she didn't want to make Brix angry and she didn't want him to think she was a child. She wanted him to call her a woman again. He could do whatever he wanted and it would be all right, because he knew so much more than she did and he loved her and she loved him, and this was part of being in love. If she pulled away now, he'd think she didn't love him.

She heard a small rustling sound and opened her eyes. Brix was sitting beside her, opening a small package. Oh, she thought; I forgot. But Brix always knows what to do. She closed her eyes again and waited for him and then she felt him spreading her legs and running his hands up the inside of her thighs. "Gorgeous doll," he said again, and lay on her. Emma sighed with pleasure at the warm, heavy weight of him, and Brix, thinking she had sighed from passion, raised himself up and plunged into her.

Emma gave a sharp scream, then bit it back, ashamed and afraid he would be angry. But he was not angry. He lifted his head and looked at the tears in her eyes. "This is incredible, you know that? I've never had a virgin. God, Emma, you're such a doll."

He bent down and sucked on her nipples, biting them and playing his tongue against them. But this time, Emma barely was aware of his mouth. She felt as if a fiery poker were tearing her apart, and her breasts hurt when he lay on her again. She wanted to curl up into a little ball, with her face in the pillow, but Brix kept her stretched out and she could not move. Then she thought she had to do something to make Brix happy, and so she tried to raise her hips to meet him, but he was too heavy, and moving made the pain worse.

"It's okay," Brix muttered. "Relax, baby doll. I'll take care of everything."

Emma squeezed back the tears in her eyes and put her arms around Brix, digging her fingertips into him, hoping he would think that was passion. "Brix," she said, so that he would remember this was something they were doing together. "I love you." Her voice was high and quavering and it seemed to come from a long way off. Brix moved faster inside her; his breathing was loud, and sometimes it sounded like a grunt. "Oh, God, you are so good," he said. "So good, so good, so good, so good. I could stay here forever. So fucking good."

The word was like a thorn, pricking through Emma's pain, but it vanished because it meant that Brix was happy.

POT OF GOLD

Brix said she was good, Brix wanted to be with her forever. "I love you," she said again; it sounded to her almost like a sob.

Brix thrust into her with a kind of fury, once and again and again, and then a groan burst from him, followed by a descending line of groans, growing fainter, until at last he lay on Emma without moving, silent. His breathing slowed. In a few minutes he turned his head to look at her. He grinned. "Now, *this* is the way to see Alaska," he said.

Emma's eyes widened. She shrank into herself. Brix rolled off her and sat up, using a corner of the sheet to wipe himself. He turned back to Emma, who had not moved, and leaned down to plant a kiss on the tip of her nose. "You are one terrific doll. I could play with you all the time." He looked at the spots of blood on the sheet. "That's probably the most exciting thing the maids will see all week in this dump." He stretched and glanced out the window. "God, it's weird to have it still light out. Do you want something to eat? A midnight snack? Maybe the bar has pretzels or something." He gazed at her. "Poor doll. Listen, I know it hurts the first time; it gets a lot better, I promise." He ran his hand over her hair and slowly around her shoulder, then cupped it over her breast. "Why don't you just relax and I'll run downstairs and see what they've got in the bar. We'll go slower next time; you'll like it better. Come on, Emma, gorgeous Emma, let's have a smile; you know I like you cheerful. You know I *love* you cheerful."

Emma stretched her mouth into a smile. "Much better," Brix said. He bent over her and kissed her slowly, lazily moving his tongue against hers. Eyes wide, Emma looked at the ceiling. Brix took his shirt and pants into the bathroom, leaving his jacket and socks on the floor, and in a moment came out, dressed, his shoes slipped on his bare feet like slippers. "Back in a few minutes," he said, and left the room.

Emma pulled the sheet and blanket over her and stared dry-eyed at the ceiling, wondering when she would feel happy. The exaltation she had felt with him every day of the cruise, the feeling that she would burst with happiness and excitement, was gone, and she did not know how to get it back. She loved Brix with a sinking helplessness; she wanted him next to her every minute. But she was not happy.

But I will be, she thought. Things will be better. Brix said so.

She wished she could talk to her mother about it, but of course she couldn't. Her mother hadn't wanted her to spend so much time with Brix; she'd told her she didn't want her to go to bed with him. She'd be furious if she knew. And disappointed? Emma wondered, but she couldn't even think about her mother being disappointed in her; that hurt too much. Anyway, Emma wasn't sure how much her mother knew about men; she'd dated now and then, but Emma couldn't imagine her in bed with anyone, and she'd seemed sort of mesmerized by Brix's father that first night when they'd had drinks, as if she couldn't quite keep up with him. *She's shy and doesn't do very much; she doesn't look for new things to do.*

So there's no way she could understand me, Emma thought. Even if she wasn't furious, she wouldn't know what to say. And I can't go to Hannah; she'd tell Mother. There isn't anybody I can talk to. I just have to figure it out by myself: how to be happy and make Brix happy and be happy forever.

She got up, feeling shaky, and picked up the bedspread from the floor and wrapped it around her again. When she sat on the bed, she saw the blood spots on the sheet. She stared at them and felt a pang of regret; she'd given it away. All through high school she had stayed a virgin while her friends recounted their adventures; now it was gone and she could never get it back. I guess I was waiting for Brix, she thought. And that meant it was all right; it would be all right; it would be fun and exciting and wonderful again. Forever.

Because they were in love.

Because it was meant to be.

7

THE house was warm and welcoming, filled with sunlight and fresh breezes, but everything seemed tame after the mountains and glaciers of Alaska. "Goodness, isn't it quiet," Hannah marveled, though birds were singing, and in the distance, a dog barked and the faint rush of traffic could be heard. Claire was arranging flowers in a Baccarat vase she had bought that morning: the brilliant cosmos and dahlias and snapdragons of a hot, dry July. She was glad to be home; a week of drama had been enough. Emma barely noticed either of them. She walked through the rooms of the house, hollow-eyed, waiting for the telephone to ring.

They had been home a week. On their third day back, Quentin had taken Claire to dinner at a small French bistro in Westport. "I bought it last year," he told her when she admired the beamed ceiling and lace curtains, and the pale green wash on the walls. "I've invested in a few companies—computers and clothing and biogenetics—and a couple of restaurants. I like to help young men getting started; it's like helping sons grow up."

"Not young women?" Claire asked.

"Not so far. I haven't found any who do business the way I do."

Claire gazed at him. "What does that mean?"

"It means I expect a certain attitude, and women don't have it and don't seem interested in it. A kind of drive, a focused vision that doesn't allow side issues to interfere with whatever has to be done. Women prefer families and good deeds, which I admire, but I don't invest in them."

"You mean ruthlessness."

"If you like the word. I prefer mine."

"And do these young men come to you for advice?"

"Of course; I told you, they want to succeed. And I expect them to. When I invest, I expect to make money, not lose it."

Claire envisioned young men crowding around Quentin, sitting at his feet, taking dictation as he dispensed words of wisdom. "Do they resent it?"

"Why would they? They know they'll go farther and faster with good advice. Claire, these aren't schoolboys' games; they're the most important business of life, and the young men I choose to invest in will do whatever it takes to succeed."

Whatever it takes. Whatever has to be done. The most important business of life. Claire felt a small chill. Was making money really the most important business of life? She wondered how he ran Eiger Labs, and what kind of a friend he was. And what kind of lover.

But then the waiter came with a special Armagnac saved for Quentin, and she let herself sink back into the cocoon of privilege that surrounded him wherever he went. No matter how much money she spent, she knew she did not hold herself as easily or walk with the same careless assurance as Quentin and his friends, and she had not mastered their air of faint boredom at the wonders of the world. She had not learned to take abundance for granted.

But when she was with Quentin and let him take charge, she felt a little bit of what it was to be rich and powerful and to accept without question everything that came her way.

"You and Quentin look good together," Lorraine said

two nights later. She and Claire were bending their heads to each other to make themselves heard amid the din of four hundred people and a dance band in a gilt and marble hotel ballroom in Stamford. "I wasn't sure, on the ship; you seemed up and down the whole week. But you've worked it out, whatever it was?"

"I don't know," Claire said. "We haven't talked about it."

"Talked about it? With Quentin? I can't imagine that you'd get very far trying to talk something out with Quentin."

"Why not?"

"Because, sweetie, he doesn't debate; he just *does*. And the rest of us follow along."

"And that's all right with you?"

Lorraine shrugged. "Them's the rules," she said lightly. She contemplated Claire's white satin sheath embroidered across the strapless top with small rhinestones. "You look terrific; I like that dress. You could use more jewelry, but Quentin will take care of that. What's wrong? You made a face."

"Sorry."

"Well, but what's wrong?"

"I'm just not used to talking about intimate things. I don't know what you expect me to say."

"Intimate? What did I say?"

"Well, whether Quentin and I quarreled on the ship, whether he'll buy me jewelry . . ."

"Good Lord, sweetie, that isn't intimate. Intimate is how much money you made or lost last week. We're a bunch of happy campers here and we sort of keep track of each other. You'll get used to it; you might even like it. It's not bad, having people keep track of you; it keeps you from feeling like you're hanging out there with nobody to catch you if you fall. What's the use of knowing jillions of people if at least a few of them won't be on tap when you need them, is what I always say. You're a lot quieter than most of the women

Quentin's gone out with; maybe he's mellowing. Though I wouldn't count on it. But you're definitely quieter, you don't make a splash; you don't *thrust* yourself.''

"My God, I hope not."

"Well, it may not sound lovely, but it's the quickest way to climb, other than being a tennis star or royalty. You have to make people think their parties won't be complete without you because you're sort of glittery, or in with a lot of famous people, or you do major conspicuous spending, whatever. If you make them think that, it won't matter whether they like you or not; they'll invite you to everything."

Claire contemplated her for a long minute. "I haven't any idea what you're talking about."

"I know you don't, my sweet innocent." Lorraine snatched a glass of champagne and a miniature quiche from waiters passing by. Claire looked at the crowd. All the women wore black or white, the men wore white tie, and as she watched them bob and weave, drinking, talking, sliding sideways through the crowd, dancing beneath flashing strobe lights, Claire thought they looked like a movie from the thirties and wished she had a pencil, to sketch them.

Quentin and Ozzie were talking to a group of men near the bar. "It happens all the time," Lorraine told Claire. "It isn't really abandonment because it never lasts more than half the evening. They're just making good use of their time by doing some business, since they have to be here anyway. Quentin is on the board of whatever cause we're raising money for tonight, and wherever Quentin goes, we, of course, go also. Let's sit down; I want to talk to you."

A stranger, tall and rangy with unruly dark hair flecked with gray, came up to Claire. "Alex Jarrell," he said. His voice was deep and quiet but somehow cut clearly through the din. "I'd like to dance with you."

"Oh, not now, do you mind?" Lorraine protested to Claire. "This is my first chance to see you since we got back and I really do want to talk to you."

Claire liked his looks and the way he seemed to stand

POT OF GOLD

apart from the crowd. She wondered what he was doing there; he seemed more an observer than someone who had come to socialize. "I'd like to," she said to him. "Perhaps later." She and Lorraine found red velvet chairs away from the dance band and Lorraine leaned close. "I like you, Claire, and we're going to be friends. So this may sound intimate, but what are friends for, I always say, if you can't let down something and be intimate now and then. Anyway, he's a difficult man, Quentin; of course I'm very fond of him, but the fact is, he likes to . . . well, maybe that's not the best way to put it. He isn't always careful about whether he hurts people or not."

Claire's eyebrows rose. "You're saying he likes to hurt women."

"No, no, no, I said—"

"You started to say that he likes to hurt people. But I think you meant women."

"No, it's everybody, and it isn't hurting so much as having power over them. Well, it might be true, or partly true, about women, about dominating them . . ." She sighed. "You're very clever, even though you don't talk much. You'll probably be fine; you probably don't need my advice at all. But I did want to mention it, as a friend; that you should be careful about getting too involved, because you could get hurt. And I want you to know that I truly am your friend and I'm here if you ever need me."

A rebellious voice inside Claire said, oh, no, not again; I'm having a good time; I don't want any dire warnings. She looked across the dance floor again at the group of men. Quentin was the tallest; he was easy to pick out of a crowd. They had danced earlier, and she remembered the firm control of his arm around her, his hand enclosing hers, his mouth close to hers. As they swept around the dance floor, a perfect match, others paused to watch, and Claire had wanted him with a rush that made her miss a step. "Good," he had said, and pulled her closer, knowing exactly why she had stumbled.

And now Lorraine was warning her. Just as she had been

warned a long time ago. *You could get hurt.* And I was hurt, she thought; oh, God, how I was hurt. But that was then. I'm older now and I have money. Whatever happens, this time I'm safe. I'm not so vulnerable, I'll be all right, because now I have money.

She looked around the room again, at the shifting patterns of black and white beneath crystal chandeliers, the silver and gold table settings with an orchid at each place, and waiters filling crystal goblets with water and champagne in preparation for dinner. I don't need any warnings, she thought. I'm not going to try to change Quentin; I just want to be with him, a lot, because I can't stop thinking about him, and I want him to make me part of this life that I don't know anything about yet. I can't do it myself—he was right about that—no matter how much money I have; I need him.

"Of course he's an amazing man," Lorraine went on, backtracking. "Ozzie says he's the absolutely perfect businessman because he knows exactly what he wants and how he's going to get it. Personally, I think that goes a long way past cosmetics. Ozzie does, too."

"To what?"

"I don't know. I just don't see Quentin satisfied with one company, however big he makes it. I think he wants to run much bigger things, mingle with bigger people. International business? Governments? Something like that. Anyway, he makes good cosmetics, the whole Narcissus line; I use all of it. You probably do, too, by now; nobody goes out with Quentin very long without using Narcissus. Of course I use all the others—you probably do, too—Estée Lauder and Chanel and Lancôme and Clarins—I just can't pass them up when I'm shopping even though I know it's all make-believe. I mean, I know perfectly well nothing in the world is ever going to make me beautiful or glamorous, but I keep trying because they sound like magic, and magic is the only thing that actually might do it for me. And they do make me feel good, probably just because I'm doing *something*. And now he's got this new one coming out, a whole new line Ozzie told me about, it's supposed to be secret, but you probably know already, anti-wrinkle, anti-drying, anti-sag, anti-*old*—and I can't wait to try it, I mean it can't make me any worse so why not—"

Alex Jarrell was starting toward them, and Claire, bored and restless, stood up.

"And then there was all that trouble with Brix," Lorraine said.

"What?" Claire looked down at her. "What trouble?"

"Well, if you really want to know about Quentin, you have to know about Brix, because Quentin just took him over a few years ago." She looked up at Claire. "And he and your daughter were pretty tight on the ship, weren't they? And spent the night in Valdez. Maybe Brix told her all about it; I don't know whether he talks about it or not. Not that it's a secret; I mean, Ozzie knows all about it, I suppose because he was the lawyer Quentin called. And it does tell you something about Quentin, that he'd go to such lengths for his son."

Claire sat down again. She saw Alex hesitate, then turn away. "What happened?" she asked.

"Well, of course I don't know all the details, I could only squeeze so much out of Ozzie, and it was a while ago so it's kind of fuzzy in my mind, but it seems when Brix was a junior in college, he thought someone in his fraternity had stolen his wallet. I don't know why he thought that, but evidently he was absolutely convinced of it, and when the other boy denied it, Brix tried to get him kicked out of the fraternity, but no one would vote for that, so Brix took it into his own hands." Lorraine paused.

"To do what?" Claire asked.

"To get rid of him."

Claire stared at her. "What are you saying? To *kill* him?"

"Well, or maybe only hurt him, or scare him, Ozzie wasn't clear on that; I don't really know the details. But supposedly Brix set some kind of trap, and the boy fell out of the window in his room in the fraternity house—it was the fourth floor, I think—and nearly died. He may have been paralyzed; I'm not sure; I don't know all the details. But Quentin was incredible; he did everything for Brix. He lined up big donors to the college to pressure the administration to keep it quiet, and then he took Brix out of there and got him into another college so he could graduate. And Ozzie said he paid a small fortune to the boy and his family; I don't know how much, I don't know the details, but obviously it was enough to keep them from filing charges and to take care of the boy while he recovered, and probably a lot more besides. Anyway, Quentin pulled it off: it all stayed quiet. No charges filed, no nothing. And then he just took charge of Brix. Totally. He kept him on a short leash, made sure he graduated with good grades, told him he was going to work at Eiger Labs, no two ways about it. And Brix seems to be doing fine; he's got Quentin's charm and you know how incredibly handsome he is, and he seems to like his work. Well, he doesn't love cosmetics, he doesn't think they're masculine, or whatever, he never went into details with me, but he must be doing all right because Quentin took him on that Alaska cruise, and he wouldn't have, if he wasn't satisfied with him. And Ozzie says Brix would do anything in the world to please his father, and that's always a good sign. I guess."

They were silent. The music rose to a crescendo, then abruptly stopped, and the dancers, caught unawares, did a few extra steps before they realized they were dancing to silence. "Excuse me," Claire said, wanting to get away, but when she turned, Quentin was there.

"I apologize for leaving you," he said. "I didn't want to be away from you for even ten minutes tonight. Shall we find our table? They're about to serve."

"I'm really not hungry," Claire said. "It's almost eleven; I'd like to go home."

He glanced at Lorraine, then took Claire's hand. "A good idea," he said. They walked across the dance floor and out to the hotel lobby where he told the attendant to bring his car. "Were you bored? I'm sorry about that; I had to talk to someone before he leaves for Europe tomorrow. Did Lorraine talk your ear off? She'll shut up if you tell her firmly enough. What was she talking about?"

"You. And Brix. And I think you knew that."

The attendant brought the car, its air-conditioning already on against the heat of the July night, and held the door for Claire. Once past the parking lot, Quentin picked up speed on the empty road, his hands relaxed on the wheel. "Lorraine talks a lot with very little information," he said. "Did she tell you she wasn't sure of the details?"

Involuntarily, Claire smiled. "A few times."

"And that she'd stand by you, as your friend?"

"Yes."

"She meant it. But you can't trust her." He sighed. "I always have to clean up after Lorraine." He drove in silence, brooding at the beam of his headlights sweeping past a forest preserve and the startled, shining eyes of a deer. The only sound was the faint hiss of the fan blowing cool air through the car. Quentin reached out and took Claire's hand. "I'm taking you home with me."

He loomed large and commanding in the cool, speeding car; Claire felt overwhelmed by him. She had been watching the needle of the speedometer move steadily past all the numbers she thought safe; now, hurtling through the darkness, she found it hard to breathe. In the ballroom, all she had wanted was to go home and talk to Emma, but by now Emma would be asleep. Anyway, Brix had not called her since they returned from Anchorage; probably there was no need for Claire to try to talk to Emma about him at all. And she did not want to leave Quentin. She wanted to be with him. She wanted to ask him about everything Lorraine had said, she wanted to try to understand him, but more than that, over everything else, she ached with desire for him. Her body, so long alone and on edge since the evening in Quentin's stateroom in Valdez, leaned slightly toward him, languorous but jumpy, heavy with longing. Her breathing was short and rapid; she could barely sit still.

They were silent as he turned into the driveway of a

red-brick, Georgian mansion with white pillars, white dormers, rounded wings at each side, and tall, paned windows. They were in Darien, a town Claire's parents had talked about as if it were on another planet, far beyond their means. Quentin held her hand as they walked through the hot, dark stillness to the white front door, lit by a lantern with insects fluttering against the glass. Inside, the air felt cold and Claire involuntarily shivered as he let the door swing closed and, still holding her hand, led her up the curved staircase, through a large sitting room lit by a floor lamp beside a marble fireplace, and into his bedroom.

Claire saw it briefly and registered the fact that it was furnished in dark browns and blacks, but Quentin's arms were around her, blocking everything out. He pulled the long zipper down the back of her dress and it fell open. In a moment she was naked in his arms, and he paused only long enough to take off his own clothes before his hands were moving over her body, hard and sure, as if he were molding her.

Neither of them spoke. Claire was rediscovering her body in the arms of a man, how it felt to let herself be open to a flood of desire and pleasure, and when Quentin led her to his bed, whatever he did she followed without thought. He lay above her, then brought her to lie on him, then stretched over her again, and his hands moved over her as he moved inside her, bringing her to a peak, then letting her slip back, then bringing her up again until Claire felt she had dissolved into the dark room, the hard possessiveness of Quentin's hands and mouth, and his thrusts within her. A faint thread of thought tried to keep her for herself, separate from him, but she could not hold on to it; she was too open to him. He filled her; she was all rhythm and response, and she followed wherever he led until all thoughts had been left behind.

Then he brought them both up together, and they came together, and slowly quieted. Their breathing slowed and they lay still. Quentin reached down to pull the sheet over them, then lay on his side, facing her, his hand cupped over Claire's

POT OF GOLD

breast. "There's a dinner party tomorrow night," he said, as if continuing a conversation. "I want you with me."

Claire stretched, feeling loose-limbed, lazy, confident. "I should be with Emma tomorrow."

"You can be with Emma all day. And the next night and the next, if you want. Tomorrow is an important dinner. I need you."

In the midst of her languor, Claire felt a small prick of annoyance. Did he have to control everything, even the time she spent with her daughter? But she pushed it aside. It was too soon to start asking questions; she was feeling too good. There's plenty of time for arguing, she thought wryly; let me have this pleasure at least for one evening.

"You don't need me," she said. "We just met; everything you've done, you've done without me."

"So far. But now I want you." He sat up, his broad chest and shoulders blocking the light from the next room. "You don't understand what you have, Claire. You have simplicity; you're not a complicated woman. You're a cool breeze over the dung of the people I spend my time with." He paused. "Sometimes I get so tired." His face froze in a look of surprise. "I don't know why I said that. It doesn't mean anything."

"Dung?" Claire repeated. "How can you fill your life with people when you think that of them?"

He shrugged. "I don't fill my life with people." He ran a fingertip around her breast. "Though I'd like to fill it with you."

"Why? Because you think I'm simple? Lorraine said I wasn't as innocent as I seemed. You're all trying to find labels for me."

"I don't think you're simple, I know it; I'm never wrong about people. And you are innocent, in ways that Lorraine can't understand. It's as if a good part of the modern world passed you by, and when you walk through it, you're like an observer, quieter and more ingenuous than the rest of us. I find you immensely attractive, I think about you when I'm not with you; I've wanted you since we met. And you've wanted me. We're good together, you know that. Just now we were perfect together. I can give you whatever you want, show you whatever you want; bring you into my world. We could be good for each other."

Claire felt a long, slow surge of anticipation. He was saying what she already knew: that she had money and time but no experience. But he was offering her his, and his authority; she would learn what it meant to have power. There was no love in his voice, but that was best, she thought; she did not love him, or want to. She wanted him to open doors for her. She wanted him to help her, with all her money, truly begin a new life.

"Beginning tomorrow night," Quentin went on, startling her because he seemed to be finishing her thought. "I'm having dinner with some people who can help me launch a new product line, the most important one I've made, and I want you with me."

"Anti-wrinkle, anti-drying, anti-sag, anti-old," said Claire with a smile.

He frowned. "Lorraine gave you that?"

"She was telling me how impressive you are."

"She doesn't know that any more than she knows anything else. She's quoting Ozzie."

"She said you'd managed to protect Brix, when he was in college."

"She doesn't know that either."

"Then you didn't?"

"I did. But she doesn't know the details. As, of course, she told you more than once."

Claire sat up, pulling the sheet with her. "There was a boy who almost died? Or was paralyzed?"

"Neither. He was injured. He was removing a screen from his window and he leaned out too far and fell."

Claire waited for him to go on. When he did not, she asked, "Then what was the problem with Brix?"

"Some people had seen him in the boy's room earlier that

day, near the window. They knew he and the boy had had words, and they jumped to the conclusion that Brix had weakened the latch on the screen so that it came loose with just a touch. Brix denied it and I made sure he wasn't railroaded. He transferred to another school and got his degree, and that was the end of it."

There was another pause. "Did you believe him?" Claire asked.

"I would have done the same things for him whether I believed him or not. I wouldn't allow the newspapers to have a field day with Brix Eiger, or anyone to pass judgment on him; we would have lived under that shadow all our lives. And I wouldn't tolerate his being prevented from getting his degree. Those were the important points and I took care of them."

Claire gazed at him, trying to make out his features. He had called her simple, not understanding anything about her. What really was simple, she reflected, was the way he dealt with the world: to identify a goal and to reach it, whatever it took, without a sideward glance or a second thought. To master events, to dominate, to bend to his will whatever and whomever he encountered. His huge body dominated his bedroom; he towered over others when he walked down the street; he brought maître d's, salesclerks, and service people running, simply by standing still and waiting to be served. Claire had never known anyone like him, she had never had the chance to see what the world could be like at the side of someone who had so thoroughly mastered it.

Desire rippled through her, for everything Quentin Eiger was, for everything he could show her. Her life until now seemed drab and inconsequential; even winning the lottery seemed to be just a first step to meeting him. She knew, or thought she knew, that he was ruthless and self-centered, perhaps he might even be dangerous to some, but none of that was enough to make her turn away. She wanted him for as long as it took to experience everything he could bring her.

Then she remembered Lorraine's warning. *It doesn't mat-*

ter, she thought. I can walk away anytime I want. I don't love him. Nothing that happens with Quentin will have any lasting effect at all.

I have enough money to buy whatever I need; I don't depend on Quentin or anyone else for security or comfort or even pleasure. I can take care of myself. I'm perfectly safe.

But she was still worried about Emma. And so when Quentin drove her home just before dawn, she did not go to sleep, but sat in the kitchen, drinking coffee, waiting to talk to her daughter.

Hannah came in first, neat and trim in her gardening pants and a long-sleeved shirt. She carried a straw hat with a pink ribbon. "Good morning," she said, bending down to kiss Claire's cheek. "You were very late last night."

For a second, Claire felt like a teenager. "Were you waiting up?"

"No, no, it was just that I couldn't sleep and I was reading when you came in. Close to daylight, wasn't it? It must have been a very pleasant—" She stopped as Emma wandered in. "Good morning," she said brightly.

"You're up early," Emma said listlessly. She wore one of her new robes, a soft white chenille embroidered in large blue and pink flowers, and her hair tumbled about her face, shining red-gold in the morning sun, but her eyes were despairing and her slim body was bent like that of a very old woman, almost too much to carry around. Claire watched her pour a cup of coffee and carry it to the table. Her heart ached for Emma's pain, but part of her was glad, because it meant that, for whatever reason, and after whatever had happened in Alaska, Brix had gone his own way. For him, it had been a casual shipboard romance and nothing more.

So she changed what she had been going to say; there was no reason to mention Brix, but there was every reason to find a way to make Emma happy again, even if that meant Claire would have to go away from Quentin for a while. "I thought we'd go to the Cape tomorrow," she said. "We could rent a house in Wellfleet." That was something else they had never been able to afford before, but they had been there once, in a house owned by a friend of Gina's, and they had loved the stark beauty of the dunes and the tough, graceful grasses that grew on them, and the slow rolling ocean waves that left the beach glistening and spongy beneath their bare feet.

Emma's eyes slid to the telephone and back. "I can't. You and Hannah go."

"No, you go with your mother," Hannah said. "I'm very happy here; I'll work in the garden and make flower arrangements all day long. You go; you need to get away."

"We *were* away," Emma said. "We just got back a week ago and I don't want to go anywhere else; I want to stay here!" Without warning, she burst into tears.

"Oh, my poor love," Claire said. She went to Emma and held her close. "You'll get past this," she said, knowing how inadequate those words were. "It was just a week out of a whole lifetime."

"It was everything!" Emma cried. "You don't know!"

What don't I know? "I know how much it hurts," Claire said. "And I know that you'll forget it, even though you think now you never will. It won't even take as long as—" The telephone rang and Emma sprang from her arms to answer it.

"Oh, yes," she cried, and Claire watched the transformation of her face from hopelessness to joy. "Well, that's what I thought. I mean, I know how busy you are, and you've been away and all. . . . I knew you wouldn't have time to call right away. And anyway, it's only been a week that we've been home." She wiped the tears from her cheeks with the palm of her hand; her lips were trembling. "Oh, yes, tonight would be fine. . . . No, it's all right; I don't mind short notice; I mean, I'm not busy, so it doesn't matter. . . . Yes," she said, drawing out the word. "Yes, yes, yes." Her face was radiant as she turned back to Claire and Hannah. "We're going to dinner. He's been busy; his father's been leaning on him and a whole bunch of work piled up while they were in Alaska. He's missed me." Her voice broke on the word.

Claire took a breath. "Emma, I don't want you to go out with him."

Emma stared at her. "What? Why not? Of course I'm going out with him. Why shouldn't I?"

Hannah, too, was looking at her with surprise, and Claire spoke carefully. "I don't think he's right for you. You're younger and less experienced than he is, and from what I've seen, he doesn't take relationships as seriously as you do; he's willing to hurt people. You're not like that, and if you keep seeing him, I think you'll be hurt a lot worse than you have been this week when he didn't call."

"He's not like that! You don't know anything about him!"

"I know what I've seen. Emma, he could have called you; he put you through this terrible week without caring about how you might be feeling—"

"You don't know that! That's a terrible thing to say! His father kept him so busy he didn't have any time!"

"He didn't have a couple of minutes when he took time to eat—probably three times a day? He didn't have a few minutes between all that hard work and bedtime, to reach for a telephone? He didn't have a minute or two in the morning, between putting on his socks and tying his tie? Emma, think about what you're saying."

"I know what I'm saying! He didn't have time! I believe him! Why do you want to believe he's a liar? Does that make you happy?"

"None of this makes me happy. But I'm worried about you. I'm afraid you might suffer because of—"

"Is it his father?" Emma's eyes were wide. "Did his father tell you something about him? You've been out with him a lot; did you talk about Brix? What did he say? *What did he tell you?*"

"It doesn't matter what his father said. He could have told me Brix was a saint and I still wouldn't want you to see him. I watched him on the ship and I watched you go through this past week and that was enough for me. Emma, you're leaving in a couple of months for college; you'll have new friends, a whole new life. This isn't the time for you to get involved with anyone, especially someone who could make you unhappy. I want you to go to college feeling good about yourself and about the world; if you're in mourning for a bad relationship, you won't be able to enjoy everything that's waiting for you there. Look," she added as Emma's face settled into stubborn anger, "we don't have to go to Wellfleet; we can go anywhere you want. Would you like to go to Europe for a few weeks? Maybe the whole summer. Or we could go to New York first and start looking for clothes for you for college, and you'll need a computer—"

"It's all that money, isn't it?" Emma flung at her. "You've got all those millions of dollars and you think you can buy anything. You think you can buy me! All I want is to be with Brix! I'm in love with him and he's in love with me and you can't stop us from being together, you're not going to ruin my life just when it's so perfect!" She was crying again and she ran from the kitchen, and in a minute Claire and Hannah heard her bedroom door slam shut.

"Poor child," Hannah said. "Why didn't you tell her what her father told you about Brix?"

Claire's eyebrows rose. "How do you know he told me anything?"

"Because you skidded around her question, instead of just denying it. Was it so terrible, what he said?"

"I think it was very bad." Claire hesitated, then told Hannah what Quentin had said.

"And you don't think Emma should know that?" Hannah asked.

"I can't tell her. If she doesn't see him again, she doesn't ever have to know it. If she does see him ... well, there's always time to tell her. And maybe he was telling the truth, that he was absolutely innocent."

"You don't believe that."

"I'd rather Quentin had said he believed Brix. Anyway, whether Brix did it or not, I didn't want Emma to hear it from me." Claire picked up her coffee cup, found it empty, and set it down. "Whatever he did or didn't do, everything I hear about him says he's not a good person. Quentin tells me things as if they're nothing unusual—that Brix never had a lot of friends, that they couldn't keep nannies in the house because he drove them away with his temper and little tricks he'd play on them—well, his father called them little, but who knows? Quentin says Brix was acting out because he was insecure, never really knowing where his home was, and that may be true, but I can't worry about what caused his temper and the trap he set for that student, if he did set it; I have to think of Emma."

Hannah refilled their coffee cups.

"On the other hand," Claire said, "maybe if she goes out with him a few times she'll find out for herself what he's like and break off with him on her own. That would be better than her sulking at home and thinking her mother had stifled the great love of the century."

Hannah put bread in the toaster and brought butter to the table.

"I don't think she'd sneak out and meet him," Claire mused, "but she might if he suggested it, or insisted. And that would be the worst of all, because then I wouldn't know about what she was doing. And she'd see me as her enemy, and I couldn't stand that."

Hannah buttered the toast and put two slices on a plate in front of Claire.

"I could ask Quentin to tell Brix not to— No, I couldn't do that. Anyway, it could be that I'm getting all worked up over nothing. I can't know for sure what really happened to Brix in college, but whatever it was, it was a couple of years ago, and he's working now, and he's close to his father; Quentin seems very proud of him. And he's a long way from a child tormenting nannies. I'm sure he's changed a lot since then."

Hannah put two jars of jam next to Claire's plate, with a small spoon in each.

"I suppose I'll let her go out with him and see what happens," Claire said. "That way at least we won't be at war around here; I want us to stay close, the way we've always been." She picked up a piece of toast. "How nice; I'm really hungry. Thank you, Hannah. And thank you for helping me with Emma; it's wonderful to have someone to talk things out with."

They looked at each other and burst out laughing. "Well, I am good at listening now and then," Hannah said. She put her hand on Claire's. "Emma's going to need you, you know, and you'll be here when she does. You're doing fine."

Hannah's praise stayed with Claire all day. She felt taken care of, the way she remembered feeling when her mother had praised her. I guess I still need a mother, she thought ruefully. But her mother had always praised her for being good and quiet and never any trouble; she preferred Hannah's praise, for something she had done that Hannah thought was good.

What makes Emma feel good? she wondered. What kind of a mother does she want? She asked it again that evening as she watched Emma leave, to go out with Brix. Her eyes bright, her body taut with eagerness, she gave Claire a quick kiss and ran from the house as soon as Brix's car pulled up in front. She doesn't want a mother, Claire thought; she wants someone to listen, someone to agree, someone to help her create a myth. I can't do that. So we're going to have trouble.

She stood at the window for a long time after Emma and Brix left. There's nothing wrong with him, she told herself. He had a difficult childhood and maybe he had a terrible experience in college, but that's all behind him. He's older, he's Quentin's son, he's a responsible young man. And Emma will leave for college in two months. It may not even last that long; he may get tired of her sooner than that.

She turned to go upstairs to dress for Quentin's dinner party. Hannah was on the landing, wearing a gray suit and white blouse with a lace collar. A cameo was pinned to her lapel and she carried a small gray handbag. "You're going out?" Claire asked in surprise.

"Why, yes, didn't I tell you? I thought sure I did..." Hannah fussed with the clasp on her handbag. "I may have forgotten," she mumbled.

"Hannah," Claire said, and waited until Hannah looked up. "I don't mean to pry, but I didn't know you'd made friends here; I mean, we haven't lived here that long, and most of the time we were in Alaska."

Hannah nodded slowly. There was a small, almost sheepish smile on her face. "It's that young man I met on the ship. Forrest. He's spending some time in Stamford and he's taking me to dinner. I did mean to tell you."

"Forrest?"

"You met him. Forrest Exeter. He's very pleasant and has so many things to talk about, especially poetry. He's a very interesting young man."

"How young?" Claire asked. "You don't have to tell me," she added quickly. "I just wondered."

"I told you, this isn't a romance," Hannah said firmly. "He's much too young for that sort of thing. We just enjoy each other's company, and as long as he's in the vicinity, I thought, why not?" There was a pause. "Forty-eight. But I think he may be padding it. I'd guess he's closer to forty." There was another pause. "So I'll wait for him on the porch; he's a little embarrassed about coming in. He said you'd wonder about us."

"I do," Claire said frankly.

"Well, I understand that. But friendship doesn't depend on age, do you think? I think we can find good companions at any age." She walked around Claire and down the stairs. "I hope you have a lovely evening. I'm sure I'll be home before you; if you feel like talking, I'll be in my room."

Claire watched her open the front door and go onto the porch, closing it after her. Well, why not? she thought. That cruise has an amazing fallout. But, still, how strange.

POT OF GOLD

When Quentin arrived, she told him about Hannah. "Do you recall a Forrest Exeter on the ship?" she asked.

He shook his head. "He's probably going to try to get money out of her; does she have any?"

"No. If that's what he's after, he's going to be disappointed. I hope it isn't, though. Hannah would be crushed."

"I doubt it; she's probably way ahead of him," Quentin said, sounding bored, and they changed the subject. Claire said nothing about Brix and Emma, and neither did he. She was not sure he even knew the two of them were out together. Leave it alone, she thought. Whatever might need talking about in the future is between Emma and me.

Quentin's dinner party was in a private dining room in a restaurant in Fairfield. The others were already there: seven men and women Claire did not recognize. But they recognized her from the dinner dance the night before, because she had been with Quentin, and because she was new.

"Hello, Claire, good to see you again," said a man whose name Claire did not know. He held out his hand. "Jerry Emmons. And you remember my wife, Lucy. We didn't get to talk last night; too damn crowded. We were hoping you'd be able to get to our place at Southport one of these days; it would give us a chance to get acquainted. Come for a week, come as long as you want; we're pretty casual up there; no rules, no regulations."

"You should know that is a definite honor, Claire," said a tall woman wearing a green silk suit and diamonds. "Jerry usually doles out visiting times to the precise second. Only celebrities get invitations so wide open." She held out her hand. "Vera Malenka. I do heartily congratulate you on the lottery. I always was sure the winners were made up. You know, an out-of-work actor paid a pittance to play the winner for the television cameras, and then the state keeps all the money. I am so glad to know it's for real."

"At least it was once," Claire smiled.

"Ah. Yes, of course, you're absolutely right. There is no predicting about next time." Vera nodded approvingly. "We don't live so very far apart; perhaps we will lunch together, soon."

"I'd like that," Claire said, wondering if this was all because she was supposed to be a celebrity. How odd, she thought; I don't feel like one. In fact, just as on the cruise, she felt out of her depth and nervous. She was wearing a short black silk dress with a red-and-black silk jacket, and jet-and-gold necklace and earrings she had bought the day before, and she knew she looked as good as any of the others—in fact, better than some—but when she saw them in animated chatter, close together, she felt like an outsider.

"Hi, I'm Roz Yaeger," said a woman just behind her. Claire turned. "We met the other night but you don't remember because it was right before Lorraine started bending your ear. Quentin says you have a house in Wilton. I've got a farm about an hour from there; if you don't mind the drive, I'd love to have you come some afternoon, see the place, have a drink, whatever you feel like."

"I'd like that," Claire said again. Roz Yaeger was deeply tanned; her skin had the hard, lined look of years in the sun. She wore black pants, a white ruffled shirt, a black blazer, and, perfectly straight on her head, a stiffly brimmed black hat. She looked like a toreador, Claire thought.

"My husband, Hale," Roz said, introducing a small man with a bald head and ingenuous blue eyes. Claire would never have thought they were a couple.

"Roz didn't mention riding," Hale said. "If you or your daughter want to ride sometime, she loves to show off the horses."

"We don't ride," Claire said. "I wish we did, but we never could afford—"

"That's the point; you can learn at the farm," Roz said quickly, as if she could not bear to hear about anyone not being able to afford anything. "There's a young woman who works in the stables who's terrific at teaching. You could even stay a few days, you and your daughter; Hale's in New

York all week, running the agency, and I'd love to help you and Emma learn to ride."

Claire's eyebrows rose. They knew about the lottery, they knew where her house was, they knew her daughter's name. *That's what happens when you're a celebrity; they know about me and I don't know anything about them.* She glanced at Quentin and found him watching her with a brooding look that might have been desire or possessiveness. She caught her breath. Call it desire, she thought, wanting him again. But then she thought about Roz's offer. It would give Emma something new to do, something she could think about other than Brix. "We'd like to learn," she said. "Thank you." She looked at Hale. "You have an agency in New York?"

"Quentin didn't sing my praises? That's how he keeps us humble. Yaeger Advertising, Claire. Eiger Labs is our biggest client. And about to grow even bigger."

"Hallelujah," said a tall, slouching man with thinning gray hair and a sparse beard. "Lloyd Petrosky," he said to Claire, holding her hand instead of shaking it. With his other hand, he drew to his side a small woman with curly blond hair and oversize, owllike glasses. "My wife and partner, Selma."

"Partner?" Claire asked Selma.

"Lloyd's so good about that," Selma replied, "even though I hardly do any work anymore. We own Petrosky Drugs; don't say you haven't heard of us."

"Of course I've heard of you; I've even spent a good part of my salary in your Danbury store," Claire said. "Petrosky's is the closest thing we have to an old-fashioned general store."

Selma beamed. "That's the idea. I was thinking the other day we ought to put a few barrels in a back corner before the next election, so men can sit around and talk politics, the way they always did in the old days."

"You'll need a potbellied stove," Claire said, smiling. "You'll probably become the social center of town. How many stores do you have?"

"Five hundred, and we're opening another six this week.

And listen, that store in Danbury was one of our first and it's sort of dumpy; we want to remodel it. Maybe you'll give us some advice, since you're a designer."

They knew she was a designer, too. Claire wondered what else Quentin or Lorraine or someone had told them. "Of course," she said, "though I don't know anything about designing stores."

"It's the eye," Selma said. "Being able to see possibilities. We can't do that. Lloyd is the world's greatest businessman, and I'm a terrific buyer—well, I was, when we were starting out; we have a whole buying staff now, though I still go in and dabble now and then, you know, make a few suggestions, and then leave."

"Like grandchildren," Claire murmured.

Selma looked startled. "What?"

"You play with them but you don't have to have them full-time."

"Oh." The others were chuckling and Selma laughed. "It is, isn't it. I never thought of that. And it's true; I like to work but I don't like to be locked into it the way I used to be. Well, anyway, Lloyd and I definitely do not have an eye for design, and you do, so we could use some help."

"Yes," Claire said. "Of course." She was amazed to see her days filling up with lunches and shopping, cocktails and riding lessons. She had wondered what she would do with herself, now that she did not work. Now she knew. These wealthy women had it all figured out.

"Tell us about your new house," Vera said. "I love new houses; that wonderful smell of fresh paint and varnish, and every room is pure, no bad memories."

"Good heavens, Vera," Roz exclaimed. "What about good memories?"

"They fade. To a kind of pale, soupy mist." Vera finished her drink and took another from the bartender in the corner of the small room. "Good memories end up as sort of vague, nice feelings. It's the bad memories that stay sharp, like knives, and they keep hurting, every damn detail."

"Oh, Vera," Lucy said sadly, "we thought you'd gotten over it." She caught Claire's eye. "Vera's second husband drank. Well, so did her first, actually, and she left him. Both of them, actually."

"I told them to choose between the martinis and me," Vera said. "It is not good for a woman's ego to have two men choose the martinis."

"It had nothing to do with you," Lucy protested. "It's a sickness. They were both sick."

"Well, it does not make me feel good about myself to know that I fell in love with two men who were sick, and married them," said Vera. "And my father was, too. It follows me, like a demon."

"But you know you'll get over it," Roz said. "It just hasn't been long enough."

"What about you, Claire?" Vera asked. "What do you do with your demons?"

"Lock them away, like clothes I've outgrown. I don't think we ever can make them disappear completely."

"But after your husband was gone you didn't marry again, all those years. Was that because they didn't stay locked up?"

Stunned, Claire did not answer. How did they know that? She had not told anyone but Quentin. Oh, but the reporter from the *New York Times* had found it out by interviewing someone at Danbury Graphics and had put it in her story. One small sentence in one small story. Claire had cringed when she read it, but she had been sure no one would notice it. But Vera did. And how many others?

"That's too personal, Vera," Roz said briskly. "We talk about everything, Claire; you'll get used to that after a while. There's nothing we love to talk about as much as ourselves."

"I don't have bad memories," said Jerry Emmons ruminatively. "Maybe that's peculiar, but it's the way I am. I forget all the bad things that ever happened to me."

"Well, Claire isn't going to forget the lottery," said Lucy, "or have it fade into some kind of soupy mist. It keeps coming forever, doesn't it?"

JUDITH MICHAEL

"Twenty years," Claire said. "A little less than forever."

"Well, you'll invest it, you'll do fine," said Hale Yaeger. "Buy a farm, the way we did. It's good security and a good place to get away from the city."

"*Who* bought it?" Roz asked, looking at Hale.

He flung out his hands. "Buy a farm, the way *my wife* did. She does let me come out on weekends, and it's a pretty place. You wouldn't want to stay there forever, but—"

"Talk to me before you even think about buying one," Roz said to Claire. "I've never worked so hard in my life."

"But you decided to run it yourself," said Vera. "Why, I cannot understand. You could hire a manager and relax a little bit instead of staying up nights worrying about a horse not looking healthy or the hay not growing as high as it should or whatever farmers worry about . . . and my God, you could stay indoors for a change instead of being out in the sun all the time, ruining your skin."

"You keep telling me that," said Roz, "and I keep telling you I like what I'm doing. I love what I'm doing. That's my little world and I run it. And I don't worry about my skin; I'm counting on Quentin to take care of it. I let it go too long, that's the problem; I didn't start slathering fancy creams all over it, or even wearing a hat, until I was . . . well, somewhat past forty, and by then it was pretty far gone."

"What's wrong with a lift?" Lucy asked. "And a peel. You're about the only one we know who hasn't done it."

Roz shrugged. "I'm scared to death of surgery. I'd rather have a magic potion."

"Claire, what do you do?" Lucy asked. "You must have some secrets; you look like you're about thirty-five."

"I am thirty-five."

"Oh, dear," Lucy said as the others laughed. "Well, I meant you look really young. You look wonderful. And I know what you do: you use Quentin's Narcissus line, like the rest of us."

"I don't think so," Quentin said. He was watching Claire and smiling.

POT OF GOLD

"A competitor?" Lloyd Petrosky asked.

Claire hesitated, wondering how to tell these worldly people she had gone to a salon in New York to learn how to use cosmetics and now used what she had bought from them. Well, if they think it's amusing, that's too damn bad, she thought, and stood a little straighter. "I only learned how to use makeup a few weeks ago; until then I never used any one brand; I always bought a few things on the rack at the drugstore. Petrosky's, as a matter of fact."

There was a hush, as if someone had thrown a rock through a church window. "How refreshing," Vera said. "You didn't go to Petrosky's cosmetics section?"

"Yes, of course, but not for everything. I just shopped around various places for whatever looked interesting. I never paid attention to brand names until I met Quentin." She thought the discussion was absurd and looked at the men, hoping one of them would change the subject.

"You never paid attention—?" said Hale Yaeger. "Good God, my life work out the window."

"You don't read cosmetics ads?" Selma asked. "All those women who look like every fantasy you've ever had about yourself? Well, of course you're very beautiful, but even so, you never looked at them?"

Claire savored being called beautiful, but she felt she was getting deeper into a discussion that showed how different she was from the rest of them. She looked at Quentin, wondering what he expected of her, but he was talking to Jerry Emmons. I'll just have to do it my own way, she thought. "Of course I never looked at ads. I couldn't afford the cosmetics they were advertising, so why would I waste time reading them? I don't think people ever pay attention to ads that are about things that don't fit into their lives. Do you read ads for hiking boots?"

"No, of course not. But cosmetics ... good heavens, every woman adores cosmetics."

"Enough of them, fortunately, to keep us in business," said Quentin dryly. "I think dinner is about to be served." He led them to a round, damask-covered table in the corner, with nine velvet chairs spaced neatly around it. A cluster of candles in the center of the table flickered brightly over gold-rimmed china and a place card and pair of white roses at each plate.

"Claire has a good point, though," said Hale, holding a chair for Vera. "If our ads aren't about something that makes sense in her life, it doesn't matter how clever or creative we are; she'll ignore us."

"Unless you say something so fantastic she can't resist it," said Lloyd. "That's what always grabs me. I don't read ads that are ordinary, but give me a great headline or something really wild and I read the whole thing."

"Like what?" Jerry asked.

"Well, if it's Quentin's new line, something about never getting old."

"What's different about that?" Roz asked. "They all say it. And nobody believes it."

"Oh, not true," Vera said. "I know many women and a lot of men who believe they'll stay young as long as they look young."

"Really stay young?" Jerry asked.

"Well, feel young, and have energy . . ."

"And be terrific in bed until they're a hundred and two," Lloyd said. "Now there's a headline I'd read."

"You can't say that, can you, Hale?" Roz asked.

"We'd have to find a way to hint at it."

"Tireless, indefatigable, and irresistible," Claire murmured.

Hale's eyes swung to her with approval. "That's good. It doesn't say anything about performance, but it hints at everything. We'll have to play around with that. Quentin, what do you think?"

"I'll be interested in seeing the copy," Quentin said.

"Right," Hale said. "We'll see what we can come up with."

POT OF GOLD

Vera leaned back as the waiter filled her wineglass. "So what is it exactly that you cannot say?" she asked Hale.

"We can't say that a product will make new cells or alter the genetic makeup of cells or the bloodstream or the chemical makeup and long-term elasticity of skin or the rate at which hair cells die or the strength of bones or any of the dozens of factors that affect the way we look. If we do, the FDA would classify it as a drug and require it to go through the whole approval process, which can take years, and then it could only be sold by prescription."

"So if you say women will look young—"

"Nothing wrong with that; though, as Roz said, that's what they all say. I want to propose a toast." Hale raised his glass. "To PK-20. The beginning of a new era for Eiger Labs."

"I like that," said Jerry. "Great success, Quentin."

"So," Vera said as the waiters began to serve the soup. "Can you say it's magic?"

There was a pause. "You know, I'm not sure," Hale replied. "What does our lawyer say about that? Jerry?"

"I think you could show castles and fairy godmothers, the whole bit, and talk about magic and so on, but why would you? Isn't the whole idea that we're talking about science, not art, and your product is more scientific than anybody else's?"

"Right," said Lloyd. "That's what we push in the stores; people have more confidence in science than they do in magic."

"That's kind of sad," Lucy said.

"Aren't you selling hope?" Claire asked. "You don't guarantee anything, do you?"

"Guarantee?" Lloyd echoed. "God, that's asking for lawsuits. Hope? I don't know. Quentin, are we selling hope?"

"And performance," Quentin said. "These products come from scientific research; we're not mixing ingredients at random. But of course Claire is right: the bottom line is that any woman buying our products, or any cosmetics, does so because she has hope. She hopes to look younger; she hopes that looking younger means she'll look more beautiful and sexually attractive; she hopes that, as Vera said, she'll also feel younger and have more energy. Which means she can compete with younger women. In and out of bed."

"But that sounds like you're selling hostility between women," said Claire.

There was a shocked silence. "Oh, Quentin didn't mean that," said Lucy.

"Good God, of course not," Hale said. "We're not in the business of running ads about hostility."

"Anyway," Lloyd said, "there's always competition in life; ask the man who owns five hundred stores. So if women feel they have to look young and beautiful to be competitive, what's wrong with that?"

"Well," Roz said, "I can't imagine competing with other women for men—what a waste of time—but it's true that women don't use makeup and face creams to compete with *men*, so—"

"So that's the way the world is," Lloyd said with finality.

"—so they're like weapons of war."

"War paint," said Selma, and a small, nervous giggle escaped her.

"It has nothing to do with war!" Hale exclaimed. "I told you, we have nothing to do with hostility or war or weapons; we don't even talk about competition. We give women hope that they can be whatever it is they want to be."

"And a chance to pamper ourselves," said Claire, hoping to make up for what had clearly been a blunder. "All those cosmetics and shampoos and bath oils are wonderful for pampering; they make us feel special to ourselves."

"Oh, all this analyzing," said Selma impatiently. "Women want to be beautiful because it's better to be beautiful than to be ugly, just like it's better to be rich than poor. It's hardly complicated."

"I like that idea of pampering," said Hale. "Just paying attention to you and nobody else for a while. Not the kids, not

POT OF GOLD

the husband, not the boss at work, just you. I think I'll play around with that."

"That's something else," Claire said, feeling bolder. "We play with cosmetics. Like adult toys."

"Interesting idea," said Jerry.

Hale thought about it. "It could be. We wouldn't talk about toys—we want Eiger products to be taken seriously—but the idea of playing, the fun of it, not this deadly desperation to erase time, that's got possibilities."

"But we don't do it for fun," Lucy said. "We do it to look younger. Claire, you do agree with that."

"I think we want to be the best we can be," Claire said. "Not necessarily the most beautiful woman in town, or the youngest looking, but the best each of us can be. Of course, we never know what that is, so we keep trying new products to see if we can keep on getting better indefinitely, which I guess is what keeps cosmetics companies in business."

Hale and Quentin exchanged a look. "Pampering, fun, the best you can be," Hale said. "What a great way to launch PK-20."

"PK-20," Selma said. "It doesn't sound beautiful. What does it mean?"

"Nothing," Quentin replied. "One of the chemists pulled it out of the air; I think his kid's initials are PK. But it has a nice scientific sound, and we'll give it a number of variations: Super PK-20, Special PK-20, Maintenance PK-20; Eye Restorative PK-20; whatever we need."

"And what is it, really?" Selma asked. "I mean, how many products and how do we sell it?"

"We're writing the literature that goes with it now," Quentin said. "You'll get a packet describing each product in the line, and instructions, with a set of six samples, that you can give to anyone who asks about it. The whole line will have over fifty products, and what they will do is temporarily eliminate wrinkles—"

"Temporarily?" Roz asked in surprise. "Nobody says 'temporarily.'"

"Of course not," Quentin said. "But only a fool would think we're promising permanence. What we say is that wrinkles disappear when our products rehydrate the skin. As long as men and women use it, their skin won't dry out and they'll look younger. Not as tight and plump as a teenager, but the closest they'll get this side of the surgeon's knife."

"But you're going to say more than that," said Jerry. "I mean, everybody from Maybelline to Estée Lauder says they'll make you look young and beautiful and ravishingly desirable."

"No, they don't say that," Hale said. "They hint."

"We're going to come from two directions," Quentin said. "One is what Hale was talking about: pampering, fun, whatever he comes up with to attract customers through their emotions. The other is the scientific one to get customers through logic. I'll tell you briefly how that will go." He sat back while the waiters cleared the soup bowls and served the main course. When they were gone, he said, "You all know about retinol; it's been around for a long time, first used for acne, but then it was found to increase the ability of the skin to retain moisture. What we've found is an enzyme that works as a catalyst, binding a polypeptide chain to the retinol molecule. The enhanced retinol molecule works faster and with more potency; it increases by fifteen to twenty percent the ability of cells to retain moisture. By doing this it regenerates cells that would otherwise decrease with age, which is what leads to dehydration and dulling of the skin tone. This hypermolecule eliminates wrinkles, makes the skin soft, even gives it a kind of glow that literally transforms it."

"And the FDA doesn't call it a drug?" Lloyd asked.

"They've told us they'll approve it as an over-the-counter product any day now; they've decided it's not a drug. The fifty products will include cleanser, toner, moisturizer, day cream, night cream, three stages of repair formula for different ages and for moderate to difficult skin conditions, and an eye cream to eliminate puffiness. They'll be sold as a full line, and only in pharmacies and department stores; we won't sell them in beauty salons or grocery stores or drugstores that don't have pharmacies and separate, professionally staffed cosmetics sections. Our people will be trained in how to use the line, and they'll go to the pharmacies and department stores to train cosmeticians and pharmacists in how to use and sell it."

"And one assumes it will be very expensive," said Vera.

"It's unique; it's amazingly effective. Customers will pay for that."

"Do you know how much yet?" Lloyd asked. Claire saw that he was making notes on a small pad in his hand below the edge of the table.

"It depends on the product. We'll set the retail price for the cleanser and toner at as little as thirty dollars each. The repair formulas are on a sliding scale; the one for people over forty-five with serious skin problems will cost a little over four hundred dollars for an ounce and a half."

Jerry gave a low whistle.

"How long will that last?" Vera asked.

"Six months," Quentin said.

"Lloyd," Selma said. "Fifty products! Where do we get the space?"

"Somebody else's line may have to go, or where we can, we build a new counter, take space from something else in the store. We'd have to see how successful it is, first." Lloyd looked at Quentin. "We'll get our usual markup?"

"Of course, depending on quantity," Quentin replied. "You'd have to agree not to discount it, but I wouldn't expect you to, in your shops."

"Well, all that chemistry just blew past me," Selma said, "but I love the sound of the rest of it. When do I get to try it, Quentin?"

"Early next year, if we stay on schedule. Hale's budget for advertising is fifty million to start; we want to be in the women's magazines with teasers in January, and we'll ship to the stores in March." He looked around the table. "Have I answered all the questions?"

"Is it safe?" Claire asked.

"Good heavens," Lucy gasped. "What a question."

"Eiger Labs has never, ever, had a problem with a product," Hale said definitively.

"The FDA takes care of that," Selma said. "They don't let unsafe products in the stores. I never think about things like that; I let the government take care of it. That's what they're there for."

"Which reminds me of our city council," Hale said, and the conversation turned to local politics and Claire only half-listened, not knowing the people they were discussing. But later, over coffee, dates were made: a weekend for Claire and Emma in Southport with Lucy and Jerry—"and do bring Quentin," Lucy said with a smile that made Claire and Quentin an established couple; lunch with Vera; an afternoon with Roz, "and when you're there, we'll figure out when you and Emma want to have riding lessons"; a visit to Petrosky's in Danbury with Selma and Lloyd; and a shopping expedition to New York with Lucy. Claire's small, leather-bound datebook was beside her on the table, and as she penciled in dates for the next few weeks, she thought of Emma and Hannah and Gina and her other friends. When would she have time for all of them?

I'll find time, she thought. I'll fit it all in. I don't want to miss this; it's too new and different. She listened to the conversation around the table, on recent trips to Europe, and then heard Lucy and Jerry Emmons suggest that she and Quentin join them at Lake Como in September. I must have passed, Claire thought. She was keyed up and alert and she thought she was having a good time. She was with people who had money and made things happen and were more polished than the people on the cruise; she had held her own with them and they seemed to like her; at least they wanted to see more of her; and she was with Quentin. It was very heady; more proof, if she needed it, of how far she had come in just two months.

"Well, you sure have," Gina said the next day. They

were shopping in the Danbury Mall, talking as they browsed through the stores, slowly making their way to a coffee bar for a cappuccino. "You look different, too."

"How?" Claire asked.

"You don't slouch. You used to walk with your head down; now it's mostly up. I like the new you; is it money? Or the new guy?"

"Oh, probably both. There's nothing like money to take away a whole bunch of worries, and maybe those are what made me slouch. And I wouldn't have this particular new guy if I didn't have money."

"You mean he doesn't like poor working women?"

"I don't think he notices them. I think it's important to Quentin that the people he's close to have money. He doesn't like surprises; he likes to be in control, and one way of doing that is keeping people around him who all take the same things for granted."

Gina's eyebrows rose. "You mean cruises and private dining rooms and owning five hundred drugstores and thousand-acre farms and all that sort of thing."

Claire gave a small laugh. "Something like that."

"And you're taking all that for granted now?"

"No." Claire thought about it. "But I don't look surprised when people talk about those things. I guess I'm *not* surprised. It's so different from that first day, when Emma and I went to Simone's. We were wide-eyed at everything. Now it more or less rolls off me; I really can understand how people begin to take money for granted. You kind of slide into things when you can afford them, and then they're familiar, so you're not surprised by them anymore. It just seems quite natural that they're there, and within reach, and when that happens, the prices lose their meaning. It's very strange. I didn't plan it; it just happened, and now it's very confusing: I don't know the value of things anymore. I used to know if fifteen dollars, or fifty or five hundred, was too much for something, but now those are just numbers, and if they're attached to things I want, I buy them and I don't think about whether it's a good price or not."

"Like that blouse this morning," Gina said. "That terrific blouse. The most terrific blouse I ever saw. And it cost eight hundred and fifty dollars."

Claire flushed, because coming from Gina the number sounded crazier than it had when she read it on the price tag. "Maybe that was a good price for that blouse. I don't know anymore."

"You just knew that you wanted it, so you bought it."

"Well, why not?"

"Damned if I know. If it doesn't make a huge hole in your checkbook—"

"It doesn't, that's the whole point; Olivia took care of that. I keep buying and my account stays the same. I told you about that."

"Automatic transfer of funds," Gina murmured. "Something like 'Open sesame.'"

"It is. The whole thing is a fairy tale."

"But you can't spend more than two million a year. I mean, that's all you've got."

"Yes." Their eyes met and they burst into laughter. "That's all I've got," Claire said mockingly. "And I'll never be able to spend more than a part of it."

"The house," Gina said.

"Well, yes, but that was one time. I'm not going to buy a house every year and add to the mortgage payments I've already got."

"Well, you'll find other ways to spend it. If you run out of ideas, maybe I can think of a few. Or what's his name will, so you can keep up with his glittery social life. I'll bet he's good at having ideas. What else is he good at?"

"He's good to talk to—a little too self-satisfied sometimes, but always interesting. He knows good restaurants. He's a good dancer. He has a way of making other people look up to him and stay close, as if they might learn something important and valuable if they hang around and listen to him long enough."

"And?"

"And he's very good in bed."

"That's last on your list?"

"They're all about equal, Gina, you know that."

"They're only equal when you've got somebody. If you're sleeping alone, it tops the list. Have you forgotten that?"

"No, I remember. It hasn't been so long ago."

"Are you in love with him?"

"No."

"But you could be?"

Claire hesitated. "I don't know. I don't think so. He's not very lovable. He's just impressive."

"Well, I guess I could use some of that," Gina murmured.

"Lovable or impressive?"

"Both. Lovable for my nights and impressive to find me a job."

At the coffee bar, they sat at a small table in the corner. Claire picked up the menu, trying to think of what to say. For fifteen years she and Gina had been as close as sisters, working hard at their jobs, always worrying about having enough money, wondering if they would ever find someone they could love and live with. Gina had been a kind of second mother to Emma. Now all that had changed. It was still easier to talk to Gina than to anyone else, but Claire did not know how long that would last. *I can't lose Gina,* she thought as she stared blindly at the menu. *She and Emma are all that's really solid in my life; everything else is still a fairy tale. And Hannah. Hannah is solid, too.*

They gave their order to the waiter. "Listen," she said. "I know you said you didn't want me to help you—"

"I said I didn't want to start sponging."

"Well, okay, you won't sponge. I don't want you to. But what if I asked Quentin to find you a place at Eiger Labs?

They're starting a whole new line now, and they might be needing lab technicians. Would it be all right if I asked him? You'd have to commute to Norwalk."

"That's nothing." Gina's eyes were bright. "Could you really do that? God, Claire, that would be your good deed for the decade." She picked up a shaker of cocoa powder and turned it around in her fingers. "This has been the damnedest time for me, like some kind of midlife crisis. I've been trying to figure out who the hell I am. I'm thirty-seven years old and I'm not interested in getting married and I'll never have kids and I don't see much of my parents and I don't have a job. So what am I?"

"You're my friend. You're Emma's . . . oh, sort of second mother; you've been part of her growing up. And you're definitely part of our family."

"Claire, I love you, but all that doesn't give me a peg to hang my hat on. If I don't have a family of my own, not even someone I love to live with, then I need a job, so I know what to call myself."

"What's wrong with Gina Sawyer?"

"It's not enough. You have to be attached to something. Gina Sawyer, lab technician, isn't bad; it gives me a whole industry to be part of, and a job description, and other people to work with who know who I am. And it's been incredibly awful to be without that. Every day I get up and tell myself this is the day I'll get a job and be in charge of my life again and know who I am; and then at night I go to bed with no job, no money, and no reason to think tomorrow will be any different. Nobody can know how that feels until you get fired; like you're out there in space, not connected with the rest of the world that's busy going to work and doing things; you're drifting, and you feel like you're not real and not alive because you're not doing anything. Except looking for a job, and that's not a satisfying way to spend the day." She looked at the cappuccino the waiter set before her. "I'm sorry; I didn't mean to dump on you."

"You're supposed to dump on me; that's what I'm here

for." Claire held out her hand for the shaker, and when Gina gave it to her, she sprinkled cocoa powder onto the froth in her cup. "I'm sorry; I've been so busy spending money and meeting people and wallowing in luxury that I didn't pay much attention to what was happening to you."

"No, that's not fair; don't blame yourself. I could have talked to you anytime; I knew that. I just got in a bind: I wanted to solve all my problems myself. Now I've had enough of that and I want help, and whatever you can do will be wonderful." She paused. "And if you can't, if it doesn't work out, I may get out of lab work forever."

"And do what?"

"Something with horses. I've always loved riding, you know, ever since I was a kid. I just wasn't able to do it unless I found somebody who'd let me hang around stables. And it occurred to me the other day, when I was trying to figure out who I am, that I really like horses better than I like most people, and a lot better than any laboratory I've ever worked in. So one of these days, when I have enough money put away, or maybe even if I don't have enough money put away, that's what I'd love to do: go to work for a pittance, taking care of somebody's horses."

"I met someone last night who has horses. I'll introduce you to her."

"My, my, you're going to answer all my prayers in one day," Gina said lightly. "Your being rich is definitely the best thing that's happened to me so far."

They exchanged a smile. "I've been thinking about work, too," Claire said. "Sometimes I miss it, at least the creating part of it. I miss sitting with a pencil or watercolors and seeing something take shape on the paper, starting with an idea—not even a whole idea sometimes, just part of one—and becoming something that has its own integrity, and life. I loved that. Maybe someday, if I get tired of all this, I might go back."

"To the same job? Taking orders from people who aren't

as good as you and letting them take credit for your ideas? You've already forgotten that part of it?''

"No, I wouldn't want to go back the same way. But I might be able to get jobs on my own, maybe working at home."

"Why don't you start your own company? You can afford it. Then you wouldn't have to work for anybody, just yourself."

Claire looked surprised. "I could. I hadn't thought about that. Well, it's all pretty vague; I haven't the faintest idea when I'd have time to work even if I wanted to. All of a sudden I'm so busy . . . you wouldn't believe how days can fill up with lunches and brunches and shopping, and thinking about the next lunch or brunch or shopping—" She caught Gina's mocking look. "I know, it's ridiculous to complain; I'm having a good time. And I want you to get a job, and I'm sure Quentin will take care of it. I'll call him when I get home. No, I'll call now. I'll be right back."

She went to the pay phone in the corner and returned in a few minutes. "He says they do have openings and you should see the personnel director; she'll have your name. He says, any friend of mine and so forth."

"I'll go tomorrow, first thing. And we'll celebrate tomorrow night. I hope."

There was a brief pause. "Fine," Claire said.

Gina tilted her head. "You've got a date tomorrow night."

"I'll break it."

"No, we'll celebrate the night after. Assuming we have anything to celebrate. And assuming the night after is free."

Claire took her leather-bound calendar from her purse and checked the date. "It's fine. I'll tell Emma we want her, too."

"Is she seeing what's his name?"

"Brix. She's seen him once. He hadn't called this morning before I left to meet you."

"Will he, do you think?"

"I don't know. I don't know what he wants unless it's just to play around for a while. He drove Emma crazy for a week and then called yesterday, and she came out of her funk and was ready to dance the night away with him. Or spend it in his bed; I don't know if they're doing that. He scares me because he can do that to her."

"So tell her you don't want her to go out with him."

"Spoken like a woman who doesn't have a teenage daughter," Claire said with a smile. "I did tell her. It doesn't matter."

"Claire, she's still dependent on you for everything."

"So what does that mean? That I'd threaten to take away her food and clothing and shelter if she doesn't do what I want?" Claire shook her head. "Look, I can't fight with her; I've never been able to. And I want her to be strong and independent and ready to make decisions about her own life."

"So what are you going to do about this guy?"

"Nothing, right now. I hope he'll move on to somebody else after he's taken her out a few times. I don't imagine he wants anybody permanent; he just wants a beautiful girl, and I guess a young one, too."

"So is he making her happy?"

"He's making her happy and miserable. That's why I can't do anything. I want to put my arms around her and keep her from being unhappy, ever, but I can't do that; she's already told me she wants to make her own mistakes. I could just hear myself, saying the same thing to my parents. All I can do is be here for her if she needs me. I can't yell at her or tell her she doesn't know what she's doing, because then she won't trust me, and if she doesn't, she won't come to me at all, even when things get terrible. If they do. So right now I can't even tell her what I really think of Brix. Or what I'm worried about."

"You can't tell his father to keep him home?"

"How could I do that? I don't want to plot behind Emma's back. And what if I did ask Quentin? Quentin talks to Brix, and Brix tells Emma what I've done. Then where are we?"

Gina shook her head. "I guess I haven't got any good

answers." She finished her coffee. "Except . . . you're having fun and you're happy. Emma's having fun and she's happy, at least part of the time. Hannah is happy and secure for the first time in years. And if I get a job, I'm going to be ecstatic. So it sounds like things really are wonderful and we should be dancing in the streets."

Claire smiled. "You're right, it's ridiculous to worry. This is the best time we've ever had. Everything has been wonderful since I won the lottery. I'm not going to ruin it by looking for trouble."

She met Gina's eyes. "Time to go," she said. "I want to do some dancing in the streets."

8

"YOU'RE gorgeous," Brix said, looking down at Emma's glowing face. They were lying on a blanket in a park in Greenwich. In the background, a rock band played, while fireworks filled the sky with huge starbursts that soared outward, then slowly descended in long, brilliant streamers that faded as they fell and vanished into the moonlit sky. It was the first week of August and Brix was giving a party for everyone who had missed being with him on the Fourth. He did not say, and Emma did not remind him, that the reason she had not been with him on the Fourth was that he had not asked her to be. They had gone out three times after they returned from Alaska, and then he did not call her for two weeks; when he did, he was cheerful and buoyant. "Did you have a great Fourth? I went to some guy's party, one of the worst, and I kept missing you, so I figured I'd better make my own. We'll have a party with fireworks, and then we'll make our own, later, when we're alone. How about Saturday night?"

"I'd love it," Emma said, weak with relief. She knew Claire was listening, but she did not care. Two of the longest weeks of her life had just passed, worse even than the first long silence because after those three wonderful nights she had thought he would not be able to bear being apart from her, just as she couldn't bear to be away from him. But now the silence was over; Brix wanted to be with her, he wanted fireworks with her . . . oh, God, she thought, whatever he wants, he can do whatever he wants, just let him want me, just let him not go away.

"You're more gorgeous than all those fireworks put together," Brix said, and kissed her, lying on her, his hand on her bare legs below her shorts. His tongue, confident and probing, took possession of her mouth, and when he finally raised his head, Emma saw nothing but his face, with the fireworks behind him, like a halo. He was wearing shorts and an open-necked, white, short-sleeved shirt that made his summer tan darker, and the curly hairs along his arms and on his chest a deeper black; Emma thought he looked like a god. "I can't stand this," he said. "You're driving me crazy. Let's go."

"But it's your party. All your friends . . ."

"They've got fireworks and booze; they don't need me," he said impatiently. "Do *you* want to stay? Is that it?"

"No," Emma said quickly. She held his face between her hands. "I want to be with you wherever you want me."

"What a sweetheart. You're the sweetest little doll in the world." He found his glass of Scotch in the grass and drained it, then stood, bringing Emma with him, so he did not see the frown that formed a crease between her eyes and almost immediately disappeared. One of these days she would tell him she didn't like that; one of these days, when the time seemed right, she would tell him. "Finish your drink," he said, bending to retrieve her glass, and even though Emma did not like the taste of Scotch and had barely touched it, she took it when he told her to and drank it like medicine, getting it all down. In an instant, she felt it snake hot and piercing through her body, which was already heavy with wanting Brix, and suddenly the world tilted and began to revolve around her.

"Brix," she said, and leaned on him.

POT OF GOLD

He laughed and put his arm around her and held her tight. "I'll have to teach you to hold your liquor, my sweet little country girl. That's what you are: my little country girl. Not used to the big time. But Brix is here; Brix will take care of everything."

A wild rush of exhilaration swept through Emma. The Scotch burned like a fire inside her, the flames lifting her higher and higher so that she felt she was dancing, weightless and without fear, far above the earth. But Brix was with her; she was dancing in the air and walking beside him at the same time. How amazing, she thought; how lovely. It's magic. Brix makes things magic. I want this forever. "I love you," she said to Brix. "I love you forever."

"Good," he said, and tightened his arm around her.

Whatever she had meant to tell him about the way he talked to her had vanished as completely as the long filaments of fireworks that fell toward earth. Tonight was for love; tonight was for magic. Tonight was for Brix. Every night was for Brix. Please, Emma prayed. Please make every night for Brix.

They made their way among the blankets and stretched-out bodies of Brix's guests, the air sweet with a pungent smoke that rose from glowing cigarettes. They passed the long table where the caterers had set up trays of food, and another table where two bartenders were busy all through the fireworks display, refilling glasses and handing out bottles of beer. They passed the musicians, who beat out a rock tune that filled the park, punctuated with the cannon booms of the fireworks being set off some distance away. And then they were at Brix's car and driving to his house, and Emma tried to sit still, though inside she was bubbling with excitement and love, and still she was dancing, far above Brix's car, looking down on it as it sped along the highway toward his home.

He led her inside, his arm around her waist, his hand under her blouse, hot against the heat of her skin, and as soon as the door shut behind them, he pulled Emma to the living

JUDITH MICHAEL

room and down with him to the soft gray carpet that shone palely in the moonlight. The flames in Emma burned higher and faster; she was feverish and heavy, and she drew Brix to her with a passion she did not know she had. His mouth was everywhere on her body where she had never felt, and barely imagined, a man's mouth, and then, suddenly, she was using her own mouth and hands as he was, and she had never imagined that, either, but now it seemed all right because it was daring and somehow dangerous, and she could not imagine anyone she knew doing it, and Brix was moaning, "Oh, good, good, God you are so good," and she knew he was happy, and the flames inside her flared wildly, until she pulled Brix on top of her and brought him inside her, deep and tight, wanting him forever. And then, finally, they lay still on the carpet, drenched and gasping, staring unseeing at the window, black now: the moon had set.

"Wow," Brix said at last. "Wow. You are one incredible doll. God, what a way to celebrate the Fourth; real fireworks, the real thing. Emma, Emma, Emma, Emma, Emma." He sighed deeply. "The best. The best ever."

Emma felt a surge of pride. The best ever. But then she wondered, out of how many? The flames inside her fell back and died away; she was chilly and a shiver rippled through her. *How many? And how many of them is he with on those endless days when he isn't calling me?*

Brix sat up and leaned back against the couch. He picked up his shirt and took a small envelope from the pocket. "Dessert," he said, and tapping a small line of white powder onto the back of his hand, he held it toward Emma. A thin glass tube had somehow appeared in his other hand.

Emma turned her head and stared at the powder. She felt helpless and filled with anxiety. Brix would think she was stupid and ignorant; he'd brush her aside because he didn't need her the way she needed him. He had everything he wanted and all the girls in the world, just waiting for his call, and he'd want to be with them, not her, because they knew the things he knew and lived the kind of life he lived. He didn't really want a country girl; he said that, but he really wanted someone who knew how to live. I'm sorry, she thought, I'm so sorry I never learned, I'm sorry. She shivered again, nothing left of the flames now but ashes. She could not imagine what it had been like to dance above the earth.

"Come on," Brix said. "I can't do it for you, you know."

"I'm sorry," she stammered. "I've never . . ."

He stared at her. "You're kidding."

"No." Her teeth began to chatter. She sat up. An afghan was on the couch behind Brix and she pulled it around herself. "I never did. The people I hung around with didn't do it, so . . . I didn't." She did not tell him she had never drunk more than a glass of wine before she met him, either. It did not matter, since now she drank Scotch; now she was experienced, and she would never have to admit to him how ignorant she had been.

Brix shook his head. "Poor little country girl; nobody taught you anything. Well, come on, I'll help you." He sat close to her and showed Emma how to inhale the powder, slowly and deeply. Then, after he did the same himself, he put his arm around her and settled her against him, humming a little tune.

Emma began to feel warm. Her teeth stopped chattering and her body relaxed into Brix's. Her bones felt light and fragile; she seemed to be a flower, lying along Brix's chest or in his lapel—but how can he have a lapel, she thought, when he doesn't have any clothes on? She tried to stifle a giggle, but it bubbled out between her lips, and Brix held her tighter and brought his hand farther around her so that his fingers played with her nipple. Oh, Emma thought, what a lovely feeling, it goes all the way through me. Everything seemed so easy. Why had she been worried? There was nothing to worry about. She was with Brix; his strong body supported hers and he was humming; he was happy. She had made him happy. He knew everything in the world, he had so many women waiting for him, but Emma Goddard made him happy. He would never brush her aside now; now she knew everything she had to know.

It was almost dawn when she got home. Brix always brought her back late, but Claire was always awake, reading in bed, the door to her room open. "Have a good time?" she always asked casually as Emma walked past, on the way to her room, and Emma always said, "Yes," walking quickly. After the night of the fireworks, she mumbled, "Awfully sleepy," almost scurrying to her room, because she was afraid if Claire asked her to come in for a minute, something would show: the whiskey or the cocaine or making love, something would give it all away. And when she got to her room and looked in the mirror, she barely recognized herself. Her pupils were so big they seemed to fill her eyes, making them look black and empty; her lips were swollen from Brix's kisses; and her body was different: her breasts seemed fuller and her back and neck had a languor that made her seem to sway as she walked.

But the next morning her eyes were back to normal, and when she came downstairs to breakfast, she thought she looked the same as ever as she sat in the bay window, looking at the glass of orange juice Hannah had just squeezed and placed before her.

Hannah gave her a piercing look. "You're losing weight."

"I am not," Emma said.

"Last time I looked, we didn't own a scale. How do you know?"

"I just know. I ought to know what I weigh."

"You weigh less than you did a month ago. And you're not drinking your orange juice."

Emma picked up the glass. She did not want it, but she forced it down. "Now are you satisfied?"

"I'm getting there. What do you want for breakfast?"

"I'm not hungry."

"Well, there you are. That's why you're losing weight.

Emma, you've got a problem; you're not happy and I want to help—"

"I don't want your help!" Emma jumped up. "You can't talk to me like that, you're not my mother, you're not even part of our family, and if I can't sit here without this—"

"Hold on a minute." Hannah stood straight. Her shoulders were squared but there was a slight tremble to her lips. "I know perfectly well I'm not your mother; I'm not anyone's mother. I wish I were, but we don't always have any say in getting what we want most in the world. And I suppose you're right that I'm not really part of this family, though I thought I was making a little place for myself, not through cooking or anything like that, but just because I love you and your mother, I care about what happens to you, and if I lost you . . . if you sent me away . . . I wouldn't have much to . . . to hold on to . . ."

"I'm sorry." Emma's face was flushed. Hannah looked small and vulnerable in the center of the room, but somehow, surrounded by sleek modern appliances, she reminded Emma of an old-fashioned woman, maybe a pioneer, standing in the doorway of a cabin with a rifle in one hand and a child in the other, while soup bubbled on the stove behind her. She seemed fierce, protective, loving, and formidable, and in the midst of Emma's anger and confusion, she felt a rush of love for Hannah, and a kind of awe. "I'm sorry," she said again. "You are part of our family, of course you are. It's just that I can't stand it when people keep going on and on, like an inquisition, and if that's what you're going to do, I'll go someplace else."

"Well. I thank you for part of that. But this isn't an inquisition, this is a conversation. Or it would be, if you'd sit down. And I have a comment to make. That's all it is, a comment, an observation. You're losing weight and you're drooping, and of course the problem is the young man. This is August eighth, and he's called you a total of four times, which is probably a tenth of the number of times you want him to call and a fifth of the number of times he's led you to believe he'd call, and I watch you wander around here eyeing the telephone and drooping, and my heart aches for you. You start—"

"I don't want you to ache for me!"

"It's not something you or I can control. Just listen. You start to droop the morning after a date with him; that's the whole point. You know he won't call today or tomorrow, even though I'll bet he promised he would—"

"No, he didn't. He wouldn't promise because he's so busy at work he can't tell when he'll be free."

"Oh, Emma, smarten up. We all fall for that once, maybe twice, but then we wake up. What's taking you so long?"

"You don't understand. You don't know anything about it."

"Well, I do, as a matter of fact; I know a lot more than you think," Hannah retorted. "Sit down and I'll tell you." She looked steadily at Emma until Emma sat down. "I was a popular girl in my time; I was beautiful and boys liked me, and a lot of them wanted to marry me. A lot of them wanted to take me to bed, too, but in those days we didn't do that. At least, nobody I knew did, and that was what counted."

Emma's face grew warm. She looked at her empty glass and said nothing.

Hannah brought coffee cake and a pot of coffee to the table. "Now, if I were you," she said casually, concentrating on slicing the cake, "I'd move past what you've done so far, chalk it up to experience, and work on getting this relationship straightened out so that you have a little clout of your own. Turn him down next time he calls. Tell him you have another date or you just don't feel like going out, whatever you want to say. Tell him Hannah says he's a cad and a lout and you don't go out with men like that. You want to shake him up a little."

Emma looked up. "Did you talk like that to boys when you were my age?"

"Well." Hannah sighed. "No, I didn't. But if I'd had someone like me giving advice, I might have." She handed

Emma a piece of coffee cake and filled her mug. "I know you're not hungry, but eat some of it."

Emma held the mug in both hands. "You sound like my mother, only worse. What did you mean, move past what I've done so far?"

"Put it behind you." Hannah looked at her steadily. "It shouldn't control you. Every relationship has lots of pieces, like a puzzle, and no one of them should be so powerful it becomes an engine that drives everything else."

Emma opened her mouth to say something, then shut it. She struggled between confiding in Hannah and not confiding. Then she sighed. "Everything's fine, Hannah; I know what I'm doing and everything's fine."

"Well, maybe it is and maybe it isn't, but as far as I can tell, just from watching you—"

"Well, stop watching me!" Emma drank some coffee and scalded her tongue. She gasped, and tears came to her eyes. "You don't have a right to watch me or tell me anything; you go out with this guy with the funny name, and he's a hundred years younger than you are and that's awfully peculiar, if you ask me, so why—"

"I've had dinner with Forrest four times. Don't you think we can have friends who are any age? Or maybe you think I shouldn't have any friends."

"No," Emma mumbled. "I mean, you can have anybody you want. It's just that I can't keep explaining . . . it's not fair. Just leave me alone, can't you! Stop trying to tell me what to do! I can't help it if your daughter died; if you want another one, find somebody else."

"That's a cruel thing to say," Hannah said quietly. "And I don't think you meant it."

"I'm sorry, I'm sorry, I'm sorry," Emma wailed. "I didn't mean to hurt you. If you'd just leave me alone—"

"You see, the thing is," Hannah said reflectively, "when I was eighteen it was the height of the Depression, and my mother didn't have any money to send me to college. My father had been killed in the First World War, and there were just the two of us and we lived in a little town in Pennsylvania. My mother was a secretary to a lawyer, and she taught me shorthand and typing, and I got a job in a real estate office. I thought everything was fine; we were better off than most because we were both working. Then the owner of the real estate company took a fancy to me, and I must say I thought he was something: he was tall and handsome, a widower in his forties, a top-notch tennis player, a horseman, a tycoon who owned buildings and land all over Pennsylvania, and he lived in the biggest house in town. And he wanted me. I couldn't believe my good fortune. Of course I was very lovely in those days, but still, I was a poor girl who hadn't done anything in the world and he'd done just about everything there was to do. So I'd go up to his big house and cook in his kitchen, and we talked about everything he'd seen in his travels, and he taught me to play tennis. He was a good teacher. And of course we slept in his bed. He was a good teacher there, too. And I thought any day we'd be married; we'd stop playing house and do it for real, because I couldn't imagine ever wanting anyone else, and I knew he loved me because he kept telling me how wonderful I was, and I was sure he'd take care of me and make me part of his life and lead me through any troubles that came along. It never occurred to me that I could make a wonderful life on my own. I melted every time I saw him; I couldn't think of anything but him; he filled up my world. I couldn't see beyond him. I didn't want to see beyond him. I wanted him forever and I told him so."

Hannah paused to refill her coffee cup. Emma was staring at her, mesmerized. "So what happened?"

"Well, it went on that way for almost two years. I'd go to his house—oh, it was a magnificent place with oversize furniture and oil paintings in carved gilt frames, and Oriental rugs on dark-wood parquet floors; my goodness, I remember every inch of that house; it was like a palace and he was the king who lived there—I'd go there whenever he asked me, once or twice a week, and we'd have an almost-marriage—

POT OF GOLD

that was what I called it—and in between I'd go home to my mother and my job and wait for him to call. And then one day he was gone."

"Gone?" Emma stared at her. "Where?"

"He just vanished. Unbeknownst to me, he'd opened an office in Pittsburgh and he had a lady there he'd been seeing, and she was the one he married. I learned about it from someone else in his office. So I was alone. And I was pregnant."

Emma stared at Hannah. She could not move.

"Now, it didn't seem so bad to have a baby; I thought this was one good thing that would come from the whole awful time: that I'd have something of my own to love and love me. But I couldn't stay in that man's real estate company and I had to support a child. So when I had my baby—her name was Ariel; I thought with a name like that she would certainly have a happy life—with my mother's help I went back to school to become a teacher. And I did."

There was a long silence. Hannah saw Claire standing in the doorway, listening, a puzzled frown on her face. "And what happened then?" Emma asked.

"Oh, a lot of sad things. Ariel died, and—"

"How did she die?"

"Well, that's another story. It's still hard for me to talk about it. And then my mother died about ten years later, so I was about as alone as could be. I'd had lovers after Ariel died, but none of them made me feel as excited and hopeful as the real estate man had, and I couldn't see getting hooked up with somebody just to have another warm body in the house, so I decided my place in the world was to be alone. A friend found me a teaching job in St. Louis and I moved there. And never had another lover. There was many a time I wanted one, but I got past it; in the long run it was a lot less trouble. And I'd made two major discoveries: that I didn't need a man to support me or lead me through life; I could do it myself and feel pretty good about myself. And I found out that I had good advice to give to people. You'd think that wouldn't be true, since my own life wasn't exactly a model, but for some reason, as long as it was somebody else's life, I knew all the right things to do. And that's why I'm telling you to stand up to that young man and tell him to go to the devil until he learns to treat you with respect and compassion. And love. If you ask me, I'm not at all sure he really loves you."

"He does!" Emma cried. "He does love me! He loves me and I love him, and I don't know why you told me all that, but it doesn't make any difference how many people you give advice to because I don't want any, I don't want your help, I don't even want to listen to you." She turned to go and stumbled over the chair, banging her hip against the table. "Oh, damn it! Damn you, Hannah, damn you, damn you, everything's fine until you start talking! Just go away and leave me alone!"

"Emma, sit down," Claire said sharply, coming into the room. "And don't swear at Hannah. I've never heard you talk like that before." She sat at the table. "I'm worried about what's happening to you. You may think Brix is special and wonderful, but you've changed since you started seeing him and it's not a good change. Whatever the two of you have together, it's making you unhappy and it's making unhappiness in our family and I think it's time it stopped."

Emma was still standing. "Stopped? What stopped? What does that mean?"

"Please, Emma, I asked you to sit down." Emma's mouth was tight and stubborn, but after a moment she sat opposite Claire. "I want you to stop seeing Brix. You're leaving for college in three weeks; we have a lot to do to get ready, and you won't have time for going out or moping around the house waiting for him to call; we'll be too busy. I want him out of your life, Emma; he isn't good for you. I think you know that, but somehow you've gotten trapped and can't get out by yourself."

"That's not true! I don't want to get out! He is good for me; he's the best person in the world for me. You don't know anything about him! You go out all the time with his father;

POT OF GOLD

why can't I go out with Brix? His father isn't so great; you should hear some of the things Brix says about him. I don't think *he's* good for *you*. He's not a nice person; he never stays with any woman very long; he's cold and mean and all he cares about is telling other people what to do. But you keep going out with him, and Hannah doesn't tell you to stop; you can do whatever you want, and that's just fine with her! Well, I'm fine, too, I'm very happy, and I'm not going to tell Brix any lies; I want to see him, I want to be with him, and whenever he wants me to, I will, and if you say I can't I'll just take care of myself, I don't need you, I don't need either of you, I don't need anybody to tell me anything. And I don't want to talk about it anymore!''

She ran from the room and up the stairs, the last words swallowed in her gulping sobs. She slammed her door and sat by the telephone and stared at it through her tears. She reached for it, then pulled her hand back, then reached out again. *I have to do this. Otherwise they're going to ruin my life and I might as well be dead.* She knew his phone number at work by heart, though she had never used it, and after another minute of steeling herself, she called it.

"Brix Eiger," he said when he answered, and Emma hesitated, struck by the formality of his voice.

"Brix," she said at last, but it was barely a whisper. She cleared her throat. "Brix. It's Emma."

"*Emma?* What the hell—I told you not to—what's the matter? What's going on?"

"My mother says I can't go out with you anymore."

"Oh, for God's sake. Wait a minute, hold on a minute." Emma heard a door close, and then he came back. "We could have taken care of this tonight."

"You didn't call me about tonight."

"Well, tomorrow night, then."

"You didn't call me about tomorrow night, either."

"Hey, Emma, what is this, are we having a fight?"

"No, no, I didn't mean . . . I'm sorry, I'm just so . . . Brix, *my mother says I can't see you anymore.*"

187

"I know, I heard you. Look, doll, we can take care of this. It isn't the end of the world, you know; we can get around it. If you really want to."

"*Want* to! Brix, I couldn't stop seeing you; I think I'd die. But then, there's college, too; she said I'll be leaving pretty soon . . ."

"God, we haven't talked about that at all. How come you never talk about it?"

"I just . . . haven't wanted to think about it very much."

Something was bothering Emma, a nagging thought that pricked beneath her words. *Brix isn't asking why my mother said I couldn't see him anymore. Isn't he surprised? Or curious? Or has this happened to him before?*

"Well, when is it?" Brix asked. "When are you going?"

Doesn't he care? He's not even upset. "About . . . three weeks, I guess. It's hard to think about."

"Then don't. What's the big deal? You don't have to go, you know. You can't let your mother run your life."

Emma sat frozen on her bed. She had never thought about not going to college. Her mother had been saving money for years, so she could go. And now that they were rich, she had started buying her a whole new wardrobe, and all kinds of things for her room at school: a stereo, a computer, a television set, a VCR . . . all the things that had been just dreams before the lottery. They had always talked about college, and it was never *if;* it was always *when.* Of course she had to go.

"I have to go," she said at last. "I can't tell my mother I'm not going."

"Sure you can." Brix's voice had taken on a mischievous lilt. "If you have something better to do, you could stay here and she couldn't say a thing."

"Something better to do?"

"I had this idea yesterday," he said happily. "I was going to tell Dad first, but what the hell. Listen, we're starting a whole new ad campaign for a new line of cosmetics we just invented, and Dad and Hale—that's his advertising honcho—were saying they want a new face and they're going to have

POT OF GOLD

a search for it. The search for the perfect face. So, what if I tell them you're it?"

"You mean, a model?"

"You got it. I told you, doll: you're gorgeous; you've got a great smile, and you're sweet and sexy as hell. You're just what we need. And you've got to have your own thing to do; you can't stay under your mother's thumb. She's in the way too much. Look, you come down to my office tomorrow and I'll have Dad and Hale here and we'll talk about it. They'll have to do a lot of photo tests, but you've got me behind you, and I know you're the perfect face, and that means you're as good as in. How about it? Your mother can't expect you to bury yourself in college if you're the famous new model for Eiger cosmetics."

Emma was clutching the telephone. A model. The famous new model for Eiger cosmetics. Sweet. Sexy. The perfect face. Her heart was pounding. I'll be somebody big, she thought. Not just a little student at college, but a model that millions of people will see. They'll recognize me. They'll stop on the street and recognize me.

And I'll be with Brix.

We'll be working together; we'll be closer than ever. I won't have to leave him, ever. And he'll never leave me. We'll be part of the same company. His father's company. His company. It will be like being married.

"Hey," Brix said, "you still there?"

"Yes," Emma breathed. "Oh, Brix, I'd love it; I'd love to do it. I've always wanted to be a model."

"So be here tomorrow morning. Can you do that? Can you get away from your mother?"

"Oh. Oh, of course I can. My goodness, it's not like I'm in jail. When should I be there?"

"Ten o'clock. Tell the receptionist you're here for me."

"Yes." *Yes, I'm here for you. I'm always here for you.* "I'll see you tomorrow."

"That's my girl." She waited for him to say something about tonight. "I've gotta go, doll; we're pretty busy around here. Ten o'clock tomorrow. Don't wear a lot of makeup."

Emma sat for a long time on the bed, her hands folded in her lap. If Mother hadn't won the lottery, I never would have met Brix, she thought. I never would have fallen in love. I never would have been a model. My whole life would have been dull and awful. I ought to tell her, and thank her. But I can't, because she doesn't understand. Someday I will. When she gets to know Brix and everything is fine again.

"But that doesn't make sense," Claire said the next morning when Emma told her she was going to Norwalk. "Why would you try out for a modeling job three weeks before you leave for college?"

Emma fumbled with her car keys; her head was down. "I'm not going to college."

Claire stared at her. "What are you talking about? Of course you're going to college; it's all settled."

Still looking down, Emma shook her head. "I know we talked about it, but—"

"Talked about it! Emma, we decided."

"Well, but everything's different now." She looked up and met Claire's eyes. "I want to stay here. And be a model. I've always wanted to be one; you know that."

"Emma, just a minute. You can't spring something like this... Listen, you can be a model, you can be anything you want, but first you're going to college. You might think of a hundred other careers you want to try, but if you haven't gone to college, you can't even get a start in them. I'm not going to let you miss out the way I did. Why do you think I never headed my own design group? The company wouldn't let me. Their clients wanted people with college degrees; they liked a lot of framed diplomas on the walls. Emma, I want you to have all the chances I never had; I want you to do better than I did."

"I will, I'll do everything better; I know a lot more than you did when you were my age. I'll be famous and rich, and I'll do it myself, without having to win a stupid lottery or anything, and I'll have a better job than you ever had, and I have a man who isn't going to leave me, ever." Emma caught a glimpse of her mother's frozen face, but she was in full flight and could not stop. "You don't have to worry about me; I know what I'm doing, and I have Brix to take care of me. My whole life is changing and it's wonderful."

She started to walk out the front door, but then her steps slowed. She stood still, fumbling with the car keys. "Please don't be mad at me," she said, half turning back to Claire. "I want this so much. I'm sorry if I said things that weren't nice. I'm really sorry. But I have to do this, I have to, and you can't stop me. I'll be back this afternoon."

People turned to look at her as she drove in her red Mercedes sports car with the top down, and after a while she pushed aside her anger and frustration and forgot that she had been feeling guilty about her mother, and a little afraid, and she began to smile. The sun was bright, and the hot summer wind whipped her hair, and she felt like a princess riding in her carriage to the castle where her prince was waiting.

Brix was very formal, as if he barely knew her, as if they had not been in his bed just two nights ago, the cocaine making everything seem easy and beautiful, their bodies together, everything perfect. "Emma Goddard, Hale Yaeger," he said, not touching her, not standing beside her, barely looking at her. "Hale's head of Yaeger Advertising, and this is Bill Stroud, the creative director at Yaeger for Eiger cosmetics, and Norma Colter, the copywriter, and Marty Lundeen, the associate creative director. And you know my father."

Emma shook hands with everyone, feeling exposed beneath their appraising eyes. She wondered if her short white sundress was too casual; she wondered if she should have worn makeup, in spite of what Brix had said; she wondered if she was smiling too much.

Brix turned. "I'll take you to makeup for your photo test."

"Let's talk a little, first," Hale said.

JUDITH MICHAEL

"Good idea," said Marty. "Let's get acquainted."

"You understand, Emma," said Bill Stroud, "this isn't the usual procedure for selecting a model. Ordinarily we have portfolios of candidates and we choose five or six girls to test with our own photographer. And in fact we've already tested four girls, and from them we've narrowed it to two. But Brix wanted this and he has a way with him, so this is a special session. I just want you to know where you stand."

Emma nodded. She glanced at Brix, but he was looking out the window, as if he were bored, and that was when she realized that no one, certainly not Brix, was going to help her. Bill Stroud was holding out one of the black leather chairs surrounding an oval rosewood table in the center of Quentin's office, and Emma suddenly understood that it was for her. She held herself as tall as she could. "Thank you," she said, and sat down.

The others sat around the table, filled water glasses from tall pitchers, and asked Emma about school, about her friends and hobbies, about what kind of clothes she liked, and about her new car. She answered everything, telling herself not to smile too much and not to fidget. When they asked where she lived and what she had been doing in the summer, she told them about the new house in Wilton and her Mercedes and the trip to Alaska.

"You're the lottery girl!" Norma Colter exclaimed. "Or, no, you're not old enough. That was your mother?" Emma nodded. "Isn't that quaint! I've never known a single person who's ever won a single prize. How much was it?"

"Sixty million dollars," Emma said.

There was a stunned silence. "My, my," said Bill Stroud. "A little more than quaint."

"Six oh million dollars," said Marty Lundeen in a kind of reverie.

"So how come you're looking for a job?" Norma Colter asked.

"I want to be a model. I've always wanted to be one.

POT OF GOLD

Anyway, the money is my mother's; it's not mine. I want to be somebody on my own."

"What about college?" asked Bill.

"I want to be a model."

"I'll bet your mother wants you to go to college," said Hale.

Emma shrank back a little. "Does that matter? I mean, she does, but she's always helped me whenever I really wanted something, and she wouldn't stop me from doing this; I know she wouldn't. If it works out, I mean. If you want me."

"Well, we'd have to have her okay," Bill said. "You're underage."

"I'm almost eighteen."

"But you're not there yet." He looked at Hale and Quentin. "I'm not sure we should even go into a photo test if we're not sure we can use her."

"You can!" Emma exclaimed. "It's all right, I know it's all right. She's never said no to me; she won't this time."

"Never said no?" Norma asked, her eyebrows raised.

"Not when I really wanted something."

"Well, I'm willing to go ahead," said Hale. "But you understand, Emma, even if this works out and we do want you, we won't offer you a contract right away. We do a few dozen magazine ads and we test them in what we call focus groups and marketing surveys. If our customers like you, then we talk about a contract."

Emma nodded. She had not even thought about a contract.

"So, let's see," Hale added. "Let's go down to the studio."

They left Quentin's office and, in two cars, drove into Norwalk, to a square, stucco, windowless building. Inside, a small, round woman, with a round, rosy face, was waiting for them. "Emma, this is Lea Partz," Hale said. "She'll do your makeup. Lea, how long do you need?"

Lea contemplated Emma. "Nice bones," she said to Emma with a complicitous smile, and Emma smiled back,

JUDITH MICHAEL

feeling she had found a friend. "Less than an hour," Lea said, and turned to leave the reception room.

Just outside the door, Emma hung back. She heard Bill say, "Nice mouth, sexy eyes; young looking but not a teenybopper."

"She could be any age," said Norma Colter. "In fact, I think it'd be hard, especially in a photo, to guess how old she is."

"And we've got to have that," said Bill. "We can't be locked into a teenage look."

"I don't know," Marty Lundeen said. "She doesn't come across as strong; she seems kind of indecisive. Weak."

"Well, we all sort of pounced on her," said Hale. Emma wanted to thank him, but Lea was waiting impatiently for her to follow her into the makeup room, and so she did not hear what Brix or Quentin said about her, if they said anything. They had been silent the whole time the others were questioning her.

It took almost an hour for Lea to put on Emma's makeup, while she chatted nonstop about actresses she had known and worked on, so that Emma would be diverted and relaxed for the camera. When, at last, Emma looked in the mirror, she barely recognized herself. She was more dramatically beautiful than she had ever imagined. "It's not really me," she whispered. Lea laughed. "It's you and me together, honey: your face and my concoctions. Eiger concoctions, I ought to say, if I value my job. You look good. Come on now." She led the way down a corridor to an enormous, white-walled, white-floored room hung with klieg lights and furnished with cushions, a few scattered pieces of furniture, and tripods holding more lights and reflecting screens. "I didn't do her hair," Lea said as they entered. "I thought it was fine."

"It's fine," said Bill Stroud. He looked closely at Emma. "Very fine."

They were all there and Emma heard a kind of collective sigh as they looked at her. They looked for a long time, with unwavering stares. She flushed and looked down, to escape those stares. "You'll have to get used to people looking at you, Emma," Bill said. "If they don't look, you're in trouble. And so are we. Okay, let's put you here for starters." He led her to a pile of cushions on the floor. "Find yourself a comfortable position. This is Tod Tallent, our photographer; you do whatever he tells you."

Emma sat on the cushions, tucking her legs under her, while Tod contemplated her in silence, hands on hips, head tilted. Lights came on, hot and blinding, like drenching sunlight. "Okay," Tod said at last. "Emma, stretch your legs out in front of you, lean back on your hands, and let your head fall back. You're looking at the sky or the sun or a bird or whatever. Dreamy look on your face. No, that's just sleepy, give me another one. No, you look bored. Hale, how about some music?"

Someone put on a tape, and a crooning love song filled the white room. "Dreamy, Emma, dreamy. You're in love and you're dreaming of tonight. Or you're remembering last night. Ah, better. Not bad. Raise your shoulder, stretch your leg, good, good, I like it." Emma heard the rapid clicks of his camera. "Now turn to the right, just your head. No, too far. Good, that's good. Now the left, as far as you can, and lift your chin. Higher. Yes, good, hold that. Now put your arms around your knees and look past my shoulder. Not at me, past me. And hug the knees. Nice, nice, good, turn to the left, good, perfect, fold your arms on your knees, look all the way around like somebody's behind you. Good, nice, fine. Okay, we'll change the lighting."

Emma held her pose, frozen, barely breathing.

"You can relax, Emma. Couple of minutes."

Emma tried to see past the blinding lights, but she could not; she was alone. Then, abruptly, the lights went out and she closed her eyes against the colored circles that revolved behind her eyelids. In a minute, she opened them. Brix was leaning against the wall, arms folded, looking straight at her. Please smile at me, Emma begged silently. Tell me I'm doing all right; tell me you're proud of me. Tell me you love me.

The three advertising people were in a huddle with the photographer. Quentin was talking to Hale, then Emma saw them leave together. She gave a little sigh of despair. She looked back at Brix, but he had wandered over to watch the two lighting men set up a group of reflectors.

"Emma, stretch out on that black couch," Tod said, gesturing toward another part of the room, and Emma moved to the couch and lay down, leaning on her elbow, her head on her hand. She looked at the camera, her lips parted in a small smile. "God, that's good, don't move," Tod said. Emma held the pose, then subtly changed it without being told, moving her shoulders, her hips, her legs, changing her smile, flowing from one position to another. It was as if her body had learned what the camera wanted and, by itself, had become malleable and supple, while her eyes and mouth focused on the dark eye of the camera, beckoning to it. She loved it; she loved being part of something bigger than herself—the camera, the photograph, the advertisement, the whole magazine, everything that all these people were doing together, dozens of people making something happen that would be all over the whole country, maybe the whole world, and she was at the center of it. She loved it. "Good, good, great, nice, perfect," Tod said, his camera clicking rapidly, and then, taking up another camera, he sent Emma to an armchair, and then to an ordinary playground swing, hanging from hooks in the ceiling. "Okay," he said at last. "Good shoot." It had lasted almost four hours.

Exhausted, Emma slid off the swing and stood uncertainly beside it. The others had left the room and returned and now stood some distance away, talking in low voices. Emma stood beside the swing for what seemed like a long time, and then Bill Stroud turned around and his voice echoed in the room as he called, "Thanks, Emma, you were fine. We'll let you know."

Emma stood still, waiting for Brix to come for her. But no one came; the others, still talking, were moving away from her, and Brix was with them.

"Come on, honey," Lea said, taking Emma's arm. "You have a car at Eiger Labs? I told them I'd drive you back. We go this way."

Emma looked one more time toward Brix, but he did not turn. She saw Lea peering at her. "You did good," Lea said. "I can always tell."

"Oh, Lea, I love you," Emma said impulsively. And all the way home, driving in her red car, she thought of Lea and what she had said. You did good. I can always tell. But no matter how many times she repeated Lea's words to herself, she still saw Brix's back as he left the room.

"Well?" Hannah asked as Emma came in the kitchen door from the garage. "Are you the famous new face or not?"

"They said they'd let me know. Where's Mother?"

"She had a lunch date with somebody and then they went shopping. My dear, you look all worn-out."

Emma slumped in a chair at the kitchen table, tears in her eyes. "I am, I'm so tired, and I don't know if I was any good."

"Good heavens, Emma, you're always good; you're wonderful. If they don't want you, it's because they want another kind of wonderful, that's all it means."

Emma looked up. "Thank you," she said, and thought of Lea. Why were women nice to her, and not Brix and his father? "Was Mother furious at me?"

"She's never furious at you. She's worried and she's unhappy."

Emma's head drooped. "I know. But she can't run my life. I wish she'd try to understand me and help me do what I want, instead of what she wants."

"I thought you agreed on college," Hannah said mildly.

"Well, I don't anymore, that's all, I've got something better, and if she loved me, she'd help me—"

"Don't you ever accuse your mother of not loving you!" Hannah said fiercely. "You know she does, more than anything, and she'd do anything she could to make you happy.

She thinks you're making a mistake; should she keep quiet about that, if that's what's worrying her?"

Emma toyed with the salt shaker. "I think, if they want me, I'll move out and get my own apartment. I was thinking about it, driving home. It just wouldn't work if I stay here; Mother would hate it, watching me go to work every day instead of—"

"You won't move out, Emma, my Lord, what are you talking about? You belong here; this is a family and you're part of it, and your mother isn't the hating kind. She'd keep on loving you the way she always has. What in heaven's name would you get by moving out? Except a private place to sleep with your young man."

Emma felt her face burn. "That isn't what I meant."

Hannah waited, but Emma kept her head down and was silent.

"Well, if that's not what you're looking for, you stay right here," Hannah said. "We love you and we want you here, not running around the countryside as if you don't have a real home. You just forget this foolish idea; don't even mention it to your mother; it would make her even unhappier than she is."

Emma looked up. "Hannah, is she going to marry Quentin?"

"Why don't you ask her that?"

"Because I can't talk to her about him. Or about Brix. Or about anything. We used to talk all the time and now we hardly do at all. He's very strange, you know, Quentin; Brix hates him and loves him and he's afraid of him, too, I think, and I don't think he's at all nice, underneath."

"Who's not nice, Brix or his father?"

"His father, of course. Brix is wonderful."

"But he didn't say you were good today?"

Emma winced. "He couldn't; he was with his father and a bunch of advertising people."

"Really? He couldn't come over and say thanks, you were very good, I'll talk to you soon? Is that the same as he

POT OF GOLD

can't call you for a week or more at a time because there's no telephone where he works or where he lives?"

"Oh, leave me alone!" Emma cried. "I believe what he tells me; I love him and I know he loves me, and if you keep talking that way, I will move out; I can't stand it if you keep accusing him all the time."

"Okay, I won't. I won't say a word." Hannah bustled about the kitchen, making dinner. "I'm trying something new: the most interesting recipe. It's so good to have a family to cook for; I was bereft when it was just me. Did you know I was a caterer once?"

Emma shook her head. "You said you were a cook. You cooked for friends, you said."

"Well, I did, but I was a caterer, too, not for long, but I had some major clients. Corporations and some very wealthy folks out on Long Island, that sort of thing."

Distracted, Emma looked up. "Was this before or after you had the affair with the real estate man?"

"Oh, after," Hannah said casually.

"But I thought you went to college to be a teacher afterward."

"I took some time off from being a teacher. Then after a while I went back; I decided catering wasn't for me." Hannah opened the refrigerator and took out cucumbers and sesame seeds. "I don't remember the exact dates. You don't remember those things once you hit seventy."

"But—" Emma began, and then the telephone rang and she grabbed it.

"Hi, babe," Brix said. "How'd you like to be the new Eiger Girl?"

Emma caught her breath. "They liked me?"

"They're crazy about you. They rushed through the proofs from the first two hours and they're fantastic; everybody's whooping it up. I'll probably get a medal; maybe even a bonus. They think I've got the greatest eye in history. They never even knew I thought about our ad campaigns; now they'll keep me in the loop when they start making plans. I'm not daddy's little boy anymore, and if things go the way I think they will, this is one vice president who's finally going to get to act like a vice president. This is the best thing that could happen to me; when I decide to get out of here, I'll have a title that means something. It's a—''

"Brix. Excuse me, but when do they want me?"

"Monday, nine o'clock, at Yaeger Advertising. You'll get a call from Marty Lundeen pretty soon. And we ought to celebrate, right? How about dinner tomorrow night? Get all dressed up; we'll go someplace classy. And tell your ma you'll be home late."

"Yes," Emma breathed.

"Congratulations," Hannah said when she hung up. "How much are they paying you?"

"Oh, I don't know," Emma said happily. "I forgot to ask. I'm sure I'll find out pretty soon."

"And are they giving you a contract?"

"Not right away. Later, maybe. Later, I hope." She jumped up and walked around the kitchen, picking things up and putting them down, bouncing on her feet. "They liked me, Hannah; they really really liked me. Brix said the proofs were fantastic. There were two other girls they were ready to choose from, but they picked me instead; they liked me best. The Eiger Girl. Doesn't that sound unbelievable? I'm the Eiger Girl. I'm a model!"

"Well, I'm so proud of you." Hannah hugged Emma and kissed her on both cheeks. "Didn't I say you're wonderful? I'm proud and happy for you."

Emma snuggled into Hannah's arms, breathing in the warmth of her small, compact body. So much was happening; so many changes, so much to think about. "I'm so happy, so happy, so happy." But even though she said it over and over, underneath her excitement she was sad and she did not know what to do about it. She tried to ignore it, she tried to will it away, but it stayed there, like a haze over the sun, so that nothing was as bright as it should be. And so she clung to Hannah, and thought about being happy, being a model, being the Eiger Girl, being Brix's girl. *But he didn't even think of me when they chose me; all he thought of was himself and how this would help him.* "I'm so happy," she said again, to Hannah, and pushed away that disloyal thought about Brix and pretended the sadness was not there.

And then she thought, he's just waiting until tomorrow night. I know he is. When we're together, when we're celebrating, then he'll tell me I was good. Tomorrow night Brix will say he's proud of me.

9

CLAIRE stood in Quentin's office, looking at photographs that covered two walls of the room. Eiger Laboratories was in a long, low brick building on the outskirts of Norwalk, and Quentin's office was in a corner, his large windows looking out on a wide, sloping lawn planted with trees, gardens, and flowering shrubs. The trees blazed with the colors of October, and the sun filtered through in a deep coppery glow; driving up, Claire had thought it looked like a college campus: a place where serious work was done in serenity and harmony by people who cared about what they were doing, who shared ideas, and formed friendships. *The kind of place Emma was supposed to be in, starting the end of August. The kind of place she should be in, instead of spending her days in front of a camera and the rest of the time pushing the hours away between dates with Brix.*

Quentin's office was high ceilinged and furnished in oversize rosewood and leather furniture and a massive stainless steel desk. Standing in the center of the room, Claire felt as if she had shrunk, and she wondered if it had been designed deliberately with that in mind: to make visitors feel small. She looked again at the photographs, many of them artistically blurred pictures of Eiger products, the others photographs and

POT OF GOLD

drawings tracing the expansion of the original, small building to its present size.

"It's very impressive," Claire said. "You just keep growing, as if you never stop to take a breath."

He smiled, pleased with her, and Claire noticed, with a little shock, that she relaxed as soon as she saw that he was pleased. Like so many of his friends, she thought. When did I start doing that? "We don't stop or slow down," Quentin said. "We still have a lot of catching up to do. We'll never be as huge as Avon or Helene Curtis—that isn't what I want— but we can be at the top if we don't make any mistakes."

"What kind of mistakes?"

"Imitating other companies, tagging along at the tail end of a fad, waiting too long to bring out a product so that others get in first. A lot of it is timing. What do you think of our packaging?"

Claire looked back at the photographs of Eiger products. "I like some of them."

"Which ones don't you like?"

She found herself tensing up again, worried about criticizing designs he had probably approved. But this is my business, she thought, I know more about it than he does. I should believe in myself enough to say what I think.

But still she hesitated. Because even now, after five months of lunches and cocktails, shopping trips and matinees in New York, she still was not as insouciant as the women who were guiding her. They had a way of being oblivious to their surroundings that Claire could not seem to master. Whether it was the playful monkeys painted on the walls of Le Cirque or the huge floral displays at Le Bernardin or the limousines lined up outside Broadway theaters on Wednesday afternoons or the homeless huddled in shapeless bundles in Fifth Avenue doorways, she always paused in her conversation or in walking along the street to take it all in, to reflect on it, and to wonder that she was really there and living this kind of life. Someday, she thought, she might be as sophisticated as Roz and Selma and Lucy and Vera and Lorraine, as familiar and casual with all the things of the world.

"Tell me which ones you don't like," Quentin said. It was an order. "And why."

Claire took a deep breath and touched the labels in a photograph of a group of oval jars. "This group; all these slashing lines and angles. Cleansing cream ought to be soft and silky, and these probably are, but everything about the labels is hard and aggressive. I might use them on something aimed at men, but not for the face or hair. Athlete's foot, maybe. Or insect repellent."

He chuckled. "What else?"

Emboldened, Claire moved to another photograph. "If you're going to use a black case for lipstick, it ought to be more sensual. This looks like a weapon to me. I'd round the top, or maybe . . . oh, this would be better: curve it in, like a shallow bowl, and make the bowl gold. And I'd make your black-on-black design gold, too, but I'd use something with longer lines, scrolls, maybe, so the fingertips would feel a smooth, unbroken curve, not a lot of little flower petals, or whatever these are." She stopped short, afraid she had said too much.

Quentin's face was impassive. "Anything else?"

"No."

"You like everything but those two? I don't believe it."

Claire hesitated again. "I have some thoughts about most of them. But I don't know anything about your company or whether you're aiming your designs at young women or older women, or male and female executives, or what kind of image you want to project, and I'd have to know—"

"You'd know all those things if you were designing from scratch. I asked you, as an expert, to comment on our current designs, and I want your comments on all of them. That black lipstick case was a total failure in the stores; we pulled it after six months. The photograph should have been pulled, too; I don't know why it's still there. The cleansing cream isn't doing as well as we thought it would, and you may have told

POT OF GOLD

me why." He pushed his high-backed leather chair away from his desk and stood beside Claire to look at the photographs. "You have a good eye. I need that here, but for much more than a critique of our current lines. I gave a contract to Bingham Design—you know them?"

"Yes. They're very good."

"I haven't seen any sign of it. I gave them a contract for the PK-20 line four months ago, and I haven't got anything, a label, a package, point-of-sale material, anything that I like. I've told them I'm replacing them. I want you to take it over."

Claire looked at him in surprise. "As what?"

"Head of design for PK-20, consultant, temporary chief designer, whatever you want to call yourself. I'll give you an office here, and you can hire your own group if that's what you need, whatever it takes for you to get something to me in a hurry; we're behind on our release date because we can't get decent designs. I want you to do this, Claire."

She was staring at him. "I don't believe it," she murmured.

He looked annoyed. "What don't you believe? I didn't expect coyness from you, Claire, or some kind of theatrical modesty. You know you can do it; why would you say anything but yes?"

"It's not that; it's the timing." Claire shook her head in disbelief. "My whole working life, I dreamed about someone saying just those words to me. All the years I was an assistant to other designers, all I wanted was for someone to say to me, 'I want you to take it over.' Do you know how that sounds to someone who never had a chance to take over anything? *Head of design.* Do you know how *that* sounds? And now that I don't need a job at all, you're handing it to me."

"Then you'll do it. We'll have to start right away; we'll get you an office this afternoon."

Damn you, Claire thought. He had no idea how she felt, nor did he care. His agenda was all that was important to him. It was as if he had shut a door on her or reduced her to one small, anonymous cog in the engine of Eiger Laboratories.

But then she told herself that it made no difference what Quentin said or didn't say; she did not need him or depend on him. What was much more important was the realization that she really did need this job. It had nothing to do with money; it had to do with how she felt about herself. It had to do with what she was, and what she made of herself. And for some time now, she hadn't known what that was.

She understood now what Gina had meant just before she got a job here at Eiger Labs. Because for the past few months, Claire had thought of herself as a woman who had won the lottery, a woman who went to a lot of lunches, a woman who did a lot of shopping, a woman who was a mother—though her daughter wasn't letting her do much mothering these days. She did not know any more what to call herself.

Nobody can know how that feels until you get fired; like you're not connected with the rest of the world that's busy going to work and doing things; you feel like you're not real and not alive because you're not doing anything.

You don't have to be fired, Claire thought. You can just lose your way.

She wanted to do something she was proud of. She wanted to be able to say, I'm Claire Goddard, a designer, and this is what I've designed. It's my creation, no one else's.

If I can. I've never designed anything on my own. I've never been a success.

"And you'll make a list of people you want to hire," Quentin said. "It may even become a permanent group; if this works out, I'll want you to look at all our other lines as well. Once you've critiqued them, you can redesign them." He contemplated her for a minute. "You understand, I don't expect you to be here as an employee. You'll decide how much you want to work. That's one of the reasons you should put together the best group you can find, so you can trust them when you're not here. I want you mainly as a consultant; you've been busy with Roz and Vera and the rest of them, and

POT OF GOLD

I don't want you to let anything interfere with that. Once we get PK-20 taken care of, that is."

I have to try, she thought. I have so much money and I still don't know what I can do with myself. And no amount of money can give that to me; I have to do it by myself.

"Yes," she said, "I'd like to do that. All of it."

He looked surprised; he had assumed it was all settled. "When you come in tomorrow, call Carol Block in Personnel for whatever you need; she'll call the people you want in your group, too. You can take them from any other company; we'll make it worth their while. Which reminds me, we haven't talked about your consultant's fee."

"No," Claire began, afraid he would not think her worth whatever amount she said. But then she thought, he wants to work with me, he wants us to work together, and he thinks I'm worth a lot. Why not agree with him? "Two hundred dollars an hour. And I'll meet whatever deadline you set me."

"Done," he said without hesitation. He pulled her to him and kissed her, and Claire leaned against his bulk and felt a new kind of triumph: a sharing of his power. He was the one who bestowed gifts and made dreams come true, and she was the one he admired; she was the one he was asking to work with him.

"This is becoming quite a family business," he said with a smile.

Claire looked at him somberly. "We haven't talked about Emma's modeling."

"I've told you I think she's very good; what else is there to say? Her modeling isn't our affair."

"It may not be yours, but it's mine. I'm responsible for her."

He shrugged. "She can be responsible for herself. She's a mature young woman. Why haven't you brought it up before now?"

"I wanted to wait. I thought it might not last."

"Of course it will last. I told you what Hale said: she's a

natural model and she photographs superbly. He says she's his find of the decade."

Claire felt a surge of pride in Emma and she thought, if Emma was hearing the same praise, she could understand her excitement. But she knew it was not that simple. Emma was troubled, as well as excited, and Claire had begun to think she might still convince her to begin college in the winter semester. "I'm glad Hale thinks she's good, but I don't think she'll stay with it very long. She has a lot of other things to do, college for one."

Quentin was amused. "I don't think so. She's smitten with Brix and with modeling and with doing her own thing, as they say. You can't stop her, and why should you try? It's about time she broke away from you."

Claire stepped back from his solid, powerful body. "Of course I could stop her if I thought I should. I'm her mother and she's not eighteen yet."

"But you won't do it. You already gave permission for us to hire her. Claire, leave her alone. She's having a good time and she's earning her own money. Do you know what she can make if she's popular with the public? We'll give her a contract for a hundred thousand or more, and if she's smart and willing to work hard while she's still young, she'll go a lot higher than that."

"She doesn't need money; I have more than enough. She needs other things—"

"She needs to be left alone."

"—and I'm not sure she's having such a good time. She doesn't look happy to me."

"Well, what do mothers know about it?" he said, making it a joke. He looked at his watch. "We should leave soon, to get to the theater on time. Do you want to wait here while I finish up or would you rather look around the building?"

"I'd rather look around," Claire said, masking her annoyance. He knew nothing about mothers, she thought, or fathers, either; that was clear. For the first time, she felt some sympathy for Brix.

POT OF GOLD

"Claire," Quentin said as she opened his office door. She looked back. "Emma has an unusual beauty that is perfect for our ads; we've been looking for someone like her for a long time. We'd just scrapped a whole campaign because I wasn't satisfied with the girl Hale was using; it's an enormous saving to us that we found Emma so quickly. We're going to use her in print and in personal appearances; Hale's already modified his marketing plan so it's built around her. Don't interfere with that."

Don't tell me what to do with my daughter, Claire thought angrily. But she could not say the words. She could picture his face darkening and turning cold; she could imagine him not being pleased with her. And maybe she was wrong; maybe this was a wonderful chance for Emma. What right did she have to try to prevent it? "I'm her mother," she said at last. "I can't just turn my back. But I've never forced Emma into anything, and I won't start now."

"And you won't urge her to do anything else," he said, pressing her. "Or make her uncomfortable with her decision to work for us."

Claire stood half in and half out of the doorway. "I want her to be happy. I'll help her, if I can, with whatever she wants to do."

He gazed at her for a long moment. "I hope so," he said. "We'll leave in half an hour. I'll meet you at the front desk."

Claire nodded and closed the door behind her. She was angry, at herself and at Quentin, and she was confused and uncertain about what she should do next, whether she wanted to work for him. No, work *with* him, she thought, but she knew that he had never said that; she was the one who had thought it. And she knew then, facing what should have been obvious from the start, that he thought of her as working for him, beneath him, part of the company he ran with an iron hand, and subject to his will.

She walked down the brightly lit corridor that bisected this part of the building, glancing into small laboratories along one side and the open doors of a long laboratory on the other.

Men and women sat on high stools at white, laminate-topped workbenches, writing, using microscopes, weighing powders on small balance scales, mixing ingredients in flasks and bowls, and on flat pieces of glass, like a painter's palette, using water from a small sink on each counter. At one open door, Claire stopped. Gina was working at a bench near the windows.

Claire did not worry, as she usually would, about interrupting; she needed to talk and Gina was here. She walked past other benches and stood at Gina's, waiting. In a moment, Gina looked up, frowning. "Hey," she said, and slid off her stool and hugged Claire. "This is terrific; you get to see my lair." She stood back and eyed Claire's face. "What did he do, tell you he expects you to climb Mt. McKinley Sunday morning before lunch?"

"He told me to stay out of Emma's life."

"He didn't. The son of a bitch. And you told him to stay the hell out of your business."

"I told him I'd do whatever I could to help Emma be happy."

Gina gave a small grunt. "Not exactly a declaration of independence." She watched Claire's face flush. "I'm sorry; I know he makes it hard. For you and everybody. And you know, they've gone totally bananas about Emma around here; I hear them talking about her all the time. The whole advertising team was here the other day; they're going to do a bunch of ads with Emma in the labs and offices and out on the grounds. Nice idea, actually; I think it was Quentin's."

"He says she has an unusual beauty." Claire's voice was low and she knew there was a note of defeat in it. "They're building a whole campaign around her."

"In other words, taking her over."

"Yes." Claire felt a rush of relief. Gina always understood.

"You know what else they're saying?" Gina asked. "That she has a unique kind of beauty: youthful but not young. Bill Stroud said she looked more experienced than most seventeen-year-olds, sort of worldly-wise, he said; no more illusions, which I hope isn't true. Marty Lundeen says she's got a lot of sadness in her eyes, which I also hope is not true."

"She is sad. Or at least not happy. And I don't know what to do about it."

"Maybe nothing. At least not right now. You can't smooth out every pitfall so she'll be happy all the time."

"I know that. But I ought to be able to make things easier for her; isn't that what age and experience are for? What good is it if every generation has to repeat all the agonies of the generations that went before? It's like reinventing the wheel. Why *shouldn't* we be able to smooth out all the pitfalls, at least the ones we know something about?" Her voice trailed away. "Well, maybe things will get better between us; we're both working for Quentin now, so we have something new to share."

"You're working for Quentin? You're *working*? I don't believe it. Why? Doing what?"

"Being a designer. Didn't I tell you I might want to go back to work someday?"

"You're honest to God going back to work?"

"Well, not really. Quentin wants me to design the packaging for a new line he's bringing out, and after that—"

"He wants you to do it? You're in charge? How about that, it's what you always wanted!"

Thank God for Gina, Claire thought; I don't have to explain anything. "That's why I couldn't turn it down. And after the new line, he wants me to redesign the packaging for everything else. But I'll hire a group for that and I'll be a consultant, not full-time. How much do you know about this new line? PK-20, such an odd name."

"Not a damn thing. You'd think it's something the Pentagon dreamed up; it's got *secret* and *confidential* all over it. And I would dearly love to get a look at it." She picked up a pencil and began to draw concentric circles on a pad of paper. "It looks like they've got a hell of a lot riding on it. I mean, there's this new advertising campaign built around Emma, and now you're designing the packaging, for a line that's supposed to be released next March. They might make it—I'd guess with Quentin pushing everybody, they will; I've never seen people jump the way they do for him—but it'll cost a fortune in overtime, hiring extra people . . . so somebody, and I guess it's Quentin, thinks the line is so important it's worth whatever it takes to make it a smash."

"Wouldn't you do whatever you could to make sure something would be a smash?"

"If you could make sure, which you can't. I guess that's what they're doing: trying to be absolutely sure. Which could be why they're still testing. It's taking a hell of a long time. More money; testing eats up money, you know." Gina tossed her pencil aside. "But then I'm a lowly lab technician; nobody asks my advice. Are you taking a tour of the plant? Do you need a guide?"

"I'd love it."

Gina took her through the laboratories, the lab kitchen, the cafeteria and its kitchen, the long wing of offices, with Quentin's at the far end, and, on the opposite end of the building, the manufacturing wing, connected by a walkway to a separate building for packaging and shipping. The main building was filled with quiet activity, men and women talking in low tones or bent over their work counters, oblivious to those around them. Everything was clean and bright, with large windows brushed by tree branches shedding red and gold leaves, gardens bronze and orange with the last of the fall chrysanthemums and asters, and beyond them, the smoothly sloping lawn. Claire thought again of a college campus. What a wonderful place to work, she thought, and then remembered she would be working there. She would have an office, and a team of designers. She felt a rush of warmth and gratitude toward Quentin. Whatever problems she had with his arrogance, she owed him, already, a great deal.

POT OF GOLD

"Do you see much of Quentin?" she asked Gina as they walked back through the laboratory, their tour complete.

"Not a lot. But enough to be reminded that he's in charge. He wanders through now and then, looking at what we're all doing, as if he really understands it, and who knows? Maybe he does. He's clever enough to keep his mouth shut and just look very closely at everything, so nobody knows whether he's faking or not. And of course it's the smart thing to do; everybody works harder and nobody takes many breaks, because he could pop in at any minute, and there's this damned feeling you have that you want to impress him, please him, make him notice you. I find that scary, you know; it's what turns people into dictators."

"But he is one," Claire said, a little surprised that it had taken her this long to see it clearly. "This is his empire and he runs it his own way, and there's no one to challenge whatever he decides to do."

"Is that true? Doesn't he have a board of directors?"

"He does, but it's only two investors who bought the lab with him, and I think they let him run it without interfering. I suppose if he started losing money, they'd step in, but so far that hasn't happened. He changed the name from Norwalk Labs to Eiger Labs, and he hired consultants to modernize it, and he hired his own executive committee and office staff and a new team of chemists without going to his board for any of it. It's really his."

"As long as it's a private company."

"Well, yes, if he decides to go public that would change. And he's talked about doing it. But—" Claire gave a soft laugh. "He is so incredibly confident—"

"Arrogant."

"Well, I've called him that, too. He never talks about failing. He doesn't look left or right; he doesn't wait for other people to catch up to him; he doesn't even worry about people who might not like what he's doing, might even get hurt by it. He just assumes everything will go the way he's planned it. And so far that's what's happened, every year. He's the

JUDITH MICHAEL

perfect American businessman. As long as he's successful, no one asks any questions. I told you: it's his empire."

"And we all do his bidding."

Claire gazed around the laboratory, at the rounded backs of chemists and technicians, the gleaming equipment, the powders and liquids and creams that had led *Fortune* magazine to call Eiger Labs the fastest growing and most innovative cosmetics company in America. Emma and I do his bidding, she thought. Gina goes home every day to a completely different life, but Emma is with Brix, at least she's with him as often as he allows, and I'm with Quentin at least three or four times a week. Part of his life. Trying to please him.

They walked down the corridor to the reception room. "I don't know," she said slowly. "It's not as if any of us has made a commitment. Everything could change tomorrow."

"Sure," Gina said.

Quentin came through the doorway to the reception room, so tall he seemed to brush the top of it, his broad shoulders filling its width. He nodded a greeting to Gina. "Ready?" he asked Claire.

"Yes." Claire slipped the gold chain of her small blue evening bag over her shoulder. She kissed Gina's cheek. "Thanks for the tour. I'll talk to you tomorrow."

"I hear good reports on your friend," Quentin said as they walked to his car. "She asks a lot of questions, learns fast, and comes up with interesting ideas. She'll have a job here for a long time, if she wants it."

"I'm glad." Claire again felt a wave of gratitude toward Quentin, and relief that he was pleased with Gina, and with her for sending Gina to him.

That night they went to a musical, a benefit for a hospital on whose board Quentin sat, and then to his home, where Claire was his hostess for dinner. By now she moved easily through his house; she was familiar with its rooms and the routine he had established for himself, and she was at ease with his butler and housekeeper and gardeners. At first, when he had told her to plan this dinner party, she was nervous and hesitant in giving instructions to his staff, but then she saw that they took it for granted that she would give orders; clearly, Quentin had paved the way. And so, for the first time in her life, she hired caterers and chose the menu and selected the china and silver, and the tables and chairs and table linens they would bring; she bought wine and hired bartenders and selected a musical group; she ordered candles and flower arrangements for the tables and, on her own, filled vases and bowls throughout the house with branches of autumn leaves and berries from the countryside; and she hired two men to park cars for Quentin's guests.

Our guests, she corrected herself, but still, no matter how many arrangements she made, she did not feel that this was her party, or that this was her home. All the guests knew her: they had taken her to lunch and dinner and shopping; she and Quentin had visited their weekend homes; they had gone in groups of four or six or eight to polo matches, horse races, and on overnight sailing trips. And they greeted her at the entrance to Quentin's living room as if she belonged there. With Quentin. Or to him. But the more casually they assumed it, the more she pushed that thought away.

She kept it at bay all evening, not acknowledging how much a part of Quentin's home she was that night, flawlessly orchestrating a dinner for forty guests. And when they left, praising her for the evening as she stood at Quentin's side to say good-night, she felt his arm brush hers and knew he was pleased and knew she had passed another of his tests.

"You'll stay with me tonight," he said when they were alone. His arms were around her, one hand caressing the back of her neck. "I don't like your leaving. And driving back alone."

"Which is it? You don't like my leaving because you want me next to you when you wake up, or you're worried about my safety?"

"Both." He kissed her, slipping her short silver jacket off her shoulders. In an instant, Claire was open and longing, straining toward him. He could always arouse her to a tumult of desire simply by wrapping her within his arms and holding her as if she were fastened to him, a vessel he could enter and leave at will. He knew it; he felt her desire, and Claire saw him smile as he led her to his bedroom.

"But I can't stay," she said, forcing the words through the fog of her desire. "I want to be home when Emma wakes up."

He shook his head. "Not tonight." He began to unbutton her dress. "Tonight you belong here. No one else has a claim on you."

"Quentin." She wanted him so urgently she could almost feel him inside her, feel his bulk lying on her, pressing her into the bed with a weight that was careless and possessive, a weight she missed when she slept alone. But at the same time, she was pulling back against his arms, and she saw in his eyes a cold flare of anger because he knew she was about to refuse him. "I have to be home in the morning; I don't want Emma to wake up and not find me there."

"Is this a game you're playing? You think she doesn't know you're sleeping with me, just as she's sleeping with Brix?"

Claire tightened inside. "I suppose she assumes it; I haven't told her. But whatever she believes, we have a home and I ought to behave as if I live there instead of running around like someone with no responsibilities."

"For God's sake." He leaned against the doorjamb. "You have a responsibility to yourself, and to me. Emma is a grown woman, and you and I have our own affair and it has nothing to do with anyone else." He smiled, but his face was hard, and the smile had no meaning. "It has to be that way, Claire; I've been patient with you, but I'm not in the habit of rearranging my life every time someone has a new idea about how something should be done."

I'm not "someone"; I'm the woman you're sleeping with.

"Why is it so important?" she asked. "What difference does it make whether we have the morning together or not?"

"It's what I want."

Claire waited, but that was all. She gazed at him, feeling trapped. He stroked her hair, then gathered her to him. His breath was warm in her ear. "You'll have to decide. I can take you to your car now, if that's what you choose."

His body seemed to surround her; Claire felt she was disappearing into him. He kissed her cheek, her closed eyes, and then her mouth, his tongue moving over hers, making it his. He slipped his hand inside her open dress and covered her breast, enclosing it, locking her in. A low moan escaped her, her tongue met his, and they both knew she would stay.

Emma leaned over the worktable in one of the small Eiger laboratories, resting her head on her hand, and looked at the camera. "Should I smile?" she asked.

Tod Tallent circled her like a hunter stalking a prey. "I don't know," he muttered. "Something's missing. Bill, give an opinion here. You're the creative director, not me."

Bill Stroud contemplated Emma. Beside him, Marty Lundeen did the same, their heads tilted at the same angle, raking Emma with their stares. Her electric blue silk blouse and red-gold hair seemed to shimmer in the stark white laboratory; there was no other color, anywhere else. Emma, accustomed by now to being stared at, gazed absently around the room. An open jar of face cream was on the counter, and she slid it toward her. It was so smooth, with a perfect swirl in the center, that she could not resist it: she dipped her finger in and began to stir. It was like stirring cool whipped cream and she smiled.

"Good, good, good," cried Tod Tallent. His camera clicked rapidly as he moved forward and back, crouching, standing, then leaping on a chair to shoot from a higher angle. "Dynamite. Fun, fun, fun; I love it."

"Emma, a little smaller smile," said Bill. "Sort of mysterious, you know? Tod?"

"Right. Good." He circled Emma, absorbed, muttering to himself. "Maybe looking over your shoulder. Like somebody just came in and you're surprised . . . that's it, good, nice, hey, what a sweetheart. Okay, now lean forward, move over the table, sort of lying across it, good. Now back, sit up more, like, turn on the faucet . . . oh, good, good, keep doing that, the hand cupped under the water, terrific . . ."

"How about those flask things?" Marty Lundeen asked. "They look so scientific. Couldn't she sort of do things with them?"

"Here, dry your hand," Bill said, handing Emma a tissue. "Like what, Marty?"

"Oh, you know, pour something or look at something blue—no, red, it ought to be red . . ."

"Pretty dull," Tod Tallent said.

"Get somebody in here," Bill said. "Somebody in a white coat."

"You mean one of the chemists?" Marty asked. "Oh, I like that." She went to the large laboratory across the corridor. "We need somebody to be in some of our shots," she said to the room at large.

"Gina, you do it," one of the chemists said.

"Gina?" Marty's look swung to her. In a minute, as if she approved of the fact that Gina was not beautiful and would not compete with Emma, she nodded. "Nice idea. Women make cosmetics; women use cosmetics. Come with me."

"No," Bill said flatly when they walked back to the small laboratory. "We'd confuse the people who see the ads. They wouldn't know who this woman is."

"She's a *scientist*," Marty said. "She's wearing a white coat. That's what you wanted."

"People don't think scientist when they see a woman. A scientist is a man. Get me a man."

"Lots of women are scientists these days," Marty said stubbornly.

"Probably, but we're not in the business of raising the consciousness of magazine readers. Get me a man. In a white coat."

"I'm sorry," Marty said to Gina.

"This sort of thing happens all the time," Gina said easily. "Can I watch, now that I'm here?"

"Sure," Marty said. "Could you get us a man first?"

Gina left the room and returned with a male chemist, and Marty and Tod and Bill bustled about, setting up a series of shots. The chemist held a simple pose, changing only the flasks and bottles and tongs and jars he held, while Emma moved as she was told, standing with him, sitting on a stool beside him, or on the counter, taking things from him or looking closely at some flask or other as he explained something to her, until at last Bill said they had enough. The chemist left, but Emma sat still for another moment on one of the work stools, her head drooping.

"You okay, sweetie?" Tod asked.

"Fine," Emma said, and sat straight. The first few minutes after a photography session were always a letdown; she felt empty when no one was telling her what to do, and she felt sad, as if no one needed her anymore. She wanted Brix. Marty had said he might stop by if he had a free minute; if he walked in now, he might ask her to dinner and she could get home really late and not have to be cheerful in front of her mother and Hannah. But there was no sign of him.

The others had left, all except Gina, who sat quietly in the corner. "Are you staying for a while?" she asked.

"Oh. I guess." Emma looked around the laboratory, and then into the hall.

"He's not here," Gina said casually. "At least, I saw him go out a few minutes before I came in here. Shall I keep you company?"

Emma flushed. "You don't have to baby-sit; you must have lots of work to do."

"Tons," Gina said cheerfully. "But I'd rather talk to you." She sat on the stool next to Emma. "How do you think it went, the photography?"

"Oh, fine; Tod gets excited and everybody seems happy. It's not hard, it just goes on an awfully long time. Tod must have a million pictures of me by now, but he keeps taking them and sometimes I think he'll never stop."

"I guess you like it, though."

"Oh, I love it. It's better than I ever thought it would be. It's so big, you know, all these people, not just Bill and Tod and Marty, but *hundreds* of people, here and at Yaeger Advertising and at all the magazines . . . and then the readers, *millions* of readers, and I'm in the middle of it, really important in it, sort of the symbol for it. I love that. I love being important." Her voice fell away on the last word.

"So you're happy," Gina said after a moment.

"Oh, yes. Of course I am."

"But?"

"Nothing."

"There's something. Come on, Emma, what is it?"

"I told you: nothing. Everything's fine. Really."

"Except Brix. Come on, Emma, I've known you a long time and I love you and I'm a hundred percent reliable with secrets. I won't tell your mother, or anybody else, if you don't want me to. Why don't you dump on me a little bit? Like, sometimes Brix's behavior leaves a lot to be desired?"

A small laugh broke from Emma. "That's such a . . . *soft* way to say it. It's more like he's . . ." She hesitated a long time. "Mean," she said at last. "He acts mean. But then all of a sudden he's on the phone or he comes into a photo session and he acts like he's . . ." Her voice broke.

"In love with you," Gina finished quietly.

Emma nodded. "But then I've been here a lot the last couple of weeks and we've only been out once, and once we talked after a photo shoot . . . and, you know, he's so close, he's right here in the building! It's like I could touch him but I can't."

"He won't let you."

"Well . . . he's awfully busy. You know, his father keeps him running all the time, he doesn't really have a life of his own—"

POT OF GOLD

"Bullshit." There was a silence. "Why don't you talk to your mother about it?"

"How can I? She's going out with his father all the time; she wouldn't understand. She doesn't care anyway. Hannah's the only one who cares about me; at least she stays home at night."

"Hey, how many times has your mother stayed out all night?"

"Twice," Emma muttered.

"And the second time she got home while you and Hannah were eating breakfast. Right? So you hardly knew she was gone."

"I don't like her being with him!" Emma cried. "And I can't even imagine . . . I can't think about her, you know, *with* him. And I hated it when I came downstairs for breakfast and she wasn't there those times; it was like she'd died or something, like she didn't love me anymore. She didn't even call and tell me she wouldn't be home!"

Involuntarily, Gina smiled. "It's usually the teenager who's supposed to call home and doesn't."

"It's not a joke! She should have told me so I'd know ahead of time. But all she thinks about is him. She's even *working* for him now!"

Gina's eyebrows rose. "Aren't you?"

"That's different! She's got all the money she needs, but I have to have a career; I can't depend on her forever. She's just always with him! And then she stays out all night like she doesn't even care what I think."

"Well, do you tell her what you think?"

"She doesn't want to know!"

"Do you tell her? Do you ever just come up and say, 'I've got some problems, Ma, and I'd like to talk about them'?"

Emma gave a nervous giggle. "I don't call her Ma."

"That's true. You never did. When you were little, about four or five, you called her Claire for a few months. She'd taken you to work with her because your sitter was sick, and you heard somebody call her that, and you picked it up. Do you remember that? Everybody thought it was pretty cute, but Claire wasn't sure whether she liked it. Then you got back to Mommy and everybody was happy. You two really had a good time; it was fun being with you. You made me feel good because you loved each other and you showed it. So do you tell her what you're thinking? Ever?"

"No. I don't want to."

"Why not?"

"Just . . . because."

"Because why? Because you don't feel good about what you're doing?"

"No!" Emma cried. "I'm not ashamed of anything!" She slid off the stool and looked around vaguely, wanting to get away, but afraid she might miss Brix. "I guess I have to go."

Gina stood up and put her arms around Emma. "Honey, I think you ought to talk to your mother. Give her some credit for being smart and able to understand you. She loves you so much, you know; all she wants is to help you be happy." Emma was stiff and silent in her arms. She sighed. "Okay, but think about it." She pulled back and searched Emma's face. "Look, you're going crazy here; why don't you wait for him in his office?"

Emma stood uncertainly. "I guess I could. I never have."

"Why not? He'd be glad to see you, wouldn't he?"

"Of course he would! Except . . . he doesn't really like surprises, you know."

"You go ahead. You'll feel better. And listen, let's try this one more time. When you go home tonight, why don't you and your mother sit down and talk? About anything. Little things, big things. Modeling, food, clothes, politics, sex, the *weather,* for God's sake, if that's all you can think of. The trouble with you two is you don't connect; you live in the same house but you don't connect. It isn't enough that you talk to Hannah; you have to talk to your mother."

"Hannah doesn't try to get me to give up everything and go to college."

POT OF GOLD

"Give up *everything?*"

"Well, you know what I mean."

"Hannah's not your mother, Emma; she doesn't have the same responsibility your mother does. And I'll bet Claire hasn't talked about college for a long time. Has she? Has she once mentioned it since you started modeling?"

"No," Emma said almost inaudibly.

"So what's the problem? You're modeling, and you love it, and she's doing graphic design, which she really loves, and she always wanted to do her own projects and now she can, so you two have a lot to talk about. So why not give it a try?"

After a long minute, Emma shrugged. "I can try. She's the one who doesn't talk much these days."

"Well, that's what I meant. Neither do you. So you'll give it a try, right? Promise?"

"I'll try. I know you want to help, Gina, it's just that you don't know how hard it is. And nobody really understands how I feel." She gave Gina a quick kiss on the cheek and walked away, down the long corridor to Brix's office, a few doors from his father's corner office.

The room was dark; he had pulled the drapes against the low November sun, and the lights were out. Emma turned on a floor lamp and wandered around, glancing without interest at the photographs of Eiger products on the walls. She picked up a magazine and flipped through it, then threw it down; she was so nervous she was shaking. *I ought to go; he'll hate it when he finds me here. He hates it when I call him on the phone. He only likes things when they're the way he plans them.*

She wandered across the room and looked at the two silver-framed photographs on his desk. A woman who maybe was his mother, and a younger woman. Who was she? Not me, Emma thought. He has lots of pictures of me, and he could ask Hale or Tod for a hundred more, if he wanted to. But I guess he doesn't.

She trailed an aimless hand across the polished surface of

the desk. There wasn't any reason to stay. She knew it. It would be awful if she stayed and he didn't want to see her and he looked at her with that cold look he had sometimes, as if she were something that was in his way. She bit her lip. *Brix, please want me. I love you, I love you, please love me.*

His desk was almost clean, except for a folder with some papers sticking out. Emma saw *PK-20 Human Sensitivity Test* on the top one. My PK-20, Emma thought. It made her feel good to think about it. She wasn't just any girl waiting for Brix. She was the Eiger Girl for PK-20, and Brix said PK-20 was going to make Eiger Labs one of the biggest cosmetics companies in the country, maybe the world. *I'm in the middle of it, really important in it, sort of the symbol for it.* And Brix was working on it, too. They were working together. Maybe he wrote something about her, she thought. Maybe these papers were about how good she was as the Eiger Girl. Or ... maybe not as good as he thought she'd be. She opened the folder and leaned over to read the top page.

Date: March 30
To: Quentin Eiger
From: Kurt Green
Subject: PK-20 human sensitivity tests (preliminary report)

As per our meeting earlier today I want to summarize part of the latest test results of PK-20 Eye Restorative Cream on human subjects: 4% of test subjects experienced a variety of minor allergic skin reactions. A few subjects exhibited conjunctivitis, which may have been caused by the bacteria Pseudomonas aeruginosa *or from an allergic reaction to one of the compounds in the product, either of which could cause corneal damage. The lab should have their report on the cause in a few days. Of course, as you pointed out, we cannot be certain at this time that the observed reactions were not caused by something other than the PK-20 products. Test #2, which begins tomorrow, will enable us to isolate the cause of any adverse reactions.*

POT OF GOLD

Puzzled, Emma read it again. It didn't make sense. She knew about Eye Restorative Cream because they'd done a whole day of photo shoots, outdoors and indoors, focusing on her eyes. They were going to run the ads and ship the cream to the stores in March, with the other fifty or so products of the PK-20 line. So how could anything be wrong with it? Somebody had made a mistake.

She lifted the sheet of paper and looked at the one beneath it.

Date: July 21
To: Quentin Eiger
From: Kurt Green
Subject: PK-20 human sensitivity tests (test #2)

The latest test results of PK-20 products confirm a 4% to 5% incidence in test subjects of allergic skin reactions. Subjects experienced some of the following: minor burning, itching, irritation, folliculitis, acneform eruptions, and allergic contact dermatitis. In addition, 1% of the subjects who used the Eye Restorative Cream experienced an allergic conjunctivitis, and one subject had a severe reaction, which resulted in blindness in one eye. (Note: we may be able to show that the subject used the product improperly, in spite of our careful instructions.) Additional tests have confirmed that the source of the allergic reactions is in the proprietary ingredient of PK-20. I will be ready to present a full report to you early next week.

Emma shivered. She looked behind her. The office was shadowed except where she stood near the lighted floor lamp, and so quiet it felt muffled. *It's a mistake*, she thought again. *I'll ask Brix. There couldn't be anything wrong with PK-20; he said it's wonderful.*

Don't ask Brix. It was as if a voice within her had spoken. She stood still, her head down. She loved Brix, but how could she talk to him about this? Admit she read something on his desk she was not supposed to see, and hear him say . . . what? What would Brix say?

Gently, silently in the silent room, she closed the folder. Gina, she thought. Gina works in the lab; I'll ask her.

She turned off the lamp and tiptoed out, though she did not know why she did that, closing the door softly behind her. "I guess I can't wait," she said to Brix's secretary without pausing as she walked past her desk. "It wasn't important anyway. I just wanted to say hi." And she retraced her steps, to the laboratory where she had been photographed, and then to the next one, where Gina worked.

But it was after five, and Gina was gone. "Can I help?" one of the chemists asked. Emma shook her head. "I'll leave a message." She scribbled a note, asking Gina to call her, and put it on her worktable, then went to her car. Driving at a crawl in the heavy late-afternoon traffic, she tried to think about what she had read, but instead she thought about Brix, and the last time they had been together, ten days ago. It had been wonderful, but it had been terrible, too.

In the first part, the wonderful part, they had gone to a movie that she couldn't even remember, and he had held her hand the whole time, his finger making little circles on her palm until she thought she would melt in her seat, she wanted him so much. Afterward, they'd gone to his house and he'd undressed her, very slowly, teasing them both, and she was so wet she was embarrassed, but he grinned when he touched her, and he put her down on his bed and kissed her all over with little licking kisses. And then, without a word, he was inside her, pounding into her, and just as suddenly he was still, lying heavily on her breasts, his mouth on her neck. "Gorgeous baby doll, fantastic," he said.

Emma lay still, wanting him inside her again, but slowly and sweetly, so that she could come in her own way as he had in his. But Brix got up and brought to bed his store of powder and the slim tube that sparkled in the light, and they leaned against the headboard, hips and legs and shoulders touching, and took long snorts, drawing the powder deep inside them.

POT OF GOLD

No matter how many times she did it, Emma marveled at how perfect it made everything seem. Brix knew how to make everything so clear and beautiful, just for them; no one else mattered. He put an arm around her and clicked on the television set, and they sat still, staring at the screen. There was no sound, but the colors danced so blindingly in the dark room that Emma was mesmerized by them. They swelled and shrank and flickered in and out; they seemed to sing in a high-pitched chorus that reverberated in her head. She reached up to Brix and kissed him deeply, and the chorus rose around them until she thought she could not bear so many sensations at once. "I love you, I love you," she said, her lips moving against his. "Please love me, please, please."

"Anytime you want," he said, and pulled Emma on top of him and was inside her again before she could tell him that was not what she meant.

"Brix," she said, but he had his hands on her breasts, and as she bent over him, he took her nipple in his mouth and played with it with his tongue and Emma forgot everything else. This time he let her move at her own pace until he heard her cry out, and then, with his hands on her hips, he moved her until he made the gasping sounds that Emma knew meant he was satisfied with her. Lying full length on his muscled body, she kissed him lightly, lovingly. "Thank you," she said, and Brix accepted it.

They were still a little high when he drove her home late that night, and the way the car drifted across the empty road terrified her and she said something, she could not remember what, about not using so much coke if he was going to drive. He was furious, and when they were a few blocks from her house, he suddenly swerved to a stop and reached across her to shove open her door. He sat still, looking straight ahead, waiting for her to leave.

"Brix, it doesn't mean I don't trust you," she said weakly, terrified at his stony face. She leaned over and kissed his cheek and tried to reach his mouth, but he refused to turn. "Brix, I love you, you know I do. You can do anything you want . . ." She began to cry, silently because she knew Brix hated to hear sobbing. Finally, she stepped out of the car and stood beside it. Without looking at her, Brix reached over again and pulled the door shut and drove off, leaving her on the dark street, with just a few lighted windows shining through the bare trees to make her feel she was almost home.

That had been ten days ago, and he hadn't called her since. She had counted on seeing him today, after her photo session. She wondered if he had left the building on purpose, while she was being photographed, to avoid her. Maybe she would never see him again.

She turned the corner onto her street and realized she was shaking. Her hands could barely hold the wheel. She made it up the driveway and into the garage, next to Claire's car, and sat still, telling herself to calm down. I'm in terrible shape, she thought. I can't go inside like this.

She wondered what was happening to her. She had never felt like this before, so helpless, as if everything were too big and too hard to face, as if anything could come along and knock her down. She cried a lot and jumped every time she heard the littlest noise, and she was so nervous she could hardly sit still. The only time she felt really wonderful was when she was doing drugs with Brix. I have to stop this, she thought. I can't face Mother like this.

The trouble with you two is you don't connect; you live in the same house but you don't connect.

I can't, Emma thought. I can't talk to her because I'm afraid to look at her. She'll see there's something wrong with me; she'll know I'm sleeping with Brix. She'll know about the drugs.

All through her body, Emma ached to feel her mother's arms around her, holding her close. I could sit in her lap, she thought, and felt the tears come again as she pictured herself curled up against her mother, warm and safe within the circle of her mother's protective arms. *Oh, that's what I want, I want it so much. But I can't ask her, I can't tell her anything. Oh, God, I wish I'd never been born.*

POT OF GOLD

I could kill myself, she thought. Close the garage door, start the car, and just go to sleep. But Mother and Hannah would hear the door close; they'd wonder where I am; they'd come looking. "Oh, stop it," she said aloud. Her voice sounded strange, as if it belonged to someone else. Stop, stop, stop, she told herself; you're acting like a terrible baby. Stop crying and whining; you don't need your mother; Brix told you you don't. You're a grown-up; all you need is yourself.

Behind Emma, a car pulled into the driveway. She squinted to see who was driving. A tall man got out of the car and stood beside it looking at the house in the floodlight that illuminated the driveway. He didn't look dangerous, Emma thought; he looked nice. He wasn't nearly as handsome as Brix, but he was older and seemed somehow more definite, and he held himself straighter than Brix. Brix, Emma had to admit, slouched a lot. This man was lanky, with dark hair turning gray, curling on the back of his neck and blowing a little in the late-afternoon breeze. He wore only a sports coat, though it had turned cold, and he carried a briefcase. He saw Emma and walked into the garage, to the open window of her car.

"Emma Goddard? I'm Alex Jarrell." He held out his hand and Emma reached through the window to take it. "I'm sorry; this looks like a bad time," he said as he saw the streaks of tears on her cheeks. "I can come back tomorrow."

"No, it's okay," Emma said, thinking that was a nice thing for him to say. "How did you know my name?"

"I've read about you and your mother, and I met your mother once at a party in Stamford. Is she here?"

"Her car is so I guess she is." Emma opened the car door and Alex stood back. "She's probably inside. What do you want her for?"

"A magazine story. I'm a writer, and *Vanity Fair* wants me to do a feature on the two of you. I just want to set a date to spend some time here, with both of you."

Emma shook her head. "Not me. Mother won the lottery;

I didn't. I'll bet those people told you to write about her and didn't say a word about me."

He smiled. "You're right; they didn't. But I write what I want. And from what I've read, you two are so close that I couldn't leave you out."

Emma flushed. "This way," she said, and opened the door to a hallway that led to the kitchen. Hannah and Claire were sitting at the table in the bay window; Claire was sketching on a large artist's pad, and Hannah was peeling apples and talking. Emma stopped in the doorway, with Alex just behind her. She heard him draw in his breath when he saw her mother, but she paid no attention; tears were in her eyes again because the room looked so beautiful. It was bright and warm, cozy against the November chill, with a tall, steaming pot on the stove, and the comforting smells of soup and bread filling the air. Emma walked in, forgetting Alex, barely seeing Hannah. "Hi," she said, and sat down close to her mother. But Claire, eyebrows raised, was looking past her. "Oh," Emma said. "This is Alex—uh—"

"Jarrell," Alex said, coming in, his hand outstretched. "We met," he said to Claire, "at a benefit in Stamford."

"I remember." Her hand met his and she introduced Hannah. "But I don't understand . . ." She glanced at Emma.

"I met Emma outside and told her I wanted to set a time to interview you. I've been asked to do an article on you for *Vanity Fair*. I apologize for barging in, but I was driving back to New York and took a chance on finding you home. If we could just make an appointment, I'll be off."

"You work for *Vanity Fair?*" Claire asked.

"No, I work on my own. I've written for most magazines, at one time or another."

"And you want to do a story on me because of the lottery? That was last May."

"And this won't be published until next April or May. It isn't the actual lottery I'm interested in; it's how wealth has changed the way you live, how you feel about it, how money affects all of us, how you balance the life you had with the life

230

that's now open to you, all those doors opening for the first time."

Claire looked at him with interest. "Did the people at the magazine talk about doors opening?"

"No, that's me. Why?"

"It's the way I thought about it. But I don't think . . ." Her voice trailed off and she looked at Emma again, and Hannah.

"Look, we'll only get as personal as you want," Alex said. "You set all the guidelines. I don't pry and I don't violate confidences. That's a promise."

"And what does Claire get out of it?" Hannah asked.

"Publicity. That's about all. I'll get paid and I'll have another byline to my credit; the same goes for the photographer; and the magazine will sell more copies—at least they hope they will. A lot of people with money want publicity," he said to Claire. "If you're one of them, this is a great way to get it. If you don't . . ."

Claire was still looking at him with interest. "You think I don't."

"I have no right to think one thing or another." He smiled, a broad smile that softened the sharp line of his jaw and the ridges of his cheekbones. "But I'd guess you're not hungry for it."

Emma saw them look at each other and felt a spark of excitement. They liked each other. Her mother hadn't even looked at another man since she met Quentin. But if she liked Alex and got to know him better and liked him more, she might drop Quentin. After all, she had to find out sometime that he wasn't nice; Brix knew it and so would her mother, eventually—and then everything would be so much better. Emma began to cheer up. Things always got better, if you waited.

She looked at Hannah and saw her watching Claire thoughtfully, almost as if she were plotting something. Hannah agrees with me, Emma thought, her excitement growing; she wants Mother to get away from Quentin, too. And she could do something about it; Mother listens to her. "Why don't you stay for dinner?" she asked abruptly. "You could start your interview right away."

Claire and Alex looked startled, and Claire began to frown. But Alex shook his head. "Thanks; I like the idea, but I'm on my way to New York. Another time, I'd like to take you up on it." He took a small datebook from his jacket pocket. "Would you be willing to set a time?" he asked Claire. "I think it could be a good story and I'd like very much to do it. And I can promise that you won't be embarrassed by it or ashamed of anything in it."

"How can you promise that?" Claire asked. "I thought journalists follow their story wherever it leads."

"I don't think this story will lead to murky bogs or back alleys," he said, smiling at her. "If I'm wrong, you can call it off at any time."

"That's generous," Claire said. "I think I'd like to see what you write."

His smile broadened. "Good. Can we start tomorrow?"

"Oh. Well, why not? I'm working, but if you want to come at three ... no, four would be better. That gives me most of the day."

"You're working?"

"We can talk about that tomorrow."

"Four o'clock, then." He put away his datebook.

"You didn't write it down," Emma said.

"There's no chance I'd forget it." He handed Claire a card. "Call me if you have to change it. Otherwise, I'll be here. Emma, thank you for bringing me into your house. Hannah, I hope you and I will talk, too."

"Oh, I'd like that," said Hannah brightly.

Emma watched Claire walk with Alex to the door and close it behind him. "He's nice."

"I think he's honest," Hannah said, and Emma knew that was the highest praise she had for anyone.

"Isn't it nice that new things keep happening?" Emma asked Claire.

POT OF GOLD

"It's only an interview," Claire observed. "You haven't forgotten all those others, have you, back in May? This one may be a little different, but they all come down to the same questions and answers."

"This one might be a lot different," Emma said stubbornly. "How do you know?"

"You could talk about the work you're doing," Hannah said. "And Emma's modeling. You may not want publicity, but I'll bet your friend Quentin does. And lots of it."

The telephone rang and Emma raced to answer it. When she came back, she danced into the room. "That was Brix; a friend of his is having a party at the Hilton in New York tomorrow night. Dancing and some kind of singer. And we'll stay overnight." She looked at Claire, daring her to say something.

"I'd rather you were home," Claire said after a moment, "but it's probably safer than driving back late." She hesitated. "Emma, are you happy with him?"

Do you ever just come up and say, "I've got some problems, Ma, and I'd like to talk about them"?

I can't do it, Emma thought despairingly. I can't, I can't. "Of course," she said, the words coming in a rush. "He's wonderful. I love him. And I love the modeling and I've never been so happy." She heard the quaver in her voice, and the thread of defiance, but there was nothing she could do about that. "Are we going to have dinner?"

"Well, it's nice to hear you ask for food for a change," Hannah said, her cheerful voice filling the spaces left by Emma's thin one. "And I want to hear all about the modeling session today, what it was like at the lab, what the photographer—what was his name? Tallent? Such an amazing name—what poses he had you do, what you wore, just everything. Maybe Alex will put it in his magazine story and you'll be a famous model a lot sooner than you expected. And if you talk about your work, Claire, you might get jobs on your own, if you want them; you wouldn't need Quentin for anything you decide to do. And how pleasant to get to know Alex; he seems so different from those newspaper people we met." She carried the bowl of peeled and sliced apples to the counter where a pie crust waited. "My goodness, isn't it wonderful, how many reasons there are to look forward to tomorrow."

10

ALEX set a tiny tape recorder on the arm of his chair. "I hope you don't mind," he said to Claire. "I like to talk to people without taking notes." He sat back and looked around. "This is a wonderful room."

"Yes, isn't it?" Claire said. "I just had it redone so I could work at home. It's the most perfect studio I've ever had. In fact, it's the only studio I've ever had. Would you like coffee? Or tea?"

"Coffee, thanks. How come you never had a studio?"

"No one ever offered me one and I couldn't afford my own." She opened a white door and revealed a white cabinet with a small sink, a refrigerator beneath the counter, and two built-in burners. "When I worked at Danbury Graphics, I worked in a room with twenty-four other people—twenty-five drawing tables lined up edge to edge—and at home I had the dining room table or a pad of paper on my lap." She poured two cups of coffee from a silver thermos. "And now I've got an office at Eiger Labs, and it's all right, but it's not a studio and it's not my own."

Alex watched as Claire arranged stems of wine-red grapes on a blue-and-white willowbrook plate. She wore white jeans and a dark red turtleneck sweater; a red band held back her hair, and a pencil was tucked behind her ear. Her beauty was not as soft as he remembered it from the day before, when he had seen her in the kitchen; here, in her own workspace, she seemed sharper, and Alex saw details he had missed: the prominent lines of her cheekbones, the clean curve of her jaw, her generous mouth and level brows, the quick intelligence in her eyes. A lovely woman, Alex thought, and he felt the same pleasure watching her as he felt when he gazed at a fine painting.

In fact, the whole room gave him pleasure. Everything in it reflected a superb sense of color and scale. It was large and square, furnished with a white couch and two white armchairs grouped closely around a granite coffee table on a boldly patterned Azeri folklore carpet. Two drawing tables stood beside the bare windows, with white rolling cabinets of artist's supplies next to each; a wall of shelves was crammed with books and magazines, small sculptures, African baskets, ceramic vases, and silver candlesticks seemingly placed at random among the books but somehow looking as if they were in exactly the right place. Abstract paintings and framed posters were on the walls, brightly lit, as was everything in the room, by more lamps than Alex had ever seen in one place. There were lamps on every table, floor lamps, wall sconces, ceiling track lights, and flexible lamps stretched over Claire's drawing tables, and every one of them was on, filling the corners of the room against the early-November darkness beyond the windows.

Claire saw him looking around, counting. "I don't like dark rooms," she said, then gave a small laugh. "That's pretty obvious."

"What isn't obvious is how you've done this." With a gesture, he took in the whole room. "I haven't the faintest idea how to create anything so embracing."

"Thank you. I like that word. Where have you tried?"

"Well, that's the problem. I live in what is called in New York a one-bedroom apartment. You'd call it a variation on a closet. In fact, it's a living room-dining room-office that's not too bad, a bedroom just big enough for a double bed and one chair, and a galley kitchen built for one person who has no aspirations to be a chef. I tried to keep the furnishings to a minimum to get a feeling of space; it wasn't hard since they're various families' castoffs that I picked up in garage sales in New Jersey. Where did you have the dark rooms that you don't like?"

"In our apartment, before we bought this house."

"The one with room for a pad of paper on your lap."

"Yes, but it wasn't only small; there was no light. It was on the ground floor of a duplex, one of those old houses off Main Street in Danbury that had been carved into four apartments, and then one of them had been divided into two, and the back one was ours. It looked onto an alley and the street along the side, but the windows were small and faced north. We never saw the sun. Were you living in New Jersey?"

"Yes." When Claire did not speak, but waited for him to go on, he said, "I lived there with my wife and son. My wife died and I moved to New York."

"With your son?"

"I brought him to New York, but not to live with me; he lives with my sister and her husband, a few blocks from my apartment. I sold the house and everything in it; I couldn't look at any of it." He shifted in his chair and knocked the tape recorder to the floor. "Well, now." He grinned at Claire as he bent to retrieve it. "If there's a god of writing, that's him or her reminding me I'm here to work. Tell me about the dark apartment and your journey from there to this very beautiful house."

Claire smiled. "It is a journey; what a good way to put it. But it keeps changing directions. Or the destination changes. I don't seem to know where it's going. Where I'm going." Her eyebrows rose in surprise. "I don't know why I said that. It isn't anything I'd want in a story."

"Then we won't use it," Alex said easily. "Is working for Eiger Labs part of that?"

"Probably. I'm sorry to be so vague, but so many things

are happening it's hard to find a center." She paused. Alex waited, sitting back in his chair, relaxed, not hurrying her. "I think I always thought that money would help me find a center: that, if only I had enough money, I could organize my life around whatever I thought was most important; that money would buy, first of all, the time I needed to look around and put things in some sort of order of importance and then go after them. Organize and plan and then live. Really live, following my own feelings and wants. And in some ways that's what I've done. But it gets muddied by other things. It isn't simple."

"You mean control isn't simple."

She looked surprised again. "Yes, exactly. I thought control was the first thing money would buy, after time. And I do have more control now than I've ever had, at least over part of my life." She rose and brought the silver thermos to the table and refilled their cups. "I bought this house half an hour after I first walked in to look at it, and we left the apartment as soon as we could buy furniture and move in. And even now I can't always believe it's mine; I wake up in the morning and think how amazing it is that I'm here, that I've made this . . . leap, from what I was to what I am now."

"And what you are now is different from what you were?"

She gazed at him thoughtfully. "I don't know. I hope not, but I think about things differently, and so does Emma; I can see it in the way we talk about what we're going to do and what we want. . . . I don't know. I have to think about it."

"Well, we'll come back to that," Alex said, though it was what interested him most in the story, and the reason he had accepted what otherwise had seemed like a frivolous assignment. "What changes have you made between the time you bought the house and now?"

"This room, for one. The rest of the house was perfect, but there was no studio, and I decided to give myself the place I'd dreamed about. That was unbelievable, too: that I really could do it just the way I wanted; that as soon as I made the

POT OF GOLD

decision, I called a contractor and had it done. I didn't wonder whether I could afford it or scale back any of my ideas because they were too expensive; I just did it. But that has nothing to do with controlling what happens so you can build a life around the things that are most important to you; that only has to do with spending money. Which I've gotten very good at."

"Did you have to learn how?"

"Yes, but it's amazingly easy to learn."

"Just by doing it?"

"Mostly. But there's an art to spending money well, getting the best of everything, and I'm not sure I could have figured that out by myself. I've had help from experts, a few women I've met, who've pointed out ways to spend money I never even thought of."

"I hope it's fun."

She smiled. "Lots of fun. A lot of the time it's like a game: every time you spend money you win. And you're always winning; that's a powerful feeling. It used to be that I'd block out whatever I read about trips or concerts or the theater, and look the other way when I passed window displays in department stores, especially around Christmas when everything is exaggerated and everybody goes crazy with the idea that if you don't buy and buy and buy, you won't be worthy or a good parent or normal or whatever the message is. Anyway, I'd tune it all out because none of it was within my reach, so as far as my life was concerned, those things just didn't exist. But all of a sudden there they were, all of them waiting for me."

"Very real and at your fingertips."

"Yes. That was almost the first thing I thought: close enough to touch. It was so strange; I couldn't get enough of it."

"Something like being hypnotized."

Claire gazed at him. "It is hypnotic. Like a drug, I suppose."

"You suppose. You don't know?"

"No. I've never used them."

"Haven't you been curious?"

"Oh, a little, and I did think about it, but I didn't know how I'd react, and I was worried about Emma. I was all she had and I didn't want to risk not being there for her all the time. And I thought if I never used them, I'd have a right to ask her not to, and she hasn't. But all my friends have, and when they talk about it, it sounds to me like money. You lose perspective; you lose precision in defining things that have no clear boundaries, like value. Everything around you changes, gets bigger and brighter and even more desirable than it was before. It's as if everything you see has arms, hands, fingers, and they're beckoning to you, urging you on, and there's no obvious reason to resist. I don't know if this makes sense; does it? You said *at your fingertips,* as if you knew. Did any of this happen to you?"

"Nothing like yours. There was a time when I made a lot of money from my writing and spent it happily and easily, but that's in the past. And of course—"

"Writing for magazines?"

"No, there's not much money in magazine writing. Too many people are willing to work for a pittance just to get their pieces published, so the pay is outrageously low. I was at the top but it still wasn't what you'd call impressive. In those days I wrote novels."

"Oh," Claire said abruptly. "A. N. Jarrell. Are you? Is that who you are? I should have thought of that. I've read your books; they're wonderful. No one writes about families as well as you do, and the way we use the past, the way we learn . . . that is who you are?"

He nodded. "But what I was saying—"

"I was wondering why I hadn't seen a new book from you in—oh, years."

"Five. But what I was saying was that I never had your experiences with money, nor would most people—and that's what we're talking about—because almost no one comes even close to winning what you did."

POT OF GOLD

"I don't get it all at once," Claire said defensively.

"It wouldn't be terrible if you did. I wasn't criticizing you. Do you always do that? Get your back up when somebody talks about how much money you have?"

"Of course I don't. Well, I don't know. I hope I don't. I'm not ashamed of it."

"No? Is that honest?"

"I'm not ashamed of it," Claire said hotly. But then she remembered thinking that she had not earned her sixty million dollars; she had not even inherited it; she had simply bought a ticket. "I don't know," she said again, slowly.

"Would you be ashamed if you won it?"

"Not for a minute."

"Why not?"

"Because we should always be grateful for good luck; there's not such an abundance of it in the world, and most of us deserve some now and then. You got a lot more than some, but why shouldn't you? You're a good person, why shouldn't you have a stroke of great good fortune? Besides, you didn't snatch it from under anyone's nose; you didn't swindle old people out of their life savings or loot the pension funds of trusting workers or destroy small companies and lay off thousands of innocent employees in a leveraged buyout; you played by the rules and you won. What is there in that to make you ashamed?"

Claire was laughing. "Not a thing. Thank you. I'll remember that. Why haven't you written a book in five years?"

"I don't know. I just stopped. No desire, no motivation, and it takes a hell of a lot of both to turn out a book."

"But something must have happened."

Alex leaned forward and filled their cups from the thermos. "You were the one who talked about not having control. It happens to all of us."

His wife died. He lost his family and his home. Five years ago? Probably.

"But you talked about controlling what happens so you

JUDITH MICHAEL

can build a life around it," Alex said before she could ask about his past. "What is it you can't control?"

"Oh, a lot. Too much, I think. At least, sometimes it seems that way." She reached out and broke off a small bunch of grapes and held them in her hand. The firm spheres were cold and smooth against her palm, at the height of ripeness, at the height of perfection. She never bought less than that now. But she had no control over what happened to Emma, and she was beginning to wonder how much control she had with Quentin. And none of that was Alex Jarrell's business. But the silence was lengthening and she searched for a way to change the subject.

"I was hoping Emma would be here this afternoon," he said, and Claire shot him a sharp look.

"Did you talk much yesterday, before she brought you into the house?"

"Hardly at all."

Claire waited for him to say that Emma had been crying. It had been so obvious: the streaks of tears on her face, her red, puffy eyes, the tremor in her voice. But Alex said nothing, letting Claire keep to herself whatever she wanted. "You're a very nice man," she said quietly. "Emma is out; I think she went shopping. She should be back by six."

"Well, I'll call her, if I may; I'd like to talk to her."

Of course that's what he wants, Claire thought. Because this isn't just a pleasant conversation; it's an interview. It all has a purpose. In an odd way, she felt let down. For a while, she had forgotten that he was gathering information; she had thought he liked her and understood her. But whatever he said had nothing to do with his feelings. He had a story to write and his way of getting information was to be casual and conversational, rather than rattling off questions as had the reporters who wrote stories on her in May. Alex Jarrell, novelist, journalist, interviewer, would have been just as warm and thoughtful, just as nice a man, with anyone; it was his job.

She stood. "I think we've covered just about everything you need."

POT OF GOLD

"Not quite." At that moment, his tape recorder clicked off. "One side of a tape; that's just a beginning." He stood with her. "Did I do something to make you uncomfortable?"

"No, you've been very good. I forgot it was an interview."

"So did I. In fact, I have a terrible fear that when I go home and play this tape, I'll hear far too much of my own voice talking about me."

Claire smiled. He really was a very nice man. "What other questions do you have?"

"Some basic ones about this house and whatever else you've been doing that's different from the way you lived before you won the lottery. I don't mean buying a car or a fur coat, though that's part of it; I mean different patterns in your life. Like these experts you mentioned, the women who helped you learn the art of shopping; I assume you wouldn't have known them before you had money, or at least spent time with them. Organizing your life, I remember you saying. And then I'd like to talk about your going back to work; how you feel about it now that you don't need a salary; and whether your work has changed because of the money, become more free, perhaps, or more daring, or maybe none of the above. I find that an interesting question. And I would like to know what you're having trouble controlling, but if you're firm on not talking about that, we won't. I think, at bottom, what I really want to do is go back to that question I asked earlier: whether you're the same person. I'd like to know whom you see now, when you look in the mirror."

Claire gave him a long look. "Someone who feels more comfortable looking in the mirror. And everywhere else." She glanced at his recorder. "It isn't running."

"I won't forget what you've just said. But I would like to talk about all my other questions, with the tape running. Would tomorrow be all right?"

"Yes."

"In the morning? I'd like to see the house by daylight. Ten o'clock if that's a good time."

"Yes," she said again.

They walked downstairs together and Claire opened the front door. Alex pulled on his leather jacket; it was scuffed and faded, with suede patches on the elbows. "Thank you for your time," he said. "I've enjoyed this."

"So have I." Their hands met briefly, and then Claire watched him walk with long strides to his car.

"Well, whatever you talked about, he certainly feels good about it," said Hannah, coming up behind Claire. "He wasn't that jaunty yesterday."

"Jaunty?" Claire closed the door. "I didn't notice."

"Well, what did you think of him?"

"I think he's the most interesting man I've ever met."

"My goodness. The most interesting? That's very exciting."

"No, Hannah, he's an interesting man and that's all. Interesting does not mean a romance."

"It does a lot more often than you think. He obviously made quite an impression on you. And was it a good interview?"

"It was different. We seemed to ramble a lot; we didn't focus on anything for very long. I think he'll be more specific tomorrow."

"Tomorrow? There's more?"

"I don't think he'll ever run out of questions. I just hope he has a deadline."

Hannah chuckled and led the way to the kitchen. "Forrest brought fresh trout that he caught in Montana. Will Emma be home?"

"She said she'd be here at six."

"Then she shall have trout and oven-roasted potatoes." Scrubbing the small red potatoes, Hannah hummed a few bars, cleared her throat, then hummed a few more. "Claire," she said at last, "I have a favor to ask. Could you loan me some money?"

"Loan? I'll give you any money you need, Hannah, you know that."

POT OF GOLD

"You think I couldn't pay it back. But I can and I will. With interest. I'd much rather it was a loan."

Claire frowned slightly. "How much do you want?"

Hannah took a long breath. "Twenty-five thousand dollars."

Claire stared at her. "Hannah, what—" She stopped. She had no right to ask Hannah what she needed money for. She had never mentioned any debts, but perhaps she had been ashamed and now could not put them off any longer. But how did she expect to repay a loan? More likely she was helping someone else. One of the friends she made in her trips to town, to the grocery store, the farmers' market, the meat market, the fish store, the pharmacy. She always brought back stories; it seemed she was a sounding board for whomever she met. "Of course," Claire said. "I'll write you a check tonight."

"Oh, you are wonderful." Hannah crossed the kitchen to hug Claire, and it was only when she moved that Claire realized how rigidly she had been standing at the counter, waiting, holding her breath. She went back to scrubbing potatoes and was cutting them into halves when the door from the garage opened.

"Hi," Emma said, entering in a flurry. She dropped a garment bag from Simone's on one of the kitchen chairs. "I found a coat. It's not the best, but it's okay and it was getting late so I bought it."

"Why don't we go to New York and find what you really want?" Claire asked. "We used to have a good time shopping together."

Emma dropped her eyes. "I know. I just don't have a lot of time."

"Are you getting a cold?" Hannah asked. "You look feverish."

"I'm fine, why do you keep asking how I am?" Emma asked angrily. "Anyway, was he here? The guy from the magazine? Alex?"

"Yes," Claire said. "He said he wants—"

"I thought you'd ask him to stay for dinner."

"No, why would I? Emma, he's a journalist writing a story and he's interviewing me. That's all. He said he wants to talk to you, too; he was sorry you weren't here."

"Oh, well, it doesn't matter. I don't have anything to say to him. But you liked him, didn't you?"

"Yes, very much. He's a likable person. And interesting. He'll be back tomorrow at ten; will you talk to him then?"

"He's coming back? Is he coming for breakfast?"

"Emma, what is this need you have to feed people?" Hannah asked.

Emma flushed. "It's a way to get to know them. Mother always says sitting around a table is the best way to really talk to people."

"But he's a professional interviewer," Claire said, "and he does just fine without food. Will you talk to him tomorrow?"

"I suppose, if you want me to. I have to go; I'm going out for dinner."

"You didn't mention you had a date tonight," Claire said.

"I don't. I mean, I do, with a friend. We're just going to dinner in Westport, then I'll be home. Early."

"We have fresh trout," Hannah said. "Caught this morning."

"Well, you can freeze it; I'll have it some other time."

"Then it won't be fresh."

Emma shrugged. "I'll see you later." She turned in place and went back to the garage. *I didn't really talk to them,* she thought. *I should have sat down and talked for a little while; I wasn't even friendly.* She got into her car and backed out of the garage. *I stayed by the door the whole time. Ready to escape.* She drove down the narrow street, her headlights illuminating little eddies of fallen leaves stirred up by the moving car. It wasn't that she thought of her house as a prison; it was that everything these days seemed constricting and she was always wanting to move, to get away, whatever she was doing. Except with Brix. She couldn't imagine ever wanting to get away from Brix.

She parked in front of a small restaurant with white curtains and red-and-white-checked tablecloths and found Gina waiting for her in a corner booth. "You look beautiful as usual and I'm glad to see you," Gina said, getting up to kiss her. She put her hand on Emma's cheek. "A little warm, though; are you getting a cold?"

"No! Oh, I'm sorry. It was just that you sounded like Hannah. Somebody's always asking me how I am these days."

"Well, how are you?"

"Fine. I don't know why people keep asking. I'm fine."

Gina contemplated her. "Honey, what have you been trying out lately?"

Emma felt a moment of terror. "What? Trying out? What does that mean?"

"You know what it means. Grass? Coke? Probably coke. How much are you doing?"

Emma stared at her, hollow with fear. If Gina could see it, everybody could. Her mother could. Her mother had been so proud of her for not doing drugs all through high school. She loved it when her mother was proud of her. "What's wrong with me?" she whispered to Gina. "Don't I look right?"

"You're wound up like a spring, is how you look, and you don't concentrate—look at you now, you're looking all over the place, not at me, and I'll bet you're thinking of a dozen other things besides what I'm saying. You're always on edge these days, sweetheart, and I know what that's like because I've been through it. So how much are you doing?"

Emma's head drooped. "Not very much. Just when I'm— just once in a while."

"When you're with Brix. Right? And when else? Come on, Emma, you're not with him that often."

"Just . . . once in a while. He gave me some for when I get nervous. And it helps when I'm really hungry. You know, sometimes, when I'm worried about Brix or something, I get really hungry; and when I've been working for hours, and all of a sudden it all stops, I'm just starved, I can't wait to eat, but I can't, you know, or I'd gain weight, and Brix told me if I did, they wouldn't want me anymore; they'd drop me and find another model. So if I use coke—just a little, you know, it doesn't take a lot—I'm not hungry anymore, and I feel fine.'' She looked up. ''Does Mother know?''

''I don't know. I'd guess that she doesn't. And I haven't talked to her about it, if that's what you're asking.''

Emma's breath came out in a long sigh. ''Don't tell her. Please.''

''I'd like you to tell her, Emma. I'd like you to talk to her about everything that's bothering you.''

Emma shook her head. ''I didn't know you'd done it, too,'' she said after a moment.

''Coke and a lot more. I did major experimenting with a spectacular variety of controlled substances when I was your age and on into my twenties. It was the thing to do; everybody was doing it and I didn't want to be left out. And I have to say, a lot of it made me feel pretty terrific, at least some of the time. But not enough of the time. It's a dead end, Emma; that's why I cut it out. Drugs don't make things easier or better or nicer in the long run; all they do is make you want more. I'd stop doing them if I were you.''

''Well, but you did it for years and you're fine.''

Gina sighed. She looked up as a waiter appeared. ''Two glasses of Chianti, two pasta puttanesca, two house salads with oil and vinegar on the side. Okay?'' she asked Emma.

''Fine. I'm not really hungry.''

''No kidding. I'll bet you're never very hungry anymore.'' Emma shrugged.

''And you haven't taken any riding lessons, either, even though your mother wanted you to.''

''Did she tell you that?''

''No, Roz did. Your mother's friend; the lady who owns the horses. I'm there a lot these days, riding and helping out. It's a gorgeous place, Emma, a little piece of paradise, and

POT OF GOLD

Roz is a very special person. You'd like it if you gave yourself a chance."

"I haven't got time. Maybe I will later, when I have some time."

They were silent for a moment. "Well, how about my other good advice? Can you tell your lover boy you've decided no more coke?"

"He likes doing it with me. Doing it together. He likes doing things together."

"Sure." Gina picked up the glass of wine the waiter set before her and sipped it. "Not bad. Do you want to talk about him?"

"Not really. I get confused when I do. It's best when I'm with him and we're not talking at all."

"Oh, Emma," Gina sighed. They sat quietly for a few minutes, until their dinners came. "Okay, why are we here? You wanted to talk to me about something. If it isn't Brix, what is it?"

"It's sort of about Brix. Gina, I know you don't think he's wonderful, but I'm worried about him and I don't know what to do and I don't know who else to go to." She leaned forward and lowered her voice. "I saw two memos on Brix's desk, about people who were tested with the PK-20 eye cream, and they talked about . . . about adverse reactions . . . something about four percent of the people . . ."

Gina put down her fork. "What reactions?"

"Something in Latin that I couldn't read, and conjunctivitis; I knew that, because I had it once. And . . . and there was something about . . . about blindness . . ."

Gina's hand grabbed Emma's. "You're sure of that?"

"I read it. It's there. Something about maybe the person didn't use it properly. . . . I read them pretty fast, but I couldn't make up something like blindness. It's what I've been thinking about since I read them." Emma paused. "Gina, could you find out what it's all about? I'm sure they're taking care of it—Brix wouldn't be involved in—well, I mean, he'd want everything to be right, I know he would—

but maybe he could get involved without knowing—well, not really, he's very important in the company—oh, I don't know, it's just that something sounds awfully wrong and if you could find out . . ."

Gina nodded. "Did you think of asking Brix?"

"Yes, but I . . . couldn't. I just didn't see how I could."

"I don't either. Okay, I'll see what I can dig up. It doesn't sound good, Emma; they're planning to release the line in March."

"I know. They're all going a little crazy, you know? Tod and Bill just thought of a whole new idea, so we'll be starting again next week, a whole new series of ads. It's like it never ends and they haven't even used the first one yet. They all act like it's the biggest thing in the world."

"It may be, for the company anyway. From what I hear, they've put everything into it. It's either going to be the splash of the century or the end of Eiger Labs."

"The end? The end of the company? It couldn't be; they make lots of other things."

"But they may be betting everything on the new one. I'm not up there with Quentin and whoever he talks to, but I'm hearing rumors in the lab, and all of them say about the same thing: that they're overextended and everything's riding on PK-20. Well, I'll find out what I can tomorrow and let you know. Come on, now, cold puttanesca is as good as hot, so let's eat. Come on, Emma, I want you to get some food inside you."

Emma sighed. "Yes, ma'am."

"Hey," Gina said, and waited until Emma looked up. "I love you. Remember that. So does your mother. But if you'd rather come to me sometimes, I understand that, and I'm always here, whenever you want to talk. I'm here even if you don't want to talk. Think about what I said. It was said with love."

Emma nodded. "I know," she said, but tears were rising inside her and so she stopped talking and tried to eat. She looked up briefly and saw Gina staring into space, absorbed in her thoughts. She loved Gina. She loved the way Gina had always treated her like a grown-up, even when she was a little girl, having long talks with her, and listening seriously to whatever Emma had to say; and she loved the way Gina talked about women: that they could do a lot more than men thought they could do, and that they were usually smarter than men and had a lot more stamina and understood people better. Emma couldn't believe that she was smarter than Brix, he was so much more experienced than she was, but she had to admit he wasn't really thoughtful or understanding of other people. She didn't know how much stamina he had, but then she didn't know how much she had, either. Gina always said women endured trials by fire and came through them better than men. Emma wondered how she would come through a trial by fire. I wish I could have one, she thought; I wish something really terrible would happen and I could come through strong and victorious and everybody would say how fine I am. And Brix would think I'm wonderful and he'd want to protect me from any more trials by fire because he wouldn't want to lose me.

Where is he right now? she thought. He hasn't called for eleven days. He's probably with somebody, somebody beautiful and— But that thought hurt too much, and Emma wrenched her thoughts away from it. Maybe he's thinking about me; planning something special for us to do together. He likes to surprise me. I'm sure that's what he's doing. Planning a surprise for me.

"Well, let's talk about your modeling," Gina said. "And I'll tell you about my horseback riding in that glorious place, and about Roz. I think we should talk about everything that's important in our lives."

Brix sat across from his father and sipped his Scotch. He was hungry but he couldn't go to dinner until his father decided their little meeting was over. He tightened his stomach to stop its rumbling and concentrated on what they were talking about, trying to keep his voice level so he wouldn't sound as if he were whining. His father hated it when he whined. "Kurt's my friend; that's why he gave them to me. Why shouldn't I see those memos? Jesus, Dad, I'm a vice president of the company; I ought to be the first person you talk to when we've got problems."

"Who else saw them?"

"Nobody; Kurt's not stupid. He warned me a couple of months ago that some things were coming through that looked bad—"

"You didn't tell me about that."

"He told me he'd sent you a memo on it so I thought I'd wait until the final test reports came in. I thought you'd want to talk to me about them; I thought we'd have a meeting as soon as you got them."

God, I sound like I've been sitting by the phone, waiting for a call. I sound like Emma.

He cleared his throat. "Anyway, there's something else. Kurt told me this morning that they've got early reports on the newest tests and they don't look good. In fact, some of them look pretty bad. He said he's sending you a memo on it. There's this pattern, you know, well, Kurt called it a pattern but I think it's just a fluke, well, not a fluke exactly because it keeps happening, but it's less than four percent who had bad reactions, not a lot less, but, still—"

"They've only got early results? Those test reports are due this week. What the hell's going on over there?"

"I don't know. Kurt didn't say anything except—"

"Do you have his home phone number?"

"Kurt's? Yeah, but Dad, I'll take care of it. I can find out when they'll be—"

"What's his number?"

Brix let out his breath in a small explosion. The rumbling in his stomach sounded to him like thunder. He wanted another Scotch, but his father didn't like it when he had more than one drink. Well, the hell with that, he thought, and went to the bar and refilled his glass. He leaned casually against the bar and, as if it weren't really important, gave Quentin Kurt's home telephone number.

He pretended to be absorbed in looking at the photographs on the wall, though he had the same ones in his office and thought they were boring, and he did not turn when he heard Quentin hang up. "Sit down, I want to talk to you," Quentin said. Brix sat down. "How much do you know about Kurt?"

"Not a lot. We go running together and sometimes we go out drinking. And tennis sometimes. He lives a few houses from me."

"Alone?"

"Right; he's divorced. No kids."

"How old is he?"

"Thirty-four."

"How long has he worked here?"

"Four or five years, something like that. He was here when I started and that was two years ago, and he'd been here awhile."

"Where did he work before?"

"I don't know; we never talked about that."

Quentin sat back. "He's worked here for almost six years, his parents live in Arizona in one of those retirement villages, he came here from Helene Curtis in Chicago, and he was made head of the testing lab here at the beginning of the year."

Brix was staring at him. "If you knew all that, why did you ask me?"

"I know it because it's my business to know the department heads in this company. Do you think you're exempt from that? You like to remind me that you're a vice president, but you don't know your own top people. And this one you run with and drink with, and you still don't know the most basic facts about him." Quentin waited, but Brix was silent, scowling at his drink. "What I don't know are his personal habits. Does he like expensive things?"

"What? Oh, well, I guess so. I mean, yeah, he spends a lot. Shoes especially; he's really into shoes, Italian, mostly.

253

And Justin cowboy boots; he's got every color they come in. And cashmere sports jackets."

"On his salary?"

"I don't know what he makes. I suppose you do."

"Eighty-five."

"Well, he spends it all on himself, I guess. No kids or anything."

"But he probably never has enough."

Brix shrugged. "Who does?"

"For Christ's sake, try to keep up with me. If he had inside information, he might want to sell it to a high bidder."

"Sell it? Kurt?" Brix shook his head. "I don't think he's smart enough to think of that."

"Just because you weren't doesn't mean that he isn't."

Brix lurched out of his chair and went to the bar.

"Three in a row?"

"Right, I'm thirsty." He filled his glass and returned to his chair. "I would have thought of it except I know Kurt. He doesn't think like that."

"How does he think?"

"Like he wants to make a lot of money, but he only thinks about his job, I mean, you know, nothing illegal. He's really into his work; he's proud of it. He just wants to earn a lot here or some other lab."

"He's talking about going somewhere else?"

"No, but, you know, everybody talks about where they might go someday. He says he really likes Europe; there's some big cosmetics companies in Switzerland and France."

"He doesn't have any loyalty to Eiger Labs?"

"Well, yeah, sure he does. He thinks we make good products. That's why he's worried about the tests."

"What did he say?"

"I told you: that they looked pretty bad. He thinks we'll have to change the formula, at least on the Eye Restorative, or pull it from the line."

"Why did he say that?"

"Because, he ... Dad, four percent isn't a lot, but it's hard to ignore."

"What about women?"

"What about them?"

"Kurt and women."

"Oh. He says he has a lot of them; nothing serious. I don't see them, so I don't know for sure."

"All right. I want to make sure of his loyalty, that he'll keep quiet about these tests. I'm not worried about the testing company in Chicago; I picked them for this project because they've never had a leak. But I need to be sure of Kurt. You'd better talk to him ... no, I'll do it, tell him we expect him to cooperate while we evaluate the tests. And I'll do something with his Christmas bonus and a raise at his regular review in January. I'll take care of him, but I want you to keep an eye on him. Jogging, drinking, tennis, whatever it is, I want you sticking with him, and I want to hear from you about him: what he's doing with his time, if he looks like he's hungry, if he's running too close to the edge on his salary, if he's looking at other companies. Is that clear?"

"Sure."

"The other thing I'm going to tell him, first thing tomorrow morning, is that we've found out the test results have been doctored to get rid of the four percent. I'll say we don't know who did it, not yet, anyway, but of course whoever it was couldn't get a job in any other lab in the world, ever again."

"Doctored? But they weren't. They're—" There was a long silence. "You want me to do it."

"A few minutes ago you said you'd take care of it. I want you to take care of it. I assume I don't have to explain to you why this is necessary."

Brix stared at his father as if mesmerized. God, he thought, he just ticks off all these ideas, one after the other, like he's thought about them for months. Why can't I do that? He puts things together, he covers all the bases ... fuck it, he's so far ahead of me I'll never catch up.

JUDITH MICHAEL

"Do I have to explain it?" Quentin asked.

"No! I mean, I understand, Dad, I know that everything's riding on—"

"I could handle it myself, but I want you to do it. Is this something I can trust you to take care of, or not?"

"Sure, Dad, you know you can; I'll take care of it; no problem. I'll do it now. Are we through here? I mean, if you don't need me for anything else—"

"Go ahead. I want to see all the reports after you've been through them. And I don't want to wait too long." Quentin opened a folder and began to read. Brix stood uncertainly, then walked out of the office, closing the door behind him. When he was in the corridor, he realized he was still holding his glass. Well, I need it, he thought. He can damn well do without it. He probably won't even notice it's gone. Like me.

I could handle it myself. Is this something I can trust you to take care of, or not? Fuck it, he can handle everything; he doesn't need me, or anybody. Why the hell didn't I think of fixing the reports when I saw those memos? That should have been the first thing I thought of. Then he would have been proud of me. But he isn't. He's never going to trust me or need me; I'm too fucking slow. Unless I can think of something that's really important that I can do and he can't ... whatever the hell that could be. I'll have to think of something. Come up with something. I will come up with something. I just have to give it a lot of thought. But first I have to do this. And do it right.

Slowly, listening to the hollow knocking of his footsteps on the hard floors and the clink of ice cubes in his glass, he walked the length of the building to the testing lab, unlocked the door with his pass key, and closed it quietly behind him.

11

"JUST one more piece of coffee cake," Hannah urged, her knife poised. "I'm sure Claire will be back any minute."

"It's excellent cake," Alex said. "I enjoyed it. But no more. I'm not used to being spoiled and I can't start now."

"Why not?"

"Because I have no one at home to spoil me. Why would I indulge in a luxury if it would only be whetting an appetite for something I know I can't have?"

"I don't believe it. No women friends? I thought writers can't write without a muse."

"This one learned how."

Hannah poured more coffee and sat down. "Claire said you used to write books."

"Yes."

"Why did you stop?"

"She didn't tell you?"

"No, why would she? It's your story, isn't it?"

"Yes," he said, bemused. "But that doesn't usually stop people."

"Claire isn't 'people.' She's very special. So why aren't you writing books anymore? Or don't you talk about it?"

"Not much. What I told Claire was that I lost the desire

and the motivation. I'd begun a book; I was about a third of the way through it when a lot of things happened in my life, all at about the same time. My wife died, very suddenly—''

"Oh, I'm sorry. How old was she?"

"Thirty-six."

"Terrible. Terrible." She shook her head. "So young, such a terrible thing. And you had children?"

"A son. David. He's fourteen now and lives with my sister and her family, and no, Hannah—I can see the question coming—I can't have him with me. I travel on writing assignments and he needs a stable home and family, not an itinerant father. And no—I can see the next one coming, too—I'm not as close to him as I should be. I wish I were, but I don't know how."

"Goodness," said Hannah mildly, "do you always conduct both sides of a conversation? I suppose that comes from writing everybody's dialogue."

Alex chuckled. "You could be right. I don't think I do it often."

"So that's when you stopped writing books? I don't get the connection."

"I'm sorry. It's not easy to explain."

Hannah checked the thermos and poured what was left into Alex's cup. "I'll make another pot," she said, and went to the sink.

Alex sat back, idly watching her, recognizing that she had backed off to give him time to decide whether he wanted to talk or not. He was very relaxed, waiting for Claire to return, feeling good about the story about her that he had already begun to organize in his mind. But it was not a time to talk about himself, however seductive Hannah was with her eyes fixed on him with interest and friendship.

Beyond the large window, heavy steel-gray clouds lay low above the treetops and the bare black branches stretched starkly upward as if in prayer. The tree trunks pressed in upon the house like dark sentinels standing in formation on a carpet of faded, crackling leaves. The copper chandelier over the table shone steadily, holding back the November gloom. Alex thought there was nowhere in the world he would rather be at this moment than right here.

"I'd rather talk about the present than the past," he said as Hannah sat down again. "If you ask me what I'm doing now or what I'm thinking of doing, we could talk about that."

"What are you thinking of doing?"

"Oh, any number of things. I might try being a waiter. I've been watching them, the good ones, and there's an art to it; it could be a challenge."

"You'd be a waiter so you could write about one?"

"No, writing has nothing to do with it. I'd be a waiter because that's what I'd decided to be. Or I might be a longshoreman. I've been going down to the docks for the past year, watching them; there's no art to it, but it has a rhythm and a pattern that one could sink into."

"You'd stop writing entirely."

"That would be the idea. I thought of doing construction, too. Whenever I see a crew working on an office building I think what a good sense of accomplishment they must have, seeing those huge monuments go up and knowing they've had a part in them."

"You'd stop writing even though it's what you do best. And it's what makes you happiest."

There was a pause. "You don't know that," Alex said quietly. "And I'm not sure of it."

"Well," Hannah said after a moment. "In a way I can understand it. Once I thought of being a cleaning woman in office buildings. You know, late at night, everyone gone, all the lights blazing on empty desks and corridors. It seemed to me I'd be like a ghost, drifting through those strangely silent spaces, cut off from all people and the busy world, not involved emotionally with anyone. I thought, that way, if I had time to think and not deal with other people, eventually I might be able to stop feeling like a ghost and feel whole again."

Alex was creasing a paper napkin, seeming to concentrate

on it, but he had heard everything she said. "A ghost," he repeated. "What kept you from feeling whole?"

Hannah clasped her hands on the table. "I had a daughter. Her name was Ariel and she was a lovely child, full of curiosity and love. We lived with my mother in a small town in Pennsylvania. My mother was a secretary, I taught school, and together we made enough to buy a little house, so small you wouldn't believe it, but it had just enough room for the three of us. My mother and I shared one bedroom and Ariel had the other, facing east; she woke up each morning with the sun touching her face. There is nothing more wonderful than to help a child discover the wonders of the world and of her own mind and body; I loved it. We did everything together: we took walks in the woods and went swimming in the local pool and spent hours in the library finding books for both of us, and once in a great while we'd take a bus to Philadelphia to go to museums and walk around the city. In those days I was angry and envious of rich people who could buy their daughters anything, fabulous clothes, trips to Europe, fine houses. We couldn't even replace our sagging couch or buy a dining room table. Of course we didn't have a dining room, either. But even without money, we were very happy. And then she died."

Alex's body jerked, as if he had been struck. "She died? How old was she?"

"Eight. One day she was deciding she'd be a ballet dancer and showing me a pirouette in our backyard, and the next day she was dead. Of course I couldn't believe it; I refused to believe it. I refused to say the words *Ariel is dead*. I'd go out looking for her, to all the places we'd gone together. I'd take those walks in the forest and sit by the local swimming pool and wander around the library, expecting to see her sitting at one of the tables, the way she always did, leafing through books, making a stack beside her that would get her through the week. I even went to Philadelphia, which of course made no sense at all, because how would she have gotten there without me? But I went anyway, to our favorite museums and up and down the streets with all the buildings from the Revolutionary days that we'd liked so much, and when I went home without her, I'd start again, with the walks in the forest and sitting by the pool and walking through the rooms of our little house. It was so little I could get through it in a minute and a half, but I took longer, I took slow little steps, as if the longer I took the more possible it was that Ariel would be around the corner or through that door, in the other room, waiting for me."

Alex saw himself in his house in New Jersey, walking through the rooms one slow step at a time, looking for his wife, listening for her laughter and her soft voice humming as she cooked dinner. He moved to Hannah's side and put his arm around her. "What did she die of?"

It was as if he had not spoken. "Such an awful time," Hannah said, slowly shaking her head. "Somehow, I was still teaching and living what looked like a perfectly normal life, but I knew I was being absolutely crazy, and my mother didn't know what to do with me. After a while, of course, I snapped out of it. But it took a long time. The point is, we do get over terrible times; we're built to do that. Most people learn again to laugh and love and respond to beauty and fight ugliness and clasp hands with friends, even though they've lost a kind of joy that they'll never get back. There's an unlit corner in their hearts and no light will ever penetrate to it. It will always be dark."

She paused, looking at her clasped hands. "That's why it's so important to be close to those we love, not to take them for granted, not to give up when we're baffled by how complicated it can be to understand and be understood by another person. And that's why you should open up to people; not just ask questions like a journalist but share your feelings with them, because that's what makes us close and loving and human. If you don't, you may wake up one day and find your chances for love and closeness gone, and that's another kind of death." She looked up at Alex. "Tragedy is no excuse, you know. However long it takes, we do recover."

"Yes," Alex said quietly. "I believe that."

Claire walked in from the garage, carrying a flat leather artist's case. "Am I interrupting something?"

"Not at all," said Hannah, slipping from within the circle of Alex's arm. "We were getting acquainted. Goodness," she added, looking at Claire, "you're all lit up."

"It was a good meeting. I'm sorry I'm late. I thought I could just drop these off, but the marketing people wanted to talk about them. Is there any coffee left?"

"There's a new pot. And coffee cake. We've been through both of them; Alex came early."

"The traffic was light," Alex said to Claire. He could not take his eyes off her glowing face; she was happy and excited and her beauty seemed lit from within. "And I was eager."

"Then we should get started." Claire took the tray Hannah had filled with two mugs and the coffeepot and a plate of cake. "You've seen the house? Where would you like to talk?"

"Hannah showed me the house; I'd like to go to your studio again."

They took the same chairs they had taken the afternoon before. Once again, all the lights were on, and the brightness made the gray clouds beyond the windows look even darker and more lowering. Alex, still under the spell of Hannah's story, took a long breath. "I'm glad to be back here; it's a very soothing room, and gladdening. Especially when the world looks bleak. Hannah was right; you look very happy. They liked your designs?"

"All of them. That's unheard of in this business. And they're all completely different from anything on the market today, but no one looked shocked or even raised an eyebrow. Of course they'd already approved the first group; I think they may even be in production, but this was a whole new group and all they did was ask some technical questions about the materials I'd specified for each piece, and they wanted to see color charts and samples of lettering. That was all. They told me to go on and finish the line. I couldn't believe it. I still can't."

"Are they confidential? Or can I see them?"

"They're confidential when it comes to anyone connected with the cosmetics industry. That doesn't include you." Claire opened the flat briefcase she had carried into the house and took from it a stack of drawings on heavy paper, each protected by a sheet of tissue. She laid them on her drawing table and Alex joined her there. Together, they bent over them and Claire adjusted the light. "There are two objectives in design. One is to convey a message, briefly, quickly, unambiguously and memorably. The other is to make an impact, to jump out, so it's the first thing a customer notices, or, if not that, to be the one design that leaves a lasting impression. Everything is so crowded now—store shelves, display cases, magazine and newspaper ads, billboards, even the yellow pages in telephone directories—it's hard to make something stand out, especially something that's done in a traditional way. So I decided to be untraditional."

Her voice had changed, Alex thought, making a mental note of it for his story: she was poised and professional, not hesitant or diffident as she had been the day before when she talked about money. This was her field and she was comfortable in it; she was comfortable with herself in it.

He concentrated on the drawings. Some were in crayon, some in different colors of ink, a few in watercolor paints. Each heavy sheet held two actual-size drawings of a product, seen from the front and the back, sometimes with a third, side view. Claire said little as Alex slowly turned the sheets; another sign of her professionalism, he thought: she let her work speak for itself. And he was impressed with its strength. All the packaging was in shades of amber, but the variety was extraordinary: there were jars sculpted like free-form female torsos, bottles curved like scimitars with jeweled handles, tubes imprinted with sinuous gold and silver bands, jars in undulating shapes that seemed to stretch out from the page, others like quiet teardrops. One of the most intriguing, Alex thought, was a case labeled EYE RESTORATIVE, a flat amber oblong with a hinged lid set with a single jewel.

"They're very different, and very beautiful," he said as he turned the last sheet. "And most cosmetics packaging isn't, is it?"

"No, most of it looks as if it came straight out of the laboratory, which is what most companies have always wanted. But, no matter how much scientific research went into them, there's still a lot of fantasy and a kind of ritual in using cosmetics—most of it is people trying to convince themselves whatever they just bought is going to do all the magic they want it to do—and that begins when they pick up a jar or bottle or tube first thing in the morning and feel the texture and shape of it before opening it. That's where their fantasy begins. I think that's where they want beauty to begin."

"You think it's a fantasy, people trying to convince themselves something will work."

"Mostly." Claire looked at her drawings. "Are you about to ask me how I can help lure people to spend their money on products I don't believe in?"

"I wouldn't have put it that harshly."

"How would you have put it?"

"I would have asked you how important you think those fantasies are for people, and if that's why you brought such enthusiasm and skill to the job you did."

"That's a more interesting question than mine." Claire picked up a pencil—I know that instinct, Alex thought; we both think better with a pencil in our hands—and leafed through her drawings. "I think fantasies are essential to our well-being," she said slowly. "That's why I bought lottery tickets; it was a game I played with myself, a fantasy, like a little spark in a very quiet life. And I think the best designs always touch somehow on fantasy. But the reason I put everything I had into these designs is because I don't think about the product when I'm designing the package. I just love to design. I discovered that after I quit my job. I missed it.

POT OF GOLD

There was an emptiness, and I didn't know what it was at first, but as soon as I started designing again, I knew it was the space left when I wasn't creating beauty."

Alex nodded, almost to himself. *There was an emptiness.* He knew that, too. He felt it every day that he did not, could not, write the books he loved to write. An emptiness. A need that nothing else could satisfy.

"Well, you've created beauty," he said at last. "I'm glad you were able to go back to it."

At the pain in his voice, she looked at him quickly. "Perhaps you'll go back to it, too," she said quietly. Then, to give him time, she turned away and returned to her chair. "Something else happened today. I got a call while I was at Eiger Labs from the president of a chain of restaurants; apparently Quentin had shown him copies of a couple of my preliminary sketches, and now he wants me to design publicity brochures and new menus for his restaurants. And he's talking about new china and glassware. I've never done that."

"So you said yes?"

"I said I'd talk to him about it when I finish this job. I'd like to do it, but if I'm going to work for other companies, I have to think about secretarial and design help, which means forming my own company. I'm not sure I want to make that commitment right now."

"You're still having too much fun."

She smiled. "I guess so. I love being able to do what I want."

"And you also love design."

"Well, if I'm lucky, I'll be able to pick and choose."

Alex sat beside her again and took out his tape recorder and pressed the small button that set it going. "How do you feel about work, now that you don't need it to survive?"

"More sure of myself," Claire said promptly. "I think the biggest problem with working for someone else is there's no time built into the job to think about what you're doing and how you could do it better. When people do that, they're accused of daydreaming. You're lucky; you don't have that problem, working on your own; you must spend a lot of your time thinking."

"More time staring, thinking, daydreaming, than writing. But the payoff is, if the thoughts go well, so does the writing. You haven't told me why you decided to work again."

"To know where I belong," Claire said, suddenly somber. "Sometimes, when I'm dashing around New York with a friend, if I stop and ask myself why I'm there and how I feel, I can't think of an answer. It's not that I don't have a good time shopping with friends; I do. It's just that, when that was all I did, I began to feel at loose ends, as if I needed an anchor. When Emma was growing up, she was my anchor, even more than my job. But our lives are so changed ... where *is* Emma? She told me she'd be here this morning, to talk to you."

"Hannah said she was still asleep."

Claire gazed across the room, as if she could look into Emma's room at the other end of the house. "She sleeps so much lately," she murmured.

Alex said nothing, waiting for her. In a moment she turned to him. "Well, that's why I work. Because when I'm sitting at my design table or my computer or even taking a walk at night and thinking about a design problem, I have something to focus on and a place where I know what to do and how to do it. I know exactly why I'm here and I know how I feel."

"How do you feel?"

"Wonderful. I'm doing something I'm good at, that I like to do, and that's mine, not anyone else's. I'm making something of my very own, and when I come up with something that I know is good, there's no better feeling in the world. You must feel the same way with your writing. That's why I can't understand how you could give up writing novels. They give you so much more room to build and create, to stretch out ... it seems to me that magazine articles are like small rooms and a novel is the whole world."

"Exactly," Alex murmured. He sat at ease in the bright studio, talking to a woman who was responsive and whose

POT OF GOLD

mind worked much as his did, and he felt wonderfully at home. *You should open up to people; not just ask questions like a journalist but share your feelings with them, because that's what makes us close and loving and human.* Finally, he said, speaking slowly, "I didn't make the decision to stop writing novels, Claire. One day there just weren't any novels inside me waiting to be written. I was empty."

Claire thought about how that would be if it happened to her. She shivered. "That's a little like dying, isn't it?"

He gave her a quick look. "Yes. Not many people understand that."

"But did they really just disappear?"

"Probably not. Though that does happen; writers never know when they'll suddenly run dry and be finished for good." He paused, but he was still under Hannah's spell—and Claire's—and the words came more easily than ever before. "A lot of things happened to me at once, a few years ago. I told you that my wife died; it was very sudden, completely unexpected. She was healthy and busy—she was a fabric designer and she'd just gotten a major order—and one afternoon she said she felt tired and lay down to take a nap . . . and never woke up."

Claire drew in her breath. "What was it?"

"A heart attack. No warning, no history of heart disease in her family, no clues. She was just gone. And if there was one thing that wiped out my writing books, that would be it. Sending my son to my sister and her husband, selling the house, moving away from everything that had given me a sense of having a stake in life . . . all that was very bad. But what was worse was the sudden feeling that there was nothing I could count on. I couldn't imagine writing novels—making up stories that progressed in an ordered world—when I didn't believe there was an ordered world. I haven't been able to get past that."

"You mean you can't predict what will happen."

"More than that. There was a time when I was very sure of what my life would be, and how it would unfold, and for years everything went exactly as I'd thought it would. My stories were published in literary reviews from the time I was in high school; I won a full scholarship to college and then a fellowship to graduate school; I won the PEN award with my first novel when I was twenty-eight. I married the woman I loved; we had a son, we had good friends, we bought a house and a dog and took in a couple of stray cats who turned out to be wonderful pets. And my wife was making her own reputation as a designer. It wasn't just that everything was happening the way I'd plotted it, it was that it was happening on schedule, as if someone, somewhere, was directing this play the way I'd ordered, and keeping the action moving."

Restlessly, he stood and walked about the studio, stopping at Claire's drawing table to gaze absently at her drawings. "Then someone pulled the curtain. That perfectly plotted life collapsed and so did my belief in my own power. The Greeks call it *hubris*, you know: pride. Defying the gods; believing you can plot your life and the lives of those you love. I was guilty of that: I thought I could control our fate."

He came back to sit in the armchair, leaning forward, elbows on his knees. "I felt I was being knocked around by invisible forces, malevolent and invincible, and there was nothing I could do but give in. That was when I sent David to my sister and sold the house."

"And had no more books to write."

He nodded. "Writing a book is a leap of faith and a declaration of love. You believe you can put on paper the ideas that are so clear and vivid in your mind; you give yourself to what you create with a kind of love that can't be duplicated even in the most passionate affair; you believe that someone will publish your work and others will read it and libraries will buy it so that future generations will discover it. You believe you can create stories that resonate with the readers of your own time and also those future generations: that you can find universal themes and present them in ways that give people hope or greater understanding or the rare pleasure of an escape from the shadows of the world around

POT OF GOLD

them. Or all of the above. In other words, you believe in the future and in your ability to make a place for yourself in it, on your own terms. I stopped believing that."

The tape recorder clicked off. Alex gazed at it. "Damn it, I've done it again." He shook his head. "This won't do, you know; I've got a deadline on this story and there's more of me here than there is of you."

"What would you like to talk about?" Claire asked gently. Her heart ached for him, for his sadness and emptiness and for all his lost loves: his wife, his son, his books. "Do you think we can do it in an hour? I really have to get to work after that."

Alex inserted another reel of tape in the recorder, pocketing the one that had run out. "An hour will be fine. Let's start with this house and the different patterns in your life. And I'd like to hear you talk some more about your work. And then, if Emma is awake, I'd like very much to talk to her."

Claire poured coffee for both of them and sat back. The room was quiet, muffled, and she glanced at the window to see large flakes of snow drifting through the branches that brushed the glass, already turning white. The studio seemed even brighter, a snug haven, and Claire listened, as if she were an observer standing in the doorway, to the murmur of their voices as she and Alex talked, the sound of their laughter, the soft clink of coffee cups. In that warm place, she felt comfortable, with nothing to prove and no tests to pass. He was easy to talk to, subtle but not sly in his questions, and quick to understand when she was fumbling for the right word. She realized she was having a very good time, and when she thought about work, she let the flow of the conversation sweep the thought away.

The telephone broke the mood. They both jumped slightly when it rang. Alex stopped the recorder as Claire answered it. "Yes," she said, and Alex heard the sudden tension in her voice. "I thought it was eight o'clock," she said after a moment. "Well, yes, I can be ready at seven." With a red pen she drew circles on a pad of paper beside her, circles within circles. "We're going to Roz and Hale's? . . . No, I didn't know, but that's fine; I love it there. And you're right; it's at least an hour's drive." She linked the circles with smaller circles, forming a chain that looped around the page. As she listened, a small smile appeared on her lips. "It's only been four days." There was a pause. "Yes, of course I am. I will. Until seven."

She hung up. "I'm sorry. Where were we?"

Alex was feeling a strange sense of loss. There had been a sensual note in her voice that had not appeared in any of their conversations; neither had that small inward-turning smile: they were only for the person on the telephone. They made her seem different to him, less singular, in a way less interesting. He had the melancholy sense that something had gotten away from him.

"We were talking about this house," Claire said. "But, you know, I really think we've covered everything." She looked at her watch. "I'll see if Emma is awake."

She left the room and Alex did not try to stop her. She was right: they had covered everything.

"You've been busy," Quentin said. His headlights picked out a low fence he had been watching for and he turned onto the unmarked, narrow dirt road that led to Hale and Roz Yaeger's farm. A few tire tracks stretched away ahead of them in the newfallen snow.

"Yes," Claire replied, because she had refused to see him twice in the past four days. She had thought about him and missed him, but she had been so busy the days had flown by, and it had been enough to know she would see him on Friday. "Has it been a good week for you?" she asked.

"Nothing special. One amusing thing: we're getting mail for Emma."

"Mail? I don't understand. From whom?"

"Women who see her in the ads."

"What ads?"

"The first set. You do know we've started running them."

"No. No, I had no idea. Does Emma know?"

"I assume Bill or Hale told her. They're teasers, saying something special is coming from Eiger Labs in March, PK-20, a revolution in stopping the clock . . . and so on and so on. You know how these things go. We've done it before, but with just a few lines of copy and a jar with a handwritten name or formula on it, and a lot of white space. This time we decided to use Emma, with a prototype of one of your designs. I assumed you knew."

"Where did they appear?" Claire asked coldly. She was furious. She was sure Emma would have told her about the ads, had she known, so it seemed that neither of them was considered important enough to be kept up to date about a program that used Emma as its symbol and Claire as its designer.

"Calm down," Quentin said absently, watching for the entrance to the long driveway. "You're taking it as some kind of personal insult. Someone slipped up, that's all. If you knew more about how companies function, you wouldn't be surprised."

"Where did they appear?" she repeated.

"In the December issues of *Vogue* and *Elle* and a couple of others. They're not on the stands yet, but subscribers have them. And we're getting mail for Emma." Snowflakes danced in his headlights as they caught the white gateposts and the white and gold sign saying CLEARVALLEY FARM, and Quentin turned into the driveway, following a single set of tire tracks already there. "Hale can tell you more than I can. Just don't make an issue out of not knowing about the ads."

Claire started to retort that she knew how to behave when she was a guest in someone's home, but she bit it back; when she was this angry, it was better to be silent. The tire tracks in front of them curved and disappeared behind the barn, but Quentin parked where the driveway opened out for guest cars, beside the front walk. The house stood before them, white with black shutters, graceful in its symmetry, its porchlights blazing and every window illuminated against the November night. Pumpkins and Indian corn, and a wrought-iron shoe scraper in the shape of a dachshund, decorated the front porch, and when Hale opened the door, the first thing Claire saw was a welcoming fire in the entry hall fireplace. And then she saw Gina.

"Almost one of the family," said Hale as Gina and Claire embraced. "She's here all the time, seems like; as crazy about cleaning up after horses as Roz is. Claire, let me take your coat. I know Quentin doesn't have one; he never does. Only man I know who's never cold. There's some people in the living room waiting to meet you, Quentin, and plenty to drink, as usual."

Roz put her arm around Claire. "I'm glad to see you; last-minute parties are always the best, don't you think? Did I ever thank you for sending me Gina? She's wonderful on the farm. She's wonderful, period. I'm getting a lot done that I've been planning for years and just never got around to. You'll have to come out in the daytime and see what we're doing. And take those riding lessons you never took."

She was talking a little too fast and Claire wondered why she was nervous. "You girls coming?" Hale asked, closing the door to the coat closet and turning toward the living room.

"In a minute," said Roz. "I want to talk to Claire."

"More secrets," he said with a mock sigh. "Things going on all the time and I don't know half of them. I come out from New York for a day or two and it hardly feels like my own house anymore."

Roz and Gina were watching him. "Well, I know, I know, it never was," he said with a short laugh. "Roz bought it with her money, runs it with her money. I'm not allowed to forget that. Claire, you want me to bring you a drink?"

She shook her head. "I'll have one later. And I want to talk to you about mail for Emma that's coming to Eiger Labs."

"For Emma?" Gina said. "How could that happen?"

"I've got a few in my briefcase if you want to see them,"

POT OF GOLD

Hale said to Claire. "They're a little dim, these women, but at least we know that Emma's making an impression. And that's what we want, you know; that's what we need. And Emma's terrific, you know; I think we'll be offering her a contract one of these days, a damned good one. A good contract. For a good model and a good girl. You say the word when you're ready and I'll get you those letters."

Claire watched him go into the living room. "Why is everyone so nervous around here?" she asked.

"Come this way," Gina said, and led the way down the hall to a small den with a leopard-patterned rug and a curved green velvet couch. A fire was burning in the marble fireplace, and the heavy, fringed draperies were pulled shut. Gina put another log on the fire, poked it a little, then said, "Let's sit. Are you sure you don't want a drink?"

"Do I need one?" Claire asked. "What's going on?"

"Well, I wanted you to know about Hale and me," Roz said. "If you want to know why he's nervous, it's because his latest lady friend called from New York this morning and demanded to know why I was refusing to divorce Hale so he could marry her. I told her there was no problem; if she wanted to marry Hale, she could start making plans."

"You're getting a divorce," Claire said. "Am I very slow or something? I didn't see this coming."

"You're not slow, Claire; you see more than most people. Nobody saw it coming. I thought it would probably happen someday, but I couldn't swear to it, and Hale didn't have a clue. Well, he wouldn't. He tells all his women I won't divorce him; it's his security blanket."

"But something happened?" asked Claire. "You've made up your mind to do it now?"

"As fast as I can. I'm going to tell him tonight, when—"
"He doesn't know?"
"He probably sees the handwriting on the wall, but if you mean have I talked to him about it, I haven't. But I will, tonight, when you've all gone home to your peaceful beds."

"And what will you do then?"

"Stay right here, my favorite place in the world. It is mine, you know, and Hale's always resented it. At first he resented the time I spent here; he wanted me in the city with him. But then he started in with his young chicks—this was about ten years ago, when our kids were both gone—and then he didn't care where I was. But he didn't like the money I put into it, either; he's always thought of it as ours even though I kept it in my own name. Maybe he expected me to leave him my fortune in my will. But that would mean he assumed I wouldn't outlast him. Or he didn't really think it through."

"It sounds very unpleasant," Claire said.

"Well, then, I'm exaggerating. We really get along pretty well. We haven't had a fight in the longest time; I can't even remember the last one. We didn't even fight this morning when that stupid woman called. Maybe that's one of the problems. Neither of us cares enough to fight. Anyway, I'm staying here, I live here, I love it, and Gina's helping me run it, and I feel better about myself than I have in a long, long time."

She looked at Claire almost defiantly. "I'm glad," Claire said, thinking how odd it was that Roz seemed as defensive about this divorce as if they were living a hundred years ago instead of in a time when everyone they knew was either divorced or close to someone who was. "I'll do whatever I can to help."

"Oh, love and encouragement are all I need right now. And between you and Gina I'll be fine. I just wanted you to know. I didn't want you to hear about it from someone else. And I hope Emma won't think less of me. I mean, she's only been here once, but I'd like her to come a lot and really learn to ride, and if she thinks things have changed here—"

"Think less of you? Of course she won't. Good heavens, Roz, I'm divorced; Emma doesn't surprise easily about the way people live these days. She'll like you as much as she always has. If she has time to think about anybody but Brix, that is."

"Is she still seeing so much of him?" Roz asked.

"She never sees him more than once every week or ten days, and a couple of times it's gone as long as two weeks. But when she's not with him, she's agonizing over his silence, or whatever he said or didn't say on their last date, or whatever it is she's worried about with him. Sometimes I think she's afraid. Not that he'll drop her, though I'm sure she's afraid of that, but also of something more serious. I don't know what that could be, but I sense it."

"She doesn't talk to you at all?" Gina asked.

"She's tried, a couple of times, but it's as if she's so sure I'll criticize him that she can't take the chance. And I guess she's right; I would. Did you tell her to talk to me?"

"I told her she'd be a lot better off if you two connected."

"Well, we're not connecting. And I don't see it happening soon."

Quentin appeared in the doorway. "There are people who want to meet you," he said to Claire.

"I'm sorry." She went to him, then turned back to Roz and Gina. "Thank you for telling me," she said, and followed Quentin down the hallway.

"Telling you what?" he asked.

"About a project they're going to do together."

He dismissed them without interest. "Hale invited these people for me," he said, holding her back at the entrance to the living room. "Their name is Collop and they own a small food company in New Hampshire."

"Collop's jam. I've bought it. It's very good. They make breads, too, I think, and cakes and cookies, though I haven't bought those. They have a beautifully designed catalog."

"You should make a point of telling them that. They're thinking of selling the company and I may decide to buy it. I want you to find out all you can about it and about them. Design is a good place to start."

Wait a minute. Claire looked into the living room where twenty people stood about in small groups or sat near the fire. *I'm at a party. I'm not at work, and neither is Quentin. This isn't the time or the place for him to be giving me assignments. And besides, I'm a designer, not a spy.*

"Hale is going to show me those letters," she murmured, and walked quickly into the living room. "Can I see them now?" she asked Hale, who was standing near a coffee table almost covered by a cast-bronze, galloping horse.

"Sure thing. Did you have a good talk with the girls?"

"Yes. Hale, if this isn't a good time for you to leave your guests—"

"No, it's okay; come on, we'll do it right now." He led the way to a library at the end of the house, illuminated by another fireplace. "Roz likes fires," Hale said. "It's like living in the seventeen hundreds, like nobody ever invented furnaces and light bulbs; you expect to see Pilgrims marching by. Probably burning somebody at the stake," he added gloomily. He opened a briefcase. "I brought about a dozen; we have more in the office. You can have them all, if you want. Emma might get a kick out of them."

He watched Claire open an envelope and scan the letter. "Listen, Claire, your PK-20 designs; they're terrific. I know we've told you that, but I'm looking ahead and I think you ought to be thinking about taking other clients. You wouldn't have to worry about me telling Quentin; he always feels he's bought us when we work for him, so he doesn't have to know. But if you decide to do it, I've got a couple of clients, major companies, Claire, not piddling stuff, who'd like your work. You don't have to answer right now, but think about it. You know, you were so far ahead of the other two firms Quentin called, there wasn't even a contest.... Is something wrong?"

Claire was frowning. "The other two firms?"

"He didn't tell you? Well, that's Quentin. He never trusts anybody to do what he wants; he always puts two or three people on something, at least until he's absolutely sure of them. He trusts me and Tod Tallent by now ... well, you know, I couldn't swear to that. He might be getting proposals from all kinds of people every time he starts a new campaign; how do I know, I'm only the hired help."

"You're his friend."

He shrugged. Claire returned the letter to its envelope and slipped the small bundle into her black evening bag. "We should get back."

"Is Roz going to leave me?" he asked abruptly.

"Hale, the only person who can answer that is Roz."

"Right. I'm afraid to ask. She thinks I don't care about her because I . . . dabble now and then, you know, sort of test the waters to see if everything's still working the way it ought to, and if I'm . . . oh, shit, you know, desirable, what a lousy word, but it doesn't mean anything, you know, it's like a game, it doesn't mean a damn thing; I'm crazy about Roz, that's never changed."

"Claire," Quentin said from the doorway.

"I'm sorry," she said, and went to him. He put his arm around her and she felt the long wave of desire that he could arouse with the slightest touch. "Thank you for the letters," she said to Hale as Quentin turned her with him and they left the room. "I didn't mean to stay away so long," she said, and wondered why she was apologizing.

"It's important to me that you're with me," he said. "Not just in the vicinity, but beside me. I've told you that before."

"I know."

"Was he asking you to work for him?"

Claire hesitated. "He said he had some clients who would be interested in my work."

Quentin stopped beside the fire in the foyer fireplace, before they reached the living room doorway. "You work for me, Claire. I have enough to keep you busy for a long time, especially working part-time. I don't want you working full-time; I told you that when we began this project."

"What you didn't tell me was that you talked to two other firms about the PK-20 line while you were telling me I'd be the head designer for it."

"Of course I did. I'd have been crazy not to. Did you really think I'd give this whole project to someone who'd never been in charge of one before?"

"You told me you liked my ideas."

"I did. Good God, Claire, stop being childish. You keep reducing things to a personal level. This had nothing to do with whether I thought you were good or not; it had to do with getting the best designs in the shortest time. Your kind of person works best when you think you're in charge: you're more creative and you work harder. I have a lot riding on this—"

"More than you have on our being together."

"What the hell does that mean?"

"You could have told me. If you'd cared about how I felt, you would have explained it to me and I would have understood. I know a good deal about business; I spent a lot of my life dealing with businesspeople. But even if I hadn't, you owed me the courtesy of telling me what you were doing. And I would have thought you'd want to share your thinking and your worries with me—"

"I don't share my thinking with people who work for me."

Claire pulled away from him, her eyes furious. "I work for Goddard Designs. At the moment, you're a—"

"Goddard Designs?" He chuckled. "Do you really need that, Claire? Is it to compete with me? You don't have to be a business; your work is excellent and you're an extraordinarily lovely woman, and none of that would be helped by a corporate logo."

"At the moment, you're a client," Claire went on. She knew she was being reckless, but having created a company out of thin air in the last twenty seconds, and suddenly feeling excited about it, she had to defend it. "And if I decide I have time to take on other clients, or if I decide to hire a staff, that's what I'll do. We don't even have a contract, Quentin."

His amusement was gone. "Has one been necessary?"

"No, of course not." She cringed inwardly as she saw his face darken. "And it's not now. But I have to think about . . ."

"What?" he demanded when she fell silent.

"Having something to focus on," she said at last.

"You have me. You have your friends and your home and your daughter. You're comfortable enough to make work a pastime instead of a daily drudgery. Why can't you learn to live like a woman with money?"

Claire gazed into the fire. The flames were low, curling long fingers around the remnants of logs. "It isn't drudgery. Someone told me, just this morning, that writing is a leap of faith and a declaration of love. I didn't realize it until he said it, but that's what design is, too."

"I have no idea what you're talking about."

"I'm sorry to hear that. You don't feel something like that in your work? That you're creating something new, with a kind of commitment that is like passion?"

"I wouldn't use those words for it."

"No," Claire said softly. "I can see that."

"Do you lack for passion in your life?"

Claire sighed. There was only one acceptable answer to that. "Of course not, Quentin."

He put his arm around her again. "If you insist on forming your own company, we can work it out so that it's satisfactory to both of us, perhaps as a subsidiary of Eiger Labs. We'll deal with it tomorrow. Now I want to introduce you to these people, and I want to leave right after dinner; I want to be home, with you."

Claire rested against him briefly. She wanted that, too. But it would not last. She knew it would not because her sexual desire was so deeply entwined with the mindless comfort she still found in his authoritarianism that she knew as soon as she rebelled against his authority that desire would vanish. But for now, she could not ignore it, or even diminish it.

Emma and I, she thought; and wondered if Emma realized what had happened to her with Brix: that she was caught with a man who seemed so powerful she could not escape her own desire and so became submissive. I have to talk to her about it, Claire thought. But she knew she could not until she had broken away from Quentin.

That's what I have to figure out how to do, she told herself as they joined the party in the living room. But first, tomorrow morning I'm going to form Goddard Designs, Incorporated, and it won't be a subsidiary of anything.

12

EMMA saw Brix watching from the doorway and her heart leaped. Her body leaned toward him. "Hey," Tod Tallent said.

"I'm sorry," she murmured, and resumed her pose, leaning back on her hands, her long legs stretched out, her head thrown back and her eyes closed, as if soaking up the sun. She was wearing white shorts and a white bikini top and she sat in a circle of blinding light.

"Nice," Tod muttered, circling her. "Okay, Emma, that's it. The last shoot of the campaign, unless somebody has a brilliant idea and we start again. You've been terrific; I hope we work together again sometime."

Emma stood and hugged him, catching him unawares. "You're so nice, Tod. Thank you for being nice and making me look good."

"Sweetheart, *you* made *me* look good. It's been a blast. You'll be on the road in January, right? Personal appearances and all that?"

"I don't know. I think so. Nobody's said anything definite."

"Well, whatever. You'll do great. I guess you want to get going."

Emma blushed because she knew he had seen her glancing at Brix, longing to go to him. "It's just that—"

"No sweat, it's okay. Listen, Emma, before you go."

"Yes?" she said when he paused.

"You need an agent. You're going to be too big to handle this yourself, even if it's you and your mother doing it."

"Too big?"

"Hale's been getting calls. Ralph Lauren. Donna Karan. One or two others. These are not little ma-and-pa outfits, as you well know; these are major players, and they're interested in you. They know you've been getting mail; they know all about you. Plus, what do you do when Eiger offers you a contract?"

"Are they going to?"

"That's what I hear."

"How do you—"

"I listen. You wouldn't believe how much I hear. People think the guy with the camera is deaf, like all my faculties are tied up in the viewfinder; it's very weird. Anyway, I just thought . . . you know, a suggestion . . ."

"Hale didn't tell me about Ralph Lauren or Donna Karan, or anybody."

"Well, maybe I'm wrong. Ask Brix; he knows about it. Good-bye, sweetheart; you take care of yourself."

Emma stood still, frowning, when he left. Brix crossed the empty room and stood close to her, running his hands over her warm, bare arms, her back, around her waist. He slid his fingers inside the bikini top and held her breast. "Emma, you are one fantastic girl. I just about went crazy, watching you."

He put his other arm around her, pulling her roughly to him, and kissed her, holding her so tightly she could barely breathe. Emma's skin prickled beneath his tweed suit, her bare toes pressed against the glossy shine of his shoes, her fingers lay along the starched crease of his shirt collar. She felt embarrassed by being almost naked while he was so completely and professionally clothed and she opened her eyes, confused by too many sensations. "I have to get dressed."

"No, come over here." His voice was thick. "You can't leave now. You drove me crazy, you know, the way you were coming on to Tod . . ." He pushed her onto the couch in the corner of the studio and pulled off her shorts and underpants, ignoring her hands, fluttering uncertainly against his chest, and her bewildered eyes. "You don't know how you look, what it does to people," he muttered. He unzipped his pants and lay on her and then was inside her.

His belt and open zipper cut into Emma's skin, shattering her arousal. He had never made love to her with his clothes on, and she did not know what to do with her hands; it seemed wrong to embrace his suit jacket, it made her feel even more embarrassed at her nudity, and wicked, as nothing else had. When he groaned, much more quickly than usual, and lay still, she was grateful because she knew he would move off her. She had never before wanted Brix to go away from her.

He did not look at her when he stood up, and his back was to her as he zipped his pants and tucked in his shirt and adjusted his jacket. "Going back to work," he said. "I'll see you later."

Slowly, Emma sat up and pulled on her underpants and shorts. *He's ashamed because he couldn't stop himself,* she thought. She felt sad for him, as if he were a child who had had a tantrum. It was the first time Emma had ever thought of Brix as younger or weaker than she was.

But he can't be weaker; he's the strongest person I know. He takes care of me and I need him. She went to the dressing room to change into her clothes for the evening. *What happened this afternoon was something that never happened before and won't ever happen again,* she thought. *So we won't talk about it. We'll forget it happened. It doesn't mean a thing.*

She drove to Eiger Labs, but when she walked into the building, she stood in the lobby, undecided, suddenly reluc-

283

tant to see Brix right away. Instead, she went looking for Gina.

"Just in time for tea," Gina said. She gave Emma a hug and then held her away from her. "You look a little down."

"Oh, I guess I am. We finished the PK-20 photo shoots today and I feel sort of sad." As she said it, she realized it was true. Brix had not given her a chance to think about it, but now it struck her: she had no more work to do. Even if they decided to send her to stores to promote the line, that would not be until January, and it was only the middle of November now. "I guess I feel like nobody needs me."

"I know the feeling. But it's not true, you know; you've still got a job. And you deserve a rest; they've been working you awfully hard."

Emma shook her head. "It was wonderful. And it kept me busy."

Gina handed her a mug of tea. "I checked out those test reports, Emma. There aren't any problems; nobody had any kind of bad reaction, Latin or otherwise, and there wasn't a word about blindness. Are you sure you read those memos right?"

"Of course I am. Well, I think I am. I mean, I was kind of in a hurry, but I know I saw something about somebody going blind in one eye, because it was so awful, and I didn't dream up any Latin words, and I didn't make up conjunctivitis, either."

"Well, you've got me. Kurt Green, he's the head of the testing lab, showed me the cumulative reports on all the tests they've done so far, and they were perfect, no red flags, nothing. Of course I didn't look at the individual tests—there are thousands of them—and I couldn't spend too long on the ones he did show me because all I'd told him was that I was curious about how PK-20 was shaping up, but if there'd been a problem, it would have shown up on the cumulatives. In fact, that's where problems show the most, because the numbers are bigger."

"Somebody changed them," Emma declared.

"Ssshhh, bite your tongue. It's a criminal offense and you don't want anybody around here doing that. It could sink the whole line, not just the eye cream, and at this point that could sink the whole company. Nobody would take that risk."

"Well, I know what I saw," Emma said stubbornly. "I didn't dream it. What are you going to do now?"

"There's not much I can do. In the first place, I never had anything to do with PK-20, and I can't start asking questions or demanding to see more data now, assuming there is any. But the main thing is, Emma, I don't expect to be here much longer."

"You're *leaving?* Why? Because you think the lab is in trouble? It might close down?"

"No, there's no reason to think that, Emma; I'm leaving because I've found something better. And listen, I haven't told them yet, so I want you to keep this quiet."

"Well, I will, but where are you going?"

"Someplace where I can do work I like better than being a lab technician."

"The horses!" Emma exclaimed.

"You've got it. At least, that's part of it. There's a six-hundred-acre farm there that needs managing; I'll be helping with that, too. And we're planning to manage some of the farms nearby that are owned by New Yorkers as a hobby, so they can have a place for weekends."

"That's nice." Emma's attention was wandering; it was hard for her to concentrate on anything but Brix for very long. He'd been telling her lately how important he was to the company these days; how his father trusted and needed him and wouldn't even be able to release the PK-20 line without him. But what if Quentin was getting Brix involved in something so he could blame him if anything ever went wrong?

I've got to find out, Emma thought. Brix would never think of that on his own.

"Gina, I have to go," she said abruptly. "I'm meeting Brix; we're going to dinner."

Gina leaned forward and kissed her cheek. "Have a good

time. And don't worry about those memos; there's probably a simple explanation somewhere. And I'll do a little quiet scouting before I leave, okay?"

"Okay."

"And I'll see you on Thanksgiving."

"Oh. I hadn't thought about Thanksgiving. Is Mother having a lot of people?"

"Well, you could ask her, of course, since you live with her, but as long as you're here, I'll tell you that she's not. Just the three of us, as usual, and Hannah."

Emma nodded, thinking about Brix again as she walked away. I have to help him, she thought; I have to protect him.

Unless I'm wrong. I don't really know anything about his work; he doesn't want me to. I might make him really angry if I ask him anything.

But what if he's in trouble and doesn't know it? Then he'd be so grateful, and he'd love me more than ever.

"He's with Mr. Eiger, but you can wait in his office; he'll be back any minute," Brix's secretary said, and once again Emma found herself standing next to Brix's desk, alone. There were papers on it, some of them sticking out of folders, but she looked away from them; she already had too many things to think about. If I had a drink, I could relax, she thought, and walked around his desk to the small cabinet near his chair and took out his bottle of Scotch. He won't mind, she thought; he likes me to drink. She poured a small glass and closed her eyes and gulped it down. Fingers of warmth spread through her and she poured just a little more. It would be all right to talk to him, she thought; whatever she told him, he'd understand, because he loved her. She wished she had some cocaine because that was what made her feel best of all, but she did not know where he kept it in his office, and anyway, she always felt strange doing it alone; the few times she'd done it in her bedroom she'd been scared and ashamed, and she almost never felt that way anymore when she was with Brix.

"Fix me one, too," Brix said, coming in and closing the

POT OF GOLD

office door behind him. "Christ, he's loaded for bear today; I don't know what the hell's wrong with him. Everything's bad until somebody convinces him it's okay."

"Somebody meaning you?"

"Well, right, he listens to me. Most of the time. Shit." He drained the glass Emma gave him and held it out to her for more. He had forgotten what had happened that afternoon, Emma thought; if he really had been embarrassed, he certainly wasn't anymore. Maybe she had imagined it. Maybe she had imagined the whole thing. Sometimes, when she was drinking and doing coke with Brix, she wasn't sure what was real and what wasn't. Brix swirled the drink in his glass. "I know he's uptight about everything going on schedule for the PK-20 release, but he's on everybody's back and it's driving people crazy. It's driving me crazy."

This isn't the time; he's not in a good mood; don't bring it up. But I have to; what else can I do? "Brix, I have to ask you something."

He took the bottle from her and sat in his chair, leaning back and putting his feet on his desk, pushing aside a stack of folders. "You look cute; is that a new dress?"

"Yes. Brix, there were some—"

"Come over here, you're too far away." He straightened up in his chair. "I don't like it when I can't feel you."

Emma sighed. His lap was her favorite place in the world to sit, but she had to talk to him. She sat on his strong thighs, her back straight, but he pulled her against him and ran his hand up her leg, beneath her dress. "That's better. You know, I may keep you right here; it would make this place a lot more interesting. Would you do that? Sit here all day and keep me feeling good while I get all my fucking work done? Well, what the hell," he said when Emma was silent. "Nice idea, but the lady isn't interested. So where do you want to go for dinner? I thought the Silvermine; you haven't been there."

"Wherever you want. Brix, one time when I was waiting for you in here, there were some memos on your desk and I . . . read them."

He shook his head. "Jesus, Emma, how many times have I told you to keep your pretty nose out of business? So what did you think? Did you understand the formulas? Or were they marketing plans? Then you probably read about yourself, our dynamite little Eiger Girl. *My* dynamite little Eiger Girl." His hand moved between her legs, sliding on her nylon hose, higher and higher, pressing into her.

Already flushed from the drink, Emma felt herself grow hot and limp. She struggled against it. "No, Brix, listen, this is important. They were about some problems with PK-20, the eye cream, an ingredient in it that caused conjunctivitis and some other thing, some Latin words, and . . . and somebody who went blind in one eye . . ."

Brix's hand had stopped moving. "You didn't tell me."

"No, I thought—I wasn't sure—"

"Those were confidential; what the hell were you doing reading confidential memos on my desk?" He took his hand from under her skirt and sat back. Emma, perched on his thighs without support, suddenly felt ridiculous. She stood up and walked to the chairs on the other side of the desk. With that expanse between them, Brix reminded her of his father.

"I'm sorry," she said. "I didn't mean to read them, I mean, I just happened to see them and when I saw they were about PK-20—"

"You 'just happened' to see them? Bullshit. You were spying."

"I wasn't! Brix, why would I?"

"Who've you talked to about this?"

"What?"

"Talked to, Emma, talked to. Girls can't keep things to themselves; they like to be little messengers, running around telling everybody what they see, being important." He stood and leaned over the desk, resting on his hands, thrusting his face toward her. "Who've you talked to about those memos?"

"Nobody." Emma blurted out the word before she had time to think. She stared at Brix's furious face and thought he might strike her; for the first time, she admitted to herself that she was afraid of him.

"You're lying."

"I'm not, Brix; really, it's true." She was trapped, now, in her lie; she stared wide-eyed and fearful at the dark rage in his face and knew she could never retract what she had said. She could not tell him she had lied, and she could never tell him about Gina. "I didn't run around, I didn't think I was a messenger, I just—" Suddenly, through the fog of alcohol and fear, it struck Emma that they were talking about the wrong thing. The question wasn't whether she had told anyone, it was whether those memos were ... "They weren't right, were they?" she asked abruptly. Brix was scowling, deep in thought, and she spoke more loudly. "It's not really dangerous, is it, Brix? PK-20? I didn't see how it could be, but—"

"Keep your voice down! Of course it's not dangerous, for Christ's sake, are you out of your mind?" He walked around the desk to stand over her. "You little fool, sneaking around here ... I got you this job; you're only here because of me, and I could get rid of you just as fast."

"Brix, you wouldn't! I didn't do anything, I was just waiting for you and I—"

"Why were you in here? You could wait in the reception room like everybody else; who the hell do you think you are, waltzing in here anytime you want?"

"But I'm not 'everybody else,' Brix; we're together!" She was looking almost straight up at him, and from that angle he seemed huge and menacing, as if he could bend down and crush her and she would disappear forever. "Brix, could we just forget this? I wouldn't have said anything, but I was—"

"No, we can't forget it; what the fuck do you think I am? I find somebody sneaking around the company, reading confidential memos, and you want me to forget it? I'm not sure I want you working here anymore; I don't think it's good for the company to have you wandering around, spying on us,

JUDITH MICHAEL

and I sure as hell don't want a girlfriend who's sneaky and disloyal—"

"Brix, please, please don't." Emma tried to take a breath, but it caught in her throat and she began to cough and cry at the same time. "Don't make me leave, please let me stay, I'll do whatever you want, Brix, please . . ."

"How do I know you'll do whatever I want? Jesus, I can't trust you for a minute. I thought you loved me, but then you come spying on me—"

"I wasn't! I do! I do love you, Brix, you know I do, I love you and I'd do anything for you."

"Sure, like fuck me up with my father."

"I didn't! I don't know what you're talking about." Crying wildly, Emma slid off the chair and crouched beside his feet. "Brix, don't send me away, please say I can stay, please, please, please . . ."

"For Christ's sake, Emma, shut up, they can hear you all the way to New York." He looked down at her crumpled form, her face hidden, her red-gold hair spread on his carpet. He felt a moment of wild exhilaration at her abject surrender, but it was gone as quickly as it came: he had his own fears to deal with. "Get the hell off the floor," he said harshly. He gripped her arm and pulled her up until she was in the chair again. "Shit," he muttered, and sat on the edge of his desk, his foot swinging in an arc.

Emma took long ragged breaths, gulping air. She wiped her cheeks with her palms and watched Brix. His head was down, as if he were concentrating on his swinging foot; his hands gripped the edge of the desk. And suddenly, through the turmoil inside her, Emma thought, *he's afraid. He's doing this to me because he's afraid. Fuck me up with my father.* He was afraid of Quentin, afraid that Quentin would find out Emma had read the memos, afraid he would be held responsible. Especially, she thought, if the memos told the truth. But she could not face that possibility now. Now she had to think of Brix. Brix needed her. "I was only worried about you," she said, her voice low and shaking. "I don't care about anybody else; it was just you."

He looked up, frowning. "Why were you worried about me?"

"Because"—*oh, thank God, we're talking, we're not fighting; we're talking again*—"because you're so important." She took a breath and tried to smile, but her face felt stiff and she thought she probably looked awful, and Brix would hate that. "You're in the middle of everything because you and your father run the company . . . and I thought if something was going wrong and somebody wanted to blame somebody, they'd pick you."

"Somebody meaning who?"

"Oh, I don't know. Whoever would be . . . your father, maybe . . ."

"My father and I run this company," Brix said harshly. "You just said that yourself. He trusts me with everything. If anything goes wrong, we take care of it together. He needs me."

"I know, I know. I know how close you are and how much he needs you. But sometimes when things happen . . ." Her voice faltered, but she went on because he had to understand that she wanted to help him. "Sometimes there's trouble and somebody has to get blamed . . ."

"That isn't going to happen here; there isn't any trouble; nobody's going to get blamed."

Afraid to bring up the memos again, Emma looked at him helplessly, trying to understand. Gina had said the same thing. But if they weren't true, why would Brix be afraid?

Brix was scowling at his swinging foot, thinking. "Okay, now listen and pay attention," he said at last. "We got a couple reports on tests that hadn't been done properly. Those are the ones you saw. You got that? They weren't done right, they were done wrong. So we're doing a bunch of new tests and everything's fine."

"Oh." The word came out in a long sigh. She looked at

JUDITH MICHAEL

him searchingly. "Everything's fine." It was part question and part statement.

"That's what you can tell all your friends."

Emma looked at him with fresh alarm. "I don't talk about the company to my friends. I don't tell them anything."

"That's what you say."

She started to tremble again. "Please, Brix, don't do this again. You can trust me; all I care about is what happens to you. I want you to be all right. And us to be together." She waited, but he was silent. "Brix, are you . . . are you going to say anything to your father? Or Hale? About my being the Eiger Girl?"

"I don't know. It depends."

Emma shrank into her chair as if her body understood that it had just been put on a leash. "I'll do whatever you want. You know I will."

"You can keep your mouth shut. You can keep out of my office. Keep out of my business. Just do what you're told and we'll see how things go. Come on." He stood up and shook his pants straight and reached for his suit jacket. "Let's go to dinner."

"I don't think . . . if you don't mind, Brix, I'm not very hungry. I'd rather just go home."

"Hey, we had a date, remember? Don't pull any primadonna stuff on me. We can skip the movie if you want; I'd just as soon go back to my place early." He lifted a few strands of Emma's red-gold hair and let them fall. "It's been—what? A week?"

"Eight days."

"Well, then we've got a lot of catching up to do. Maybe you'll stay the night."

Emma looked at him dully. Her mother expected her home. After those two nights her mother had stayed out, it had never happened again, and it was as if they had made a silent agreement that as long as they lived there, they would sleep there. But if Brix wanted her to stay with him tonight, she had to do it. She could call later and say she'd had a flat

292

tire or something. *Lying again; I'm turning into a liar.* She felt a stab of despair. She did not want to lie to her mother; she wanted to love her and be loved by her with that unalloyed kind of love that mothers have, like a great velvet cape sweeping her up, surrounding her, making her feel safe and warm and so sweetly happy. Tears filled Emma's eyes again. She had always had that kind of love from her mother; she had taken it for granted. Now, she could remember it, but it seemed so far away she could not imagine ever getting back to it. Her mother was far away, too. They had lost each other. And Emma had lost her way back.

"Okay, you go wash your face and whatever, and then we'll go," Brix said, and held out his hand to her. "I'll tell you all about my quick trip to Florida last week; did you know I went scuba diving?"

Claire adjusted the light and gazed at the large sheet of paper in front of her. She was working on the last group of PK-20 packages, sketching shapes that would blend with the others she had designed. The only sounds in the room were the swish of chalk on paper, the knocking of branches against the window in the high wind that had come up earlier in the day, and music playing softly in the background. A cup of tea steamed near at hand; shapes appeared and disappeared beneath her fingers, colors merging and glowing softly in the light. She loved the feeling of dominion that came with working in her own space and creating something from nothing; especially she loved this moment of beginning, when ideas, images, memories, and feelings floated freely through her mind until, from them, order suddenly appeared, a way of showing and saying something, a shape that revealed itself as if it had just been born.

Everything should have been perfect, Claire thought, but it was not.

Emma was avoiding her, sleeping late, leaving the house when Claire was upstairs in her studio or out with friends, coming home late. They never had a conversation anymore;

when they saw each other, they exchanged a few words that had no meaning for either of them. She and Emma had lost each other, and Claire missed her. It was as if she had moved out, but it was worse than that because her ghostly presence still drifted through the house, a constant reminder of what they once had had together. At first Claire had thought that what kept Emma away was normal adolescent rebellion, delayed in her case: she had never gone through the turmoil all her high school friends had had with their parents. But now Claire had begun to think there was something very wrong in Emma's life, something she could not talk about because she was afraid or ashamed or both.

When Claire had brought home the letters Hale had given her, she and Emma read them together, amazed and touched that people would take the time to write to a stranger and tell her they thought she was beautiful—a lovely, all-American girl—and if she ever came to their town, they would like to meet her. Claire and Emma laughed together and exchanged smiles, and for a few minutes they found each other again. And then it was over, and Emma went to her room. She had no date with Brix that night, nor with friends, since all of them had left for college, but still she went to her room right after dinner and did not come out until almost lunchtime the next day.

Thinking about her, Claire had stopped sketching. When she heard footsteps on the stairs, she came back from her thoughts and looked down at her paper. In one corner a half-moon intersected a circle and a long wavy line. Claire took up a pen and outlined the shape at the intersection, then gazed at it. It was slender and graceful and she could almost feel its cool, smooth curve in her hand. A bottle, she thought, with a stopper going in sideways at the top of the half moon. She was smiling when she heard a knock at the door and turned. "Yes, Hannah," she began, and then saw that it was Alex.

"I'm sorry to bother you. Hannah told me to come up."

"It's all right." Now that she knew what her drawing

was, she was anxious to get back to it. "I thought you had everything you needed from me."

"So did I. But when I was writing it, a few loose ends came up. That always happens. If this isn't a good day, I'll come back."

She sighed. "Come on in; I know you have a deadline. What can I tell you?"

He shook his head. "You've got something good; you should work on it. I'll come back another time."

Claire's eyebrows rose. "How do you know that?"

"I know the signs. When you've hit on something exciting, you should stick with it before it drifts away. I'll come back."

"Why don't you wait? You're right; I'd like to work on this a little bit, but once I have the concept, I can put it aside. Can you give me half an hour?"

"As long as you want. Thank you."

He took an art magazine from the bookshelves and sat in the armchair, turning the pages quietly. When she looked up from her drawing, Claire saw his strong profile, the firmness of his mouth, the comfortable stillness of his tall body filling the deep chair. He seemed at home and she found herself with a different feeling about her studio: her sense of dominion was the same; it was still her space where she created from her own ideas, her own self, but now it was shared. Not invaded, she thought, but occupied in a way that was neither threatening nor competitive. She smiled to herself because it was pleasant, and she worked in silence for almost an hour. "Now," she said at last. "What can I tell you?"

Alex put away the magazine and took out a small notebook. "Emma told me about your first shopping trip; she said the owner tried to make her feel young and stupid, and you stopped it and she thought you were wonderful. Could you tell me about that?"

"She said she thought I was wonderful? What a long time ago that seems."

Claire sat on the couch and told him about shopping at

Simone's. "But please don't use the name of the store; there's no reason to. They're all the same; salespeople, even owners like Simone, don't like customers who seem to have no money because they're afraid they'll spend a lot of time for nothing. I understand that, but it's still atrocious to categorize people by whether you'll make money off them or not."

"Aren't some of your new friends the same way?"

"In a way. Most of them don't think about making money off the people they meet socially, but some of them do rate people by money or notoriety. At benefits they talk about 'A' tables and 'B' tables, meaning where the famous or chic or rich will be sitting, so they can sit with them and not get stuck with people who don't impress them."

"Does that make you angry?"

"Angry enough that I'm beginning to want to stay away from them and their 'A' tables. But it makes me sad, too. I don't like categories anyway, and when they're based on money, they reveal such a poverty of spirit that it's very depressing."

"What else is depressing?" Alex asked, almost offhandedly.

Claire looked at him in surprise. "Why do you think something is?"

"I think you're feeling melancholy about something. It has nothing to do with this article, so of course you don't have to talk about it."

Claire gazed at him. Having been with Quentin for several months, she was not used to a man who was sensitive to her feelings. "I'd rather not. Do you have any other questions?"

"A couple." He glanced at the notebook in his hand. "You said you'd be doing some volunteer work as soon as your life got organized. Are you doing any?"

"Not yet." She told him about the after-school art and design classes she would teach in nearby schools after the first of the year, and about the students who had already signed up for them. "I've never taught; I'm looking forward to it."

POT OF GOLD

"I taught for a few years, in New York. I liked it a lot, but I was frustrated a lot, too. You get such a sense of how much you can accomplish, and then, just as powerfully, you know how much you can't."

"Why not?"

"Because you're fighting forces that are beyond you. The kids who do best are the ones whose parents read to them and talk to them as if they're intelligent human beings, and share thoughts and feelings with them, and experiences, too: concerts, theaters, trips to the zoo, all of it. Those kids have pride in themselves, they think they can move mountains, and they soak up whatever you give them like a sponge. But kids who are parked in front of television sets or farmed out to indifferent sitters or left to roam the streets would look at those mountains and shrug their shoulders and say they can't be moved because they're too damn big. Some of those kids, with lots of attention from good teachers, move beyond that, but most of them never really believe they can be movers in the world, and so they don't believe that anything we teach will help them."

"Emma was with sitters. I worked."

"And at night, when you got home, I'll bet you read to her and talked to her and took her for walks and all the rest of it. That's all it takes, you know: a few hours a day. And I know not everybody can do it. If we had a good system of day care in this country, it would help . . ." He gave a short laugh. "I'm sorry, I didn't mean to make a speech; it's been fifteen years since I taught, and I still get wound up about it."

"I like that," Claire said, thinking of Quentin, whose passion seemed to be reserved for acquisitions and power. "I like it when people get passionate about something besides themselves and money. Did you stop teaching because you were frustrated?"

"Partly. But mostly I wanted to write and I gave myself a year to sell a book to a publisher. If I hadn't been able to, I would have gone back to teaching."

"Was that the book that won the award?"

"It was. And I never looked back."

"You don't want to go back to teaching now?"

"No, now I'm thinking of being a waiter or a longshoreman. I told Hannah all about it. Hannah is as good a listener as you."

"Hannah taught for forty years," Claire said thoughtfully. "She's never told us how she felt about it, except to say she loved helping young people when they came to her for advice. I wonder if she was frustrated."

"Probably not for long. My guess is, she'd turn a school or a town upside down to correct whatever was frustrating her. She's an impressive lady."

"She is, but I think she may be in trouble. Or maybe both of us are, because I'm paying for it." She told Alex about Forrest Exeter, who, Hannah had finally told her, wanted to build the Exeter Poetry Center, partly with Hannah's money. "And I suppose he's got other women like Hannah, elderly, maybe lonely, all eager to help him. She met him on the cruise we took to Alaska, and I'm sure she told him about my winning the lottery, and that was probably all it took for him to become her instant friend. Hannah is usually the most levelheaded person, but I'm worried about her because she really likes him. She keeps saying they're only friends, and I'm sure that's true, but he seems to be able to stir in a little romance, so she's entranced by him. He must be a brilliant actor."

"You haven't met him? After all this time?"

"She meets him somewhere or he waits outside, in his car. Either he doesn't want to meet us, or Hannah doesn't want it."

"How much have you given her?"

"Fifty thousand. Twenty-five at two different times about ten days apart. She calls it a loan, of course. But I've told her I can't loan any more without meeting him and seeing some documentation of what he plans to do with the money: blueprints, building permits, something."

He gave her a long look. "You're very generous."

"With Hannah I am. I love her and I've trusted her since we met. But I do worry. A friend of mine thinks she's being taken, and of course he could be right."

"Would you like me to look into it? I have friends at the *New York Times* who ought to know if there really is an Exeter Poetry Center on the drawing board; they might even be able to check on the financing of it. They can check on him, too."

"Thank you; yes, I would. Unless . . . I don't want to spy on Hannah."

"You've paid fifty thousand dollars for the right to find out what's going on; I wouldn't call that spying."

"Thank you," Claire said again. "And thank you for listening. You're easy to talk to."

Their talk moved to other things, their conversation easy and relaxed, as the windows grew dark and the afternoon slid smoothly into evening. "I'm sorry," Alex said at last when Claire looked at her watch and gave an exclamation of dismay, "I didn't mean to do this. I keep saying that to you, don't I? The atmosphere around here is very seductive. I'm leaving, right now."

"I guess you'd better," Claire smiled, "or I won't finish this job."

"Would it bother you if I write some of this up before I go? I didn't have my tape recorder and I'd like to get a few things down while they're fresh."

"It wouldn't bother me," she said, already moving to her worktable. "Why don't you use my computer? It uses Word-Perfect, if you're familiar with that."

He looked at the broad desk with its computer and printer, neatly organized scratch pads and artist's sketch pads, coffee mugs holding pencils and scissors, and piles of photographs and design magazines. It was a space four times as big as the one he had in New York. "It's the one I use," he said. "Thank you."

Claire sat on her high stool and looked at her drawing. The shape was still good; she still liked it. She gave a sigh of relief. Often, for reasons she had never been able to fathom, she would come back to a sketch a few hours or days after she had drawn it and find it weak and uninteresting, even though, earlier, she had thought it fine. But that did not happen today, and in two hours she had smoothed the lines, made the bottle longer, and drawn it from two different angles and from above, and another view with the stopper drawn out and placed beside it. She reached for a fresh pad of paper, and as she did so, she became aware of the quiet tapping of computer keys.

Still here, she thought, surprised, and turned around. Alex sat before the computer, frowning in concentration, glancing now and then at notes spread on the desk beside him. A pencil was stuck behind his ear. He was as absorbed in his work as Claire had been, and after a moment, smiling, she turned back to her drawing table. She felt very good. She liked the feeling of comradeship in the bright studio with the darkness outside, the energy that flowed from the two of them as they created in their different ways, the friendship of their conversation and the silent sharing of her space, even better, now that they were both working, than it had been when she worked alone and he waited for her. Still smiling, she opened out a fresh sheet of paper and bent over it, making final renderings of all the views of her new bottle in ink and watercolor.

When she was finished, she had four sheets, and she spread them out for the paint to dry. The tapping of keys had stopped and she turned. Alex was turning on the printer, and he met her eyes with a rueful smile. "I've made myself at home. I apologize again; I don't usually overstay my welcome."

"You didn't. I've enjoyed having you work here."

"Well, it's been a wonderful respite for me; I haven't had a space like this since I had a house with a separate office."

"Why don't you use it again?" Claire asked, surprising herself. Did she really want someone to share her space on a regular basis? "I know it's a long way from your home, but you're welcome to work here whenever you want, whether

I'm here or not." I guess I do want it, she thought, and thought again that he did not feel like an intruder; he felt like a friend.

Alex's eyebrows had gone up. "That's a very generous offer."

Hannah stood in the doorway. "Alex, are you staying for dinner?"

"No," he said firmly, and stood up. "I'm going home."

"You haven't printed out your work," Claire said, smiling.

He smiled ruefully and sat down again, then turned back to her. "I'd rather make a copy on a disk, if you have an extra one, and load what I've written into my computer. I'd bring it back in a day or two. Would you mind?"

"No, of course that's what you should do." Claire opened the bottom drawer of the desk and brought out a blank disk, newly formatted. "There's no rush to return it; I have plenty."

Alex nodded as he struck the two keys that recorded his text on the screen onto the disk. He removed the disk and turned off the computer. "Now I really am going. I've almost finished the article, by the way; I've written more in the last three hours than I have in a week. I should have a copy to you tomorrow or the next day."

"Dinner?" Hannah asked, looking at Claire.

"No, I'm going out. I thought I'd told you."

"You had. I thought you might change your mind."

Not a bad idea, Claire thought, and wondered what Hannah saw that told her Claire would rather stay home than go out with Quentin. She shook her head. "I'm committed for tonight. Some other time, I hope you'll stay," she said to Alex.

"I'd like that." He slid the disk and his notebook into his briefcase.

"I'll be downstairs," Hannah said. After she left, the room was quiet. Claire began to gather up her chalk and pens to put them away.

"I like Hannah," Alex said. "Whatever else she's up to, she seems to keep a devoted watch over your house."

"You're amazing. No wonder you're a wonderful writer; you see things so clearly. Yes, she watches over us. Once I called her our fairy godmother."

"I like that; we all could use one. Ask her if she has a friend." He slipped the dustcover over the computer and went to Claire. They shook hands. "I'll send you the manuscript, probably tomorrow. And I might take you up on that offer of dinner."

"I hope you do." She glanced at her neat desk. "You don't leave any sign that you were here."

"I hope I leave something behind," he said quietly. "At least friendship."

"You do," Claire said. "I'll see you out." She led the way to the hall and glanced back once before going downstairs. The studio seemed brighter than ever, for having been shared.

Gina and Roz paid for the new riding boots, and Roz looked at her watch. "We have time to buy you some riding pants. You can't keep borrowing mine."

"Why not?" Gina asked absently. She was holding up a denim, fleece-lined jacket. "This is perfect for this time of year. I have to try it on." She pulled off her leather jacket. "Your pants fit me perfectly; why shouldn't I keep borrowing them?"

"Because you need your own clothes, and you know it. If you want to ride competitively—"

"I want to be in the Olympics."

"In borrowed pants?"

Gina grinned. "Probably not. But I'd rather not spend the money right now; things are a little tight."

"For God's sake, Gina, I'll pay for them; you'll pay me back later."

"I'm quitting my job, remember?"

"And you'll be working fifty or sixty hours a week at the

farm. You're good for it, Gina. Come on; as long as we're in New York, we might as well do everything at once."

"You're right. And I want you to know that I'm having a wonderful time. Probably something like Claire and Emma, when they went on their first shopping spree. There's nothing like seeing something and saying, 'I'll take it.' I'll take it," she said to the salesclerk, holding out the denim jacket. "And could you bring me a few different pairs of riding pants to try on?" She watched the clerk walk away and leaned back against the counter. "Roz, I have a hypothetical question."

"Do you want a hypothetical answer?"

"No, I want to know what you think. Suppose you heard that something was going on that would make something else illegal, and the something else is going to happen in a few months even though the people in charge know it shouldn't happen. Are you following this?"

"So far. You don't want to make it simple and just tell me what you're talking about?"

Gina sighed. "I guess so. What if you heard there was something wrong with one of the PK-20 products, like causing severe reactions in some of the women testing it?"

Roz stared at her. "That's what you heard?"

"I heard it from someone who saw a couple of memos about test results on the eye restorative. There was semi-serious stuff like conjunctivitis, and, this is the killer, somebody went blind in one eye."

Roz shook her head. "It can't be. I would have heard. I was still with Hale when the tests were done."

Gina put out her hands. "I don't know. Either it's true, which means somebody doctored the test results, or it isn't, which means the person who told me dreamed it up. And I don't think she did."

The salesclerk returned and they followed her to a dressing room with two armchairs and a rod for hanging clothes. Roz sat in one of the chairs. "If it's true, they'd have to put off the release date until they find out what's causing the problem, and fix it."

"It may not be fixable. It sounds to me like a chemical allergic reaction. You know, like some people are allergic to peanut butter; most people do fine, but a percentage actually die from it. If that's what's happening, and if the reaction is to a key ingredient, maybe even the proprietary one, they'd have to scrap the whole line and start from scratch. Do you see Quentin doing that?"

Roz looked at Gina. "You think it's true."

"I lean that way. On the other hand, I saw the cumulative test reports and they didn't have a single word about allergic reactions."

"So it isn't true."

"Well, that's the problem. It is or it isn't." Gina stepped out of her slacks. "Which one should I try on first?"

"The black. Very classy. How could you find out?"

"I haven't the faintest idea. I thought you might think of something."

"Is anybody talking about changing the release date? Or not releasing the line at all?"

"Not a soul. They're going ahead full steam. You never heard anything?"

"I'm not part of their inner circle anymore. They've all decided Hale got a rotten deal."

Gina met her eyes in the mirror. "I'm sorry."

"It's okay. I expected it, and most of them I won't miss. I'll miss Quentin; he's such a cold, calculating son of a bitch he always makes me feel better about my life, just because I've got room for love in it."

"He doesn't?"

"Not that I've ever seen. Though maybe he's different with Claire; he hovers a lot when they're together. Is she in love with him?"

"She says she's not, but she seems to be fascinated by him, probably because he's so different from anyone she's ever known. I think I'll take these."

"Good. Now try the brown. He's got a lot of charm, when he wants to use it. Get him talking about his travels and he's wonderful; he's been everywhere and he's got a good eye and he doesn't forget anything he's ever seen. But he makes his own world, and the people who want to be close to him have to follow his rules or they're out."

"Would he release the PK-20 line even if some of it might be dangerous?"

Roz was silent. "Sure," she said at last. "He makes his own rules." She watched Gina try on the other pants. "I suppose I could talk to Hale, but he'll guess it came from you."

"You can't do that," Gina said swiftly.

"Why not? They're not going to come after you, like the Mafia or something."

"I don't know what they'll do; you just said Quentin makes his own rules."

"Gina, they wouldn't do anything to you. Why would they?"

"It's not me." Gina hesitated. "I hadn't even thought of this, but I don't like what I'm thinking. Look, the person who told me about the memos was Emma—she saw them on Brix's desk one day when she was waiting for him—and if they think I'm involved, they'll get to her; they know how close I am to her mother, and to her, and how else would I know about it? I've never been involved with the PK-20 line. So, if Brix thought Emma had seen the memos, and told me, or anybody, about them, would she be in danger?"

"No, of course not. They're businesspeople; they don't go around knocking off people. Anyway, whatever Emma saw might not be true. Maybe somebody made a mistake and saw problems where there aren't any. If the reports are fine, doesn't that settle it?"

"It ought to." Gina stepped into her skirt and tucked in her blouse. "And maybe it does. You could be right; lots of times the people who run tests come up with different interpretations of the data."

"What happens then?"

"They run more tests or they get more people to read the

JUDITH MICHAEL

data and see what interpretations they come up with. Testing is tricky, you know, because your subjects don't live in sterile glass bubbles: all the time they're using your new product they're eating and drinking and washing themselves and putting on makeup and traveling God knows where, with what kinds of pollution . . . you just can't control what they do and you never know how much of that affects their reaction to your product."

"So why were you so worried?"

"Because." Gina pulled on her suit jacket and picked up her raincoat. "Because everybody who watches television or reads a newspaper has heard about corporate cover-ups—Ford, Dow, GM—and for every one we hear or read about I wonder how many hidden ones there are, that never get found out."

Roz thought about it. "You said they run more tests. Are they running more tests on PK-20?"

"Emma says Brix told her they are."

"Then it sounds like they're taking care of it. I don't think you should do anything. Are there some people in the lab you can call after you've left, to find out the results of the new tests?"

Gina nodded. "I can keep up with things pretty well. That's what I'll do. And I might nose around a little bit before I take off. I have to be careful, though. If it weren't for Emma . . ." She shook her head. "I can't take that risk."

They left the dressing room. "But listen," Gina said. "If I hear anything else, I'm going to have to find a way to blow the whistle on those guys. I have a responsibility to do that; I can't just turn my back. Except, what do I do about Emma?"

"She can hide out on the farm," Roz said as they walked to the sales counter. "But it won't come to that; I can't believe it would. I love you, Gina, and I love your imagination, but this time you've gotten carried away by it. This whole business is one of those things you read about and see on television; it never happens to anybody you know."

13

"So much to be thankful for," said Hannah, carving the turkey. She stood at the head of the table, her face flushed from bustling about in the warm kitchen since early morning. With a neat stroke she severed the drumstick and laid it on the silver platter. "Claire won the lottery, and now she has her own company, and Emma's started a brilliant career, and we have this splendid house, and we've added Gina and Roz to our family."

"And Hannah came to us," Claire said.

"Well, yes, absolutely." Hannah's crinkly face beamed. "I've never had such a Thanksgiving, with so many good things all at once."

"I'll second that," said Gina. "I want to propose a toast to—"

"Oh, wait until I've finished carving," Hannah said. "Only a few more minutes. And I forgot the corn bread; it's in the oven. Would somebody—"

"I will," said Claire, and went to the kitchen.

Gina followed her, letting the door swing shut behind her. "I wanted to get you alone for a couple of minutes; it's been so long since we had some time together."

"Not since the horses won you over," Claire said, smiling.

"Well, that's what I wanted to talk to you about; I wanted to tell you before we tell anyone else. There's a lot more going on than the horses."

Claire nodded.

"What does that mean? You nodded."

"Gina, why don't you just tell me what you have to say? I think I know, but I might be wrong."

"You're not usually wrong about people. Well, the thing is, Claire, it's not just the horses and it's not just that wonderful farm. It's Roz."

"Yes," Claire said.

"So it's not a big surprise." Gina looked at her hands, then opened them out. "I didn't know. Honest to God, Claire, all these years, I never knew. I would have told you if I had; of all people, I would have wanted to be honest with you. But all I knew was that I didn't want to get married—I couldn't even imagine being married—and I was always happier alone than dating. I hated dating. Everything about it made me feel like I was in the wrong place. You knew that; I've told you often enough. I thought it was just that I was dating the wrong guys, but there never was a right one, somebody I could just relax and be comfortable with. I thought it was something I'd grow out of, or I'd wake up one day and find I was like everybody else I knew, but nothing changed, and finally I thought, well, what the hell, I wasn't meant to be married; lots of people are happily single all their lives. And I had you and Emma for my family, and that was enough for me. At least, I thought it was enough for me, until I met Roz."

"Claire?" Hannah called. "Is something wrong with the corn bread?"

"Our drill sergeant," Gina said with a grin. "Listen. You did figure it out, right? I mean, it's not a shock?"

"Of course not. I was wondering when you'd get around to talking about it."

"I was going to, that night at Roz's, when she told you she was divorcing Hale, but we just weren't ready. But now—"

POT OF GOLD

The door swung open and Hannah marched in. "If there's a problem with the—oh, I'm sorry, I didn't mean to interrupt."

"We were just talking," Gina said. "Everything's fine. I'll get the bread." She took the covered basket from the warming oven and followed Claire and Hannah into the dining room. "Shall I pass this?"

"Yes, and now we'll have a toast," Hannah said when Gina was seated. She held up her glass of vodka and waited for the others to lift their glasses of wine. "I'd like to say, for myself, first that I'm very glad to be here, and second that it is a new and most enjoyable experience to have a women's Thanksgiving. At first I thought we would be sadly dull without men, but I couldn't think of any we might have. Quentin and Brix are out of town; Hale and Roz have gone separate ways; and Forrest is with his family on Long Island. Alex of course is with his sister's family, and who knows if he would have accepted in any case? But I need not have worried. We are a congenial and merry group with much to talk about and much to be thankful for, and that's Thanksgiving in a nutshell. And so I drink to our small and happy family."

"I like that," said Claire. "There's no other place in the world I'd rather be, tonight, and there are no other people I'd rather be with."

Emma took a sip of wine. Something was happening as she sat there: she was feeling better than she had for weeks. It was as if a weight had been lifted from her, and she felt cozy and warm and safe. Snow had fallen during the day and had begun again just before they sat down to dinner; Emma could see large lazy flakes against the window, and she imagined them piling up outside like a stockade, higher and higher, keeping them safe from danger. Looking at the festive table Hannah had set with a fine linen cloth and tall white candles in French ceramic holders, and small bunches of chrysanthemums at each place, Emma felt a sudden, piercing love for her mother and her home. She missed Brix the way she always did when she was not with him, but today, for the first time, she had to admit that it was a relief to be away from him. Like being on vacation, she thought ruefully.

She was so ashamed of the way she had crouched at his feet that she could not bear to think about it; she kept pushing the memory away whenever it flooded in upon her. But the worst part of it was that she knew she would do it again, or whatever it took, if he once again threatened to send her away, and that made her feel helpless and angry at herself. Sometimes she even hated herself. And tonight it made her dread tomorrow at the same time that she couldn't wait for tomorrow.

But right now, this moment, while she sat here amidst the comforting smells of turkey and corn bread and pumpkin pie, with the reds and yellows of the chrysanthemums shining up at her like tiny suns and the candles casting a flickering glow on the loving faces around her, Emma felt as if she were suspended for just a little while in a quiet place where she was light and relaxed and young. Hannah was right: it was nice, sometimes, to be just with women. "I have a toast," she said impulsively. "To my mother because I love her, and to Hannah because I love her, too. And a special toast. To Gina and Roz."

"My goodness," said Hannah.

"Thank you, love," Claire said to Emma. "You know I love you, always, more than anyone."

"Well, thanks," Gina said to Emma. "Is there any special reason for that special toast?"

"Oh, you're so silly." Then, abruptly, Emma blushed. "I mean . . . am I wrong? I just assumed . . . you both look so happy, you know . . ."

"The new generation," Roz murmured. "No, you're not wrong, Emma, you just took us by surprise."

"Well, you've sort of left a trail," Emma said, "haven't you? I mean, isn't Gina living at the farm? Or almost? And you're divorcing Hale, and you've been married to him forever and then all of a sudden . . ."

"Not quite forever, though sometimes it felt like it," Roz

said. "It wasn't a good marriage; it was just going along, waiting for one of us to end it. Hannah, this is a wonderful dinner. Thank you for including me."

"How do you do that?" Hannah asked. She carefully did not look at Emma. "The world is full of bad relationships that need ending. How do you make the decision?"

"Well, when it's bad enough it almost makes it for you." Roz gazed through the dining room arch into the living room where clusters of lighted candles on the mantel and on all the tables cast dancing shadows on the walls and ceiling and were reflected in the high windows. "I suppose I might have stayed with him for years, maybe forever. We got along okay: we always had a lot to talk about, we agreed pretty much on how to bring up the kids, and when they left home, there were things we liked to do together. And I gave him lots of ideas for his ad campaigns and he's been grateful for them. Sex isn't a problem because we haven't had it for years; he likes his women very young and very blond with no hips, and that is definitely not me. And, you know, when you're busy doing things you like—I was riding in competitions and running the farm, which is the place I love best in the world—the days kind of slide by and you don't say, 'I have to change this because it's terrible.' It wasn't terrible. But it sure as hell wasn't wonderful, either. It is wonderful with Gina."

"Everything is more fun when we're together," Gina said. "Everything *means* more when we're together." She looked at Hannah and Emma and Claire. "Both of us used to feel that we didn't have anyone to belong to. That's over with. We're not lonely anymore."

"That's so neat," Emma said wistfully.

"There are dozens of kinds of love," Hannah said, "but the only one that is inexcusable is the one that is a false front for cruelty or manipulation."

There was a silence. Emma looked at her plate.

"I envy you," Claire said quietly. She stood up and kissed Roz and Gina. "I've never heard a better description of the kind of relationship everybody dreams about. And I wish you much happiness."

"Thank you," Gina said. "Thank you, thank you. I was sure you'd say that, but, still, you know, there was a ..."

"Small question mark," Roz said. "Thank you, Claire. Thank you, Emma. I can think of a lot of people who probably won't be so generous."

"It doesn't matter," said Gina. "You're the ones we really care about. I mean, everybody will know, of course, it's not a secret—"

"But we're not going to march in parades or anything like that," Roz put in. "This is our private life and we're keeping it private."

"But we wanted you to understand how we feel," Gina went on, "and share it with us, before people start making cute comments."

"Like Hale," Roz said. "Hale will be horrified. He'll see it as a blot on his judgment and God knows on his sexuality, and within twenty-four hours he'll be telling everyone he always knew there was something very peculiar about me and he would have left me long ago but he had to stay until the children were grown because he didn't want to leave them under my unnatural influence."

"How do you know?" Claire asked.

"I've heard him on the subject before," she said dryly, "about a few people we know in New York. But we won't be seeing him, so it's not important. I've been dropped from Quentin's charmed circle, so we'll make our social life in other places, and I've shipped everything Hale had at the farm to his apartment in New York. It's the end of a chapter. Maybe of a book."

"But it's the beginning of a new one," Emma said. "I'm really happy for you. Brix wouldn't have nice things to say, either."

They all looked at her in surprise. They had never heard her say anything critical about Brix. "Is that so?" Hannah asked mildly.

"He's not a very tolerant person." Emma heard herself in amazement. How could she do this to Brix? But it felt good to do it; it was as if she were on a roller coaster and was picking up speed and it was exciting and liberating. She knew, at the bottom, she would still belong to him, but right now it felt so good to break free that she rushed ahead. "He can't stand it when people are really different from him; he thinks they're peculiar or sick or something, and he doesn't want to have anything to do with them. And he doesn't like it when people disagree with him; he puts them down, as if they're obviously stupid."

"So do you always agree with him?" Hannah asked.

Emma flushed. "He's usually right. And . . . it's easier . . ." A look of confusion spread over her face. She felt like crying. She could not remember that feeling of excitement and freedom; she felt like a traitor.

"Tell us what it's like to be a model," Gina said quickly. "Do you work all day?"

"Mostly," Emma said, and animation returned to her voice as she spoke. She told them about Lea, who did her makeup, and about Bill Stroud and Marty Lundeen, and about Tod and the way he prowled the room with his camera. "He's always talking, the whole time he's taking pictures. I don't think his mouth ever stops. Maybe it's connected to his camera."

Claire smiled. "Talking about what?" she asked.

"Mostly it's just words. 'Nice, nice, good, sweetie, great, good, terrific, hold that, Emma, look this way, look that way, nice, nice, sit up, stretch out, good, good, great . . .'"

They were all laughing at Emma's mimicry, and Emma felt herself sink softly into the cradle of their approval, and she loved them all. Then they all began telling stories about the way people talked, at work and play, while Hannah moved around the table, serving second helpings. Claire sat back, watching Emma, wondering what was happening with her. She seemed to fade in and out, almost as if the rest of them caught glimpses of her through swiftly moving clouds. But even when she was with them, talking and laughing, her gaiety and even her beauty had a feverish quality that made her seem fragile, on the edge of collapse: as if her happiness—and she did look happy, Claire thought—was temporary and she knew it and was cramming everything into this little space of one Thanksgiving dinner.

I'll try again to get her away from here, she thought. Maybe she's ready to take a trip to Europe. Or anywhere. Maybe she won't fight me so much.

"Have you met him, Claire?" Roz asked.

"I'm sorry," Claire said. "I haven't been listening."

"Hannah's friend Forrest; she says he talks like a poet. Have you met him?"

"No. A poet? I'd like to hear that. But Hannah doesn't give us a chance."

Hannah turned red. "I know I haven't. I've been meaning to. I really don't like to be secretive, you know."

"Did you think we wouldn't like him?" Gina asked.

"Oh, dear, it sounds as if I have a beau. It's all rather awkward; that's the problem."

"Well, tell us about him," Gina said. "Even if he's not your beau, you're spending a lot of time with him, right?"

"Not so much. Oh, we're getting low on corn bread; I'll get some more—"

"Oh, no, you don't," Gina said firmly. "Come on, Hannah, out with it. Is he a con man? Does he rob from the rich and give to the poor? Does he prey on old people and get them to—oops. Sorry. Not a great thing to say. Tell us something about him. How old is he?"

"He says forty-eight; my own opinion is that he's closer to forty." Hannah was sitting very straight, her head proud, as if gathering her dignity about her as a bulwark against what they might say, and even, Claire thought, against her own doubts. "What is more important is that he is a brilliant poet and teacher; his students love him—"

"Where does he teach?" Roz asked.

"New York University. He teaches American and English

literature and poetry, but he says they're the stepchildren of our schools today and we need to pay far more attention to them. In a time of technology worship, he says, we need a place to nurture poetry and teach people how terribly off balance we've become. Instead of being awestruck by fax machines, he says, we should be awestruck by Wordsworth and Eliot and Derek Walcott. I must say, that makes sense to me; I've never felt the need of a fax machine, but I do need the beauty of poetry in my life."

"So he wants a place to nurture poetry," said Gina. "What kind of place?"

"Well, that's the exciting part. He's going to build the Exeter Poetry Center that will be a retreat for poets to do their writing, and a place for seminars and readings and conferences."

"What's he going to build it with?" Roz asked bluntly.

"Oh, he has the money. Or almost. Someone has promised him all he needs and he's found a building, an old brownstone near his university, and as soon as he gets the money, he'll begin renovating it."

"Who's the someone?" Roz asked.

"A very wealthy person who loves poetry and believes in Forrest's vision."

Gina tilted her head. "Is this person a woman?"

"Yes."

"A woman over fifty?"

"Yes."

"Sixty? Seventy? Eighty?"

"Eighty-two." Hannah hesitated. "To be honest, he does seem to be very good with older people."

"Oh, he's got men on board, too?" Gina asked.

"No. No, the truth is, he really does prefer women. But he's very straightforward and Mrs. Manasherbes knows exactly what she is doing. She has a great deal of money and no children and she loves poetry."

"And Forrest," Gina said wryly.

"She admires him and is fond of him, as I am. And as

JUDITH MICHAEL

soon as she returns from England, they'll finish their paperwork and she'll give him the money, for the center and for an endowment to keep it going." Hannah looked at Claire. "Forrest did need cash to secure the brownstone, which someone else was bidding on. Since Mrs. Manasherbes was in England, I loaned him the money, which he will repay the instant he receives the money from her."

"What if she changes her mind?" Emma asked.

Hannah's mouth tightened. She looked down, at her clenched hands, and Claire knew this was the fear that haunted her: that the money would not be given after all, and that Hannah would have thrown away fifty thousand dollars of Claire's money. "I believe she will not change her mind," Hannah said.

"Have you met her?" Roz asked. "What's she like?"

"Well, no." Hannah was uncomfortable. "I wanted to meet her but she left for England before we could arrange it."

"Keeps his women away from each other," Roz muttered to Gina.

"That is not true!" Hannah cried, her eyes blazing. "Roz, you and I have known each other only a short time, hardly long enough for you to be in a position to pass judgment on my ability to evaluate a situation and make a sensible decision."

"You're right," Roz said immediately. "I apologize."

"How much did you loan him?" Gina asked.

"It doesn't matter," said Claire. She put her hand on Hannah's. "I trust Hannah's judgment, and if she believes in Forrest, we should, too. And we'll all assume that everything will end happily. Does anyone want pumpkin pie or should we have it a little later?"

"Oh, later," Gina said. "Let's play Ping-Pong and billiards and jump rope and work off some of Hannah's elegant feast that I ate too much of."

"Let's take care of this first," Roz said, and began stacking dinner plates. Gina gathered up the wineglasses, and after a minute, as if she had faded in again, Emma jumped up to help.

Claire met Hannah's eyes. "Thank you," Hannah murmured. "I should have told you from the first, but I remembered all those people hanging around your apartment and chasing you up your front walk and knocking on your door, all of them wanting money for what they said were good causes, winners, sure things . . . and I didn't want to sound like them."

"You couldn't have sounded like them; you're part of our family," Claire said. "I wish you had told me earlier, but I'm glad you did it now. And I hope it works out, for your sake."

"And yours. And Forrest's. Life is no fun, you know, unless you take chances . . ." Hannah sat back. "Look at Emma, would you. She hasn't helped around the house for quite a while."

"Do you think it will last?"

Hannah contemplated Emma as she moved between the dining room and the kitchen, walking a little too fast, carrying too many dishes at once. At that moment, she dropped a glass and it shattered at her feet. "Oh, no!" she cried, and dropped to her knees. "Oh, no, oh, no, why did that have to happen?" She looked up, tears in her eyes. "Everything was fine, it was so fine, I didn't mean—"

"Emma, sweetheart, it's all right." Claire knelt on the floor and put her arms around Emma. "It's all right, it's only a glass, don't worry about it. Of course everything is fine; this is the loveliest Thanksgiving we've ever had. Come on now, you go help in the kitchen and I'll sweep—"

"Way ahead of you," said Hannah. She knelt beside them with a whisk broom and dustpan.

Emma went into the kitchen, her feet dragging. Claire moved out of Hannah's way and gazed absently at the brisk movement of the broom and the small pile of glistening glass shards. She heard Gina and Roz laughing, and then Emma's subdued laughter joining in. Hannah went through the swinging door and her voice joined the others, and the next time they all laughed, Emma's laugh came more easily and was clear and sweet.

Claire stood beside the window, watching the heavy, wet flakes drift past the glass. It seemed to her at that moment to be such a beautiful world, filled with family and friends, with work, with wonders she could now afford. Maybe she'd been wrong before; maybe Emma really was coming out of her infatuation; she seemed anxious to be part of the family again, to make a place for herself among them. Her mimicry and laughter, and the way she had jumped up to help clear the table, brought back the Emma of a year ago. Oh, nowhere near that long, Claire thought. I won the lottery in May. A few months out of a lifetime, and everything has gone through such changes, swinging like a pendulum, and still not settled down.

She listened to the voices from the kitchen and suddenly thought of Alex. He had called to say he was making some changes in his article and would send it in a few days. They had talked for a few minutes, and when they hung up, she felt an odd sense of loss. She had wanted to talk longer but he was working against a deadline on another article and had been almost abrupt. He was part of her new world of friends and work and wonders, and Claire wanted to know him better. Well, I've done all I can, she thought wryly; I've invited him to use my studio, and I've talked about his coming to dinner. I don't know how much more obvious I can get.

Tomorrow night she had a date with Quentin. She shook off the thought; she would deal with it tomorrow. For tonight, she wanted only to think about what she had all around her, the people she loved, the studio upstairs where she had discovered the joys of her own creativity, all the possessions she had bought, bringing the magnificence of the world into her home, and the promise of whatever else she wanted to buy and do with her newfound wealth. For the first time, she felt she was making things happen instead of having them happen to her. Alex had talked about children who believed they could move mountains. Well so can I, Claire thought. It took me a lot of years to get there, but I know I can move mountains, and anything else that's in my way.

"It's a long shot," said Alex, pushing his chair back from the desk in Claire's studio and stretching out his legs. A box of Christmas ornaments was near his feet, and he gently pushed it farther away. "My friend Stan Gabriel at the *Times* says Forrest Exeter put down fifty thousand dollars as earnest money on the brownstone. He didn't keep any of it for himself; he put it all down. But Mrs. Manasherbes, unfortunately, is something of a flake."

"You've heard of her?" Claire asked.

"A lot of people have. You don't forget the name, you know; isn't it impressive? It curls around your tongue; you can almost chew it. I love words like that. Well, her father was Hosea Manasherbes, who made a fortune in oil in Oklahoma and died in a brawl when he was forty-five. He was divorced and left everything to Edith. His daughter."

"Why is she Mrs. Manasherbes if that was her father's name?"

"Because she's never been married. She adopted the *Mrs.* when she ran the oil company; she thought people would respect her more. She was probably right. Anyway, she cultivated a personal image of eccentricity, but she ran the company better than her father and doubled her fortune. Then she sold out and moved to New York and took up a few causes that no one had ever heard of, Hannah's friend Forrest being one of them. The trouble is, she waffles on donations; she's been known to pull out at the last minute if somebody says something she doesn't like or if somebody distracts her with a new cause that demands immediate attention. And money, of course. Would you like more tea?"

"Yes, thank you." Claire watched him take their mugs to the small built-in kitchen. How quickly he had become part of the studio, she thought. He had worked there five times in the two weeks since Thanksgiving, and now she found herself missing him when he was not there, missing his silent presence when they were both working, missing their long talks when they finished for the day. "Well, there's nothing I can do about Mrs. Manasherbes," she said as Alex put her mug on the table beside her. "I have to trust Hannah. But I'm worried about her. It isn't the money; it's gone and we won't starve if I don't get it back. But Hannah cares about repaying it, and she cares about Forrest and she'd be crushed if she found he was wrong about Mrs. Manasherbes, or if—oh, could this be possible? What if he and this woman are a team?"

"They lose the fifty thousand if they don't buy the brownstone. That much sounds genuine. She has come through on a lot of causes, you know; it's just that she's not a person you'd want to bet on."

"But Hannah did."

"And so did you. Unwittingly."

"Did your friend at the *Times* find out if there's a schedule for opening the Exeter Poetry Center?"

"No, it's vague. Exeter called Stan at the *Times* about a month ago and sent him a press release—he wanted Stan to do a story, to help with other fund-raising; I don't know why; maybe he was worried about Mrs. Manasherbes—but Stan said it wasn't a story yet but he'd be interested if it ever became one. The press release didn't have dates for renovation or ribbon cutting or anything else. Are you staying here over the holidays?"

"Yes," Claire said.

"Will you have dinner with me tonight?"

"I'm busy tonight. I wish I weren't."

"Then tomorrow night."

"I'd like that."

"And what will you do at Christmas?"

"Probably duplicate our Thanksgiving dinner. We were all happy being together; it was a good way to celebrate. What will you do?"

"Duplicate Thanksgiving. I think my sister's in-laws will be there, which will swell the crowd. When I was a kid," he said reflectively, "we had upwards of fifty people for Christmas. My parents gathered in all the strays from miles around, anyone who didn't have a family, and my sister and I made name tags and played usher, getting everyone seated and making sure they had cider to drink. Nothing harder than cider; we couldn't afford it and my parents didn't believe in it. Then we'd hand out Christmas presents that my mother had made: cookies wrapped in colored tissue paper, small loaves of raisin bread in foil wrapping paper, little jars of strawberry jam with striped ribbons tied around the lids. My mother had a passion for strawberry jam. I'd listen to all those people who didn't know each other, or didn't see each other from year to year, getting acquainted or reacquainted, telling their life stories, trying to impress everyone, even though most of them were out of work or not doing the jobs they really wanted, or just divorced or whatever it was that made them eligible for my parents' table of strays. I'd wander from one small group to another as they got together in different rooms to sing carols or play chess or Chinese checkers or help in the kitchen. It was like theater; that's when I started to think about being a writer. My sister and I loved it; we got so excited we didn't calm down until halfway into January. What did you do for Christmas?"

"We went to a neighbor's house. Their son had been killed in the war and they wanted to have the house crowded at Christmas, with us and their married daughter and her family and a few others that I guess you'd call strays. It wasn't as exciting as yours sounds; when I got older, I wanted to go to my friends' houses. In fact, I begged my parents to let me go, but they always said absolutely not; we had an obligation to help our neighbors fill their house at Christmas."

"You're like that now, aren't you? You have a strong sense of obligation."

"Yes, of course. The world would be an awful place if people didn't have it."

"A lot of people don't. They make it tough for those who do. Have you finished your work for Eiger?"

"Almost. I hope I'll have a new job, or maybe more than one by the time I'm finished; I don't want to have to look at empty drawing tables. They always remind me of a cemetery. What about your work? You still haven't shown me your article."

"It's finished." He took a folder from his briefcase and crossed the room to hand it to her.

"Is this for me to keep? I'd like to read it later."

"It's yours. Change anything that's egregiously wrong and let me know, within a couple of days if possible. I have to be going; I had a dinner date with my son for tomorrow night and I want to change it to tonight."

"Will you be able to?"

"It's a school night; he won't have any other plans. Have you a preference for dinner tomorrow night?"

"You decide."

"Is there any kind of ethnic food you can't abide?"

"None. I like them all."

"An admirable woman." He pulled on his leather jacket and picked up his briefcase. "By the way, a friend of mine has a play opening in the Village next Tuesday; would you like to go? I've read it; I think it's very good, and they've got a good cast."

"Yes," Claire said. "I've never been to an opening night."

"There's a party afterward, unless that makes it too late for you."

Claire smiled. "I don't have a curfew."

"Good. Neither do I." He took her hand and held it for a moment; what had once been a handshake had become a lingering clasp of friendship. "Good-bye, Claire, and thank you once again for letting me share this wonderful place."

"I enjoyed it. It seems empty when you're not here."

He paused in the doorway. "Thank you for telling me that."

POT OF GOLD

Claire sat on her high stool for a long time after he left, gazing at the door and her cluttered drawing table and the furnishings of her studio without really seeing them. She was content to sit. She had no desire to go anywhere.

"Won't you be late?" Hannah asked, standing in the doorway. "Or aren't you going?"

"I'm going. I just can't seem to get moving."

Hannah came in and sat in one of the armchairs. "Emma left half an hour ago. She said to tell you she'll be late."

"She's always late."

"But at least she comes home. That one night—"

"She promised not to do it again. I don't think she liked it. What do you think happened at Thanksgiving, Hannah, that made her so different? I'd duplicate it, if I knew how."

"I imagine it was a little vacation from all the things that are troubling her. And I think it was a first step. Now that she's had one vacation, she's going to want another one, and she'll look for ways to make it happen."

"Speaking of vacations, I'm going to dinner with Alex tomorrow night."

"What a fine idea. It's taken you a long time to get around to it."

"Has it? I've only known him a few weeks."

"And you've been preoccupied with Quentin. Are you still?"

"Sometimes." Claire stood and moved aimlessly about the studio, trailing her hand across the small animal sculptures she had grouped on tables and windowsills. She knew she was putting off getting dressed to go out with him.

"You know, my dear," Hannah said, "by now you ought to have some very definite ideas about him. At the very least, you ought to know exactly what he wants from you and what you want from him."

"What he wants from me," Claire mused. "A decorative companion. A hostess for his parties. An intelligent, knowledgeable listener who can discuss business and politics and the arts. A woman who enjoys sex. A loyal and dedicated employee. Someone who isn't anxious to get married."

"And you're all those things."

"He seems to think so."

"And what do you want from him?"

"Now? I'm not sure. What I did want, in the beginning, was his world: different people, different lives, different ways of thinking about people and things. I didn't know how to live Quentin's kind of life. He taught me. He took me there."

"And now?"

"Now I've seen it and it's very pleasant, but there's less there than meets the eye."

Hannah chuckled. "I know all about that. I once broke off with a man because his only goal in life was making his company the biggest in town so he could swing his weight around without interference. He was rich and good-looking and knew all the best restaurants and which nightclubs had little private rooms upstairs, but there was no poetry in his heart and no music in his soul and I told him so." She nodded as she met Claire's quizzical gaze. "I think you're ready for poetry and music."

"Hannah," Claire asked, "how many of your stories are true?"

"Oh, dear." Hannah shook her head. "Why would you doubt me? Is it easier to do that than to think about breaking off with Quentin?"

"Of course not," Claire began in annoyance, but then she thought about it. She did have doubts about Hannah's stories, but why had she brought it up now? Maybe Hannah was right: maybe she had brought it up because Hannah had given her the best reason of all to break with Quentin, and she was afraid of facing it. Poetry and music, she thought ruefully. She had been with Quentin for six months. He still could arouse her with a touch or a word, but part of that, she knew, was the aphrodisiac of power: she reveled in the attention she got at his side, and it, too, was a kind of arousal. Quentin Eiger made ease and luxury and acquisition seem the natural order of things. "It's a very comfortable way of life," she murmured.

"But would you be uncomfortable without him?"

"You mean, would I miss him? I don't know. Not a lot, I think. But that doesn't mean I want to lose his particular kind of excitement." Claire sat on the arm of the chair near Hannah. "It's heady stuff to be on his side of the fence instead of the other side, watching the fun."

Hannah sighed. "I'll tell you what I think about Quentin Eiger. I'm sure he's essential to the smooth functioning of our economy, and I should be grateful to him and people like him, all those millions of businessmen with their eye on making money and swinging their weight around, because they're no doubt responsible for food being shipped so efficiently to our grocery stores, and cars and planes being built so we can whiz about the country with ease, and clothes coming from all over the world, and all the rest of it. I grant him and his kind all of that. But it seems to me there is little joy in him."

Claire sat still, staring unseeing at the black squares of her windows and the mounded snow visible on the windowsills. *Little joy in him.* And there never has been, she added silently. She thought back over the months they had been together. He was determined and aggressive, forceful, confident, and skillful in whatever he undertook, but everything Quentin did, even his lovemaking, was without buoyancy; he never really let go. All his real energy and focus, and whatever passion he had, was bound up in the drive to succeed in one sphere, and then go on to another, wider and more influential, and then another beyond that. His friends knew that; they had told her more than once. Everyone knew, and so did Claire, that Quentin was more interested in the bottom line and the horizon than in the people he carelessly gathered around him.

He knew which nightclubs had little private rooms upstairs. Yes, he knew the little secret places of the world and how to use them. He was exciting and fascinating and sexually powerful. And there was no joy in him.

"Thank you, Hannah," Claire said, standing up. "You

have a way of putting everything in perspective." She bent over Hannah and kissed her on both cheeks. "You're wonderful at that. I have to get dressed; we're supposed to be going to dinner."

"Supposed to be?"

"I don't think we'll get there. I think I'll be home very early. In fact, if you're making dinner for yourself, save some for me."

On Saturday afternoon, in mid-December, Eiger Labs sat silent and dark beneath the heavy clouds that lay low over the land. Here and there a light was on in the offices and laboratories and signs of life could be heard: the tapping of computer keys, the clink of a coffee cup, the rush of water from a faucet at a laboratory table. Gina let herself in the side door that was kept open during the day when the rest of the building was locked and made her way along a dim corridor to the testing lab. No one was there. The testing tables and the offices along one side of the large room were still and dark; they looked abandoned, as if everyone had fled. Or died, Gina thought, because there was something ghostly about the silence.

She shook herself. Enough of that; she was there to look for ... something; whatever she could find. It was her last chance before she left. Test reports, she said silently. Always kept in the same file, but maybe there's another set somewhere. If I were altering test reports, would I keep the originals? Of course not; I'd destroy them. But people don't; for some reason I don't understand, they keep them. All those executives at dozens of companies like Dow, Ford, GM, Monsanto—even a president of the United States—kept everything, even the most incriminating documents and tapes. So it's worth another look.

She heard footsteps and froze until they faded. Have to hurry, she thought, and, in the pale light from the corridor, went to the file cabinet from which Kurt had pulled the reports he had shown her. She shone her flashlight into the top drawer. The reports were still there. She riffled through the rest of the folders in the drawer, each on a different product of the PK-20 line, but no more on the Eye Restorative Cream. She opened the next drawer and then the two below that and skimmed reports on other Eiger products, documentation, interviews, analyses. But there was nothing else on PK-20.

They got rid of the originals, she thought. Or Emma misread the memos and there's no problem and never was.

She sat back on her heels, her flashlight on the floor beside her. If there were original reports that had been altered, they could be in any file cabinet in the room, or in any of the offices. It would take hours, days, to go through them. Well, if I can't find them, I can't, she thought. I don't know what else to do. If Emma weren't so sure of what she'd read in those memos . . .

The memos. Gina raised her head and looked down the length of the room, toward the corner office. Kurt's office. Kurt is the head of testing; the memos would have come from him. And Kurt is leaving, he says, for a better job, though he won't say where. Would he bother to erase everything from his computer? I'll bet he wouldn't. I'll bet he's thinking about the future, not the past. I'll bet it's all still there.

Excitement flared within her, the kind of excitement she felt in the lab when she saw that something was going to work, the kind she felt when she first rode a horse at Roz's farm, the kind she felt about Roz. There are times when we know what we're doing is right, Gina thought; the words almost sang in her head. And this is one of them.

She shone her flashlight on the floor and made her way along the side of the room, past open doors, to Kurt's office. She turned off the flashlight. The last light of the gloomy afternoon barely penetrated the room through its corner windows, but Gina could make out the computer keys, and that was all she needed.

She closed the blinds on the windows and switched on the computer, pulling up the list of files. There were over a hundred for PK-20, each with its own identification code.

"PK-20—testpre," she read, and struck a key to bring the document to the screen. It was a preliminary plan, from two years earlier, setting out the guidelines for testing all the products in the new line. In a few minutes she found the final plan, written three months later. Gina sighed. Ninety-eight files to go.

But she soon learned which ones she could skip. The code for test results was the date of the test and its sequential number in Kurt's final plan. So, since the memos Emma saw were probably written in October, when she saw them, or September, at the latest, Gina looked for the numbers 9 and 10 and a high sequential number, and those were the ones she brought up on the screen and scrolled through.

> *To: Quentin Eiger from Kurt Green. Per our discussion with Hale Yaeger, we're expanding the test on Restorative Day Cream, Restorative Night Cream, and Eye Restorative Cream to include black women, 250 from cities in the North, 150 from the South. Test findings should come in at about the same time as . . .*

Gina exited that document and brought up another.

> *. . . early tests on the exfoliant scrub indicate minor contamination, probably from the equipment; later tests, on a different unit, were clean. We should purchase a replacement for the first unit; the cost is $175,000 and I strongly recommend that . . .*

"Damn," she muttered, and got rid of that one and brought up another.

> *. . . toner A preferred by 65% of the subjects; toner B preferred by 15%; 20% did not like either one. Of those, 17% said it dried their skin. A possible solution is to make it clear rather than pale blue; women like things that look clean.*

POT OF GOLD

"What does he know about what women like," Gina muttered, and called up another file and then another. She found nothing in October, nothing in September. She went back to August and found nothing. This is ridiculous, she thought, it can't go back this far. But, doggedly, she went on, into July.

PK-20 human sensitivity tests (test #2)
The latest test results of PK-20 products confirm a 4% to 5% incidence in test subjects of allergic skin reactions. Subjects experienced some of the following: minor burning, itching, irritation, folliculitus, acneform eruptions, and allergic contact dermatitis. In addition, 1% of the subjects who used the Eye Restorative Cream experienced an allergic conjunctivitis, and one subject had a severe reaction, which resulted in blindness in one eye (Note: we may be able to show that the subject used the product improperly...)

Gina read it again. Just what Emma had said. And they knew it last July. But where's the Latin Emma said she saw? Oh, she said there were two.

She turned on the printer and printed out the memo, then turned back to the computer and went further into Kurt's test file, scanning the documents, until she came to March.

PK-20 human sensitivity tests (preliminary report)
... 4% of test subjects experienced a variety of minor allergic skin reactions. A few subjects exhibited conjunctivitis, which may have been caused by the bacteria Pseudomonas aeruginosa *or from an allergic reaction to one of the compounds in the product, either of which could cause corneal damage. The lab should have their report on the cause ...*

Still reading the memo, Gina printed it. She rummaged through the desk drawers until she found a box of blank floppy disks, then inserted one in the computer and made a copy of both memos. *In case anybody decides to erase things.* She tucked the printed copies and the disk into her shoulder bag and turned off the computer. The room was plunged into darkness. Though it was only five-thirty, it was dark outside. Getting late, she thought; what time does the maintenance staff come in? For the first time she was nervous and thought it was better not to use the flashlight; instead, she fumbled for the dustcover and fit it over the computer, ran her hands over the desk drawers to make sure they were all shut, and left the room. And only then, as she was standing in the dark, did she realize that the memos proved that the cumulative test reports she had seen were false. And there was a chance that the originals were still somewhere in the test-lab files. And a good chance, she thought, that the computer codes for the memos might be the codes for the cumulative reports.

"A few more minutes," she muttered to herself. "There's no way I can leave now." Shielding the flashlight, she moved along the ranks of file cabinets. Three of the cabinets were organized by months, one month for each drawer. Gina flipped through the folders in March, and at the back of the drawer, behind test reports on other Eiger products. she found a folder coded as the memos had been in the computer, and inside it were test reports on PK-20 Eye Restorative Cream. They were not the ones Kurt had shown her, taken from a file cabinet at the other end of the room; these showed a report of blindness in one eye of a test subject. These listed conjunctivitis and minor burning, itching, irritation, folliculitus, acneform eruptions, and allergic contact dermatitis. These were the reports Kurt had summarized in his memos to Brix.

A feeling of triumph swept through Gina. *They kept them. The damn fools kept them. Shoved them in a file and forgot about them. So why bother to make copies? I'll just take these with me.*

She slipped the reports into her shoulder bag with the memos and the disk, turned off the flashlight, and made her way back through the laboratory. As she got closer to the

POT OF GOLD

door, she could make out tables and workbenches in the pale light from the corridor, and she moved more quickly. Once outside the lab, she heard a distant voice saying good-night to someone, and a door slam. She turned to the right and almost ran to the product laboratories and her own worktable. A carton was on the floor, partially filled with the things she would take with her on Monday, when the chemists and technicians in her laboratory were giving her a going-away party. She threw her books, an empty flowerpot, and a box of pens and pencils into the carton and picked it up. Now, if anyone saw her, she had a reason for being there.

But she saw no one. She left by the side entrance and walked to the parking lot. Floodlights illuminated the few cars that were there, and Gina turned toward hers.

"Gina! Gina, hi!" She spun about, wondering if she looked guilty, and saw Emma, sitting in her car, leaning out the window.

"What are you doing here?" Gina asked.

"Waiting for Brix. We're going to somebody's party. What about you?"

He was here the whole time, Gina thought. Both of them. I was practically breaking and entering and he was here. "It's moving day," she said to Emma, gesturing with the carton. Then she thought how absurd it was to lie to Emma. "Well, not really. I came in for something else." She hesitated. "Look, do you have a minute? I mean, when does Brix appear?"

"Not for about ten minutes. I'm early. Come keep me company."

Emma had the motor running and the heater on, and when Gina sat next to her on the front seat, she closed the window against the cold mist that had drifted in. "Did you find out anything about the memos?" When Gina hesitated, she said again, "Did you?"

"I found the jackpot. The memos you saw. They were still in Kurt's computer. I've got printed copies and I've got them on disk and they're exactly what you said they were."

"Oh." Emma's breath came out in a long sigh. "That's awful, isn't it? I mean, I knew I didn't make them up or imagine them, but now . . ."

"Now it's really true. I found the original test reports, too, Emma; I've got the whole thing. And now we have to do something about it."

Emma's eyes widened. "Like what?"

"We have to tell the FDA. They can't do anything about a product until it's shipped across state lines, but I have a few acquaintances there and they could call Quentin, unofficially, and warn him that they've got evidence that could cause them to seize his shipments as soon as he makes them. He'd cancel the release if that happened. And then there's the State's Attorney. He's intensely interested in what products are on the shelves of Connecticut's stores, so I think he'd call Quentin, too, and tell him he has evidence that would not permit the product to go on sale in the state."

"Oh, no," Emma wailed. "You can't do that. Gina, he'll blame Brix; he'll take it out on him; you can't *do* that."

"How come you're so sure Brix isn't part of whatever's going on? I know you love him, Emma, but try to think past that, just for a minute. There's a cover-up going on here. Somebody altered those test reports. If Brix is really close to his old man and there's a cover-up going on, why wouldn't he be part of it?"

"He wouldn't be! I know him; he'd never do anything like that!"

"Well, I don't see how you can know that for a fact. But whichever it is, Emma, he's a big boy; he'll take care of himself. If I were you, I wouldn't worry about him. What you ought to be worrying about—"

"I do worry about him," Emma said, her voice low.

"Well, I can't help that. What you ought to be worrying about is him finding out that you saw those memos. As long as he doesn't know, you're out of it and that's the best place for you to be. You don't want him to know you have anything to do with this. Because I have to do something about it,

POT OF GOLD

Emma; I have a responsibility here, and I can't turn my back on it." Gina had been watching the door of the building, afraid Brix would find her there. Now she opened the car door. "You know, I keep imagining that whole PK-20 line in Claire's gorgeous new packaging, filling up the Eiger warehouse: all those jars and tubes and plastic bottles in their neat little cartons piling up, higher and higher, huge piles of them, like the pyramids, and everybody in the lab, from Quentin on down, just waiting for March, to sweep them onto trucks and trains and ship them all over the country. Like an invading army. And it looks as if some of that stuff is poison, at least potentially, to a lot of people. If I ignored that, I'd be as guilty as whoever ordered the test reports changed, and whoever did it, and whoever knows about it."

"Gina, listen. Nothing's going to happen until March; you just said so. So you could wait a few days, couldn't you? Brix told me there were new tests and the results were coming in and they were fine, and maybe all that old stuff—"

"Emma, there aren't any new tests; I would have heard in the lab if there were. There hasn't been a word about any more PK-2θ tests. And I've just been reading the memos."

"Did you read all the test reports? You read the memos and the old test reports, but what about new ones? Did you read those?"

"There aren't any new test reports."

"Brix said there were. You can't be sure, can you?"

"Ninety-nine point nine percent."

"That's not fair, Gina; Brix *told* me! And even if there aren't any new tests, maybe they've changed the release date and you haven't heard about it. You're leaving; maybe people aren't telling you everything. Isn't that possible? It won't make any difference if you wait long enough to make sure. Just a few days, Gina. You could do that."

"I suppose I could, but I'd be willing to bet nothing's going to change."

"Do it anyway, please, please, Gina. Just a few days. A week."

"Why should I? What's going to happen in a week?"

"I don't know. But something might."

Gina looked at her closely. "Emma, you stay out of this. Listen to me; I'm very serious. Stay out of it. I don't want you thinking you're going to tell Brix about any of this; that would not be smart."

"No. Of course not. I just think you ought to wait and give them a chance."

Gina hesitated, then shrugged. "I'll give it a week, but I wouldn't expect much, Emma. And another thing. I think we should tell your mother. There are a lot of things going on that—"

"No!" Emma shook her head fiercely. "She'd tell Quentin! You can't tell her, Gina, you can't, you can't! Please, Gina ... oh, I can't stand this. Couldn't you just not do anything for a while? I mean, just forget all of it for a few weeks or—"

"You said one week."

"Well, okay, one week. But you won't tell anybody. Promise, Gina, please promise."

"Your mother ought to know," Gina said stubbornly.

"Know what? Nothing's going to happen to me, and I don't want her to know anything about this, and I'm asking you not to tell her. I'm asking you to promise."

After another moment, Gina shrugged again. "I'll give it a week."

"Thank you." Emma leaned over and kissed Gina's cheek.

Gina put her hands on Emma's arms. "Now, listen. Tell me you heard everything I said. You may think I'm being silly, but I'm not; and I'm asking you: don't play heroine, Emma. Stay out of this. These people have a lot at stake, and nobody should know that you saw those memos or heard anything else. In fact, you should forget that you know anything about anything. If you do that, you'll be all right. Are you listening?"

Emma nodded.

"This is very serious business, you know. Okay?"

"Yes. Yes, Gina, really. I understand."

"I hope so." She stepped from the car, opened the back door, and took out her cardboard carton. "I'll talk to you in a day or two. Give my love to your mother."

Emma watched her walk to her car and drive away. But he already knows, she told Gina silently. I told him I'd read the memos; he knows all about it. And when you talk to your friends at the FDA and the State's Attorney, and they call his father, or him, he'll blame me. And he'll be right, because it's all my fault.

So I have to talk to him. I'm sorry I had to lie to Gina, but I don't know what else I could have done. Because I have to talk to him. I have to warn him about what's going to happen.

"I thought we'd have a drink here, first," Claire said when Quentin arrived.

He put his arm around her waist and kissed her. "Everyone at the lab is ready to give you ribbons and medals. You're a talented woman, Claire, and the last designs were the best you've done. They've already gone into production. How many do you still have to do?"

"Four." Shaken by his kiss, not wanting to admit that her body had clung to his as he held her, she eased away from him and led him into the library. "But I've got two I'm pretty sure of. One more week at the most."

"You've set a record." He sat on the couch and picked up a copy of the December *Vogue*. It fell open to the PK-20 ad with Emma's luminous beauty almost filling the page, dreamlike, as if seen through a mist, above a richly colored photograph of one of Claire's amber packages and two bold lines of type:

Coming in March. The revolution in banishing aging.
Reserve yours, with your cosmetics specialist, today.

"The response has been phenomenal. We're very pleased with Emma. Both of you: our Goddard women."

Claire winced, but, still looking at the magazine, he did not see her. She brought him a Scotch and put her glass of wine on the table between them. "Quentin, I'm not going to dinner with you tonight."

He closed the magazine and looked up, frowning. "You're not well? You look fine. Of course we're going to dinner. If you really aren't feeling well, we'll go someplace quiet. Come over here; why are you sitting over there?"

Her hands were trembling. This is crazy, she thought. People end relationships all the time; there's nothing to be afraid of. "I'm not going to see you again," she said, the words tumbling out. She met his hardening frown and the quick calculating look in his eyes that always appeared when he was faced with something unexpected, and she clenched her hands to hide their trembling. She made herself speak slowly. "We both had a good time and I'm grateful to you for so many things, but I don't want to go on."

"Why not?"

"Because we've done enough together. People begin to change toward each other, after a certain point; they don't think about each other in the same way they did in the beginning or behave the same way. Sometimes it gets better. With us it's getting worse."

"I don't know what you're talking about."

"I know you don't." She drew a breath, feeling unsure of herself, as she so often did beside his overwhelming solidity. He dominated the cozy room, making the furniture seem smaller, the books fading into a blurred background. Even the lamplight seemed dimmer. It occurred to her that she could stop and reverse direction; she had not said anything irrevocable. She could cling to Quentin and the life he gave her just as her body had clung to him when he kissed her. That would be the easiest thing to do. *But it won't be the easiest if I think I'm being bullied. Or if I become a different kind of person, to keep him happy.*

"I'll try to explain." Her voice was low, but in the strange frozen silence of the room it seemed loud to her, and she lowered it even more, speaking to the black mirrors of his eyes and the hard, sculpted lines of his face. "I don't want to live up to your expectations for me, Quentin; they're not the ones I have for myself. You have a slot for me that you expect me to slip into, and I can't do it."

"You mean you won't."

Her eyebrows rose in surprise. "Of course. That's what I'm talking about. You've always made rules for me, and I went along, and I suppose that makes me an accomplice, so in a way you had a right to believe you could make whatever rules you wanted. I'm sorry I gave you that impression. But even if I did, I don't like the way your rules are changing, and I want us to stop being lovers before we stop being friends."

"You've met someone else," he said.

"Oh, Quentin, you're cleverer than that." Abruptly, as she said the words, her unsureness vanished. The inanity of what he said made her feel stronger; it almost made her feel sorry for him. She sat straighter in the chair. She knew, without question, that she was doing the right thing. "I have met someone else, as a matter of fact, but he hasn't made this happen. You're the one I've been going to bed with, and wanting to go to bed with, and you're the one who's made me change. In fact, I still want to go to bed with you, but I won't, because everything else about us is wrong."

"If you want that, nothing else is important. And nothing about us is wrong. Someone's convinced you to break off with me."

"No one has," she said coldly. "Do you really think so little of me that you believe I'd send away a man I really wanted to be with, just because someone else suggested it?"

"I think you're vulnerable to suggestion. From me, from the people I introduced you to, from everyone. Everything you are today you've learned from me and the women—"

"And whose ideas did I use in my designs?" Claire asked icily.

"Your designs seem to be your own; I grant you that. I had a copyright search made and it appears that you broke new ground. I admire your talent and you know it; I haven't stinted in my praise of you. That's why you were allowed to go on with the entire line."

"You had a search—? I could have told you—"

"Why would I have asked you? Of course you would have told me you were original; what else would you have said? I needed an outside opinion and I pay my attorneys for that. You're a good designer; how many times do you need to hear me say that? But in every other way you're a follower; you're always listening to other people's ideas. You're too accessible to other people, Claire. You should hold yourself apart more. I thought I'd made you understand the value of that. But you still aren't entirely comfortable with me, or with the things I tell you, because you're not comfortable with money and what it can do."

"That's nonsense. I've been having a wonderful time. I love having money. Is it such a sign of weakness to you, Quentin, that I listen to other people's ideas? I love to find out how other people think and live and get along with each other. Are you so sure there's nothing else you have to learn, so you can shut your ears to other people's ideas? I've had a good time meeting your friends and listening to them, and I've had a good time spending money with them."

She gazed at his impassive face and wondered if he was really listening to what she was saying. "I don't like all of your friends; I don't like all the people who happen to have money. I certainly don't like what a lot of them do with it, buying rank and status and piles of possessions and helping other people with whatever they can spare after satisfying all their whims, but that doesn't mean I've been uncomfortable. I've been having fun. And that's the problem. You don't have fun, Quentin; you don't have any joy in your life. Everything you do is so . . . *heavy*, as if you're always working through the steps of some job description. Lover, host, corporate executive, master manipulator—"

"What the hell does that mean?"

"What?" she asked, cut off in the middle of her thought.

"Master manipulator. What the hell does that mean?"

"Nothing specific. Should it? But that's the way you operate: you manipulate people; you manipulate events. You set rules and you move people and events around inside them. Sometimes I feel like one of the pieces in a game of Monopoly. It's all so calculated and measured, Quentin; you don't have room for spontaneity or for trying to see the world through my eyes. That's called sensitivity, and when we met, I thought you were sensitive, but you aren't, not in the least. You just have your guidelines, your expectations, your rules. I have no control over the rules you make for yourself, or for others, but I do have control over my own life and I can get out when I think that what's happening isn't good for me. And that's what I'm doing."

She stood up. Their drinks were untouched, and she realized they truly had nothing to share: not even a final drink together. She looked at his dark, handsome face with the frown etched between his eyes. He'll get over this very quickly. I'll probably remember him long after he's forgotten me. "I'm sorry," she said. "I'm sorry if you're angry. I haven't been, for the most part, but I'm not sad, either, and maybe that's part of the reason I'm saying good-bye. We've been talking about what we had and we haven't raised our voices or shown one tiny bit of passion. No music or poetry, even at the end."

"Poetry," Quentin snorted.

"It means something to me," Claire said quietly. "But I did mean what I said about being grateful, and about being friends. I hope we will be. I just don't want us to be lovers."

"You've made that abundantly clear." He walked to the door. "What about the last four designs?"

"Oh, for heaven's sake, Quentin, you'll have them, of course. I don't see how you can even question that. I'll bring them to you within the next few days."

He nodded. "You know, Claire, there was a time when I

would have argued with you. But this childishness about rules and joy and spontaneity and . . . what was the other one? Oh, yes, sensitivity. You're crying because you want fairy tales. But that's not the way men and women come together. Of course I had expectations for you; you had your own, for me. We all look for someone to be what we want, and when we find people who seem right for us, we grab them before they disappear. I thought I'd found such a person in you. I was wrong. You'll regret this, you know. And I don't give people second chances." He turned and left.

Claire heard the front door open and shut. She stood beside her chair, listening to the silence. The library felt empty, as if a storm had swept through it and left it bare. For a brief moment she felt Quentin's body against hers, heavy, solid, a bulwark against unpredictability and uncertainty. He was like the money she had won: protection and security. But I still have the money, Claire thought; I don't need any other security than that.

In the hushed emptiness of the library, she felt a slow wave of regret. But even as it rose, it began to fade. She looked about the room and saw it slowly grow familiar again. It returned to its normal size; the books shone brightly with their enticing colors and titles; the furniture assumed its natural proportions. The lights brightened. Claire stood in the center of the room, the solid floor and enduring Oriental rug beneath her feet, and once again felt it was hers.

I'll miss him, she thought. He filled such a large space in my life. But I am so glad he's gone.

14

"WHERE'S Mother?" Emma asked, coming in to breakfast. "Did she stay out all—"

"No," Hannah said firmly. "She had dinner with Alex, as a matter of fact, and when she came home—"

"She had dinner with *Alex?*"

"Yes, and she had a nice time, but it was very short because she was anxious to get back to work. And when she came home, she went straight to her studio and worked for a few hours, and then we had tea and talked. *You* were very late."

"I know. Brix likes late nights. Where is she?"

"Taking the Eiger drawings to the lab. She finished the whole project, all day yesterday, right up to dinner, and then when she got home, till about one o'clock. I never saw anybody work so hard to get something done and out of here." Hannah put a bowl of oatmeal in front of Emma, sprinkled it with cinnamon and sugar, and poured milk over it. "Eat this; no arguments. She finished with the owner, too."

Emma looked up, her eyes wide. "Quentin? She's not going to see him anymore?"

"That's what I said. That happened night before last. Emma, you should be in bed."

JUDITH MICHAEL

"Why?" Emma demanded.

Hannah sat across the table. "Your eyes are red and puffy, from lack of sleep or who knows what; your hands are shaking, and you're pale as a ghost. You're exhausted and you're getting the flu or a cold or something, and you belong in bed with me bringing you tea and soup. Why don't you go up there now?"

Emma shook her head. "I'm just a little tired. I have a lot to do today."

"Like what? They're not doing any photo shoots, you said; what else do you have?"

"Christmas shopping. I haven't done any."

"You can do it tomorrow. You still have a few days."

Emma sat stubbornly, looking at her untouched oatmeal. "Did Mother really break off with him?"

"Yes. You can ask her yourself when she gets back."

"For good?"

"Of course for good. What a nuisance to have to go through something like that twice." Hannah watched Emma stare at her oatmeal. "You know, I understand that oatmeal may not be the peppiest remedy when you're feeling gloomy. I promise something more lively for lunch. Shall I make you a pizza?"

Emma shook her head, but she was smiling. "I'm just not very hungry, Hannah. I can't help it."

"There was a time when I didn't eat," Hannah said reflectively. "That was after my daughter died, when it was too much of an effort to do anything."

Emma looked up. "You never told us how she died."

"Well, it's hard to talk about. But maybe this is a good time to tell you about her. Her name was Ariel—did I tell you that?"

"Yes," Emma said. "It's a pretty name."

"She was a pretty child. Lovely, really, with reddish hair, almost like yours, and brown eyes with long lashes and the sweetest smile. We lived with my mother in a small town in Pennsylvania; I've told you about that. My mother and I had managed to buy a little house with just enough room for the three of us. We shared a bedroom and Ariel had the other; it faced east and the morning sun touching her face was what woke her up each day. She always woke up happy; she'd kiss me, first thing, and say how much she loved me. Best of all, she said. She loved me best of all. People claw each other for money and possessions and power and fame, but those are poor substitutes for what we had."

Emma had taken a few bites of her oatmeal; she held her spoon suspended. "What happened to her?"

"One December, when she was eight, my mother and I took her to New York for a production of *The Nutcracker*. Ariel loved ballet. We took a bus there and stayed in a little hotel and ate in little restaurants that we could afford and saw the ballet. Ariel was so excited all she could say was, 'I'm so happy, so happy, I'm so happy.' "

She paused. "I can hear her still, her voice was so clear, and I can feel her hand in mine as we walked back to our hotel, after the ballet. She said she was going to be a dancer and dance in *The Nutcracker* and *Sleeping Beauty,* and she said she already could do some of the steps. She said, 'Stay there, I'll show you.' And she let go of my hand and walked a little way along the sidewalk and did a pirouette and tried to get up on her toes. We were laughing. So happy, so happy. And then . . . it was all gone. As if a whirlwind came down and swept her away. A driver was speeding—they said he was going sixty miles an hour on Forty-second Street, can you imagine?—and he lost control of his car and jumped the curb and . . . struck Ariel."

"Oh, no." Emma put her hands over her face. "Oh, no, oh, no." She saw it so clearly in her mind: the careening car, the crumpled body . . . After a minute she walked around the table and sat next to Hannah and put her arms around her. "It's so awful, Hannah."

"That was forty-seven years ago this month," Hannah said. "And it still hurts. I held her in my arms and kissed her and called her, I called her over and over, but Ariel didn't hear me. And her eyes were open but she didn't see me. I cuddled her in my lap to keep her warm, the way I did when she was a baby. There was blood all over her, and all over me, and I knew her bones were broken, I could feel them when I gathered her to me. The doctors told us later she died instantly. I think I was glad of that, because she would have hurt so much, you know."

Emma was crying. "Poor little girl. Poor Hannah. Oh, Hannah, what a terrible thing."

"But beside my grief there was anger: absolute, total fury. The driver was hardly hurt; cut up by smashing his head into the window, but nothing that couldn't be fixed. He was drunk, of course; and he didn't have a driver's license. But what drove me crazy was, why were we *there,* at *that minute?* If we'd left the theater one minute earlier instead of staying until the last curtain call; if we'd walked a little more slowly or a little faster; if we'd stopped for a minute to look in a shop window . . . *one minute* one way or the other and Ariel would be alive. It drove me crazy; I kept saying, 'Please let me do that walk again and change just one little thing. Please, please, please.' Those were the days when I wasn't eating; I did a lot of walking around, feeling empty and angry and so sad I thought I would die of sadness. But after a while, I started eating again and went back to teaching and functioned quite well. That's what happens, you know: we recover from tragedy. Except that from then on there was always an unlit corner in my heart and no light could ever penetrate to it. It will always be dark."

After a while, Emma's tears stopped. She realized that just as she was holding Hannah, Hannah's arms were around her waist; they were comforting each other. How did she stand it? Emma thought. I've never even known anybody who died. But to lose your little girl . . . She pictured her mother, weeping inconsolably if she died, never going out of the house, not eating, wearing black. She wouldn't see anybody, Emma thought, well, maybe Hannah, but Hannah would be mourning, too. They'd cry all day and go into Emma's empty

POT OF GOLD

bedroom and walk around it, looking at everything and remembering how much fun they used to have....

Fresh tears came to her eyes as she thought about their house without her in it. All the rooms with little things of hers scattered around—whatever book she was reading, her shoes that she always kicked off when she came home and then forgot when she went upstairs, a magazine that had just come in the mail, a blouse she'd brought downstairs to replace a missing button—poor Mother; she'd look at all those things and she wouldn't be able to stand it, Emma thought. She was glad she'd told her she loved her at Thanksgiving. She used to tell her that all the time, but lately she'd felt confused about her, loving her and not loving her at the same time, angry at her for not liking Brix, jealous of her because she always seemed to know what she was doing, wanting to talk to her and be comforted but afraid to because there was so much she could not tell her. But she knows I love her, Emma thought, and she'd be out of her mind if I died; she couldn't stand it. She might die, too. There's nothing worse in the whole world.

Not even worrying about Brix when he doesn't seem to love me. The thought was crystal clear, and Emma raised her head as if she had heard the words spoken. *Not even feeling empty when I'm sitting here waiting for him to call. Not even feeling like I'm nobody because there aren't any more photo sessions and nobody wants me for anything right now.*

Nothing, she thought, nothing can be as bad as losing your little girl.

She sat close to Hannah and thought, I've got to think about these things; I've got to think about everything. Then I'd feel better; I wouldn't be so confused. I have to think about Hannah and her little girl, and Mother and Brix and my work. I have so much to think about; my whole life needs to get organized.

She rested her head on Hannah's shoulder. "I think maybe I will go to bed for a while. I really don't feel very good. And, Hannah, would you bring me some soup?"

* * *

Brix closed the last of his ledgers and put it on the pile on the floor beside his chair. He still sat forward, not ready to relax until his father had approved everything. "So we've had heavy reorders," he said, "probably because of the PK-20 advertising—it's made buyers interested in everything we make. And the hottest things are the makeup and personal care kits; it's like they've been walking out of the stores, they're going so fast. I didn't even know you'd asked Claire to redesign them, but she did a sensational job, you know, they really look like Christmas presents." He waited for his father to say something. "Well, anyway," he said into the silence, "like I said, we've had heavy reorders, but we've kept up, no problems with shipping, and the inventory's down to where we want it this time of year. And raw materials; I already gave you those figures, where we are, and we've got another shipment coming January fifteenth." This time he came to a complete stop. He had made his report and had nothing else to say.

"And the March release for PK-20?" Quentin asked.

"It's on schedule," Brix said, taken by surprise. "I mean, I gave you the inventory figures; we're on target on those, and now that all the packaging is in production—well, some of it we've already got, the things Claire designed first—we'll keep up; we'll be right on target. We'll be shipping on March tenth, no problem. Is that what you wanted to know?"

"We're interviewing for a new head of testing. I'd like you to sit in on those sessions."

Brix's chest swelled. "Sure. Glad to."

Quentin put down his pencil; he had made only a few notes on Brix's shipping and receiving report. "I'm very satisfied. You've done a good job."

At last Brix could sit back, letting his spine curl with relief into the chair. "Kurt said a lot of the chemists and techs wanted to see the PK-20 test reports."

Quentin's look sharpened. "Is that usual?"

"Oh." His spine began to tense again. "I didn't ask him that. I guess it must be; he didn't say he was surprised."

"Didn't ask him," Quentin murmured. He shook his head slightly. "Did any of them comment on the reports?"

"Kurt said they all said they were terrific; they loved the numbers. I knew they would."

"What does that mean?"

"I knew the numbers were good because I copied most of them from that cosmetics line you took over the first year you had the company. Narcissus, remember? I changed a couple percentages, but mostly I just lifted it because if it worked once, I figured it wouldn't give us any trouble now."

Quentin's gaze was thoughtful. "A clever idea."

Brix grinned. "I thought so, too."

"And you destroyed the original reports?"

"No, I kept one, just to have. It's in my private file; nobody even knows it's there."

"Get rid of it."

Brix hesitated, then shrugged. "Okay."

"And what else have you picked up that they're saying about the line?"

"They think it's terrific, great for the company and good for them, too. They'll be expecting bigger bonuses next year, you wait and see. I haven't heard anybody having problems with it; Kurt said everybody he's seen is happy as can be."

"When is it that you're having these conversations with Kurt?"

"The other day. He's still—"

"When?"

"Day before yesterday. He's still living a couple doors from me, that didn't change just because he's not working here anymore, and we still go out drinking together." There was a pause. "Is there something wrong with that?"

"No. In fact, it's fine. I'd just as soon you kept an eye on him. But I want to hear about it if he ever says anything about the PK-20 line."

"Christ, Dad, you know I'd tell you that."

"And Emma? You're still seeing her?"

"Right. She's a sweet kid."

"That's not serious, is it?"

"No; with Emma? She's a kid. Anyway, I'm not about to tie myself down with anybody." Brix paused, wondering what was going on. His father never asked about the girls he dated. "Does it matter?"

"Your girls are your own business. I'm not sure I want that one around too much."

Her or her mother? Brix thought, suddenly having an idea. Maybe his father had been tired of Claire for a long time, but hadn't wanted to break off with her until the designs were done. Maybe, now that they were, he'd done it. Brix couldn't ask because his father became enraged when he asked anything about the women he took out, but he'd bet that was it. And then he wondered, if it was all over with Claire, if she'd make it harder for Emma to go out with him. Well, I can get around that, he thought.

"Now, what about the people in shipping and receiving?" Quentin asked. "Do you need any more, or do you want to get rid of any?"

"Well, we could use one more person in inventory . . ." Brix settled farther into his chair, and he and his father talked for an hour about their work and the coming year. As he talked, Brix's voice deepened to match his father's; he rested an ankle on one knee as his father did and played with a ballpoint pen as his father did. They sat facing each other, two executives wearing dark gray suits, having an end-of-year conference about their company, and when Brix left, he thought he had never felt so good in his life. His father had treated him as an equal.

Pretty fucking good, he thought. Everything under control, everything going ahead, everybody happy. This is my year, the year I really make it. All I have to do is get this fucking PK-20 off the ground. If I do that, I can do anything. Whatever it takes, I can do it.

On the Tuesday before Christmas, Claire and Emma went Christmas shopping in New York. They began with breakfast at Adrienne, in the Peninsula Hotel, going over their lists. It was one of Emma's favorite places to feel elegant: in pink and pale gray, with art nouveau furnishings and wall panels, a deep, flowered carpet, and mirrors everywhere. The tables were spaced far apart, so no conversation could be overheard ... though who would be so crude, Emma wondered, to eavesdrop in such a place? She sighed. It felt good to sit close to her mother, sharing the morning. On the drive into the city, they had talked about little things and laughed a lot, and Emma had loved it. It seemed to her it was the first time they had laughed together in a long time. "My list is awfully short," she said. "You and Hannah and Gina, and I guess Roz, and Brix."

"What about all your friends from school? You always gave each other little things, and you had a party."

The corners of Emma's mouth turned down, as if tightening against a painful memory. Then she shrugged. "They changed when they went to college. I guess I've changed, too. We didn't have a good time over Thanksgiving; we kept not having things to talk about and there would be these long silences and it was really awful. They were excited about seeing me in the Eiger ads when they first came out, and they asked me all about modeling, but they really just wanted to talk about their courses at school and their teachers and boys. *Boys.* They made me feel really out of it and sort of ... old."

Claire put her hand on Emma's. "You'll make new friends; it just takes a while."

Emma shrugged again. "I'm fine. I'm really too busy for friends. Your list is longer than mine."

"I've met a lot of people lately."

The waiter came to take their order. "Grapefruit," Emma said, surprised at how good everything on the menu sounded. Suddenly, she was ravenous. "And eggs Benedict and Canadian bacon, and nut and raisin bread on the side. Oh, and the yogurt terrine, too; it's so good."

Claire smiled. "There was a time when I could eat like that without thinking about all the reasons I shouldn't.

JUDITH MICHAEL

Brioche," she said to the waiter, "and melon to start. Emma, are you having coffee?"

Emma nodded; she was reading Claire's Christmas list.

"Two coffees. Black." She turned back to Emma. "I thought I'd get something for some of the women who've been guiding me around for the last few months."

"But are you still going to see them? I mean, aren't they Quentin's friends?"

"I think at least two or three of them are my friends, too. I may be wrong; I'll find out pretty soon."

After a moment, Emma asked, studiedly casual, "How come you're not seeing him anymore?"

"Oh, I changed, or maybe I began to see him more clearly. Whatever it was, I didn't like the kind of person I'd have to be to stay with him."

"What does that mean?"

"I didn't like what he wanted from me, what he expected me to be." Claire gazed absently at the steaming coffee the waiter set before her. "I don't think, until lately, I ever really thought about what kind of person I wanted to be; I was always too busy with my work, and you, and worrying about the refrigerator compressor or the car battery or whatever was fouling up my budget that month. And then, with Quentin, I was having a good time and I guess he impressed me so much it didn't occur to me that I was adjusting my life to his. I was adjusting *me* to *him*. I suppose I took it for granted, the way a lot of women do, maybe most women; there's all that tradition behind us that says we have to please men and be ruled by them, so whatever we want has to be swept into a corner. That's changing so fast, your generation won't even think that way. At least I hope not."

The waiter brought a tray of jams and jellies and a pot of honey, and Claire waited until he left. "Then, after a while, I started thinking about how I want to shape my life. That's one of the most important things about money, you know: it gives you freedom to decide those things."

"Not always," Emma said in a low voice.

POT OF GOLD

"You have as much freedom as you want, and you'll use it when you're ready." Claire knew what Emma meant, but she was not ready to talk about Emma's strange subservience to Brix. That would come later. They were just getting used to sharing confidences again.

"What did you decide?" Emma asked after a moment.

"Oh, different things, in stages; mainly that a lot of things were missing. I think that whole time, last spring and summer, was like another childhood, or maybe adolescence: sort of an irresponsible stage that I had to go through."

Emma was watching her mother seriously. She felt warm and happy because her mother was confiding in her and was talking about ideas that only grown women could understand. It made them close, and alike. They were two women who dated. Sometime back, Emma had thought that was unnatural and it had bothered her; it was as if her mother were trying to be a teenager. But now she liked it. They were both women, grown-up, with careers. And we're both beautiful, Emma thought, catching an admiring glance from two men at the next table. Mother isn't as beautiful as I am, but there's something about her; maybe being older and sort of ... finished. She's elegant, and proud, and I'm not. Not yet, anyway. But we're still alike: two women who date. And go to bed with the men we date. But that thought got shoved out of sight; it wasn't something she could ask her mother about or bring up at all.

"It shows up in sex," Claire said casually, and Emma started with surprise.

"What does?" She felt her face grow warm. She didn't want to know anything about her mother in bed with Quentin, and she couldn't talk about sex with Brix. She wished she could, but it was too wrapped up with other things.

"How independent a woman is," Claire replied. "I guess sex can be terrific if one person is happy being submissive to someone who insists on dominating, but that wasn't what I wanted. I didn't think about it at first because I hadn't had any sex for so long, it was almost as if I were a virgin, and I

351

JUDITH MICHAEL

confused dominance with strength. But after a while, it stopped being so good. I never stopped being attracted to Quentin, up to the day I told him I wouldn't see him anymore, but attraction is only a beginning. I think sex is always a mirror of a relationship, and one day I realized—Hannah helped me, in fact—that our whole relationship was exactly like what we were in bed: Quentin wanted me docile and pliable, and he assumed that would happen with a kind of arrogance that was almost mechanical. There was no light-heartedness in him. I wanted joy and lightness and I wanted a partner, not a boss. So I decided I'd been wrong: he wasn't what I wanted at all. I wanted different things."

"What kind of different things?" Emma was grateful to her mother for not forcing her to talk about anything; she never even asked if she and Brix had gone to bed together. She's just putting things out there, Emma thought, and if I want to talk about them I can, and if I don't, she'll let it go. She's really so wonderful. I wish I could be honest, like she is. But I'm too confused. Maybe someday . . .

"Work, for one," Claire replied. "Something that made me feel I was accomplishing something. I could have found it by volunteering for some organizations, and I'm still going to do that, but I wanted the discipline of doing a whole project, and I guess I wanted to prove to myself that I could do it."

The waiter brought their grapefruit and melon, and Claire watched him arrange everything to his satisfaction. "And I wanted to have my own goals and set my own agenda for reaching them, and make my own decisions along the way."

Emma frowned slightly. "Isn't that what you always did? It was just you and me, and you decided everything."

"Yes, but I didn't have a lot of choices; what I had was a salary that everything had to fit into. It was like a wall and it was always in my way. So when I won the lottery, all of a sudden the wall was gone. It was as if a blindfold was taken off and all around me were a thousand choices. Maybe a

POT OF GOLD

million. You felt it, too; remember the first time we went to Simone's?"

"That was so much fun," Emma said wistfully.

"Well, that was the problem with Quentin and me. Part of it was timing: I was loving all those choices and just beginning to concentrate on what I wanted to do with myself, how to live my life, and he'd already done that; he was used to money and choices, and he was used to making decisions, for himself and everyone around him. So after a while I felt I had to get away, to decide for myself what I wanted to be instead of being the woman he wanted, even though that would have been the easiest way."

"But what if you can't decide?"

"You can; it just takes time. You have to be able to imagine a lot of 'what ifs' and follow them through and see if they lead to a vision of the future that excites you and makes you feel at home. You have to believe in yourself, Emma; you can't make choices if you don't; you'll fail before you even begin."

"But you didn't do it alone. You said Hannah helped you."

"Hannah always helps. She said something about Quentin that was like a spotlight; it made everything clear for me. She's very good at that."

"She helps everybody. I thought she was nosy and a busybody, but she's pretty good to talk to. Do you know about her daughter?"

"No, what about her?"

"She was hit by a car and killed when she was eight. It was horrible."

"Horrible," Claire echoed. "She never told us."

"She said it was hard to talk about. I *guess*. Anyway, she told the whole story and it made me think about how people have really awful things happen to them. And I don't. Not really."

"No, we're very lucky," said Claire almost absently; she was thinking about Hannah. "But that doesn't mean we don't have sadness in our lives. Just because other people are unhappy doesn't make our unhappiness any easier to bear."

Emma gave Claire a swift, grateful look. She picked up her spoon and began to eat her grapefruit. "It needs honey. I don't know why people think it's good when it's bitter; it needs to be sweet."

Claire handed her the small pot of honey. "Does Brix make your life sweet?"

Holding the pot of honey, Emma looked past Claire, to the view of Fifth Avenue. The balloon curtains were pulled high on the windows, and she could look straight across the street, into the Godiva chocolate shop. The world is full of sweet things, she thought. Wonderful, sweet things. But Brix isn't always one of them, and a lot of the time he doesn't make my life sweet at all. "Of course he does," she said, turning back. She let a golden thread of honey swirl onto her grapefruit. But then, glancing up, she saw Claire's warm eyes on hers, so full of love, and she could not leave those words out there, by themselves. "Not all the time, of course. But that's true of everybody, isn't it? We disappoint each other in little ways all the time."

"Do you disappoint Brix in little ways all the time?" Claire asked gently.

Emma looked down. "I don't know," she said; it was almost a whisper. "I guess I do, because he doesn't want to see me a lot of the time. But then, when we're together, he can be really sweet and say such wonderful things, and when we're—" She caught herself. She had almost started talking about the free-floating nights when they used coke in his bedroom, when everything seemed so easy and beautiful, when she was sure Brix loved her more than anyone else in the world and they would always be together, when she was really happy . . . but how stupid could she be, to let herself go and almost talk about that to her mother?

"When you're what?" Claire asked.

"When we're happy together, it's the best thing in the world. But it doesn't matter what happens when things aren't

POT OF GOLD

perfect, because I always love him and I can't live without him."

"Can't?"

Emma toyed with her spoon, thinking she was talking too much. But then the words tumbled out because they had been inside her so long and she had not been able to tell them to anybody, and she loved her mother so much she hurt inside with wanting to be close to her. "It feels like I'll die whenever I think about not seeing him again. I start feeling empty inside, hollow, and I can't breathe. I know you don't feel that way about Quentin—I'm glad you don't—so you can't understand how I feel, but—"

"I felt that way about your father," Claire said quietly.

Emma stared at her. "I never think about him."

"Well, I do, sometimes. And I remember how much it hurt when he left. I stood in that empty apartment and ached all over. My skin felt stretched and full of pinpricks, and my head hurt, and I thought I would explode because I couldn't hold all that hurt inside me."

Emma's eyes were wide; she had never thought of her mother going through anything like that. "What did you do?"

"I felt you kicking, and I knew there was more than hurt inside me; there was a baby, waiting to be born. I was so glad of that: glad I wasn't alone. I still hurt and it was awful getting through the next months, learning how to live on my own, but every time I felt you move I felt better because it gave me a reason for everything I did. I don't know why it is, but it seems that the worst part of agonizing over a man is having the feeling that nothing else is really important: you don't have a reason to do anything."

"You *know* that," Emma breathed.

"We've all been through it. I know it's hard to believe, but all of us have felt exactly the same kind of hurt and the same loss of will. Alex told me about the death of his wife; he said he felt he was being knocked around by invisible forces, malevolent and invincible, and there was nothing he could do but give in. And remember what Hannah said about the death of her daughter. It's not a unique pain, Emma; it's universal. Of course, you're not mourning a loss; you're imagining one. But sometimes the imagining is almost as bad as the real thing."

The waiter brought their breakfast and Emma picked up her knife and fork. "I can't believe how hungry I am."

"You haven't eaten much for a long time."

Emma paused in cutting her bacon. "You didn't say anything."

"I let Hannah say it for both of us. I thought it might make more of an impression coming from her."

"It did, after a while. She told me she stopped eating when her daughter was killed."

"Emma, all this unhappiness . . . you've had such a hard time, and what I wanted for you were easy times, and joy."

Emma's eyes filled with tears. She looked again through the window, blinking her eyes dry. "Some things are just . . . hard," she said, trying to keep her voice from choking, guarding herself so that she said nothing about sex or drugs or drinking or the memos on Brix's desk. Too many things, she thought; how can there be so many things I can't tell my mother? "But everything's fine. Really. I've got this great job—"

"Is it a great job? Is it really what you want to be doing?"

"It is; it is; it's the best. Even if I decide to go to college"—Emma stopped momentarily, surprised at her own words; why had she said that when she didn't even know she was thinking about college?—"well, whatever I decide about anything, I always want to be a model, as long as somebody wants me."

Claire nodded. She seemed to be concentrating on spreading honey on her brioche. "So you didn't lose your appetite because of problems with modeling."

"Well, I can't get fat, you know, they'd drop me if I gain any weight. I hate it when they don't need me, though; I wish I had a lot more to do."

"Then is it Brix?" Claire looked up, holding Emma's gaze.

Emma felt helpless. They kept coming back to Brix, and she couldn't talk about him. "It's just ... everything," she said at last. "Lots of little things. But there isn't anything to worry about; I'm really fine, and when I go back to work in January—you know, they're going to send me around to the stores, they decided to do that, just to tell people about the PK-20 line and I guess say that I use it, you know, sort of a salesperson but a model, too, and then Hale said after that I can work for other companies—not cosmetic companies, they won't let me do that, but clothes or cars or something—and still work for Eiger, so I'll be awfully busy, and I'll make a lot of money, too. And I'll be fine."

"And where does Brix fit in that schedule?"

Emma tightened up inside. Why couldn't she leave it alone? "He can be anywhere he wants. I told you, I love him and I want to be with him, and that isn't going to change." She pushed her plate away. "I wanted to ask you about his Christmas present. There's a shearling jacket I want to get him—you know, suede with sheepskin—it's really gorgeous, but I know how you feel about him and it's awfully expensive."

"Emma, you don't have to ask me. You have your own credit card; you buy what you want with it. Of all the things we have to talk about, money isn't one of them. If you really do know how I feel about him, then you know that I don't care how much you spend on him, I care about your seeing him at all." Claire paused. She could dredge up the story about the college student who fell through the window, but why would she do it? Emma would defend Brix and turn against her mother ... just when they were rediscovering each other. And by now Emma had to know that Brix had a temper; why would she be so subservient, unless it was to keep him happy?

The waiter refilled their coffee cups, and when he was gone, Claire said carefully, "What I worry about is the kind of person you are with him. That's what I was talking about when I told you how I felt with Quentin. You're a strong young woman, Emma, but you turn into a little girl when you talk about Brix and when you talk to him on the telephone. You turn into a strange sort of wife-mistress, deferential, a little coy, working so hard to please . . . you don't sound like yourself, at least not to me—"

"That's not fair!" Emma nervously pushed back her hair with both hands, putting her palms over her ears. *He always calls me little girl, little country girl, babe; he calls me his little girl, his little girl, his, his* . . . After a minute, she sat up straight. "His father's a tyrant; I know all about him. I think it's really smart of you not to go out with him anymore. But Brix isn't like his father; he cares about me—he was the one who got me the job as the Eiger Girl!—and he's proud of me and we love each other. If you don't like that, I . . . I can move out. I thought of doing it a long time ago, but Hannah said I shouldn't. But I will, if you want me to."

"Of course I don't want you to. What I do want, more than anything, is for you to be happy—"

"I told you, I am!"

"—and I don't think you will be until you take the time to find yourself; who you are all by yourself, and what you want to do with your life just for yourself, not for Brix, and not with him, either, or because of him. I want you to be your own person, Emma, not someone whose well-being depends on how much attention Brix Eiger pays to—"

"Don't, please don't!" Emma said, her voice filled with despair. She pushed back her chair. "I can't change the way things are, and you just make them worse when you talk like that. I want Brix to love me the way I love him; what's so awful about that? I won't be happy without him and I can't imagine that ever changing, and if you really wanted me to be happy, you wouldn't keep running him down; you'd be on my side. I wish you were . . . I wish we could be the way we used to be . . . I thought we were, this morning, but I guess I was wrong, because you just won't leave it alone. I never told you what to do about Quentin! I let you live your own life; why can't you let me live mine?" She reached to the floor for her shoulder bag. "I'm going shopping by myself; that's the only way we're going to stop arguing."

"No," Claire said quickly. "Please, Emma, don't go. We'll stop talking about it; I really do want us to spend the day together. I think it's important for both of us, don't you?" Emma was looking at her lap, her mouth tight. "I've been looking forward to it and I thought maybe you had, too." She waited again and let the silence drag out until Emma gave a small, reluctant nod. "Look, we've got lots of things to talk about, a world full of things; we'll have a lovely day." She paused again and made her voice light. "I might even find a talent for picking out the best shearling jacket around."

Slowly, Emma relaxed. The heaviness inside her began to lift; she didn't have to be angry at her mother after all. In another minute, she was like a different person, buoyant with gratitude and love. "Thank you," she said. "I guess I could use some help. I've never bought one."

"Well, neither have I." Claire finished her coffee. "But we learn fast. We've never had sixty million dollars, either, and look how well we're doing with that."

"Right," Emma said promptly. "Things have never been so great." And a few minutes later, wearing their new cashmere coats, long and full against the December cold, they left the restaurant. Attracting glances from passersby, they smiled at each other as they set off, side by side along New York's crowded, festive streets.

Emma called Brix at home, sitting on the edge of the bed, her Christmas packages piled in a corner of the room. "I was waiting for you to call, but I couldn't wait any longer. I have something important to talk to you about; could I come down tonight?"

"Not tonight, babe, I'm going out. How about tomorrow? I was going to call you in the morning; there's a party—"

JUDITH MICHAEL

"No, Brix, I really want to talk to you. Couldn't we go somewhere quiet?"

"I'll pick you up at eight. We can talk in the car on the way to the party. See you then."

Frustrated, Emma hung up. We'll just have to go somewhere for a drink first, she thought. Maybe we'll never get to the party. I'm getting a little tired of Brix's friends' parties. But that was another disloyal thought, and she pushed it aside, and the next night, when he came to her door, she was dressed in a party dress, with a short chiffon skirt and a beaded top with thin beaded straps on her bare shoulders.

"Wow," Brix said, "that is dynamite. And so's the girl inside it." He looked beyond her at the quiet, shadowed house. "Where is everybody?"

"They went out."

"Well, then, I'm going to scoop you up"—he bent down to lift Emma in his arms and pretended to stagger forward—"God, you are a healthy, hefty lady. But I love every inch of you. You are my delicious little girl and I am going to eat you up. Come on, come on, let's go upstairs; we can be late for the party." He took her hand and held it against him. "Look what you do to me; you're a little witch, a delicious witch, casting spells . . . come on, babe—"

"Brix, I really have to talk to you." Emma was glowing because he had said he loved her, and he was in such a wonderful mood, happy, playful, loving. *I could wait; I shouldn't spoil things when he's being so wonderful.* But she was afraid for him and she felt responsible. She knew, and Brix did not, what was going to happen. "We can go to bed later, I want to as much as you do, but I really have to tell you something, so can't we talk now? We can do it here; I'll make you a drink and we can sit in the library. Let's do that; I'll make a fire; it'll be so nice."

Brix was scowling. "What the hell is so important? Well, go on, tell me; you don't have to make a fire to tell me whatever it is."

"Come on," Emma said, taking his hand and tugging him

with her. "I don't want to stand here, at least we can sit down."

He let her lead him to the library, and when she sat in a chair, he perched on the edge of a table piled high with books. "Well?"

Emma looked at him and opened her mouth. But no words came. Suddenly, she was terrified. Gina had said she should stay out of it, and Gina was one of the smartest people Emma knew. Gina had said that what Emma ought to be worried about was Brix finding out that she knew—

"That's it; time's up." Brix slid off the table and turned to the door. His face was dark. "I don't like your little games. Just because you didn't want to go to the party. Christ, what a stupid, half-assed trick."

"It's about those memos I read," Emma blurted out.

He stopped. "What memos?"

"Oh, Brix, you know, the ones about PK-20, testing it, the women who had problems with their eyes."

He was facing her now, standing with his feet apart. "I told you that was taken care of."

"I know, you said you were doing some new tests and the results were good."

"Well?"

"Well, they're saying, in the lab, that there weren't any new tests."

"*They're* saying? Who the fuck is *they*? And who's giving you this crap; they know better than to talk to outsiders—"

"I'm not an outsider; I'm the Eiger Girl; I'm part of this company just as much as you are. Well, almost as much. Anyway, people talk to me, and when I asked about new—"

"*You asked?* You went around the labs asking about tests?"

Emma shrank into the chair. "I was worried about you."

"God damn it, we went through this and you told me you'd stay the hell out of my business. You said that, right? *Right?*"

"Yes, but when I heard—"

"You were on your goddamn knees, right?"

"Yes, Brix, but—"

"Then what the fuck are you doing wandering around talking to people, asking questions, making trouble? That's the worst goddamn thing in the world!"

"No, it's not!" Emma sat straight, suddenly angry. Hannah had told her what the worst thing in the world was; Hannah had told her about really terrible things happening, and people somehow getting through them, and what was Brix doing, trying to make her feel awful about something not nearly as important? He didn't even know what she wanted to tell him! "I wasn't making trouble; I was worried about you."

"God damn it, I don't need you to—"

"Let me talk!" she cried. He stared at her; she had never raised her voice to him. Wide-eyed, her back straight, Emma met his look. She felt brave and strong; she would help him whether he wanted her to or not, because she loved him. "They're saying there weren't any new tests, only the first ones, and the results on those are good, so the line will be released on schedule, in March. But something is really wrong, Brix, because the results can't be good if those memos were right. And people know that; maybe the whole testing lab." Brix's look was impaling her and she faltered. "So what if they tell some of the . . . the chemists and the chemists go . . . they call the FDA . . . and maybe the State's Attorney? Of course the FDA can't do anything until you ship across state lines, but they could be waiting for you to do it and then—"

"Where'd you get all this shit?" Brix demanded. He had not moved from the center of the room, standing with his feet apart, his hands in his pockets. Emma could see the knuckles through the fabric of his pants; his hands were clenched. "Somebody's feeding you a line; who the fuck is it? *Who've you been talking to?*"

"It doesn't matter; what matters is—"

POT OF GOLD

"I ASKED YOU A QUESTION!"

"I can't tell you. A few people—"

"Your friend what's her name. Is that it? The one we hired because she's a friend of your mother's."

"She's not involved with PK-20, you know that," Emma said, dodging the question. "Brix, I'm just telling you to be careful, that's all. You should know what's happening, what people are saying, because it could hurt you. You're the one I care about. Maybe you really should do some new tests; you can't just pretend those memos weren't there. Maybe you shouldn't release the line in March; I don't know. I just think you have to be careful."

"Who talked to you?" he asked after a moment.

"I can't tell you."

"Who talked to you, Emma?"

"I can't tell you. Why does it matter so much? The tests are more important, aren't they? Aren't they the most important thing of all?"

"You won't tell me who it was?"

She shook her head.

"Did you tell whoever it was that you'd read the memos?"

"No; I told you, Brix—" She swallowed. He would never forgive her if he knew she had talked to Gina; he would hate her forever. "I didn't tell anybody."

"*Nobody* knows you saw those memos?"

"Nobody."

He stood looking at the floor. The room was silent. Emma waited, not moving. I did it, she thought; I warned him and now he'll take care of everything. He doesn't need anybody to tell him what to do; now that he knows there could be trouble, he'll handle it.

"Okay," Brix said, rousing himself from thought. He gave himself a little shake, like a dog waking up. "This is it. Now listen, because we're not going to talk about this again. We'll push the release date back and we'll set up another series of tests. Okay? Will that satisfy you?"

"I'm not asking you to satisfy—" She stopped. "I think that's a wonderful idea, Brix. I'm very proud of you."

"*Proud* of me?"

"Because you're strong and you know what has to be done. I think you're wonderful."

"Good," he said; he was thinking of something else. "You'd better not tell anybody about this, Emma."

"About the new tests? Why not?"

"It could hurt the company. You know, talk about changing a release date, doing more tests, you could ruin a company's reputation overnight—everybody'd be saying we had bad quality control; we rushed into a release; you know—and it would take forever to get it back. If we could at all. You're sure nobody knows you saw those memos?" Emma nodded. "Then keep this whole thing to yourself. You don't want us to shut down; then we wouldn't need an Eiger Girl, would we? Let me handle it; you just keep out of it. You got that? *You keep out of it.* If you'd done that in the first place . . . Well, Christ. Anyway, you've got it straight now, right?"

"Yes."

"Okay, then, is that the lot, or do you have any other news to give me?" Emma shook her head. "Then what are we waiting for? That party won't wait all night. Get your coat, little girl, and we'll go have us a time."

He was smiling broadly, his face cheerful, his body relaxed, but there was a falseness to his gaiety, and Emma looked at him searchingly, trying to see how he really felt. And she saw that his hands were still in his pockets, still clenched, and his eyes had no expression at all; they were flat, as if they did not see her, as if he were calculating something that did not include her and never would. A shiver ran over her and she held her bare arms, as if the weather had suddenly changed. "Go on, go on, get your coat," Brix said again, jovially. "We're going to make a night of it."

Emma stood up. I wish I could stay home, she thought. I wish I could just be here alone. But she could not do that. Brix would never understand, and he would hold it against her. I've annoyed him once tonight, she thought, going to the coat closet. A second time wouldn't be a good idea. She turned and Brix took her coat, holding it for her while she slipped into it. Then he put his arms around her from behind, imprisoning her. "Love me?" he asked in her ear.

"You know I do," Emma whispered.

"Well, then, we've got nothing to worry about, have we? Let's get going, my little sweet, before the rest of them drink up all the booze."

15

THE theater was long and narrow, an old, converted movie house in Greenwich Village with seats that tilted and sagged and poked springs into unwary buttocks. But opening night had brought out a full house; the reviewer from the *New York Times* was in the third row, looking pleased and making notes; and Claire thought the play was one of the best she had ever seen.

"Would I think it's this wonderful if the theater were plush?" she asked Alex at the intermission. They stood in a little circle of privacy in a corner of the crowded lobby.

"I hope so," he said, smiling. "I admit the setting makes it seem more of an uphill battle, so you tend to be amazed at what they accomplish, but they'd be good anywhere. In fact, they are: most of their plays have gone on to Broadway. And they're known for their acting classes, too; a dozen or more of the top film and TV stars you see today came from this company."

A group of people came by and Alex introduced them to Claire. "How do you feel about our little family?" one of them asked Alex.

He grinned. "As good as you; it's a good night for all of us." When they moved on, he said to Claire, "We've all put

POT OF GOLD

money into this company; they have a lot more in it than I have, but for all of us it's like a family."

"Does it make money?" Claire asked.

"Never. We're happy if they break even. There's usually a loss at the end of the year, but we've always been able to make it up with our annual fund-raising routine. Most of these small theaters don't make money, you know; they can't charge enough for the tickets to pay the expenses. Broadway is supposed to make money; if it doesn't, the plays close. But it's very special down here; don't you feel it? None of the slickness of uptown, but with a magic all its own. I'd give more, if I could."

Claire thought of Quentin, who invested in restaurants and computer companies and insisted on seeing a profit. "Yes, it is wonderful."

They stood silently, watching the crowd. Alex tossed his styrofoam cup into a wastebasket. "Do you want another coffee?"

"No. Thank you."

They were silent again. Around them, the chatter of the crowd bounced off the tile floor and the cracked, peeling walls covered with posters and photographs of other plays the company had performed, magnified and echoing until it was like the screech of a train coming around a bend, isolating Alex and Claire in their corner. A couple approached Alex and raised their voices to ask about putting money in the theater company. "End of the year, you know, we're making all our donations." They were knowledgeable about theater groups in other parts of the country, and the three of them talked about income and expenses, acting classes, touring, publicity, and crossover into movies.

Claire watched Alex's animated face, liking his enthusiasm, liking him. He met her eyes and for just an instant his look changed: it was private and warm . . . and loving, she thought suddenly as he turned back to answer a question the couple had asked. She clasped her hands in front of her, as if to hold on to the thought. Loving. That had not occurred to her, before this moment.

But they had been moving beyond friendship, she thought, ever since they went to dinner a few nights earlier. It was the first time they had been together outside of her studio and at first they were a little stiff, their conversation slow and self-conscious, until Claire told him she liked the magazine article he had written about her: "It was much more interesting than I thought it would be."

"Are you saying you don't think you're interesting?" he asked. They were in a booth in a small restaurant in Greenwich, with wooden floors, red-checked tablecloths, whitewashed walls hung with hundreds of baskets of all shapes and sizes, and a wide stone fireplace with a leaping, hissing fire. On the table between them was a carafe of Chianti and a basket of crusty bread.

"Oh, to ourselves we're always interesting," Claire said, "and to those who are close to us, but I never assumed I'd be interesting to strangers. What I liked in your article was that I came across as a person who thinks about things: what it means to have money, how we think about the world when we have money, and how other people think about those who are wealthy, how we all have to decide what kind of life we want to make for ourselves, what money does to people in a society where a lot of people don't have even enough to get through a week. You brought all those questions to life; you made them real and universal; you went beyond me and made the whole subject something people could relate to and find parallels to in their own lives. I think that must be very hard to do."

"Thank you," he said gravely. "That means a lot to me."

"But this isn't the first time you've been praised for your writing; you've always had people tell you how good you are."

"There is no such thing as enough praise to a writer," he said with a grin. "We hunger for it; we look for it shamelessly. It makes up for all the solitude and self-doubt and hours of staring out the window as if something out there will give us a clue to how we'll write the next sentence or paragraph or even the next word."

"Well, I've told you I think you're wonderful. Your books are very powerful; they've all given me ideas and feelings that seem to be my own, to think about and use in my life. Your article did that, too."

"Thank you," he said again. "I couldn't hope for better praise."

"Do you get letters from readers?" she asked.

He nodded. "They mean a lot to me, too; that people take the time to write, to say they're grateful, or to tell me what a terrible person I am."

"Terrible? Why?"

"Oh, some are angry at the four-letter words I use; they don't want to read them even when they fit the characters who speak that way. And some are angry at descriptions of pain—when I describe the cruelty people manage to inflict on each other—they say they're reading for pleasure and they don't want to see the dark side. Some of them think I should use my gift to be inspirational because the world needs that. And they're right—the world certainly needs inspiration—but when I answer them, I tell them it should begin with all of us, not just the writers."

"You answer all of them?"

"All of them. If people take the time to write, I take the time to answer them. You don't get any of that pleasure, do you? You create a design and it appears on millions of boxes of shampoo or book jackets or soup cans, and you never know how people feel about it. Even if they wanted to tell you, they couldn't, because they don't know your name, much less how to reach you."

"The designer is always the invisible person," Claire said with a small smile. "Sometimes we get credit, usually in something like an art book, but otherwise, designs just seem to appear from thin air. I think most people hardly notice them, though they're influenced all the time by the designs around them."

"I remember one from when I was a kid. Probably because it had a baseball player in it." Alex looked up in surprise as the waiter appeared to take their order. "We haven't looked at the menu; give us a few more minutes." When he turned back to Claire, he met her smile. "I forgot where we were. But you wanted to get back early and finish your designs, so I think we'd better eat."

They picked up their menus and ordered, but later neither of them could remember what they had eaten. What they remembered was the talk, all through dinner, without pause, as if they could not fit everything they had to say into the brief time they had.

"I'm sorry," Claire said as they left the restaurant. "I wish I could make it a longer evening, but I really want to finish the whole project tonight."

"You have nothing to apologize for; I've worked against deadlines most of my life." And when he pulled up in front of her house, he turned to her. "It's a rare and special pleasure to have someone to talk to and the talk be inexhaustible."

"Yes." Impulsively, Claire leaned toward him and kissed his cheek. "Thank you for a wonderful evening."

She was thinking about that evening as Alex talked to the couple in the theater lobby. When they moved on, he apologized. "I didn't mean to leave you out; but they could become major contributors, and I had to make them feel wanted. Which, God knows, they are."

"You know so much about it. And I remember, one of your novels was about an actor. Have you been in the theater?"

"No, I just hang around and pick up information. I may be a frustrated actor, though I don't think so; as far back as I can remember, all I've wanted to do was write books."

"But you're not even doing that."

"Not at the moment." Claire looked at him in surprise,

and he smiled. It was a little boy's smile, she thought, almost sheepish, trying to be casual but not quite containing his excitement. "The fact is, I've had a couple of ideas in the past week that I'd like to explore. That's always the way my novels have started: with one or two ideas that interest me and make me curious to see where they lead."

"That's wonderful. Isn't it? Aren't you pleased?"

"I think so. I really didn't plan to write novels again, you know."

She shook her head. "I don't see how that could ever be final. It would be like saying you hadn't planned to look at a sunset again, or listen to music. Or eat."

He looked at her with interest. "You think writing a novel is like listening to music and eating."

"I think it's as deeply a part of you, the same way design is a part of me."

"Yes, I liked that, in one of our interviews, when you said that you found you couldn't just stop doing it."

She nodded. "Because, in a way, it would be like saying I'd decided to stop breathing. There are some things we have to do to feel alive. I don't think you'd feel alive if you went for years and years without writing books."

"I might not. That may be what I'm discovering."

"That the world just doesn't feel right, or you don't feel comfortable in it, because you've lost something that's so much a part of you."

He smiled. "Not many people understand that."

"And I hope it's a good feeling. It was for me, it was wonderful, as soon as I went back to it."

"It is good. But I feel tentative, too. It's a little like moving back to the town where you grew up. You know it won't be the same; it probably will have painful memories; and almost certainly it will be harder to become part of it than it was the first time."

"You think the writing will be harder this time."

"It's always harder, the older a writer gets. It takes longer to think of the exact word you want, the best metaphor, the most lyrical description; it's more difficult to be fresh and sharp in your ideas; and if you care about not repeating yourself or unconsciously lifting from authors you like, you have to have an encyclopedic memory for everything you and all your favorite writers ever wrote."

"But that wasn't what you meant, was it? I thought you were talking about going back to a way of life with so much of that life gone. As if you'd found yourself in a different country but you still had to perform the way you used to. Or even better."

"A different country," he repeated. "That's exactly what a great loss does: there's a shift, like an earthquake, and you find yourself staggering because suddenly everything is off center, the same but devastatingly not the same. Shadows are longer; people are more distant from you, but their voices are louder and they all seem happy; and buildings seem to tilt inward, over your head, like a cap someone is pulling low over your eyebrows, so that you can't see the sun. Everywhere you go, there's a feeling of the foreignness of things."

"Yes," Claire murmured, remembering how she had felt as if she were staggering through the days when she finally understood that Ted really would never be back. "And will you write differently, do you think?"

"I don't know. I'll be interested to find out. You told me, in one of our interviews, that you're designing differently."

"Yes, but it had nothing to do with my loss; that was eighteen years ago. It's what I told you: the lottery made the difference; it gave me confidence."

"Winning the lottery?"

"Having sixty million dollars."

"You told me that, and I put it in the article, but I didn't really understand it. What does sixty million dollars have to do with how well you design?"

She looked at him wonderingly; it seemed so clear to her. "The world is an easier place; I'm more comfortable in it. I can concentrate on what I want to do instead of what I have to do."

"But your eye hasn't changed; the way you look at the world and see shape and color and harmony hasn't changed; the desire to excel hasn't changed."

"No, but now I'm willing to experiment."

"So you're more daring?"

"Yes."

"And you think you can't be daring unless you have money?"

Claire was uncomfortable. "The answer to that ought to be no. But there's something so powerfully affirmative about money, as if having it gives permission for almost anything. If you lost something, you can buy another; if you fail at something, you can afford to keep trying until you succeed; if you make a mistake, you can buy a second chance. Money is control. And I never felt in control of my life until I had it."

"Or something else changed in your life."

She looked at him reflectively. "Maybe. Maybe I just wasn't ready to be daring until now. Maybe the money had nothing to do with it."

"I like that the best," he said with a smile. "We all have to grow up sometime."

"Well, I hope you do," Claire said, her smile meeting his. "And whether you write differently or not, I'm very glad you're going back to it. I never really bought the line about your turning into a longshoreman."

"But I was serious; I wasn't posturing. It was an alternative I really thought about, a way to get out of a rut and into something alive and useful."

"What was the rut?"

"Being in that foreign country. Mourning, feeling sorry for myself, wrapping myself in my own sorrow as if I were trying to be dead, too. As if it would be a betrayal of my wife and our love if I started to live again. Something had to pull me out of that because I sure as hell wasn't doing it for myself."

"And what pulled you out?"

"Partly time: enough time passing. But mostly, I think, it was you."

The lobby lights dimmed and brightened and there was an immediate responsive surge in the crowd. Claire and Alex were pushed back into the corner, their faces very close together. "Time for the second act," he said.

Casually, he took Claire's hand to follow the audience into the theater, and when they were in their seats, he held it again, glancing at the program in his other hand. "Watch the young girl in the first scene; I think she's going to be a great actress." From then on, they concentrated on the play, their eyes meeting now and then when something struck them both as memorable. After a while, Claire became aware of how often that was happening: she would look up and find Alex's eyes meeting hers in appreciation or amusement at something on the stage, and it happened every time she looked up, as if their thoughts were identical.

The next time she found herself turning to look at him, she deliberately kept watching the stage. From the corner of her eye, she saw the movement of his head and she felt his eyes on her. After a few seconds, it was too hard to look straight ahead; she turned, and as their eyes met, they broke into quiet laughter. It was the first time ever, Claire thought, that she had shared a private joke with someone without either of them having to speak.

When the final curtain came down and applause filled the theater, Alex turned to her again. "I have to show up at the party; it goes with being a sponsor. But I'd like to leave early; I want to be with you. Will you come back to my place after we spend half an hour or so with the others?"

"Yes."

"A woman of swift decisions," he murmured, and after repeated curtain calls and the slow exit of the audience, they left the theater and walked up the street to the Gargoyle Cafe, bright with low-hanging colored lights, like theater spotlights, and swirling with energy. "They know it was good, even with all the opening-night glitches," Alex said between greeting people and introducing them to Claire. "In fact, they know it was great; you can feel it in the air. There's a unique kind of excitement when people know that everything they hoped for has come to pass; it's like a special blessing embracing everyone even remotely connected with it. There's no other feeling like it in the world."

He and Claire stood beside the bar talking to the director and producer of the play, the backstage crew, the office staff, and the patrons and sponsors who, like Alex, kept the theater alive. The talk grew in volume and excitement, and when a new crowd came into the restaurant, they were surrounded again. It was almost another half an hour before Alex turned to Claire and smiled ruefully. "I wanted to stop in for a few minutes and then leave. Are you ready to go?"

"Yes, but I've enjoyed this. It's so different from any party I've ever gone to. I've learned a lot and I've had fun."

"I was hoping you would." He took her hand and led her through the crowd, saying good-night to everyone they passed. They all paused in their conversation to talk to Claire.

"Come backstage some night; we'll all go to dinner afterwards."

"If you want to watch rehearsals or some acting classes, feel free."

"We're having a donors' dinner in January at the Rainbow Room; I'm sure Alex has asked you, but I want to tell you how glad we'd all be to see you there."

Claire recalled the invitations she had received from Quentin's friends when she first met them. Two different worlds, she thought, so far apart. Alex held her coat and she slipped it on, and they walked to his car, parked near the theater. "I didn't ask you to the donors' party," Alex said as they drove up Christopher Street, "because I didn't want to ask you to give us money."

"Why not?" Claire asked. "You know I have the money, and you know how many organizations I'm involved with; they're in your story."

"None of them are theater groups; you've narrowed it to

education and music and anything connected with children."

"I don't know much about the theater. I'd like to know more; I think I will come to rehearsals and acting classes, to learn how they work. But that wasn't why you didn't ask me to the dinner."

He stopped at a red light and looked ahead, at the Christmas lights strung on shops and restaurants and, on the floors above, the trees blinking in apartment windows. Once, this had been the worst time of year for him, when everything was a symbol of home and family, when carols and candy canes and fake Santas seemed to mock his singleness, when he missed his wife with a deep, dull pain that seemed to have no end. And even when it did, finally, ease and then disappear, what remained was emptiness, and he had wondered if he would ever feel, or love, again. Now he thought he knew the answer to that. Tonight, he felt only happiness. Tonight, he had to admit, he was absurdly happy.

"You're right," he said, driving on as the light changed. "I didn't ask you for money because, however personal the request—and the ones that bring in the most money are always personal—it's a business transaction, and I don't want to be doing business with you."

Claire was silent, gazing out her window. Traffic was light and they were moving swiftly up Eighth Avenue, past bedecked apartments, past stores whose neon signs blinked and flashed and quarreled with the meek Christmas lights beside them, past record stores with music blaring through open doors, and nightclubs with solid, secretive doors, and apartments with uniformed doormen in white gloves standing guard. Only a few people walked on the streets, stepping briskly past shapeless bundles of sleeping people in the doorways, men walking their dogs, and groups of young people swinging arm in arm down the sidewalk.

Claire felt the life of the city: a constant, rumbling vibration that quivered through the streets; the air was tense and alert, perpetually in motion, as if a steady gale kept everything spinning a few feet off the ground. Coming from the forests and fields of Connecticut, she felt like a stranger, but, still, something drew her to the growling, humming intensity of the city, and for the first time, she found herself thinking that she would like to live there.

Alex had glanced at her once as he drove, but he said nothing and they both were silent, absorbed in their thoughts. Claire liked it that he did not feel he had to keep noise going between them, whether they had anything to say or not. But that had never happened, she thought; they had always had something to say. She thought back over the past few weeks, to the long hours in her studio when they had put away their work and sat over tea, talking, talking, talking, about everything in the world, and about themselves. She had never talked so much or so comfortably to anyone but Gina and Hannah; she had never had a good friend who was a man.

I don't want to be doing business with you.

Alex turned off West End Avenue onto a quiet street, and she was struck by the sudden difference in the atmosphere. Here there were no tall apartments or bags of garbage on the sidewalk or the rush of taxis; here tall trees lined the street on both sides, screening elegant limestone row houses facing each other with severe grace. The noises of the city seemed to have vanished; it was as if they had driven into a small corner of another century, and as Claire looked around with pleasure, she almost expected to see varnished horse-drawn cabs clip-clopping along past young boys with soft caps hawking penny newspapers.

They drove the length of the row houses to the end of the street where a square, graystone apartment building stood on the corner of Riverside Drive. Beneath bright yellow streetlights, Alex pulled to the curb, maneuvering to fit into the small parking place. "You may not appreciate this, but you are witnessing a minor miracle: a parking place on 105th Street." He took Claire's hand as she got out of the car and led her to the door, opening it with his key. "No doorman; we all voted it down. Too expensive. We do have a maintenance man who seems to excel at catnaps; now and then he finds an odd job or two, like taking out the garbage, that he's willing to expend some energy on."

The lobby was enormous, dimly lit and bare of furniture, with a black-and-white tile floor and, at each end, an elevator with scarred and chipped doorframes. "The idea is not to look like a Fifth Avenue building, to discourage anyone who thinks we have anything to rob. In fact, I don't, but some of my neighbors do; the apartments are very good. You'll see."

They rode the self-service elevator to the eleventh floor and walked to the end of the corridor, to another scarred door. Alex opened it with his key, and Claire went inside and walked farther into the large room while he hung up her coat. It was a combination living room, dining room, and office, with a galley kitchen on one side and a small bedroom on the other. The furnishings were Spartan—a couch and armchair with a hassock and a glass coffee table; a small, square dining table with four chairs; two desks, one for a computer and printer, and several filing cabinets—but Alex had brought warmth to it with a dark red kilim rug, floor lamps with dark red shades, a rare Toulouse-Lautrec poster with life-size figures, floor-to-ceiling bookshelves, crammed and overflowing, on two walls, and more shelves running up the sides and over the top of the large windows on the fourth wall.

"They overlook the Hudson," Alex said. "You'll have to come during the day, to see it. We get exceptional sunsets here, too. I have Stilton and fresh pears and a good Bordeaux; would that please you?"

"Very much." Claire was at the windows, looking down at the bright lights of Riverside Drive and the river's edge. "You seem so far from the city here."

"An illusion, but a happy one. I've come to enjoy the city, now that I have my own retreat." He set the food and wine on the coffee table and sat on the couch, then watched Claire turn and hesitate between the armchair and the other end of the couch, and choose the couch.

He leaned forward and filled their wineglasses and handed her one. "I haven't brought anyone here in the four years I've lived here," he said casually. Claire looked at him in surprise. "It isn't that I've been a monk; far from it. But I haven't been able to bring anyone here. Somehow, from the day I bought it, it seemed to be a part of me that couldn't be opened to scrutiny, like the house I'd sold, and the people who'd lived in it. That was the private core that never made it to conversation."

There was a silence. "I'm glad to be here," Claire said.

Alex nodded slowly, contemplating his wineglass. "It's a wonder to me, how you always say what I hope you'll say." He leaned forward again and filled a small plate with cheese and fruit and handed it to Claire. "I don't think I made a deliberate decision to keep out of any involvements; it just happened. I couldn't imagine living with any of the women I knew, or even staying with them very long. I couldn't imagine living with anyone, even my son. For the first year, I craved solitude as if I couldn't hold myself together except in silence. After that, I wanted people, I needed them, but not in my own space and not permanently. Until I started working in your studio. After the third or fourth time, I didn't want to leave. Or, if I had to leave, I wanted to take you with me and bring you here. Because I couldn't imagine staying here, without you."

Claire sat very still, letting his words settle within her. She felt a long, sweet sense of expectancy, like a child contemplating Christmas. It was nothing like the thrill she had felt when Quentin and his friends took her into their lives; this was slower and deeper. She felt as if the pieces of her life were falling into place and she was finding order and harmony. She felt she was coming to a place where she belonged.

Alex was waiting for her to say something; he would not go on if she stopped him. But he knew she would not; their thoughts were as close now as they had been in the theater when their eyes met and they shared those special moments. "Something I've been thinking about," she said, "is how slowly things used to happen, before our world speeded up, especially the way people got to know each other. There was a rhythm to it that they understood, a way of moving gradually and gracefully from one stage of friendship to another, instead of lurching from the first drink or dinner into bed."

She gazed at him for a long moment, liking the look of him: the sharply defined bones of his face that made him look as purposeful and intense as she knew him to be, his brown hair, turning gray, curling on the back of his neck, his mouth that pulled down at the corners, and his deep-set eyes that never wandered when they were talking, but stayed on her face, as if the most important thing to him was to keep in close contact with her. "I like the way our friendship has grown, and what it's still becoming," she said, and watched his face change, the corners of his mouth lifting, his eyes seeming to grow lighter.

He moved to her on the couch and they held each other as naturally as if they had done it many times before. And when they kissed, that, too, seemed familiar to Claire, her mouth and his opening together, welcoming each other, as if their bodies were homes, each giving the other a place to belong.

They held each other more tightly, feeling the beat of each other's heart. Within Claire, something seemed to let go; she felt loose and at ease, with nothing to prove. *Not a contest.* The words sprang to her mind; it was the last time she would think of Quentin when she was in Alex's arms.

They stood and she felt Alex's lean body pressing against hers, his shoulder bones and the long, hard muscles of his arms beneath her hands. For the first time since they had met, they were silent, their bodies taut and locked together. *Not a contest. A journey that two people take, together.*

They pulled back and looked at each other. "Wonderful," Alex murmured. "Filled with wonder. I love you, Claire. I love what you are and what we are together, and the way the world seems filled with possibilities since we met, instead of—"

"Alex, even writers ought to know when words are unnecessary." She curved her hand on the back of his head and brought his mouth to hers again. Together, they moved toward the bedroom, their arms around each other. And then they heard a key in the front door.

Alex's head shot up. "David," he muttered. "What the hell . . ." He took long strides toward the door, but it opened before he got there, and a tall, thin young man came into the room with casual familiarity. He was a young, gangly version of Alex, with the same curling hair and deep-set eyes, but his face was not as sharp and his mouth not as thin. He was handsomer than his father, and soon, Claire saw, he would be irresistible.

"Hi, Dad," he said. Then he saw Claire. "Oh." His palm struck his forehead with a dramatic slap. "I am the world's most incredible jerk. I never even thought . . . Well, you know, you never have anybody up here—"

"It's all right," Claire said, coming to him with her hand outstretched. She was trembling, and she had no idea how disheveled her hair was, but in a way, David's bursting in was like a farce, and the corners of her mouth were lifting with the humor of it. "I'm Claire Goddard."

"David Jarrell," he said, taking her hand and pumping it, "and I'm really and truly, *fervently* sorry. I'm not usually a total dork, but, you know, usually when I come here—"

"David," Alex said. His voice was husky and he cleared his throat as David turned to him and they hugged each other. They were almost the same height.

"Hi," David said again. "It's okay, Dad, I'm gone; I'll come back tomorrow, or, you know, whenever."

Alex was studying him. "What's wrong?"

"Nothing. Why should anything be wrong?"

"Because it's almost midnight and it's a school night—"

"Nope; Christmas vacation."

"Do Diane and Jake know you're here?"

"Uh, not exactly."

"What the hell does that mean?"

"Well, I didn't exactly punch the time clock."

"You just left? Without telling them you were going out?"

"They were out."

"And you didn't have the courtesy to leave them a note."

"Hey, Dad, could you not get all bent out of shape? I mean, I'm going; I'm sorry I butted in."

"No, hold on. I'm sorry I got angry. Get yourself something to drink and we'll talk. But you've got to call Diane and Jake first."

"We sort of had a fight. At dinner."

"Over what?"

"This place some guys are going to tomorrow night. It's in New Jersey, and Diane said I couldn't go and then so did Jake."

"What place in New Jersey?"

"I don't know. I don't know anything about it. Some place that has music, you know, rock stars. They said it's sort of a barn. Lots of guys go there."

"You want to go someplace, but you don't know where it is or what it is or who goes there or what goes on there, and you're fourteen years old. And you're surprised Diane and Jake said no?"

There was a silence. David shrugged and went to the kitchen and took a soft drink from the refrigerator and flipped the metal tab into the wastebasket. Then he went to the telephone at Alex's desk.

"I'm sorry," Alex said to Claire. "That is a meager, inadequate word for the way I feel."

"You can't do anything else." They were speaking quietly, with David's low voice in the background. "He's a lovely boy."

"Yes, he is; I think he's wonderful. In fact, I'm crazy about him, and most of the time we get along pretty well, but then I get worked up, feeling helpless because I don't always know the right thing to do, except back up whatever Diane and Jake do, because they're the real parents right now, and I always remember—and so does he—that I gave him up."

POT OF GOLD

"You think he holds that against you?"

"I'd be surprised if he doesn't."

"Maybe he does," Claire said reflectively. "But you gave him to loving people when you were in a crisis, and you moved to a place close by and never stopped loving him and being part of his life, and he knows all that. And I'll bet he doesn't hold anything against you. He looks to me like a boy who's as crazy about his father as his father is about him."

Alex watched David talking on the telephone, slouched against the desk, absentmindedly probing with a finger in one ear. "Thank you," he said. "I'll hold on to that. You're very generous." He hesitated. "I'm sorry you had to see this side of me; it hardly fits a romantic image of—"

"Alex." Claire briefly considered David watching them from the corner of his eye, then thought, oh, the hell with it; he's fourteen; he can handle it. She stood close to Alex and laid her hand along the side of his face. "I don't want a romantic image; I want you."

Alex took her hand in both of his, turned it over, and kissed her palm. "Do you mind waiting while I talk to him?"

"You might not want me to be part of this. I could take your car and bring it back in the morning."

He thought about it for only a moment. "It's up to you, but I'd like you to stay."

"Then I'd be glad to. Unless David objects."

David turned from the telephone, holding the receiver. "Diane wants to talk to you, Dad."

Alex went to the desk and David dropped into the armchair with a long groan. "They forget what it's like."

Claire returned to the couch, to the same place she had been sitting, and picked up her wineglass, still full. We were too preoccupied to eat and drink, she thought wryly. "Maybe they do remember, and that's why they're worried."

He shook his head gloomily. "They're too old." He looked up. "Have you known my dad long?"

"For a few weeks."

"So, is this something special? I mean, you're here, which

I have to tell you is a major surprise, so is this something I should know about?"

"Does your dad tell you about his friendships?"

"Sure, but he never said anything about you."

"Did he tell you he was writing a magazine article on someone who won the lottery?"

"Yeah, somebody in Connecticut. She won megabucks. She has a big house in the woods, in Wilton; he showed me pictures. Oh. *That was you?*"

Claire nodded.

"You won the lottery? That's cool. I never knew anybody who won anything. So Dad interviewed you; is that how you met?"

"Yes." Claire was amused, and touched, that nothing could distract him from talking about his father.

"He never dates people he interviews; he tells me about his interviews, he tells me about everything." Claire sat quietly, smiling at him, and he squirmed lower in his chair. "Well, I mean, he *can,* there's no rule or anything that says he can't; he just never did. But I guess he likes you better than the other people he's interviewed."

"I hope so."

"You like him a lot?"

"Yes."

"And he likes you a lot?"

"That's what he told me."

David contemplated his soft drink can. "So, if you got married, would you live here or in your house in Connecticut?"

"We haven't gotten that far," Claire said gently.

"I'll bet your house has lots of bedrooms."

"Yes, it does."

"But they're all full, I guess."

"A couple of them are. My daughter is in one, and my cousin—or maybe she's my aunt, I'm not sure which—is in the other." She thought of suggesting that he come for a visit, but decided not to. That was something she should work out

POT OF GOLD

with Alex. She tried to change the subject. "What do you and your friends do besides go to rock concerts in New Jersey?"

"I don't go to rock concerts in New Jersey," David muttered. " 'Cause I'm treated like a little kid instead of somebody who's in high school. They haven't got a clue how to be parents; they never had any kids of their own. My mother and dad knew; we had a house, I guess Dad probably told you, and it was just the three of us, and they let me do whatever I wanted."

Once again he was talking about his father. Claire was impressed with his determined single-mindedness. "Is that so?" she asked. "That's amazing. You were nine years old—is that right?—when your mother died, and they let you do everything you wanted?"

"I was almost ten. It was three weeks and one day before my birthday. Do you know, I'm the only one in my class who has a dead mother? Everybody else, their parents are divorced, nobody lives with everybody in their family, but they don't have anybody dead. Just me." He had sunk deeper in the chair, holding the soft drink can on his chest. "My parents never ever said no about anything. If they did, I'd remember it."

"Remember what?" Alex said. He put a hand on his son's shoulder, then walked to the other end of the couch and sat down.

"If you and Mom ever told me I couldn't do things."

Alex dodged it. "Are you still talking about the barn in New Jersey?"

"She asked." He saw his father's frown, the stern tightening of his lips. "Claire," David said hastily. "Claire asked what we did, you know, where we went, stuff like that."

"Well, tonight where you're going is right here."

David's eyes brightened. "I'm staying over?"

"Isn't that what you just told Diane on the phone?"

David ducked his head. "Well, sort of. I mean, I said I hoped I could. I mean, I said . . . well, uh, yeah, I guess I did. Say I was staying here."

Claire's eyes met Alex's, as they had in the theater, sharing, this time, pleasure in David's honesty.

"But I thought maybe you'd, you know, want privacy or something, like, I didn't want to be in the way."

Alex glanced again at Claire. Not anymore, they thought together, and shared a smile. "You're not in the way," Alex said. "This is your home, too, you know; that's why you have a key."

"So you could let me go with the guys tomorrow night."

"To New Jersey?"

"Right."

"David, you know without a shadow of a doubt the answer to that; you're too smart to try this game." Alex waited. "Look at me." David looked up at him from under his brows. "You know I wouldn't second-guess Diane and Jake; you know I wouldn't undercut their decision; you know I have no reason to let you go and every reason to say exactly what they did. You can't go."

David stared at his feet, crossed on the coffee table, at the same level as his head. Suddenly, he shot up, crossed to the kitchen, and took another can from the refrigerator.

"David," Claire said suddenly as he slumped back in his chair, "how are these guys going to get to New Jersey?"

He flashed her a look. "Driving."

"Then they aren't freshmen, or even sophomores. They're probably juniors and seniors. Are they guys you're close to?"

"Not usually."

"What does that mean?" She waited. "What is it that you have that they want?"

"Sheesh," David muttered. He stared at his feet. "They have to write a computer program, it's a group project, and they're having trouble, and they want me to write it."

"That's cheating," Alex said.

"It's okay to get help," David said uncomfortably. "They asked the teacher and he said they could get help."

"What kind of help?"

"You know, showing them ways they could write it."

"But you're talking about writing the whole program. Which is unethical and could also get you into a hell of a lot of trouble."

After a moment, David nodded. "Yeah, I know. It was just, when they asked me . . . it was . . . you know . . ."

"They made you feel grown-up and part of their group," Claire said. "And that was exciting."

David looked at her, frowning. "Yeah."

"I had that happen once," she said casually. "It was as if doors were opening to a whole new world. It was a lot of fun for a while, but then it sort of wore out and I decided I wasn't crazy about it. I didn't feel I really belonged there."

"Yeah?" David asked.

Claire looked at Alex, thinking she was interfering too much, and caught her breath at the warmth in his eyes and a love she had never seen in a man's eyes before. She turned back and contemplated David's newly interested face. "I think you should forget the barn in New Jersey and writing computer programs for anybody but yourself. I guess you're pretty good at it, and they're not—"

"They're awesomely stupid," he blurted. It was as if a load had been lifted from him. He sat up. "But, you know, they're cool and they said this place was the greatest . . ."

"Then you can go on your own, when you're a senior," Alex said.

"If I have a car when I'm a senior. Diane and Jake said—"

"Well, that's a discussion I'll be part of," Alex said. David's eyes widened, but Alex stood up, forestalling any more conversation. "Now, look, it's getting late. I'm taking Claire home. If you're still awake when I get back, we can talk some more."

"Well, but couldn't I—"

"No," Alex said.

Claire looked at him, her back to David. "I think it would be a good idea," she said very quietly.

Almost without hesitation, Alex nodded. "Okay," he said to his son. "You come along for the ride."

David sat up. "Right. Thanks." He unfolded his long body from its contorted position and stood up, in front of Claire. He leaned down and kissed her cheek, then kissed the other cheek. "You're great. I'm glad you won the lottery." He looked from Claire to Alex and back. "I'll wait outside," he said, and in the next minute he was gone.

In the silence, Alex took Claire's hand. "You were wonderful. You made it seem easy."

"It's always easier with someone else's child," Claire said ruefully. "But I was right about him, Alex: he is a lovely boy. You should be very proud; your sister and brother-in-law didn't do that alone."

Alex stood, bringing her with him, and took her face between his hands and kissed her. Claire held him and she felt the warmth of his arms, encircling her, pulling her to him. Their bodies seemed to flow together; Claire wondered at it, that everything they did made them seem to be one. She had never felt that before. Their kiss grew in intensity until she was dizzy and a low moan started in her throat, and then, simultaneously, they both pulled back. "We'll never get out of here if we don't do it now," Alex said. "Tomorrow night . . . can I see you tomorrow night?"

"Yes. Oh, yes, of course, but do we have to wait for nighttime?"

He laughed, a joyous laugh that brought lightness to his face and buoyancy to his step. "We can start at the crack of dawn, though that's only a few hours away. Tell me what you'd like."

"I'll call you in the morning." She was regaining her sense of separateness. "I want to see what's happening at home."

Alex helped her on with her coat and kissed the back of her neck. "It doesn't matter what time we start. We have a lifetime ahead of us."

16

HANNAH had invited Forrest Exeter for lunch and he arrived early, impeccably dressed in a dark suit, striped tie, and a homburg that sat squarely on his head. He swept it off as he was introduced to Gina, whom Claire had invited. Then he bent over Claire's hand, lifting it reverently to his mouth. "It is an honor to meet you, Mrs. Goddard; you are one of our special friends."

Claire looked at him quizzically. "You mean, I've given you money."

"Ah, no," he said, brushing it aside. "No, no, no; I never equate friendship with money; I do not speak of them in the same sentence. Friendship is a sacred trust: within it we flourish and bloom; without it we wither and die. Poets know this; they write of friendship. It is the bankers, a barren lot, who write of money."

"Indeed," Claire murmured neutrally, and led the way to the library, where Hannah had set a lunch table before the fire. "If all I offered you was friendship, there would be no poetry center."

"But friendship is the first and most beautiful gift, dear lady, and from it flow other gifts. Your two checks, desperately needed and received with boundless gratitude, sprang from your sympathy to my cause, your confidence in me and your belief in my stewardship. In other words, you were a true friend."

Claire did not say that he was right about the friendship but wrong about the person: she had given the money because she loved Hannah; it had nothing to do with him. And she was sure she would never get it back.

In the library, she and Gina sat at a round table set with a green and red cloth that reached to the floor, and holly-patterned plates and bowls. Hannah served soup, and Forrest stood before the fire, one arm resting on the mantel, looking down at them. His mouth was half-hidden by his beard; his brilliant blue eyes held Claire's with unwavering sincerity. Claire, who was sure he was a charlatan, found herself liking him.

"The world is a treasure trove of such glories that we can barely begin to apprehend them in our short lifetimes," he said, and Claire was sure this was how he sounded when he lectured to his college classes in New York. His voice was a resonant bass, and it gained in fervor as he spoke. "The world is fresh each dawn with promise; look around! We are surrounded by wonders and possibilities; we stand tiptoe on a precipice, arms outstretched, one foot in space, poised to fly. My God, what a blessing to be alive, to stretch and feel our limitless grasp and embrace the infinite wonders of this magnificent world! What a blessing, to wake each day to such a splendid world!"

Claire glanced at Hannah and Gina; their eyes were on Forrest and they were smiling. Claire thought she must be, too; she felt buoyed up, as if his voice were a river, carrying her outward, beyond the house. But it was more than his voice: it was his outspread arms, his body, almost springing forward with robust enthusiasm, and a kind of innocence, too, such as a very young child would have, walking through an enticing world where everything beckons and nothing is taken for granted. It was as infectious as an invitation to dance.

"It is our responsibility, as intelligent, sensitive human

beings," Forrest went on, his voice dropping, then rising eloquently to new heights, "to increase the glories, to make them fruitfully multiply, and fall as the gentle rain from heaven to sate the thirsts of the spiritually forlorn throughout the world, so that violence and degradation and unhappiness disappear from the face of the earth forever."

"I agree," said Claire easily, stopping him in midflight. "I can't imagine anyone quarreling with that."

He looked at her for a long moment, as if trying to find his place in a script. Then he spread his hands wide, smiled a sunny smile that seemed to radiate happiness, and took the fourth chair at the table. Gina was gazing at him in admiration. "You're very good. I'm not surprised people give you donations. How many projects have you been out beating the drum for?"

A look of pain at Gina's grammatical lapse rippled across Forrest's face, but he banished it in an instant and turned his smile on her. "Alas, none. I would have welcomed other opportunities, but the times were always out of joint. This is a dream I have had for a long, long time. We live on dreams, of course; we would shrivel to dried weeds without them; they nourish us and keep us human and alive, in harmony with the universe, itself a web of dreams. Awake and asleep, we dream; we merge with the ages to become what was, and what will be; we strive to become the invisible future. Now, with the miraculous generosity of Mrs. Manasherbes, all the stars of my destiny have turned in their orbits and arrayed themselves with infinity, and I am prepared to turn my energies and affections to a life's work that fully justifies my existence; I will leave this poor, bruised world a better place when I leave it than when I arrived."

"How?" Gina asked bluntly. "The generous lady has to come through first."

Claire, who was enjoying Forrest's performance, looked at him with interest, waiting for his answer.

He gave several slow, sagacious nods. He draped his napkin across his thighs, took a spoonful of potato leek soup, and

JUDITH MICHAEL

delicately dipped his tongue into it to test its temperature. Claire shot a glance at Hannah, uncharacteristically silent, watching Forrest with a quiet smile on her lips.

After a moment, when it became clear that he was not going to answer, Hannah put down her spoon. "Forrest does enjoy being dramatic," she said. "It's what makes him a great teacher. You should see him in the classroom: filled with fire and tenderness. He brings poetry and literature to life, and that brings romance and passion to the lives of his students. They think they know all about romance and passion, but in fact they know almost nothing, because they're too young and too abrupt with the world. Forrest gives them their first real taste of what it's all about, and they adore him; there are waiting lists to get into his classes."

"Have you heard him?" Gina asked.

"Oh, indeed yes. Many times. You could, too; he delights in visitors. I've been sitting in on his classes off and on since we met last June. I never get involved with anyone I haven't thoroughly checked out, you know."

Claire recalled Hannah's stories of the Italian industrialist on the cruise ship, and the realtor in her hometown in Pennsylvania, and she looked at her thoughtfully across the table.

"Over the years I've met many people who've had schemes for some big project or other," Hannah said, "and of course they all want money. Just the same as the people who camped outside your apartment, Claire, when you won the lottery. I helped some of them with the few dollars I could spare from my teacher's salary; the others I refused. And after a time I found I was able to divine which schemes would succeed and which would fail. There was something in the eyes of the people who were asking for help. I was never wrong. You, of course, never looked into Forrest's eyes; you gave money because you care about me, and you gave it freely, without even asking what I wanted it for. You are a great woman, Claire, whom money has not spoiled."

Claire was still watching her thoughtfully. She did not believe for a moment that Hannah, a third-grade schoolteacher, had been asked for money, or that she had been able to predict the success or failure of capitalized ventures.

Hannah folded her hands on the table and beamed at them. "Forrest has been playing a little game with you, Claire; he can't resist these dramatic flourishes. The fact is, he has something for you. Forrest? You are not to put it off a minute longer."

He nodded obediently. He reached into his pocket and took out a small envelope and handed it to Claire with great solemnity, as if he were acting out an ancient ceremony. "With my most fervent gratitude and admiration. You are indeed a great lady, a humanitarian, a true friend."

Claire opened the envelope and took out a check for fifty thousand, four hundred dollars.

"I estimated ten percent interest for approximately one month," Forrest said, "but I confess great ignorance in, and a strong aversion to, mathematics. If this amount is not satisfactory, tell me what you would like and I'll write another—"

"It's quite satisfactory." Claire was looking at the check. If it were a coin, I'd bite it, she thought, to see if it's real. But I can't do anything with a check but deposit it and wait to see if it bounces.

"It won't bounce," Forrest said with a boyish grin. "This is real. This is true. This is really going to happen."

"I'm very happy for you," said Claire, "and I owe you an apology."

"Oh, no, not for a moment." He put up his hand as if to stop traffic. "Those of us who are visionaries are used to being doubted. You had no reason to believe me, except for Hannah's faith in me, and I'm sure you thought I was a charlatan who mesmerized her to con her out of a pile of money. But we're past that now, yes? And we can be friends. Let me tell you about the center. We will have ten rooms, two people to a room, for poets who need a place to live and write for a few weeks; we will, of course, provide their meals as well. We'll have famous poets giving readings and lectures and conducting seminars; we'll have special films and concerts..."

He talked on, all through lunch. He spoke with fewer theatrics and even gave some hard figures on how much it would cost to run the center. "We'll always lose money; that's the way life is. We'll get grants from foundations, to keep going in a Spartan way, but that's the most we can expect. In modern societies poetry is far down any list of what people think is important in their busy lives. Anyway, it does not exist to make money; it exists to enrich our souls, and the souls of nations."

"I agree," Claire said, thinking of Alex and his theater group and all the other groups around the country whose brochures and well-written, pleading letters filled her mailbox every day. So many groups, outside the profit system, but essential for the beauty and new understanding and broader horizons they brought to those whose lives they touched. But they could not exist without money. Everything came down to money, Claire thought; it solved all problems. And she had plenty of it, coming every month, so predictably it no longer amazed her. Nor was she surprised any longer at how thoroughly she had mastered the many ways of spending it. "I'll be glad to make a donation to the center," she said, "when you know what your needs are."

"Oh, how generous. But in fact, we already know how much—"

"We'll tell you as soon as we have some figures," said Hannah firmly. She had put a platter of cookies in the center of the table and was pouring coffee. "We're not running it yet; all we're doing is getting the building ready for the grand opening next September."

"Hard to believe," Gina said. "She really came through, Mrs. what's her name."

"Mrs. Manasherbes, and some of us never doubted that she would," Hannah said. "You might have noticed that Forrest has a way with him."

Claire was frowning. " *'We'll* tell you as soon as *we* have some figures,' " she said, echoing Hannah. " *'We're* getting ready for the grand opening next September.' What does that mean?"

"Well, my dear Claire." Hannah leaned forward and took Claire's hand. "I was going to tell you later, but this is really quite a good time for it. We've actually formed a partnership. Forrest will deal with the visiting poets and writers, the public programs, and the writers who need scholarships to live and write at the center for short periods of time. But he does lack an essential practicality. Someone else has to run the place, someone who's a kind of combination resident housemother and executive director and traffic cop. Forrest has asked me to be that person. And I've accepted."

Stunned, Claire just looked at her.

"It's time," Hannah said gently. "You never thought, when I arrived, that I would stay indefinitely."

"But that was a long time ago, and we weren't sure it would work out. But it has. Don't you think so? I thought you were happy here."

"I've been happier than you can imagine," Hannah said simply. "This is my home, and I love it. But now I'm needed somewhere else, not only by Forrest and all those poets who probably have no idea how to cook or take care of a poetry center, but also by this elusive woman, Mrs. Manasherbes. Perhaps she and Forrest will need a mediator. Perhaps she needs a friend when she returns. I find this so exhilarating, you know: new people whom I can help, new territory, a new adventure. And I must tell you, my dear, I happened to be downstairs when you and Alex were talking just inside the front door last night, and it occurred to me that your life may be changing again, and it certainly would not include me."

"That's not true; you always have a place with me. You've been so wonderful I can't imagine ... You were downstairs? In the library?"

"Yes, getting a book; I couldn't sleep."

"The light wasn't on."

"I'd just come down when I heard you and I didn't want

to startle you, so I kept quiet." Claire looked at her skeptically. "Well, of course I was interested; I can't deny that. I'm interested in everything that happens to you, good and bad."

"Yes," Claire said, amused. She knew she could not have it both ways: that Hannah would be interested when they needed her, and discreetly withdraw when they decided they wanted privacy. Fairy godmothers, Claire thought wryly, are interested all the time.

"And I'll only be as far as New York," Hannah said. "Close enough for visits and long talks, and if you should ever need me, I'd come to you in an instant."

"Yes," Claire said again. But it was not at all the same, and she was feeling a sense of loss, as if she were losing her mother all over again. How amazing, she thought; once she had come to love Hannah and to love her presence in her life, it had not once occurred to her that Hannah might have a separate life and might someday leave.

"And I'm not leaving yet," Hannah went on. "Good heavens, how could I? I won't have a place to lay my head until the renovation is finished, sometime in August. So I'll be with you until about the first of September. If that's all right with you."

"Is your name really Forrest Exeter?" Gina asked. "It sounds like something out of a nineteenth-century novel."

"Of course it's all right," Claire said to Hannah. "How can you say such a thing?"

"Much older," Forrest said. "Are you a student of literature? If so, you've heard of the *Exeter Book,* a collection of old English poetry put together in about 1070. *Forrest,* as of course you know if you know literature, is my own modification of *The Forest Lovers,* a romance that was indeed published in the last century—"

"Gina, can I talk to you?" Emma stood in the doorway.

"Sure." As if freed from taking a test, Gina shot out of her chair.

"Emma, come join us," Claire said.

"Not now, maybe later. I've just got to talk to Gina now."

396

"It's one-fifteen," Gina said, following her into the hallway. "Did you just get up?"

"A little while ago." They went into the living room and Emma dropped onto the couch. "I just can't get myself to wake up. And I've got to, I've got to, because we're doing an extra photo shoot, Hale couldn't wait, and I've got to be good, I've always got to be good . . ."

Gina sat next to her. "Look at me." Slowly, Emma raised her head, blinking in the gray-white light that filtered through low clouds and a few blowing snowflakes. She met Gina's eyes, but it was as if she did not see her; she had a blurred, distant look, not focusing on anything, not interested in anything. "You're doing too much of that stuff," Gina said bluntly. "And it looks to me like you're mixing your poisons. Emma? Did you hear me?"

"Sure." Slowly, Emma's look focused. "I'm okay, Gina; it's just that we were up awfully late last night, that's all; I think it was about four or something when I got home."

"Drugs and booze, right?"

"I don't do a lot, Gina; I don't drink much, either; I don't like the taste."

"Something else, too. What is it? What else are you taking these days?"

"I don't know . . ."

"Come on, sweetheart, just tell me what you're taking. Drugs and booze and . . . what?"

"Just something to help me sleep. Sometimes I can't sleep. And I have to, because I look awful the next—"

"What is it?"

"Just an ordinary sleeping pill, Gina; it's nothing."

"What is it?"

"It's called Halcion."

"I've heard of it. Something; I can't remember." Gina frowned. "Who prescribed it?"

"Doctor Saracen; Brix knows him. It's okay, Gina, it really helps."

"How much do you take?"

"I don't know. Not a lot. Just one. Sometimes two."

"On top of drugs and alcohol."

"No. I mean, not always. I don't do a lot, Gina; just a tiny bit."

"A lot of what?"

"Coke, mostly; that's what Brix likes. And it doesn't do anything to my body or anything; it makes me feel good and happy, that's all it does; and Brix likes to drink, too, but I really don't like the taste. I like the coke best; it makes everything feel all right. It's not like I'm *addicted* or anything; it's not like I have to have it, it's just a . . . a tool for making life better, Brix says, like you use a pencil to write? Well, we use coke to make things fun."

"How original," Gina said dryly.

"He's very smart. Gina, listen, I have to tell you." She struggled to sit up straight. "I talked to Brix and he said they won't release the line, you know, PK-20, in March."

"They canceled the release?"

"He said they'd push it back until they did a bunch of new tests."

"He said that? Emma, he really said that?"

"Yes, he promised. He said I shouldn't tell anybody, so you should keep it to yourself, but I had to tell you."

"Why aren't you supposed to tell anybody?"

"Oh, lots of reasons. Mostly he was worried about the company's reputation; he said everybody would say they had bad quality control and they couldn't get their reputation back for a long time. Maybe never."

"Maybe people would say what a good company it is, extra-careful, willing to spend more money to guarantee safety."

Emma looked confused again. "I guess. But Brix didn't say that. He was really worried that people would know what was going on. Even about the memos. He kept asking and asking—"

"*The memos?* You told him you'd seen them? Emma, I asked you, I practically *begged* you, not to tell him."

"I know, but how else could I warn him? I had to tell him all of it or he wouldn't have taken me seriously."

Gina's head was bent in thought. A long sigh broke from her. She looked up. "What did he keep asking?"

"What?"

"You started to say, about the memos, that he kept asking and asking . . . something."

"Oh. If I'd told anybody about them."

"And? What did you say?"

"Well, I said no; what else could I say? He would have hated me if he knew I'd told you, and after I said it once I had to keep saying it."

Gina felt a chill. "Why did you have to keep saying it?"

"I told you; he kept asking. The memos, the tests they didn't do, the tests he said they were going to do; all of it. It's so confusing, I don't even want to think about it. I'm not going to think about it. I'm going back to sleep; I'm so sleepy . . ."

"Just a minute." Gina put a hand on her arm. "Listen, this is important. He thinks you're the only person who knows about the memos?"

"Yes, it's okay, he's not worried; he knows he can trust me." She drooped against Gina. "I'm going to sleep; I just wanted you to know. Everything's fine. Tell Mother I'll see her later, okay?"

Gina put her arms around her and held her close. She seemed very precious, and very vulnerable. "Sweetheart, pay attention. I want you to stay close to home. All right? Promise me you will."

"Why?" Emma murmured drowsily.

"Well." Gina laid her cheek on Emma's head and held her tighter and tried to sound casual. "Christmas is a good time for you and your mother to be close. Okay?" She thought she felt Emma nod. "Yes? You'll stick around?"

"Sure." Emma pushed herself to her feet. "I feel so heavy, like everything's dropping out of the bottom."

"Come on, I'll help you." She kept her arm around

Emma's waist as they made their way up the curving staircase and along the corridor to Emma's room. Gina helped her lie down and covered her with the quilt and stood over her as she fell instantly asleep. "Poor love," she murmured. "We'll have to figure out a way to rescue you." She bent and kissed her and closed her door before quietly going back downstairs.

Claire was alone at the table, gazing at the fire, her hands curved around a cup of coffee. "They're gone?" Gina asked.

Claire nodded. She looked up. "What's going on, Gina?"

"Well." She sat down and poured a cup of coffee. "Emma's been doing a lot of drugs, Claire; she's drinking, too, but probably not—"

"That's not true!" Claire looked at her angrily. "Emma's never used drugs; she and her friends never did, all through high school, and she wouldn't start now. I even asked her, a couple of times, and she told me she wasn't."

"Well, she lied."

"She doesn't lie! And she'd never lie to me! What's wrong with you, Gina? You've always said what a wonderful girl Emma is—"

"She is. This has nothing to do with how wonderful she is. She's in trouble, Claire, and it's this guy she's going with, and if you'd looked at her really closely, you would have seen it."

"Seen what?" Claire's anger was gone; she had sunk into her chair as if her energy had vanished, too. "I don't know what to look for."

"The pupils of her eyes and the way she looks past everything a lot of the time; how much she sleeps; the way her moods swing back and forth."

"I saw all that; I do look at her, you know. But I thought it was because of Brix, that she was worried about him and unhappy and . . ."

"All of the above. But mostly it's coke and booze."

"You *think*," Claire said, fighting back. "You don't really know. It's not like Emma; she wouldn't change so much; I *would* have noticed. We're still close enough that I would have seen ... And I know she never, ever, was even interested—"

"Claire, she told me. It doesn't do any good to deny it."

There was a silence. "How much is she doing?" Claire asked at last, forcing out the words.

"A fair bit, I'd guess. With him and alone."

"She's not doing it alone!"

"I'd guess she is. Maybe not the drinking, but I'll bet he's keeping her supplied with whatever it is they're doing; probably just coke."

"But she's all right, isn't she? It hasn't hurt her or made her ... I don't even know what it does."

"She's okay, but I told her to stop doing it. I told her to hang around the house, to stay close to home, and if I were you, I'd make sure she does. She'll be better off, and it would give you two a chance to do some talking. There's another reason for—"

"She doesn't talk to me," Claire said, her words filled with pain. "When we were Christmas shopping, there was only so much we could talk about and then she started to run away. She doesn't trust me anymore."

"Trust has nothing to do with it. She can't stand the thought of disappointing you. She isn't proud of what she's doing—I don't think she's proud of anything lately except her modeling—but at least she knows that *you're* proud of her, and she can't bear to lose that."

"I'm always proud of her," Claire said in a low voice. "I always love her. She knows that. She must know that."

"Sure she does. But she's scared, too, and she's not thinking straight."

"Poor love," murmured Claire, echoing Gina's words. There was a silence. "I have to get her away from here," she said at last. "I've tried before, but she didn't want to leave and I didn't push hard enough. I'll have to find a way now; she's got to get away from Brix and even the modeling; she ought to have a chance to think about what she wants to do instead of plunging in."

"There's another reason I think she ought to stay close to home," Gina said when Claire's words faded. "I don't know whether it's something to be worried about or not, but since Emma's involved, you ought to know about it." She told Claire about the memos Emma had seen, and the copies and the test reports she herself had found in the files in the testing department. "What I'm pretty sure of is, somebody's doctored the test results so everything looks fine, and they'll ship in March with trumpets playing and banners flying and have the jump on all their competitors. It's all timing, you know; whatever ingredient they're using, everyone else will have a variation of it, probably sooner than later. So a few months can make a huge difference in sales."

"All this time, you didn't tell me any of this."

"You were pretty tight with Quentin, you know, the boss, the president of the company. Emma didn't want you to know, and it didn't seem urgent, so I went along."

"But it concerned Emma. I had a right to know."

"Really? A right? Come on, Claire, we've known each other a long time, and I haven't seen you throwing your weight around with Emma, telling her about all your rights. What about if she'd gone to college? You wouldn't have the faintest idea what she was involved in, unless she decided to tell you, and I'll bet you'd think that was fine; you wouldn't expect her to tell you every detail of every day. It would probably drive you crazy if she did, because you'd be too far away to do anything about it. Anyway, you brought her up to make decisions on her own, didn't you?"

"What did she do about the memos?"

"She went to Brix and told him she was worried about him; she's got some screwy notion that he's being set up as the fall guy if something goes wrong. He told her they're delaying the release and setting up some new tests, that there was some kind of flaw in the first tests. Which I don't believe. But the point is, he kept asking Emma if she'd told anybody about the memos. She says he asked and asked."

"She told you."

"But he doesn't know that because she told him she hadn't told anybody. She was afraid he'd hate her if he knew she had. So she told him nobody knew about the memos but her. She says he had her repeat that, over and over, as if that was all he was worried about. As if—this is what I thought, anyway, when she told me about it—as if he was part of whatever was going on and was worried about his own ass." Their eyes met. "And I was thinking about that kid in college."

"No," Claire whispered. "No, no, he wouldn't hurt her . . ." She shook her head. "His father . . . everyone knows about them . . . and besides . . . these are respectable people, Quentin and Brix, they're not . . . they don't . . ." She jumped up. "Where is she?"

"In bed. Asleep. She was exhausted. Look, I don't know if they're respectable or not; you know Quentin better than I do. But whatever they are, they've got a lot at stake, and I wouldn't want to predict what either of them would do if they felt threatened. I think you're right about getting her away from here, for a lot of reasons. But if she refuses to go to Europe or someplace else, why don't you send her to us for a while? You know, the modeling is all she's got that makes her feel really good about herself right now; maybe it's not good to take that away from her. She could stay with us and nobody has to know it, and I could drive her to her photo sessions and bring her back. My first experience as a chaperon. She's comfortable with us, Claire; she doesn't even have to worry about not disappointing us, the way she does with you. It would be a good escape."

"Thank you; what a wonderful offer," Claire said. "It's probably the best thing she could do. I'll talk to her. But I'll have to tell her you've told me all this."

"Fine. She's so beaten down by now she'll probably be grateful. She's been wanting to talk to you all along, you know, but there was that business of worrying that you'd think she let you down, and then on top of that she didn't think you'd understand."

"But she didn't give me a chance." There was a pause. "Remember when we talked about not talking to our mothers? It's awful, isn't it? I was always sure my mother wouldn't understand me, either."

"Well, lots of times mothers don't. Lots of times *people* just don't understand each other. Do you think my mother would understand me and Roz? Fortunately she lives a long way off, and she'll never know, if I can help it; she'd think I was damned, in the biblical sense. And maybe you wouldn't have understood Emma. Would you have sympathized if she told you how good she felt when she used drugs?"

"No, but I hope I would have tried to understand."

"But whether you understood or not, you'd tell her to stop using them."

"Of course. You just told me that's what *you* told her."

"It's different, coming from me. And my saying it isn't going to make it happen. She sees it as a criticism of Brix, you know, and she's not ready to accept that. She doesn't even want to hear any suggestion that she could still have a career as a model if she took a few years off to go to college, because she thinks *that's* a criticism of him, too."

Claire stood beside the fire, looking down at the flames. "I shouldn't have paid so much attention to myself. I was so excited at having all that money—and then there was Quentin, and now Alex . . . I didn't pay enough attention to her."

"Hey," Gina said gently, "that is pure bullshit, if you'll forgive my elegant language. From my observations, mothers are always blaming themselves when they shouldn't. You've got a grown-up girl here, and she's a very nice girl because of the way you brought her up, and if she's got problems, it's because everybody has problems at one time or another, even people who are hovered over all the time. You have a right to a life, Claire; you gave Emma everything a mother could give a daughter, and the time came when it was right for you to break out of your cocoon and kick up your heels. And get into your own kinds of trouble."

Claire gave a small laugh. "Thank you. I sort of believe

that. But right now Emma needs somebody to hover, and that means I stay home tonight so we can talk. Excuse me a minute." She went to the desk and called Alex. Between your son and my daughter, she thought, we are having a very chaste love affair. The phone rang a few times and then his answering machine clicked on. She debated briefly, then hung up without speaking. It was a message she wanted to give him personally.

"You had a date?" Gina asked. "Alex?"

"Yes."

"Is that a good thing you two have going?"

Claire smiled. "Yes."

"Oh, that is the smile of a happy woman. I'm glad; I am so glad. You know, I never was ecstatic about you and Quentin."

"Neither was I. But it was a lot of fun for a while. Until I knew it was all wrong for me."

"I hope the day comes when Emma can say that about Brix." Gina stood up and began stacking dishes. "Let's clean up; then I have to go. Would you believe I'm going to a Christmas party at Eiger Labs?"

"Why? You don't work there anymore."

"I was invited; everybody asked me to come back for it. It's kind of a going-away for me, too, I gather. Nice people work there, you know; I hope whatever's going on with PK-20 doesn't put any of them out of work."

"I can't believe Quentin would endanger the future of the company; he's got so much at stake in it."

"Well, that's the point: what he's got at stake. I think he's looking beyond it; CEO of an international company is what the rumors say. And he's still young; who knows where he'll go from there?"

There is nothing but power; it makes everything else real. You can romanticize about love, or fantasize about money, but the core is power, and those who have it have the key to everything else.

JUDITH MICHAEL

"I don't know his plans," Claire murmured. "I don't like the way he defines them."

"Somehow that doesn't surprise me." They cleared the table and cleaned up the kitchen, talking quietly together, and then Gina left. "Call me," she said. "I want to hear about Emma. And the invitation is open, you know; she can come anytime." She looked back as she left, to see Claire standing in the doorway, a small figure framed by the gleaming house she had bought with such delight only a few months before. Only happy things should happen there, Gina thought, driving away, and as she turned onto the highway to Norwalk, she tried to think of what else she could do for Claire and Emma.

For years they had been all the family she had, and even now, when she had found her place with Roz, she felt a little bit like a daughter who has moved away, but still had her family nearby. Sometimes she thought of what her life would have been without Claire and Emma, and it was a thought that froze her heart. She would have been so alone.

What would I have done with all this love I have stored up in me? she wondered as she pulled into the Eiger Labs parking lot in the fading light of midafternoon. Years of love for Claire and Emma, and now so much for Roz. Walking into the building through the familiar side door, she felt blessed; no one could ask for a fuller life.

She was surrounded by the staff of Eiger Labs as she came into the main lab. They had decorated it with a lighted Christmas tree and strings of cranberries and holly looped above the worktables, and Gina found herself having a good time, having pleasantly nostalgic feelings. She made her way slowly from group to group, raising her voice when someone turned up the volume on the Christmas carols pouring from a tape player on one of the worktables.

"Punch," said a chemist named Len Forsberg, seeing her put down an empty glass. He handed her a paper cup. "And it has one."

Gina tasted it. "Yes, indeed; you might even call it a kick. How generous of our host. Is he here?"

POT OF GOLD

"No, but junior is. Over there, in the red tie and spiffy sports coat, looking oh-so-pleased with himself. They had a terrific year, you know. We all got the end-of-year report yesterday, and everything is very rosy for Eiger Labs."

"Except for PK-20." There was a chance, Gina thought, a very small chance, that Brix had told Emma the truth, and this was the way to find out. "How much is the delay in the release date going to hurt them?"

"What delay?" Len frowned at her.

"You don't know about one? There was nothing in the end-of-year report?"

He shook his head. "I don't, and there wasn't. Why would there be?"

So that was that, Gina thought. No new tests, no delay in the release date. "I heard, just the other day, that they were going to do a new series of tests. Something about not being satisfied with the ones they'd done."

"Not satisfied? Christ, they were perfect. Who've you been talking to, Gina? Or is it the punch?"

"No, I heard it. You know how people talk."

"Well, it sounds like somebody's dreaming. Or having a nightmare, is more like it. We're all geared up for March—they've even started training sessions for salespeople all over the country—and we're working on a second line to come out next year; different products, including a whole line for men."

"You're sure of that."

"Oh, come off it, Gina; you worked here; you know what we're doing. Everything in the whole place is focused on March; it's like D-day and Judgment Day all rolled into one. If it wasn't going to happen, it would have been through here like wildfire. But what the hell, let's ask junior. If anybody would know, he would."

"No," Gina said hastily. She was gazing at Brix, laughing boisterously at something someone had said to him ... *oh-so-pleased with himself*. "Maybe I had the wrong information. Tell me again what the schedule is."

"Same as when you were here. Why would it change?"

"No reason, I guess. I guess I was pretty gullible." *And so was Emma.*

"You better believe it. Don't believe anything you hear unless you hear it from me." Len laughed and wandered off, while others took his place, asking Gina about the farm, asking her if she would ever come back. She tried to look attentive, but she was watching Brix, and in a few minutes she saw Len in the group around him.

Oh, God, what do I do now? she thought. I could tell Emma, but what good would that do? I should stay out of it at this end. But there's no reason why I should keep those memos a secret; I only promised Emma I'd give her a little time. And why should I, now? I don't care about Brix; I care about Emma.

But if I go to the FDA, Brix will know the information came from Emma. I can't tell him I raided the testing lab one night . . . well, I guess I could, but he'd know I went there based on information from Emma. And I don't want him anywhere near Emma when he finds out the FDA has the memos. In fact, I don't want him anywhere near Emma if Len tells him I was asking about postponing the release date and scheduling new tests.

She glanced again across the lab, but did not see Brix. She turned in place, looking closely at all the clusters of people, but he was not there. That's odd, she thought; the party has a while to go yet.

"Excuse me," she said to someone who was winding up a joke about lab technicians. "I have to make a phone call."

She found an empty office and perched on the edge of the desk. "Hi," she said when Claire answered. "I've been thinking about what we talked about and it seems like a very good idea, better than ever, in fact, for me to take Emma home with me tonight. You, too, if you want to come."

"Gina, she isn't here."

"She must be—she was asleep when I left and that was only a couple of hours ago."

"I don't know how long she was asleep." Claire's voice

POT OF GOLD

was strained. "I went upstairs to see how she was, and she was gone. She left a note saying that she had to go to New York for a last-minute photo shoot, and she'd stay overnight and be back tomorrow."

We're doing an extra photo shoot, Hale couldn't wait, and I've got to be good, I've always got to be good . . .

I didn't pay enough attention, Gina thought.

"And she's going with Brix," Claire said.

Gina swore. Her hands felt cold as she pictured Len standing beside Brix. But the photo shoot was scheduled before the party. This had nothing to do with Len. This was just what it seemed to be: a photo shoot scheduled three days before Christmas, which was odd but not unheard of. Still. "Listen," she said, trying to sound casual. "I think we ought to bring her home. I think that might be a good thing to do."

"What's wrong?" Claire demanded. "What happened?"

"Nothing. Well, I just found out Brix lied to Emma about putting off the release date, and he may have an inkling that people are talking about it and he might blame that on Emma. If he thinks she might be a threat to him, he might be . . . unpleasant. And why should Emma have to go through that? Where does she stay in New York, Claire? We could be there pretty fast."

"I don't know." Claire's voice was almost inaudible. "She's stayed in a couple of hotels, that I know of . . ."

"Which ones?"

"The Plaza and the Fairchild."

"Why don't you call and see if she's registered? Or if Brix is."

"And if they're not?"

"I don't know. I think I'll come up to Wilton. I'll be there in twenty minutes. Claire, everything is probably fine. I'm probably acting like a hysterical aunt."

"Yes," Claire murmured, but there was a catch in her voice.

"Wait for me. I'm on my way." And Gina grabbed her coat and ran from the building, to her car.

17

CLAIRE was standing at the desk in the library, looking for a telephone number, when Alex arrived. "I'm early; I couldn't wait. If it's not a good time, I'll—". He stopped. "Claire, what is it? What's happened?"

"Nothing. I don't know." She was so glad to see him it drove everything else from her thoughts. She moved into his arms blindly, as children do when they are afraid, as Emma had done through the years, coming home from school to find comfort from the cruelty of another child or the pain of a romance gone astray. Claire's eyes were closed; she felt the soft wool of his jacket beneath her palms and the silk of his tie beneath her cheek; she heard the faint shudder of her breathing in the silent house. She felt none of the arousal of the night before; what she felt now was the comfort of closeness and Alex's strength.

Finally he stirred, caressing her hair and holding her head protectively against his heart. "Whatever it is, we'll deal with it," he said. "Together. From now on, my love. Together. Tell me what's happening."

"Emma," she said, her voice strained. "Gina thinks she's in danger." She began to shiver.

"Wait; come in here." Alex tightened his arm around her

shoulder and led her into the library. They sat on the couch and he took her in his arms again and cradled her. "Where is she?"

"New York. I don't know where. She left a note saying she was going in for a photo session and she'd be back tomorrow."

"She went alone?"

"She went with Brix. Or met him there; I'm not sure. I called his secretary, but she didn't have his itinerary." She told Alex everything Gina had told her. "She's probably fine; I don't know why I'm so scared. Gina said that, that she's probably fine, and I don't really have any reason to think she isn't, but when I put everything together, I can imagine . . ." She took a long breath, trying to stop shivering.

"Parents are afflicted with hyperactive imaginations; it goes with the job. What can we do?"

"Oh." Claire sprang up. "I was calling Hale when you came."

"Hale?"

"Hale Yaeger. His agency does the advertising for Eiger; he sets up the photo sessions." She was at the desk again, leafing through her leather datebook. "It's not six o'clock yet; he ought to be there . . . Hale," she said in a minute, "it's Claire Goddard."

"Claire, what a pleasant surprise." His voice was not pleasant and not surprised. But why should it be? Claire thought. Whatever he felt about me in the past few months was because of Quentin, and now that that's over he has no reason to feel friendly toward me; in fact, he has good reason to be hostile, since I'm Roz and Gina's friend. "What can I do for you?" he asked.

"I'm looking for Emma. I know you usually take care of her hotels in New York, and if you could tell me where she is—"

"That's tomorrow."

"What?"

"The photo session is tomorrow afternoon, and I told her

she ought to plan to stay over tomorrow night because we'll probably run late."

"But she went in this afternoon."

"I don't know anything about that. I just arrange the photo sessions, Claire; I don't play mother."

Claire gripped the telephone. "Hale, I'm worried about her; please help me."

"Why? What's to worry? Isn't she with Brix? He usually comes along on the New York shoots."

"Please, Hale, I've got to find her. If you'd just tell me which hotels you usually put her in . . ."

There was a pause. "The Plaza or the Fairchild, unless they stay in an apartment he borrows from a friend. I booked a room at the Fairchild for her for tomorrow night; that's all I know."

"Do you know the name of the friend?"

"With the apartment? No. And I don't know his phone number, either. Quentin might, but I never get involved in these things; young folks' screwing is their busi—"

"Thank you." She hung up and called the Fairchild. "We've stayed there," she murmured. "Emma loves it. Emma Goddard, please," she said aloud when the operator answered.

"I'm sorry," the operator said after a moment, "we have no one by the name of Goddard."

"Then Brix Eiger," Claire said swiftly, before he could hang up. "If you'll ring his room . . ."

"I'm sorry, madam, we have no one registered by that name, either."

Claire called the Plaza and again was told that Emma was not registered, and neither was Brix. Without pausing, she called Quentin, at work. "He's just left, Mrs. Goddard," said his secretary. "He did say he was going home, but I think he's going out later." Her voice went up slightly on the last word; she thought Claire would know more about Quentin's plans than she would.

"Thank you," said Claire again, and called Quentin's car

phone. But it was busy, and it remained busy for the next few minutes. Finally she slammed down the telephone and looked at Alex. "Brix uses a friend's apartment sometimes. Quentin might know where it is, but I can't reach him."

"Where is he?"

"On his way home. He lives in Darien."

"Then we'll go there, too." Alex moved quickly to the foyer and opened the closet and took out a long mink coat. "Is this all right?"

Claire looked at it absently. It stood for everything that had happened to her and Emma in the previous seven months, and she had always luxuriated in wearing it, but now she barely saw it. "Fine," she said, and Alex put it on her and she took her purse from the shelf and they went out the door, into the cold air. A few skittering snowflakes danced around them, but the clouds were breaking up and some stars and a crescent moon peeked through, and Claire had glanced up at it just as Gina arrived. "I forgot," Claire murmured. "How could I forget? Gina, this is Alex Jarrell. Gina Sawyer. I told you about her—"

"The friend who thinks Emma is in danger," Alex said as they shook hands. "Something you saw? Or heard?"

"I think I saw Brix getting the word that somebody's talking about new tests on PK-20 because the first test results weren't good. If I'm right, Brix would know that the only person who had that story is Emma. And he'd know she'd passed it on to someone, even though she told him she hadn't."

"That's worth worrying about," Alex said. He put his arm around Claire as he opened the car door. "We're going to Darien, Gina; sometimes Brix uses a friend's apartment in the city, and we thought Quentin might have the address."

"Good idea; it's a hell of a lot better than sitting around worrying. I'm coming, too, is that okay?" She saw that Claire was not focused on her. "Alex?"

"Of course. Quentin probably knows which hotels Brix likes, too," he added as he backed out of the driveway.

"He may," Claire said. "They don't seem to confide in each other very much."

Alex took her hand and held it as they drove. They were silent; none of them wanted to talk. "It's early," Alex said as they approached Darien. "They'll be at dinner in New York. We can be there before they finish. We'll find her, Claire. We'll bring her home."

His hand held hers firmly. But he's never met Brix, Claire thought. He's never met Quentin. He doesn't know what they're like: the single-mindedness, the determination. And he doesn't know that Emma is afraid to break away. She may be afraid of Brix by now, but she may be even more afraid of losing him.

But she did not say that to Alex. He was comforting her; he was at her side and he would stay there through whatever they found. *From now on, my love. Together.*

My love. My love. She could barely fathom it. Something so wonderful should be savored, its endless possibilities imagined and treasured. Instead, she felt only a swift moment of delight, her own love welling up, but then, just as swiftly, it was overwhelmed by the thought of Emma, and something so terrible ... but she was not sure of that. Gina could be wrong; she could be imagining, exaggerating. We might find Emma and Brix quietly at dinner. We might. We might.

He was removing a screen from his window and he leaned out too far and fell.

A long shudder tore through Claire. She closed her eyes and saw Emma falling. No! she cried silently. No, no, no... She forced the image away. Then, in a minute, she saw Emma, graduating on a sunny May day, wearing a yellow dress her mother had made for her, laughing and teasing with her friends after the ceremony, her eyes wide with worry when Toby disappeared. *Everything's changing.*

Please, Claire thought, unable to put anything more into words. Please, please, please.

* * *

POT OF GOLD

Brix and Emma sat at a small table along the mirrored wall of the restaurant. It was early and the room was not crowded, and sitting on a velvet banquette, Emma looked only at Brix and pretended they were alone. Around them was the hum of other conversations and the clatter of china and silver, but their table felt to her like a beautiful, private place where waiters approached silently and spoke in hushed tones, where she and Brix faced each other across a crisp white cloth set with delicate French china and crystal, a small candelabra with three white candles, and a perfect rose in a small cut-glass vase. French Christmas carols played softly in the background, and now and then Emma caught a phrase from a song she had learned in school, and then she would have the strange sensation of being two people at once: Emma in the high school chorus, excited about singing in French, and Emma in a restaurant in New York, excited about Brix.

"To the most beautiful woman in New York," he said, and took her hand as he raised his glass. "And to us."

Emma, flushed and trembling with a happiness she could barely contain, touched her glass to his. "I love you," she said.

The waiter brought their desserts and Brix let go of Emma's hand. "Maybe we'll go skiing," he said, taking a neat spoonful of his crème brûlée. "Would you like that? You'd learn in no time; we'll go to Aspen and you'll take a couple of lessons and then you'll be flying down the slopes, no stopping you."

Emma's eyes were shining. "I'd love it. I used to have a friend who told me what it was like, and sometimes I'd lie in bed at night, pretending I was skiing, and I could almost believe it, and then Toby would jump on me and that would be the end of that."

"Toby?"

"My dog. Didn't I ever tell you about Toby? I found him in an alley one day; he was filthy and so thin you could feel every one of his bones, and his ears were torn, but he had the most beautiful eyes, so I brought him home. Mother couldn't believe it, our apartment was so tiny, but he only took up a few inches, and he slept in my bed—"

"Lucky dog. Smart, too."

Emma flushed. "Anyway, he followed me around and we played games—"

"I like the way you play games."

Emma's flush deepened. She hated it when Brix made comments like that.

"What was he?" Brix asked after a moment.

"You mean what kind? I don't know, sort of a terrier, maybe; I don't know anything about dogs. All I cared about was, he loved me and followed me around, and understood almost everything I said, and sometimes we'd have conversations."

Brix cocked an eyebrow. "You talked to a dog?"

Emma gave a small giggle. "I know it sounds silly, but he always looked like he was listening so seriously, and when I wanted to think about something important, I told him about it." She giggled again. "I knew he'd keep it to himself, so I could tell him anything. I mean, how many people do you know that you're absolutely sure won't tell your secrets to somebody else? And it was good to talk because things sound different when you hear them out loud; not so *dire*. At least sometimes they don't." Her voice dropped. "I've really missed Toby the past few months."

Brix finished his dessert. "What happened to him?"

"He ran away. The day I graduated. That was the day Mother won the lottery, too; everything happened that day."

"Well, why didn't you get another one?"

"Oh, I don't know. We were doing so many things with all the money, and we took that trip to Alaska, and then I started modeling ... I don't know; I just never did." She paused. "I found him, you know."

"Who?"

"Toby. One day I drove to Danbury, to our old neighborhood, just to look around, and I saw him."

"So?" Brix asked when she stopped. "Why didn't you take him home?"

"Because he was happy. He was in the backyard of a big house, with a lot of little kids, and they were throwing a ball for him and his tail was wagging so fast you could hardly see it, and he was making those little barks, you know, sort of yipping sounds that are like a person laughing. And I thought, the worst thing you can do in the whole world is take somebody who's happy and . . . ruin it."

"Well, you can always get another one." Brix motioned to the waiter, who refilled their glasses. "Drink up, sweetheart, this is a very special Yquem in honor of a very special lady, who had the good sense to come to New York without going through the motions of asking her mother's permission. Which reminds me, what's with her and my dad? I haven't seen her at the office lately."

"They're not together anymore." Emma took a sip of wine, trying to see what was so special about it. It was the third bottle of wine they had had, and she could no longer tell them apart, even though the first one had been white and the next was red and this one was a half-size bottle and the wine was a deep gold. She thought it tasted a little like varnish. She did not want any more wine, but Brix got upset when she turned down anything he chose, so she took a sip, then put it down and touched her fork to her pear Tatin, which he had also chosen, even though she hadn't wanted dessert. "They haven't been, for a while."

"Right; that's the old man," Brix said. "He goes along for a few months, hot and heavy, and then finds somebody else. Women are always trying to pin him down, but they don't get anywhere."

Emma heard a note of admiration and looked at him, frowning slightly. "Are you like that, too?"

"Hey, what kind of a question is that? This is Brix, remember? Faithful, loyal, brave, helpful, reverent, friendly and reliable, that's me. Didn't I rescue you from that terrifying wilderness in Alaska? With wolves and lions at our heels?

And carry you like a princess to that hotel that was like the end of the world?"

Emma was laughing softly. "There weren't any wolves and lions."

"That's what you think. I saw them back there, hundreds of them, thousands, maybe, hiding behind trees, waiting to come and grab you—they're into princesses these days. But I kept them away. Whenever they made the first move, I gave them my wild-animal look and it struck terror into their hearts. Did you think I'd let anybody but me get close to you? Nobody decides my Emma's fate but me."

What an odd thing to say, Emma thought vaguely, but the thought slipped away; she felt so wonderful, so warm and loving and wanting Brix that there was no room for it. "What would you have done if there really were wild animals?" she asked curiously.

"Killed them, of course." He grinned. "I couldn't be sure just looking at them would work."

"No, I didn't mean if they were attacking; I meant, just if they were there, and we could see them."

"I'd probably kill them anyway. You don't want to give somebody a chance to get you first."

"Somebody?"

"Something. Animals. Whatever it is, you have to get there first, before they get you in a place where you can't get out. Anyway, nothing happened, nothing with the animals, anyway. A lot of other things happened; it was the best night of the cruise. It's a good thing you never looked at your watch. You almost did; I actually had to distract you a couple of times. You were a challenge, you know."

"Distract me? When? At dinner? You mean you knew . . . you *knew* we'd be late getting back to the boat?"

"If I had anything to do with it. Come on, you don't really think I'd do something like that by accident, do you? I don't miss boats, my little Emma. I don't miss anything."

"You planned that whole evening? Everything?"

POT OF GOLD

"Hey, don't talk to me like that; I'm hardly a criminal, you know. We both wanted it so I made it happen."

"I didn't want it."

"You did, but you didn't know it until I gave it to you. It's not such a big deal; most women don't know what they really want. They need the right guy, to show them."

Bullshit. Hannah's voice, clear and sharp, pierced through Emma's thoughts, which had become fuzzy with wine. *Men tell women what men want. Remember when we talked about that?* Emma clung to the image of Hannah's crinkled face, shrewd and loving. She couldn't use Hannah's language; she had never been able to say those words comfortably, but she had other words, almost as good. "That's the most ridiculous thing I've ever heard," she said.

Brix's eyes narrowed. "I told you to watch it, Emma; you don't talk to me that way."

"But it is," she said stubbornly, clinging to Hannah, remembering Hannah's sorrow, and her strength. She shook her head, trying to clear away the fuzziness. "It's ridiculous. It's stupid. Men don't show women what women want; men tell women what *men* want women to want, and then if women don't give it to them, they act like they've been cheated out of something they deserve."

His face was dark. "Who told you that?"

"Hannah. But I agree with it. You shouldn't decide what I want, Brix; people who love each other try to find out what they want and then they try to give it to them." She shook her head again. "That doesn't sound right. I mean, if we love each other, I'd find out what you want and try to give it to you. And you'd do the same for me. That's what love is. You wouldn't pretend we had lots of time when you knew I was worried about being late for the boat. And you wouldn't make up stories about my mother, either, because you don't really know her. She was the one who broke off with your father; he didn't break off with her. She ended it."

"They always say that. What else did your friend Hannah say that you think I ought to hear?"

"She did end it; I know she did. She's met somebody else."

Brix was momentarily diverted. "No kidding. What a kick. Wouldn't that give him something to think about. So"—he picked up her hand and played with her fingers—"is that what you're going to do to faithful, loyal, reverent Brix? First tell him he's ridiculous and stupid and then find somebody else?"

"No, of course not. I could never do that."

"But you just told me I'm stupid and ridiculous. Or was it ridiculous and stupid?"

"I'm sorry." She hadn't meant to say that, but the words slipped out. Hannah wouldn't have apologized, she thought, because what he'd said really was ridiculous and stupid. But she wanted the dark look on his face to be gone; she wanted him to be joking and loving again, the way he had been before.

"Well, you're my little sweetheart." Brix dropped her hand and poured more wine into her glass. "The trouble is, you don't mean it."

"Mean what?" Emma asked, feeling confused.

"You don't mean that you wouldn't leave me for somebody else. You don't mean that you'd always be loyal to me. You don't mean that you wouldn't do anything to hurt me."

The sentences fell like hammerblows and Emma shrank beneath them. "I don't know what you mean. I'd never do anything to hurt you, Brix, you know that. I love you."

"Really? Really and truly? Well, maybe we should talk about that a little bit."

The waiter came to clear their dessert plates. "Mademoiselle is finished?"

"What?" She looked up at the waiter. "Oh. Yes, I'm finished."

"Two coffees," Brix said. "And two cognacs."

"Brix, I really don't want any—"

"But I do. After all, this is a celebration, right? We're

celebrating Christmas. Oh, and Emma's love and loyalty. Mustn't forget that."

Emma felt dizzy. All through dinner he had been swinging between one mood and another, and now he had changed so completely, his voice, his face, even the way he was sitting, that it was as if she sat opposite a stranger. "Brix, please, don't do this. I don't know what you want."

"I want to know why you're out to destroy me."

She stared at him helplessly. He returned her look without expression. The waiter returned with coffee and cognac, and Brix held his glass, still looking at her. He appeared perfectly relaxed, but his eyes seemed to look through Emma, as if she were not there.

"A while back," he said after a moment, "I asked you to do something for me. Not a hard thing, but something that was important to me. I asked you to keep something to yourself. You'd been spying in my office and you read a couple of pieces of paper you weren't supposed to read, and I told you it could hurt me if you talked about them and you told me you wouldn't. Am I right about that?" He waited. *"Am I right?"*

"Yes, but—"

"Yes, but you did talk. Right? Sweet, loyal, loving Emma went out and did what she'd promised not to do. Right? In fact, that's what you said just now about talking to your dog. Right? You liked talking to him because there weren't a lot of people you could trust who you're absolutely sure won't tell your secrets to a bunch of other people. That's what you said, right? So you did. How many?"

"What?"

"How many people did you tell?"

Emma tried to keep her thoughts straight. How did they start talking about the memos? They hadn't talked about the company all evening. And what did Toby have to do with it?

"How many?" Brix repeated, leaning forward. *"I asked you a question."*

She couldn't bring Gina into it. Not now; he was too angry. She couldn't even pretend there was someone else;

JUDITH MICHAEL

she'd lied to him too many times. "I didn't," she whispered. She cleared her throat. "I didn't tell anyone."

"You're lying."

"I was worried about you; you don't tell me about your work, hardly at all, but I was worried about you and—"

"Not enough. God damn it, how many people did you talk to? There are rumors all over the lab."

"There are not! You would have said something earlier."

"Well, aren't you a clever little debater. I heard it just today, at the Christmas party, somebody asked me about putting off the release."

"But you told me that's what you were going to do. Why wouldn't people know that? Everybody would know that."

"I told you that story could hurt our reputation if it got out. Remember that? We didn't broadcast it. But Emma did. Emma didn't care, did she? Little Emma didn't care about the company, or about Brix—"

"I did! I do!" Emma knew he wasn't making sense; she knew she was right and he was twisting things; but she was confused and she was becoming alarmed. Brix had never talked to her like this. Everything that was happening seemed ominous, as if doors were slamming, as if everything was ending. She looked down at the steaming cup of coffee in front of her and wondered if it would make her feel better or worse. She picked it up and drank recklessly, scalding her tongue. Tears came to her eyes. "Brix, we were so happy, you were so nice and loving, why are you doing this?"

"Because you're not my girl. My girl is somebody I can count on. My girl is somebody who never does anything I ask her not to do. I protect my girl from wild animals and she protects me from anything that could hurt me. I thought that was you, but I was wrong, wasn't I? That isn't you, is it?"

"Yes," Emma whispered. "Yes, it is. It is. It is." Hannah's smile and clear voice were gone; Emma was cold and alone and Brix was pushing her away and she thought she would die. "I am your girl, Brix. I'd do anything for you, I'd

422

POT OF GOLD

never hurt you, I'd never do anything you didn't want me to do."

"But you did," he said almost amiably.

"No, I told you—"

"But I know you lied and you're lying now and you lie all the time, and there's nothing that I hate more than a liar."

Emma's head came up. "You don't hate me, Brix. You're just saying that to punish me. But you don't, not really; you couldn't." She struggled through the fog of her thoughts. "You've been so wonderful all through dinner, and you knew all this the whole time, and you didn't say anything, you said I was a special girl, you said I was your sweetheart, you were *loving*—"

"Well, I changed my mind," he said flatly, and stared at her as if they had never met.

Emma gave a cry and slid along the banquette to get out from behind the table. A waiter came swiftly and pulled the table out so she could stand up. "Down the stairs, mademoiselle," he said, his eyes worried at her despairing look. Emma barely saw him; she scurried between the tables, between the curious faces turned her way, to a doorway in the corner of the room, and disappeared through it.

Brix watched her go. Too bad, he thought. She's the most terrific-looking girl I've ever had. Sweet, too.

He had known for some time he would have to get rid of Emma. There was no other way he could be sure of shutting her up. He'd already waited longer than he should have, but he'd kept putting it off because he got a kick out of those big eyes looking at him as if he were God, and he'd never known a girl who turned him on the way she did. But he'd known he had to do it even before the Christmas party that afternoon. He knew damn well she'd told somebody about those memos; that was how Len came to ask him about the rumor that they were delaying the release of the PK-20 line. Whatever Emma had blabbed, it hadn't been too specific; if it had, Len wouldn't have called it a rumor. Brix had been able to stop Len cold, telling him it was just somebody going overboard with the Christmas punch. You could get people to believe anything if their jobs depended on it the way Len's depended on the success of PK-20. So it was all right for now, but Emma was a loose cannon and Brix couldn't risk letting her get to Len or anybody else, even accidentally dropping something, because a rumor doesn't have to be repeated more than a few times before it begins to sound like fact.

Of course, no one would want to believe it because all of their jobs, like Len's, were at risk. And since the company was geared up for shipping in March, probably no one would even pay serious attention to it.

But his father would.

He would lose his father's trust; he would never again be close to him as he had been lately when he really began to believe Quentin had confidence in him, needed him, depended on him more than anyone else. All that would be gone forever if his father knew he'd left that folder lying on his desk for Emma and anyone else to read, exploding what had been a perfect secret, so perfect even Brix had begun to forget it.

But there was something else, too. This was a time of crisis for his father, and Emma could blow everything wide open—unless Brix stopped her. Now, truly, even though Quentin did not know it, he depended on Brix for the future of the company. Brix would save his father, save the company, be the guardian of what was most important to Quentin: all his plans for influence on a bigger stage. Without me, it would all fall apart, Brix thought. Without me he'd be nothing. I'm all there is between him and disaster.

He took from his pocket a tiny envelope and opened it. Leaning forward as if to adjust the candles on the table, shielding his cognac glass with his body, he tipped the envelope over it. He watched the pale powder, as fine as dust, settle onto the surface of the amber liquid; he held the balloon of the glass in his palm and swirled the cognac, helping the powder to dissolve. A true chemist, he thought cheerfully; you can tell my daddy owns a laboratory; maybe it's in the genes. Still leaning forward, in one smooth motion he casu-

POT OF GOLD

ally slid his cognac glass to Emma's place and pulled hers toward him. With the stem between his fingers, he cupped it in his palm and sat back, holding it below his nose, luxuriating in its heady fumes.

That was most of it, he thought. The groundwork had been laid earlier. He had gotten the Halcion from a friend, the same strength Emma took, and ground it up in the lab. He'd purposely come early to her hotel room to take her to dinner, knowing she'd be dressing, and he'd taken her prescription bottle of Halcion from her purse and dumped its contents into his pocket, then slid it almost out of sight between the lamp and the radio. Emma would be unlikely to spot it there, but the people who found her would be looking for something like it and would find it in a few seconds flat.

There was only one more step to take; then he would have covered all the bases. And for that, he needed Emma.

She came back, pale but steady. Once again the waiter pulled out the table for her and she sat in her place. "I'm sorry; I didn't mean to make a scene."

"Drink your cognac, and then we'll go," he said.

"I don't want it."

"You've made enough trouble for tonight; drink it. I planned this dinner for the two of us, and you're going to do the whole thing."

"Brix, you know I don't like the taste—"

"Emma."

She looked at him. "Why is it so important to you that I drink? I'd be the same person if I didn't. We'd still have fun together and make love together and ... love each other."

"You don't know what love is. Love is making somebody happy."

"I make you happy. You told me I do."

"You did," Brix said, nodding judiciously. "You really did. You were a nice girl and we had a good time, and I got you your job. Maybe you forgot that. You wouldn't be anything without me; we'd have another Eiger Girl. I think you forgot that. You got so full of yourself you forgot what love means, and what trust means; all you care about is being the center of attention, getting people to think you're important. I guess that makes you a good model, but it sure as hell makes you a lousy girlfriend."

"I don't want to feel important! Brix, I told you—"

"Keep your voice down. And then when I plan a special dinner—I spent a lot of time thinking about this dinner, what we'd eat and what we'd drink, and I did it for you; I wouldn't have done it for anybody else—you sit there and say, 'I don't want it.' Christ, you don't know the first thing about love."

Emma looked at him for a long moment. "You're the one who doesn't know anything about love," she said, and picked up her glass and drained it.

She gasped, trying to get her breath. Her face and throat felt as if they were on fire. Tears came to her eyes and ran down her cheeks.

"That was a stupid thing to do," Brix said.

"Don't," Emma whispered. "Don't talk." She breathed in with a wheezing sound. "You've ruined everything."

"Then leave," he said flatly. "If you don't like the way I do things, you don't have to hang around. I can't stand crying anyway."

Still wheezing, Emma stared at him. "You want me to go?"

"That's what I said. Christ, it takes you a long time to get the point. The hotel's just across the street; even you couldn't get lost. Go on."

There are lots of different kinds of love, but the only one that is inexcusable is the one that is a false front for cruelty or manipulation.

She was still staring at him. The restaurant had disappeared; Emma felt as if they were alone in a vast, barren field, absolutely silent, with an empty horizon stretching forever in all directions. "You've set this up, this whole dinner, to destroy us."

"You'd already done that," he said carelessly, and picked up his cognac, looking past her.

POT OF GOLD

Emma hesitated, then pushed herself along the banquette before the waiter could get to her and ran through the restaurant, still wheezing, tears running down her cheeks. She ran outside. "Mademoiselle!" cried the maître d'. "Your coat!"

"It doesn't matter, it doesn't matter, it doesn't matter." She ran across the street. Drivers honked and swore at her as she dodged between the cars and got to the other sidewalk. She was shivering in her thin dress, and her tears were like icicles on her face. She stumbled in her high heels and fell to one knee, and a hand grasped her arm and helped her to her feet. She looked up, into the stern face of one of the hotel doormen.

"Didn't know when to stop, did you, young lady?" he said. "Too much to drink and now you're going to catch your death."

"Yes." Emma felt dizzy and, suddenly, so sleepy. "Please, if I could just get to my room . . ."

"You're staying in this hotel?" he demanded in disbelief.

She nodded. "Ten . . . something. I can't remember . . ."

Holding her arm, he half dragged her into the hotel, past cheerfully singing birds in an aviary, and up to the registration desk. "Ask him," he said.

Emma tried to focus on the clerk. "Emma Goddard. I can't remember my room . . ."

The clerk tapped impatient fingers on his computer keys. "Ten twenty-one," he said coldly. His eyes were hard. "Do you have your key?"

She nodded, then realized she had left her purse on the banquette. "No. I'm sorry, I . . . I left my purse in the . . . in the restaurant."

The clerk called a bellhop and handed him a key. "Take her upstairs."

"Listen," the doorman said. "I don't think she's drunk, you know. I think she's sick."

"Get her upstairs," the clerk repeated.

The bellhop put his arm around Emma and took her to the elevator. "You'll feel better when you're in bed," he said; it was not the first time he had done this, and he knew how to make his voice sound comforting. "I'll have them send up some tea."

Emma shook her head. She was so sleepy she could barely talk. "I'll just sleep. I'm ... fine ... Thank ..." Her voice trailed away in a long sigh, and as the elevator doors opened, the bellhop took a quick look behind him, in the direction of the restaurant across the street, wondering why no one had come with her to make sure she stayed on her feet at least until she got to her room.

In the restaurant, Brix finished his cognac and strode to the door. "She'll sleep it off," he said to no one in particular, but the maître d' heard him.

"Her coat, monsieur," he said.

"Oh." He had forgotten about her coat. "Sure," he said after a moment. "Thanks." He left a ten-dollar bill on the coat check counter and gave a twenty to the maître d'. "Sorry she made such a scene. They get irrational, you know; when they want to get married, that's all they can think about. Even if the other person doesn't want to."

The maître d' nodded icily, watching Brix leave. He was not interested in the problems of his customers, unless they were the ones who came several times a week, month after month. Those he would listen to with dignified interest. For this young man and his young lady, however beautiful she was, he had only contempt, because they drank too much and behaved improperly.

He saw one of the waiters holding something, striding rapidly toward him. "The young lady's purse," the waiter said. "She left it on the banquette."

"I'll take it." Sighing with exasperation—he only wanted to be through with these people—the maître d' laid it on the shelf within his podium. Later, when he had time, he would look through it for her name and address, so it could be returned. Or she would come to retrieve it. It was all the same to him.

Asshole, Brix thought as he stood on the curb, waiting for

a lull in the traffic. In another minute he walked across the street and into the hotel. He went to the registration desk. "Did my friend come back to the hotel? Emma Goddard."

"She's in her room," said the clerk. "She seemed ... unwell."

"She was upset. You know, when they want to get married, that's all they can think about. Even if the other person doesn't want to."

The clerk nodded shortly. His view of the world was strict and uncompromising. He would never abandon his girl the way this guy had, letting her run around drunk and falling apart. Of course the clerk would never go out with a girl who drank herself into a stupor, but if a girl did drink a little too much one time, and was crying and unhappy, too, any decent man would stay with her and at least get her back to her room. It's a shame we have to let that kind of people into our hotel, thought the clerk.

"My key," Brix said. "Brix Eiger, fifteen oh nine."

"Good night, sir," the clerk said, handing Brix his key. He watched him go to the elevator. At least the guy took a separate room; most of them didn't do that anymore. You could give him credit for that, the clerk thought, but not much else.

In the elevator, Brix made a comment about the cold weather to one of the strangers standing beside him. "I'll say you must feel the cold," said the stranger. "Wearing one coat and carrying a spare."

For the first time Brix realized he was carrying Emma's coat. He chuckled. "A friend left it in the restaurant. I'll give it to her tomorrow. She won't need it tonight; she's too busy sleeping off a very lavish dinner, which she drank very lavishly."

The stranger smiled uncomfortably. There was something forced and unforgiving in Brix that bothered him. He was silent, as were the other two people in the elevator. "Good night," Brix said genially at the fifteenth floor, and turned to walk to his room. He'd watch television for a few hours, he thought; he was too edgy to sleep. Then, about seven in the morning, he'd call Emma, and when she didn't answer, he'd call the desk or security or somebody. The more people he could get involved the better. It was amazing how easy it was to do what had to be done: simple, straightforward, and smart. No complications. That was him, Brix Eiger. Smart. His father's indispensable right-hand man.

18

QUENTIN'S house was brilliantly lit: lanterns blazed along the cobblestone front walk, the porch lights on either side of the white front door, and all the paned windows, shone, and even the lights in the backyard were at full strength, illuminating the trees towering above the house. "A party," Alex murmured as he stopped at the curb. "Or he's afraid someone might sneak up on him."

Claire saw the house as if for the first time. She was not revisiting a place filled with memories, she was thinking of Emma, and so all that occurred to her as she looked at it was how sleek and self-satisfied it looked, the perfect house for its owner, who could walk through troubled families, ruined relationships, perhaps even criminal acts, and remain unscathed. It looked like a mansion from another time that would house lesser royalty, a place more sheltered from the whims of fortune than her own. *But we're not sheltered at all. We can't buy what Emma needs now; we can't even buy the time it will take to get to her.*

"You go in," Gina said from the back seat. "I wouldn't be any help at all."

"I hope we won't be long," Alex said, and he and Claire walked to the front door between low, square-cut hedges

JUDITH MICHAEL

lined up like squat sentinels guarding the house. He rang the doorbell, but it was Claire whom the butler saw first, when the door opened.

"Mrs. Goddard!" he exclaimed, showing, by his surprise, that Claire had been thoroughly erased from Quentin's guest lists. "Mr. Eiger didn't tell me . . ." He saw Alex, and confusion spread over his face. "I'm so sorry; we did not expect you, or . . . anyone else."

"We're not staying, we just want to talk to Mr. Eiger for a few minutes," Claire said. She pushed past him, with Alex just behind her. "Is he in the study?"

"No, madame, in his bedroom. If you'll wait, I will tell him—"

"It's all right; I know the way." Without any sense of irony, Claire moved familiarly through the foyer, past tall vases of ginger flowers and lilies, past the open door to the dining room where she caught a glimpse of a lavish buffet, then up the wide staircase to Quentin's bedroom. The door was ajar and she and Alex stood to the side as she knocked.

"Yes," Quentin said, and opened the door. His face froze; Claire had never seen him taken so completely by surprise.

"I'm sorry to bother you," she said, speaking quickly to forestall anything he might say, and also to mask her own surprise: she had not thought she would be so stunned by the impact of his presence, even now, after weeks away from him. "We won't take much time; we only need to talk to you for a minute. We're trying to find Emma and Brix. Emma said she had a scheduled photo session in New York, but we don't know where they're staying tonight and—"

"I haven't the faintest idea where they are." He was wearing his tuxedo pants and shirt, and a silk robe Claire had bought him for his birthday. He saw her glance at it, and his mouth curled briefly in amusement. Then he looked directly at Alex.

"Alex Jarrell." Alex held out his hand, realizing how ridiculous it was to be formal, but Quentin took it.

"The novelist?" he asked.

POT OF GOLD

Alex's eyebrows rose. Somehow, it had never occurred to him that the man Claire had rejected would know his books. "Yes," he said.

"And when you barge into a stranger's bedroom, do you call that research for a new book?"

"This is not something I'll put in a book," Alex said evenly. "I'm here because Claire asked me to come."

Quentin turned his look on Claire. "You were afraid to come alone?"

"I'm not afraid of anything here," Claire replied, an edge to her voice. "I'm worried about Emma, and we came for your help—"

"How touching. I have nothing to tell you."

Claire took a few nervous steps across the hall to the study, dimly realizing that she was desperate to get away from the bedroom. "We only want to ask you—"

"I don't know anything about your daughter." His face dark with anger at having to follow her, Quentin strode past her, into the study. "She's not my responsibility. Call Brix's secretary; she always has his itinerary."

"I did call. She said it was the first time she could remember that he hadn't left—"

"Well, he forgot. I'll talk to him about that; he knows better." He was standing beside a large globe of the world that rotated within a mahogany stand, and he gave it a shove and watched it spin. Claire had seen him do that hundreds of times, and for a brief moment she felt she was back with him. It made her feel as if she had lost her way. "If they did go in for a photo session, you can call Hale tomorrow."

"We called him," Alex said. He was standing beside Claire, and when he spoke, his voice pulled her back from the tentacles of memory and Quentin's presence. "He told us Brix sometimes stays in a friend's apartment and you might have the phone number."

Quentin ignored him. "I told you: call Brix's secretary," he said to Claire. "I don't keep track of my son's friends or of his travels. What the hell is wrong with you? They go to

New York all the time, and they're both adults. I suggest you leave them alone."

"We can't do that!" Claire exclaimed. "Quentin, please, we've got to find—"

"Then do it, whatever way you want. I can't help you."

"You might, if you'd let Claire finish a sentence," Alex said. "Are you telling us that you have no idea who Brix's friend is? I don't believe you couldn't call him at that apartment if you needed him."

"Who the fuck do you think you are?" Quentin exploded. "Get the hell out of my house. Now! Get out! If Claire wants to talk to me, she can do it herself. You're not part of this."

"Yes, he is, he is part of it," Claire said. "We're both worried about Emma. Quentin, help us, please!"

Quentin had pulled himself in; his voice was under control. "You threw away the right to ask me for help."

"My God, why do you cling to this vindictiveness?" she exclaimed. "You should be worried about Brix, too."

His face grew wary. "What does that mean?"

"He could hurt Emma! If he does, he'll be—"

"Hurt her? What the hell are you talking about?"

"He may, if he's angry. Oh, God, this is taking so much time ... Listen, we think he may be angry at her. We don't know for sure, but he could be angry, and afraid, and if he is, Emma could be in danger."

"She's not in danger; she never has been; and you know it. You've let her go running all over the countryside with him, without a word, while you were in my bed. If you think I'm going to listen to this hysteria—"

Alex took a step forward and started to say something, but Claire put her hand on his arm. If Quentin was crude enough to talk about his bed, she would have to bear it; there was no way Alex could help her with that. "He's done it before," she said to Quentin. "You know he has. That student in college; the one who's paralyzed—"

Quentin's head jerked backward. "It never happened."

He stared at her, smoldering. "I told you that story. It was over and done with long ago. Brix wasn't involved."

"Lorraine said he was. She said he—"

"Lorraine is a stupid bitch who has nothing to do with her useless life but tell wild stories. I told you not to listen to her."

"If she was wrong, there's nothing to worry about," Alex said. "We'll find Emma in good shape. But now you know what we're worried about and we're still waiting. Tell us how to find her."

"Why would Brix be afraid?" Quentin asked. "Or angry?"

"He may not be," Claire said evasively, not wanting to tell Quentin what Emma had done. "Maybe nothing at all is wrong. I just want to know that Emma is all right. Please, Quentin, please give us the number of the apartment."

"Brix has his faults," Quentin said, staring at her flatly. "One of them is a weakness for inexperienced, dependent girls. But he wouldn't do anything that might risk losing my approval. I know that. He won't hurt her. Tell me what you think he might be frightened of."

"I can't. I don't know enough about it. Quentin, for God's sake, please—"

"What the hell is he frightened of?" he roared. "You'll get nothing from me—nothing!—until you tell me—"

"He thinks Emma heard something about the early tests on PK-20," Alex said.

Quentin's face closed up. This time he looked directly at Alex. "How the hell do you know anything about PK-20?"

"I don't know anything about it. I know that Emma picked up a lot of talk in her photo sessions at Eiger Labs, and we think Brix is worried about what she may have heard."

"There was nothing to hear." Quentin looked at Claire. *"There was nothing to hear!* Where did you get this?"

"I didn't. We don't know what Emma may have heard—"

"This is a trap to destroy me. You and that woman, the

lab technician; you set me up for this, didn't you? I gave her a job and she stayed a few months, and then she quit. She was your spy. Wasn't she? *Wasn't she?*"

"No, of course she wasn't. I don't want to destroy you, Quentin; I didn't send Gina as a spy; my God, how do you think of these things?" Claire was astonished. He had always dominated; now he seemed to have shrunk, his voice not as strong, his face not as firm. He's very worried, she thought, and that made her even more afraid, because it must mean that what Emma had found was true and serious and threatening.

She looked at her watch. "We shouldn't be talking; we should be finding them." But Quentin's face had closed in and she tried to make him listen to her. "The whole time Gina worked for you, she never talked about her work. But Emma . . . Emma may have heard . . . or seen . . . or somehow gotten . . . involved . . ." She was fumbling, trying to find a way to say enough to satisfy him without giving away what Emma had seen and how much they all knew.

"There was some talk," Alex said smoothly and rapidly, as if spinning a tale, and spinning it in a way, even shading the truth, to keep Quentin calm enough to help them, "about problems with the early tests on PK-20. Someone named Kurt talked about it, early on, and said he'd mentioned it to Brix, and Emma heard about it one day when she was in Brix's office. You've probably resolved those problems; we don't know anything about that, but if you've scheduled a shipping date, you must be satisfied with your tests. What we're afraid of is that Brix may be worried about his responsibility for the product, and rumors of problems could compromise its success, or the way he's handled it, even though the problems probably were corrected long ago, and since Emma seems to have heard something about those problems, he might think she's a threat to him. We're concerned for Emma, and we've got to find her, and if you have any decency at all, you'll help us instead of dragging out this agonizing debate. It's causing Claire anguish and delaying our getting to New York and finding out one way or another whether we're right or wrong."

Quentin was scowling. The silence stretched out. "If it's the friend I'm thinking of," he said at last, "he sold the apartment a couple of months ago. They're probably in a hotel. I don't know which one, but Brix likes the Regency, the Helmsley Palace, and the Inter-Continental. When you get there, you can tell your daughter we'll be using another model from now on. Someone who doesn't cause trouble."

"I have to use your phone," Claire said, and went to the desk and began dialing. Quentin walked out without a backward glance. Alex stood with Claire, his arm around her, while she called the hotels in the order Quentin had named them. There was no Emma Goddard or Brix Eiger at the Regency or at the Helmsley Palace. But they were both registered, in separate rooms, at the Inter-Continental.

There was no answer in either room when the operator rang them.

"Come on," Alex said, and they raced down the stairs, past the butler and the waiters preparing for the party, and outside, to Alex's car. They had not seen Quentin on their way out. No more, no more, Claire thought. No more of Quentin and, please God, after tonight, no more of Brix.

"Where are they?" Gina asked.

"The Inter-Continental," Claire said, and turned to Alex, who was backing out of the driveway. "Where is it?"

"Forty-eighth and Lexington." He smiled at her. "It won't be long. They're probably at dinner and we'll beat them back to the hotel. We'll be waiting for them in the lobby, the three of us, sitting erect and stern-visaged, like the three Fates, confronting them when they walk in."

Claire could picture it. She smiled.

"Are they registered under Brix's name?" Gina asked.

"They're in separate rooms," Claire said.

"What?" Gina leaned forward. "Why?"

"I don't know. Maybe they always travel that way; I never asked."

"They didn't. Emma told me." Gina was silent for a moment. "It sounds like he wanted a way to prove he was somewhere—" She stopped abruptly. "I could be wrong. About all of it."

"I hope you are," said Alex, and picked up speed as they left Darien.

The bellhop balanced Emma on one arm as he opened the door to her room. "In you go," he said cheerfully, and sat her in one of the wing chairs beside the window, propping her head in the corner of the chair. "Do you want me to help you get undressed?"

"No . . . fine . . ." Emma murmured. "Bed . . ."

"Sure thing. Oh, hold on." He knelt and pulled off Emma's high-heeled black shoes, his hand lingering on her slender feet, ice-cold in their silken stockings. His fingers curved around her ankle and moved up her long, elegant leg. Emma murmured something, and he jerked back his hand. He put an arm around her and lifted her from the chair and laid her on the bed. Then he looked at her sheer dress, crumpled around her, and lifted her again, to pull back the quilt. Stretching her out, he covered her to her chin. Her eyes were closed. "You'll be okay," he said uncertainly. "You just had too much whatever." He backed away from the bed. "Sleep tight." He reached out his hand to turn out the lamp on the nightstand and saw the empty bottle almost hidden beside it. He started to pick it up, then pulled away. None of my business, he thought. He switched off the lamp and left the room, pulling the door shut behind him.

Emma heard the door slam. *Who's there? Did somebody come in?* She felt the weight of the quilt, but she was still cold. Her body ached to be held. *Mommy, I feel sick.* Fragments of faces and bodies, and isolated words, tumbled through her mind: she saw Hannah's smile but not the rest of her and heard her say "oatmeal" and "pizza." How odd, she thought; why is Hannah talking about oatmeal and pizza? She saw Gina's legs walking through Roz's barn to the horse stalls; she saw one of Simone's eyes watching her while she tried on a new dress; she saw Hale Yaeger's bald head shining under the lights in a photo session and Tod Tallent's grin when he said "nice, nice." They were all there at once, swooping in and out, swelling and shrinking, shrinking and swelling, circling in front of her and all around her. She was dizzy from the whirling colors and voices—they sounded so loud—and she felt like throwing up, but she could not move. She saw her mother's eyes, frightened about something. *I feel so sick, Mommy.*

"Cognac," Brix said; it was so clear she thought he was next to her, and she shrank inside because she thought he would hurt her. *I love you, Brix. No, that's not right. I loved you once, but you ruined it. Oh, Brix, why did you ruin it?* "Riding," said Roz, and Emma saw herself on a beautiful horse, flying across Roz's farm, but then the horse crashed into her house, into their beautiful new house in Wilton, into Hannah, knocking her down—*oh, Hannah, don't die*—and ran over Toby—*oh, Toby, I'm sorry, I'm sorry, just when you came back to me*—and crashed into Emma's bedroom, and she fell and fell and fell into snow and ice, she was so cold, she was shivering, she could hear herself shiver and she thought everything inside her would break apart from shivering so hard; she saw a huge chunk of glacier break off and fall into the icy water with a thunderous splash, icy droplets suspended against the blue sky as if the world had turned to ice, and she felt her mother's hand on her forehead, and she heard her mother say, "Emma," as if she were calling her.

I'm here, Mommy. Here I am. I'm here, I'm here. She was a little girl, so small her mother had to pick her up onto the couch; she curled into her mother's lap, nibbling on an oatmeal cookie and listening to her mother read a book, her voice like music, warm and beautiful, making the story real. Her mother kissed her cheek and her forehead and the top of her head and held her tight, but then, suddenly, she couldn't see the book or her mother anymore; it was all dark, the whole room was dark and she wondered how her mother could read in the dark, how could she see anything, it was so dark, but her mother wasn't reading because her voice had stopped, and then Emma couldn't feel her mother's arms anymore, she couldn't feel anything, she was all alone and so cold, she was cold deep inside her and all through her, in her throat and her stomach and even her eyes, and it was hard to breathe, she was having trouble breathing because she was so cold and weak and each breath was like pushing up a mountain that was on her chest, and then a feeling of terror swept through her because she knew she was dying—*I can't be dying, I'm just a little girl*—but when she tried to breathe the mountain kept pressing on her as if she were already buried deep in the earth, and everything hurt, all over; she was cold and she hurt and she was going to die.

There was a loud sound in the room, louder and louder, a slow rasping with long pauses in between, and Hannah's voice said, "It's you, Emma, it's you, breathing, keep breathing, Emma, keep pushing, don't stop, don't stop." Reds and yellows and blues whirled behind her eyes, so bright they hurt, and then they were gone and it was dark again, and she felt herself sinking deeper and deeper into the cold, and she thought, I can't help it, I can't do anything, I'm sorry, Mommy, I'm sorry, Hannah, I can't keep going, I can't, I can't, and then she saw her mother's eyes and she heard her mother's voice, and her mother said, "Love."

"Room ten twenty-one," said the registration clerk. He looked with curiosity at Claire and Alex, a handsome couple, respectable, classy, and their friend, standing a little to the side, good-looking, not beautiful but a real lady. And they'd come to get a kid who drank herself into a stupor. He gave them the key. "The bellhop took her up."

"Why?" Alex asked.

"She wasn't in good shape. She'd had a lot to drink."

"She doesn't drink," Claire said, and the three of them ran across the lobby, to the elevators, and pushed ahead of others who were waiting. "She hardly drinks at all; she never liked it."

"She's been drinking a fair bit, with Brix," Gina said. "And she's been taking Halcion."

"What?" Alex swung on her. "How long have you known that?"

"Since this afternoon," Gina said defensively. "She took it so she could sleep. She hasn't been sleeping too well."

"She told me that," Claire said. "But she never mentioned—"

The elevator door opened on the tenth floor. Claire ran ahead of them down the corridor to 1021 and automatically put her hand on the doorknob. "Let me," Alex said. He knocked once, loudly, and then unlocked the door. The room was dark and still, the only sound a terrible, slow rasping. Gina found a light switch and a floor lamp near the bed came on, sending a pale yellow cone of light straight down, onto Emma.

She lay in the middle of the bed, covered to her chin, her face drained of color. The rasping came from her open mouth: long struggling breaths with deadly silences between. With a cry, Claire flung herself on the bed, taking Emma and the quilt and the pillow into her arms. "Emma, we're here. Emma, Emma, we're here, we love you, please open your eyes, please, Emma, oh, God, Emma, please, please; we love you . . ."

Gina sat on the other side of Emma. She found one of her hands under the quilt and rubbed it between hers. "She's so cold. My God, she's so cold."

Alex was at the telephone. "We need an ambulance. We've got a very sick girl in ten twenty-one. Now!" As he hung up, he saw a prescription bottle tucked between the lamp and the radio. He picked it up. It had Emma's name on it, it was labeled Halcion, and it was empty.

"Emma," Claire pleaded, "you've got to hear me. Open your eyes or just nod or . . . Please, Emma, please wake up."

"Maybe if we slapped her . . . ," Gina said.

"I can't," Claire said, her face against Emma's. "I can't."

Alex leaned over the bed. "I don't think it would help."

The ambulance took only a few minutes, and then the paramedics took over, ignoring Claire and Alex and Gina. "You'd better take this," Alex said to one of them, handing him the empty bottle. "If you know what she took . . ."

"Right," the paramedic said. "Thanks. These damn kids," he muttered to himself.

"I'm riding with Emma," Claire said, and she walked beside the stretcher, holding Emma's lifeless hand. A paramedic on the other side held aloft a bottle, from which an intravenous tube ran into a vein on the back of Emma's other hand; an oxygen mask covered her nose and mouth. "Which hospital?" Claire asked the paramedic.

"Roosevelt." He was checking the flow from the bottle into the tube.

"We'll meet you there," Alex said to Claire. He kissed her forehead and held his arm tightly around her shoulders as they took a back elevator and walked through a bare corridor at the rear of the hotel. He tightened his arm briefly. "There's a lot of love around here, and if that does it . . ."

Claire nodded. "I know. I know there is. Thank you." She was crying. She touched Alex's hand and then walked beside Emma, trying to hold her head to keep it from rolling back and forth, and they went through a back door, down a ramp, and into the ambulance.

At exactly seven o'clock in the morning, Brix rang Emma's room. He let the telephone ring a dozen times, then, his voice worried and anxious, he called the front desk and spoke to the assistant manager. "This is Brix Eiger, in room fifteen oh nine. I'm worried about my friend, Emma Goddard, in room ten twenty-one; she doesn't answer her phone and I'm afraid she might be ill. I think someone ought to go there and find out."

"She's not in the hotel, Mr. Eiger. She—"

POT OF GOLD

"What? Of course she's there, you idiot; she couldn't—" He stopped himself. "She was in no condition to go anywhere last night; that's why I'm worried about her."

"She was taken to the hospital by ambulance; she was indeed very ill. Her parents arrived; it was fortunate they got here when they did."

Brix sat frozen in the desk chair. Ambulance. Hospital. Her parents. Who the hell was that? She only had a mother; how could she have parents? And why would they come looking for her? How did they know where to come?

"Mr. Eiger?" said the assistant manager.

Ambulance. Hospital. Brix stirred. "Is she all right? I mean, is she alive?"

"We don't know, Mr. Eiger. She was taken to Roosevelt Hospital."

Suddenly, Brix was engulfed in waves of fear; he was drowning in fear. Something was going on and he didn't know what was happening or who was making it happen, or where it was going or how it would end. Everything seemed beyond his control. Last night he'd had it all mapped out; he'd been on top of everything. Now he didn't know anything, he didn't even know how he could find out anything so he could figure out what to do next.

Hospital. They pumped people's stomachs in hospitals; they'd find out she took an overdose of Halcion. But that was all right; that was how he'd planned it in the first place; that was why he'd left the empty bottle next to her bed. They'd think she tried to kill herself. He'd be in the clear.

The assistant manager was asking him something. Brix hung up the telephone. He'd be in the clear, except that Emma would be alive. And she would know she hadn't taken any Halcion that night. If she remembered. If anybody believed her.

Her mother would believe her.

And his father might believe her. If he did, he'd know that Brix had fucked up. Again.

He felt sick to his stomach and bent over, his head in his

hands. Everything had been so clear the night before, so straightforward and easy. She was such a simpleton; he always knew how to get her to react the way he wanted. She called it love, but he knew it was weakness. His father didn't fall in love and neither did Brix; it was the way they stayed in control.

I have to call him, Brix thought. But maybe not. Not until he knew. If Emma died, he wouldn't have to say anything; he'd taken care of her before she talked to anybody; all his problems would be solved. He wondered what time they'd gotten to her. He thought Halcion acted very fast in the body, but he wasn't sure. And there was no one he could ask. He couldn't call the hospital; he couldn't walk in there and come face-to-face with Emma's mother and God knows who else; he couldn't ask a doctor about Halcion because that would be remembered.

He couldn't do a damn thing except go home and wait.

No, he thought. My girl had a photo assignment today and she's sick. I should call Hale and tell him she won't be there.

But he'll ask how she is and I'll have to say I don't know.

He'll ask where she is, and if I say she's at the hospital, he'll ask if I'm there with her, and I'll have to say no.

He might want to go to see her at the hospital.

And if she didn't die, he had to call his father and tell him ... something. Tell him he'd tried, tell him he'd had it all figured out but something had happened, tell him he'd fucked up. Again.

God damn it! Shaking with frustration, he fumbled with the combination lock on his briefcase, and when it was open, he took out the innocuous-looking case that held his supply of coke. "Have to think about this," he muttered in the silent room, and snorted it deeply and fiercely. He sprawled in his chair, staring vacantly at the window. The minutes passed. *If she didn't die, he had to call his father and tell him ... something.*

"Christ!" he blurted, and stood up, looking wildly around the room like an animal seeking a place to hide. The coke hadn't helped; nothing had changed. It wasn't enough, he thought; I ought to know by now what it takes. . . . He laid out the coke and leaned over the table again to snort it in, feeling the tickling sensation in the back of his throat. Now he could think about things; figure them out.

Tell him he'd fucked up. Again.

With a long howl, Brix hunched over. Nothing helped. His head was buzzing but he still didn't know what to do. *Go home.* He couldn't. All he'd do would be to sit around waiting, and he wasn't good at waiting. In other times, like that time at college, he'd called his father, but he couldn't do that now, not until he knew what was happening. There was nobody he could call, nothing he could do. Still hunched over, he paced the room. Nothing, nobody, nothing, nobody.

He could not stand it. He had to move, he had to think. He grabbed his coat and left the room. A walk, he thought. Maybe a cup of coffee. Oh . . . don't forget this. He grabbed the case of coke and slipped it into the inside pocket of his sports jacket. A little more of this, and a little time, and I'll think of something. It'll all work out; pretty soon I'll know what to do, and everything will be fine.

"Coffee," Gina said, and held steaming cups in front of Claire and Alex. "And doughnuts. Probably a long way from the world's best, but I think we should eat."

"Did you call Hannah?" Claire asked.

"She's on her way." Gina sat across from them and blew on her coffee and stared unseeing at the stack of tattered magazines none of them had read. It was seven-fifteen in the morning, and beyond the door of the waiting room the hospital was bustling with the changing of shifts and the arrival of doctors on their rounds. Everyone moved purposefully through the white corridors, everyone had tasks and schedules and goals to reach. Everyone except the people in the waiting room, groups too withdrawn into their own fears to talk to each other. On one side, on a blue leather couch, Alex and Claire and Gina sat as they had all night, except for forays to the intensive care unit, seeking news of Emma, any news at all. But there had been none.

"We're doing our best," the nurses said each time; it was said in kindly but absent voices; they were thinking of their patients, and Claire or Alex or Gina, whoever had gone, would return to the waiting room with its soothing blue carpet and blue walls, and a television set no one turned on and magazines no one read and a philodendron in the corner, its heart-shaped leaves drooping over a round table.

"Why would she do it?" Gina asked, as she had a dozen times that long night. "Why would she want to kill herself?"

"She didn't," Claire said again; she had not wavered in that belief all night. "I don't believe Emma would ever kill herself. She loves life too much. It was an accident; she took something and she had a bad reaction to it. She'll tell you that when she . . . when she wakes up."

"Who prescribed the Halcion?" Alex asked Gina.

"Some doctor Brix knew."

"Do you know his name? Damn, I should have read the label before I gave that bottle to the paramedic."

"She mentioned the name, but I don't think I . . ." Gina frowned. "Something weird, something like an Arab . . . Saracen!" she said triumphantly. "I think he's in Greenwich."

"I'll be back," Alex said, and went to a pay telephone in the corridor. He was so tense his steps were stiff, and the back of his neck ached. He took into himself Claire's agony, and it seemed to him the worst kind of agony because there was nothing they could do with it. It was not like the anguish he had felt when his wife died; he had known then he had to accept it, live with it, and somehow get past it. But there was nothing they could accept now; they could only pray and wait and help each other through the hours.

But as he lifted the handset of the telephone, absently watching the nurses at their station, busy with the work of the hospital, Alex knew that by making Claire's agony his own he had at last taken the final step in breaking through the bubble of loss and anger and loneliness that had made him feel cut off from everyone else for so long; he had become engrossed in other lives, other fears, other kinds of pain. He had learned to love, and so he had learned to live again.

Now he could write. He no longer was afraid of what emotions he might dredge up when he created, and so now he could create freely. And because he was no longer afraid of feeling love and pain and fear, he could be a lover again, and a husband to Claire and a real father to David. And to Emma, he thought, and then thought, please, God, please, God, let Emma live. Let this new family have a chance to love, and to thrive.

Meanwhile, he had to do something with the tension inside him, and he did what he always did when driven by pain: he did research. He tracked down Dr. Saracen, calling his home, his office, and finally the Greenwich hospital, where the operator paged him. In a few moments the doctor answered the page.

Alex tried to put everything into a few sentences. "My name is Alex Jarrell; I'm a friend of the mother of a patient of yours, Emma Goddard. I'm with her now; she's in Roosevelt Hospital in New York; she's taken an overdose of Halcion—"

"An overdose!" exclaimed the doctor. "I can't believe— How is she?"

"We don't know yet. She's not conscious. We're trying to find out where she got the drug, and we know she went to you."

"She did, about a couple of months ago, I think. But I wouldn't have prescribed more than half a dozen pills; as I recall, she was very agitated and I wanted to see how she reacted to it."

"We found the empty bottle. It was labeled for ten pills."

There was a silence. "It may be that she said she'd be traveling and wouldn't be able to come in for another prescription; I have a number of patients who do that. I'm sure the label said no refill."

"It did. Would ten pills plus alcohol be life threatening?"

JUDITH MICHAEL

"She probably didn't have ten. I told you, she came to me a couple of months ago. She'd probably taken at least a few of them between then and now."

"Well, would five be threatening? Or seven?"

"It's unlikely. I don't know how much alcohol she had. She told me she drank very little."

"Could she have gotten another prescription anywhere else?"

"She could have gone to ten doctors in ten cities; I wouldn't know about that. She didn't get it from me."

"Thanks—"

"Will you let me know how she is? I liked her very much. She was a lovely girl."

Is. She is a lovely girl. "I'll let you know," Alex said, and returned to the waiting room. "Did she go to any other doctors that you know of?" he asked Gina. She shook her head. "Claire? You must have a doctor."

"Paula Brauer," Claire said. "She's in Danbury."

Once again Alex went to the telephone, and called Dr. Brauer. "My God, my poor Emma," she said when he told her why he was calling. "Why in the world— What do they say about her chances?"

"They're not saying. We don't know how long it will be."

"But it isn't like Emma to do something like this. She's not a quitter; in fact, she's a very stubborn young woman. I've known her for most of her life, and I don't believe she took an overdose of anything. Are you sure it's not something else?"

"The doctors here seem sure. And we found an empty pill bottle. Did you prescribe Halcion for her?"

"Absolutely not. I don't like the drug, and I certainly wouldn't prescribe it for a teenage girl. If Emma was agitated—and I didn't know she was—there are milder drugs she could take. You found a pill bottle? Who was the doctor?"

"Robert Saracen. In Greenwich."

"I don't know him." There was a silence. "I didn't know

POT OF GOLD

Emma went to any other doctors. I don't know why she would. She's a healthy, vigorous young woman; she isn't a hypochondriac, and she wouldn't be spending her time in doctors' offices. It's possible that she's been having terrible problems that I never heard about, but even so, I can't imagine that she'd try to kill herself; it just doesn't fit with anything I know about her. Poor Claire; she must be going through hell. Tell her to call me anytime; if she wants me to come to New York, I will. And tell her I'd bet on an accident before I'd talk about Emma committing suicide."

Or something else, Alex thought. If it wasn't suicide, and it wasn't an accident—and we don't have any evidence of an accident—then that leaves murder.

He had begun thinking about it driving into the city from Darien. They had gone to look for her because they thought she might be in danger, and the danger they feared would come not from herself but from someone else. He had been swayed by the way they found her: alone, her dress crumpled up as if she had crawled into bed and pulled the quilt over her, and the empty pill bottle on the nightstand near her head. *But of course all that could have been arranged. That's the first thing that ought to occur to a novelist.*

And he had wondered about her shoes, set side by side under the chair near the bed. If she was too sick to worry about her dress, would she have worried about her shoes?

And where was her purse?

Alex re-created the room in his mind. Still standing at the pay telephone in the hospital corridor, he saw the chair with black high-heeled shoes under it. The dresser with something on it, a blouse, he thought, folded up. The desk with an empty can of grapefruit juice, the kind Emma would have found in the courtesy bar in her room. One nightstand with a lamp and an issue of *Mirabella* magazine. The other nightstand with a telephone, lamp, radio, and empty pill bottle. The bed, with a quilt pulled smoothly to Emma's chin.

He had taken a quick look in the bathroom, to see if there were any other pill bottles. There had been nothing but Em-

449

ma's makeup, organized in neat rows on the marble vanity.

He called the hotel. "This is Alex Jarrell; I was with Emma Goddard's mother last night when we took her to the hospital. Did anyone find a purse in Miss Goddard's room?"

"Not that I know of, Mr. Jarrell. If you'll wait, I'll call housekeeping." In a moment the clerk was back on the line. "There was no purse. Miss Goddard's suitcase has been packed and we're holding it at the desk."

Alex stood beside the phone. He took a pencil from his pocket and held it as if he were about to write. *I forgot about the bellhop; he took her to her room. He probably took off her shoes. But why? Where was Brix?*

He went to the doorway of the waiting room. "I'm going out for a while. I'll be back in an hour or so."

Claire looked up. Her eyelids were heavy, her face drawn. "Where are you going?"

"To find out where they had dinner. By the way, I could use a picture of Emma."

"I have one," Gina said, and took out her wallet. "Oh, wait a minute. I'll bet there's a better one, bigger anyway." She shuffled the magazines on the table, pulled out a December *Vogue*, and leafed through it until she came to the full-page Eiger advertisement. "How's that?"

"Perfect. Thanks, Gina. Do either of you need anything? I can get it while I'm out."

"No," Claire said. "Just come back."

"I'll always come back." He saw the shadowy smile that touched her lips and then he walked along the corridors they had walked through the night before. He left his car where it was and took a taxi to the hotel. The night clerk had gone home, but the clerk on duty found his home number and dialed it for Alex. "I'm sorry to bother you," Alex said, "but I'm trying to find out what happened to Miss Goddard last night. When she came in alone, had she come in a taxi?"

"I don't think so," the clerk said. "The doorman told me she fell on the sidewalk in front of the hotel, and he thought she'd run across the street. He wasn't sure, but that's what he thought."

Alex stood in front of the hotel, looking across the street. There was an Italian trattoria in the block to his right, a Japanese restaurant in the block to his left, a French restaurant across the street, and two others in the next block down. There were three restaurants in the hotel itself, but he eliminated them, since the doorman had found Emma outside.

He began at the Japanese restaurant. He found an open back door and went in, interrupting the preparations for lunch to show Emma's picture to the host and to the coat check girl. When they shook their heads, he went to the Italian trattoria, and then he walked the block back toward the hotel and went into the French restaurant directly across the street.

The owner was in his office. "The maître d' will be here at noon," he told Alex. "He told me something about what happened." He looked at Emma's picture. "Close enough to his description, I suppose." He opened a drawer in his desk and brought out a small, beaded handbag. "The waiter said she left it on the banquette. There was no identification in it or we would have called."

"She wasn't alone," Alex said.

"No; the maître d' said she was with a young man."

"Whom he did not approve of," Alex said, hearing the note of disapproval in the owner's voice.

"It is not our job to approve or disapprove of our customers. The young man did allow the young woman to leave alone, and made, I am told, a totally inappropriate remark that she was upset because she wished to marry him and he did not wish to marry her."

"He said that so others would hear it?"

"He did. The maître d' and the coat check girl."

"The young lady is in the hospital," Alex said, and saw alarm fill the owner's eyes. "Not from her dinner here, I'm sure; she either took or was given a dangerously high dose of a legal drug. I'm trying to find out what happened during dinner."

"I have no idea. I was told that the young lady fled in a state of agitation, and when she was reminded of her coat, she evidently said it didn't matter. More than once, I'm told."

"She left alone?"

"Several of my people told me that."

"Was this at the end of dinner?"

"I think so. Is this important? I can call the waiter who served their table, if you'd like."

"It is important. I'd appreciate that."

The waiter sounded as if he had been awakened. "She was very lovely, the young lady, but very unhappy. Twice she has to leave the table; once I am there to pull it out for her, and she goes to the ladies' room downstairs, but the second time she is gone before I can help her, and this time she leaves the restaurant."

"Had they finished their dinner?"

"He had, monsieur; the young lady barely ate."

"And what did they drink?"

"Ah, that I remember. A Graves, a Côtes-du-Rhone, a Château d'Yquem, and then cognac."

"Full bottles or half?"

"Full, monsieur."

"A great deal for two people."

"Indeed, monsieur. The young lady seemed to drink moderately. Except for the cognac."

"What does that mean?"

"It was after she came back from the ladies' room. The cognac was there and she drank it all at once. Like a . . . what do you say . . . like a bet. It caused her some difficulty."

"You seem to have kept an eye on them."

"On the young lady, monsieur. She was so happy, you see, and then suddenly so unhappy."

"Were they quarreling?"

"I think so." There was a pause. "I think the young man wanted to quarrel and so they did."

"What about?"

"Alas, monsieur, I am suddenly very busy and I do not

get close enough to hear. That is why the young lady leaves the table without my help."

"Thank you." Alex turned back to the owner. "May I call the maître d'?"

The owner contemplated him. "You are conducting this like a police investigation."

"I'm asking questions because I don't know what happened and the young lady is very ill. I think I can safely say you and your restaurant are not involved."

After a moment, the owner nodded and dialed another number. Again, he handed the telephone to Alex. "I'm told the young lady who fled the restaurant last night said her coat didn't matter," Alex said.

"That is correct, monsieur."

"Did she say anything else?"

"No, monsieur. She pushed through the door before I could help her, and she was gone."

"And then her companion left. When was that?"

"About ten minutes later, monsieur."

"And he made a remark about marriage?"

"A totally uncalled-for remark, monsieur."

"And then?"

"He got his coat and I gave him the young lady's coat, and he left."

"Was he cheerful?"

"I have no idea."

"Well, was he upset? If they'd been quarreling, as the waiter says, he would have been upset."

"He did not seem upset, monsieur. If I had to give you a word, I would say he seemed satisfied."

"Satisfied," Alex repeated. "Satisfied," he said again after he left the owner's office and crossed the street once again. He reentered the hotel lobby and went to the pay telephone. He had made a note of the clerk's telephone number when the day clerk dialed it. "I'm sorry to bother you again," he began.

"Hey, dude, I'm sleeping," the clerk said angrily. "I work at night; I sleep in the day."

"I'm sorry; I wouldn't have called if it wasn't important. I only have a few more questions. Please."

"Well, what the hell, you got me awake now. Go ahead."

"Did Mr. Eiger say anything when he came in last night? Did he ask about Miss Goddard?"

"Yeah, he said she was upset because she wanted to get married and he didn't. Something like that."

"He told you that? Something so personal?"

"People do that."

"But he should have stayed with Miss Goddard," Alex said, probing.

"Yes, he should!" the clerk burst out. "You don't leave young girls alone in the middle of New York!"

"Right. Thanks for your help." Alex went to the front desk. "I'll take Miss Goddard's suitcase, if I may."

"Yes, sir. You'll have to sign for it."

When he left, holding Emma's suitcase, he hailed a taxi. And he was repeating the word *satisfied* as he went back to the hospital.

Hannah had arrived when he returned to the waiting room; she was holding Claire's hand, and shaking her head, back and forth, back and forth; she could not stop. "Another hospital. Another child. I should have done more, I know what dangers there are, I know what loss is. I was complacent; I thought everything was smooth ... so much money ... a home ... a family ... but I was wrong, nothing is ever completely smooth. I let Emma down; I should have said something more, done *something* to help her."

"We all tried; we didn't ignore her," Gina said. "It's not smart to sit here blaming ourselves; it's awful enough without that." She looked up as Alex joined them. "Well?"

"They quarreled at dinner and Emma left alone." He sat beside Claire and took her hand. "We have to consider the possibility that Brix somehow got her to take more Halcion than she would alone. Paula Brauer agrees with you; she says the idea of suicide contradicts everything she knows about Emma."

Hannah stared at him. "You're saying he tried to kill her."

A long moan escaped from Claire. "I let her go out with him, I didn't try hard enough to stop her."

"You did as much as you could," Alex said. "Every parent I know says the same kind of thing—'I should have done more,' 'I should have been wiser,' 'I should have been stricter'—but their kids were going to break away and do their own thing whatever happened at home. You know that, Claire; you couldn't keep her under lock and key forever. And you wouldn't want to; how would she find her own way, if you did? You're no different from every other parent; after a while, all you can do is be around if your kids need you, and hope for the best."

"But other kids don't end up in a coma," Claire said. "This wasn't just adolescent rebellion, this was a dangerous relationship and I should have done something about it."

"You didn't know it was dangerous."

"I knew what he'd done in college."

"You heard a story that Quentin contradicted, and you had nothing to help you choose between the two versions. Anyway, it was two years ago and by now he's a responsible person; a vice president of his father's company. Most mothers would have cheered."

Claire shuddered. Abruptly, she stood up and went to the nurses' station outside the intensive care unit, then in another moment came back. "Nothing. She's just the same. It's more dangerous, the longer it lasts." She stood in place, looking out the window. "She was so happy, just a few months ago. We had all that money and she was so excited; she loved that red car—she couldn't believe it when I told her it was hers—and then we went to Simone's . . . my God, it seems like a lifetime ago. We bought presents for friends and for each other; we bought the house; we bought and bought and bought, like kids in a toy store. We thought the world was wide open to us, and we could have anything in it we wanted, or the whole damn thing, for that matter, and our lives would be perfect from then on."

They were silent. In the corridor, a doctor was paged, a nurse gave instructions to a hospital volunteer, carts were wheeled past the waiting room, interns came by, trailing a doctor on his rounds, a telephone rang at the nurses' station. "What happened to me?" Claire asked, speaking almost to herself. "Why did I forget all those obvious things people always say about money? It's so trite. *Money can't buy happiness.* Everyone says it; I wonder how many people really believe it. I didn't. I thought I did, but I didn't."

"How could you?" Gina asked, "when you were barely making it from one paycheck to the next?"

"It's hard to think clearly about money," Hannah said. "It wasn't your fault." She looked to Alex, silently asking him to help.

"Most people have trouble thinking about money rationally," he said. He knew Claire was listening, even though most of her attention was on the corridor and the room at the end of it where Emma lay. "Money and power. I suppose it's because they seem simple, but in fact they're very complicated. And slippery: the more you think about them the more your ideas about them change, until, after a while, you see the world in terms of money or power, or both, instead of people. How many people do you know who think they have exactly enough money? I've met men worth hundreds of millions of dollars who go on increasing their wealth even if it means destroying people or companies or open land. They get blinded."

"I was blinded," Claire said in a low voice.

"Yes, no one could have that much money fall out of the sky without being blinded by it. There's nothing more cold and brutal than money, but it can sing, like the sirens, luring people on."

"Like Midas," Gina said. "As soon as he had the power to turn things into gold, he couldn't stop; he transformed

POT OF GOLD

everything he saw. At the end he even turned his own daughter into gold, and it killed—oh, God, oh, God." She put her hands over her face. "I'm sorry, Claire; I'm not thinking straight."

"Mrs. Goddard, will you come with me?" A nurse stood at the door of the waiting room.

They all sprang up. "What is it?" Claire asked. Instinctively, she put her hands over her ears, like a child, so as not to hear bad news.

"She's not dead," Alex said flatly, as if he could make it true by saying it.

"No," the nurse replied. "She seems to be coming out of the coma, and she may respond to her mother. If you'll come with me, Mrs. Goddard . . ."

Claire took a tottering step and Alex reached out to steady her. "Do you want me to come?"

"Just Mrs. Goddard," said the nurse.

"She'll recover now," Gina said to the nurse, daring her to deny it.

"We don't know that," the nurse said gently, "but this is a beginning."

"Go on, go on," Hannah said to Claire. "We'll be here. We'll wait as long as it takes. You go to your daughter and help her live."

19

EMMA'S bed was in a corner of a large room, bright with fluorescent lights and crowded with equipment: metal boxes, plastic tubing, wires, TV monitors with jagged peaks or waves on the screens. The narrow bed had low, barred sides, like a crib, and Emma was partially screened by a curtain on a U-shaped rod in the ceiling. Her eyes were closed; her hands were folded on her chest; an intravenous tube ran to the back of one hand from two plastic bags hanging on a chrome rack beside the bed, and she breathed oxygen through a small plastic device in her nose. Her skin was as pale as parchment; the only color anywhere was her red-gold hair, spread on the pillow. Everything else was white and chrome, sterile, cold, starkly efficient, smelling of antiseptics.

Claire sat in a plastic chair beside the bed, her back to the room. She held Emma's free hand in hers, stroking it gently and steadily, the way she always did when Emma was sick. "You're going to be fine," she said softly. "You're going to get well. You'll feel good again, and happy, and we'll have so much fun . . ." Her words caught in her throat and she took a shaky breath.

Her whole world at that moment was centered in Emma; she could not bear to think of a world without her. They had

POT OF GOLD

been so close, they had been the boundaries of each other's life for so many years that Claire thought of Emma as her other self, a self Claire had only dreamed of being, a self she willingly gave to her daughter and rejoiced at when she saw the woman Emma became. If Emma died, Claire knew she would only be part of a person, never again whole, never again able to see the world as a place of marvelous possibilities. She could not imagine any marvels, with Emma dead; it would be as if an eclipse had wiped out the light, everything in the world diminished.

She could not stand thinking about it. She wanted to scream with helplessness; she wanted to scream Emma's name, to clutch her shoulders and shake her to force her to respond. Instead, she sat still, watching Emma, her eyes burning with tears she would not allow to fall, because she was determined that when Emma opened her eyes, she would see her mother smiling and confident, absolutely certain in her love and her ability to help Emma get well, to help her forget the past.

Why would she do it? Why would she want to kill herself?

She didn't, she didn't, she didn't. The words ran through Claire's mind beneath all the words she was saying aloud to Emma. She wouldn't try to kill herself. Something else had happened. She'll tell us what it was. Soon. When she wakes up.

When she wakes up. "Emma, listen to me," Claire said urgently. "Listen. You will wake up. You'll get well and we'll do wonderful things together; I've got so many ideas about things we can do—" She stopped, holding her breath. She thought Emma's hand had moved in hers. "Emma?" She waited, barely breathing, as if she were straining to catch an elusive sound. "Emma, do that again." And Emma's hand stirred against her mother's palm.

Claire closed her eyes. In the cold brightness of the room, there were just the two of them, close together, and Emma telling her mother she was alive.

Claire put her mouth beside Emma's ear. "I'm here,

Emma, as close as I can be. Can you look at me? Can you tell me you hear me? I won't go away; I'll stay right here. I won't leave you, I'll help you wake up, I'll help you get well. Emma, can you look at me? Can you open your eyes? Can you tell me you hear me?" She sat there without moving, leaning forward, holding Emma's hand, her lips brushing Emma's ear. And then she thought of how she used to sing to Emma when she was sick. She had not done it for a long time, but now, very softly, she began to sing, old nursery rhymes and folk songs that Emma loved: songs of love and homecoming, of partings and reunions, of parents and children and again, always, of love. Her back ached, her leg was numb and tingling, but she did not move. It had been over two hours since the nurse brought her to Emma's side, but still she held Emma's hand, and talked and sang and talked again.

Emma thought it was a river, a sweet, murmuring river buoying her up. She floated on the river, and when she put her hand in the water, it was warm and gentle; there were no rocks or rapids, only softness and the low, steady sound that was so comforting as it held her and carried her forward, away from danger. She loved the river, she thought she had never loved anything as much as she loved the river, and she sank into it, giving herself up to it, letting it take her wherever it wanted to go.

I won't leave you, I'll help you wake up, I'll help you get well.

The voice seemed to be inside her, but she knew it was her mother's voice. And suddenly Emma thought, I didn't die. I was going to die but I didn't. I didn't die because my mother found me.

"I'll help you get well." This time the voice was outside her, a whisper, a soft breath in her ear. Her mother's voice. Her mother had found her and was beside her, talking to her. Her mother would take care of her. "Emma, can you look at me? Can you open your eyes?"

I want to, but they're so heavy . . .

"Emma, can you tell me you hear me?"

POT OF GOLD

Struggling, forcing her muscles to move against a great weariness, Emma opened her eyes—and looked into the eyes of her mother.

"Oh, Emma, thank God, thank God . . ." Claire leaned down, sliding her arms beneath Emma's shoulders to hug her and kiss her cheeks and forehead. "You'll be all right. I promise, you'll be all right."

Oh, my mother is so beautiful, Emma thought; nothing is more beautiful than my mother. She wanted to tell her how beautiful she was, and how much she loved her, but no words came. She tried to talk, but her throat and mouth could not push out the words. She thought them; they were in her mind, and she made sentences of them in her mind, but it was too hard to push them out; that terrible weariness that weighed on her eyes kept her throat and mouth from moving. She tried and tried, but nothing happened; she could not talk.

It frightened her. Maybe she would never talk again, or maybe she wasn't awake at all; maybe she was dreaming her mother was there and she was still dying. She remembered thinking she was dying. She couldn't remember very much, but she did remember that. She looked past her mother, at the white curtain, and looked back again, wondering where she was.

"You're in the hospital," Claire said. "In New York. We brought you here when we found you. You were very sick. When you're better, we'll take you home."

Who? Emma wondered. She looked at her mother.

"Can't you talk? Try, Emma." Claire watched Emma's lips open. No sound came out; her eyes were filled with fear. "It's all right," Claire said quickly. "It's because you're weak. You'll be fine in a little while; you'll be fine. Right now I'll do the talking; you nod if you understand. Emma? Do you understand?"

Emma nodded. It was hard to move, but her chin rose and fell enough for her mother to see.

"Good, that was very good." Claire squeezed Emma's hand. "You're going to get stronger every minute; you'll see.

Well, what shall I tell you? Gina and Alex and I found you. Hannah's here, too; she came just a little while ago. All the people who love you best—"

"Oh, this is wonderful," the nurse said, appearing beside the bed. "Hello, Emma, we've been waiting for you to wake up. Excuse me, Mrs. Goddard." Claire moved back, and the nurse took Emma's blood pressure and temperature. She checked the intravenous fluid, adjusting the valve slightly on one of the bags, checked the oxygen flow, watched the monitor showing Emma's heart rate and breathing. "Welcome back," she said, and her voice was tender and thankful. "I have a daughter," she said to Claire. "She just had her fifteenth birthday." She paused, and Claire knew what was going through her mind. Because we all have the same nightmares, she thought; all the parents in the world. There's nothing I can tell this woman that she doesn't already know; in fact, she's seen worse than Emma and worse than anything I can imagine. "I'll get the doctor," the nurse said. "She's in the hospital; she'll be here in a few minutes."

"Emma's all right now, isn't she?" Claire asked. "Now that she's awake . . . ?"

The nurse hesitated. "I don't know. Sometimes there's damage that we don't see for a . . . I can't really say, Mrs. Goddard; the doctor can tell you much more." She leaned over the bed. "Hang in there, Emma; you're doing fine."

Emma was struggling to understand what had happened. Her throat hurt; she hurt all over, especially in her stomach, as if she were bruised inside, as if she had had a terrible fall or she'd been in a fight, but she could not remember falling and she had never, ever, been in a fight. But she hurt, and it made her feel heavy, but at the same time she felt empty and light-headed, the way she felt sometimes when she hadn't eaten and she and Brix were in his bedroom, doing drugs with the television on, just the picture, not the sound. She felt she wasn't connected to anything, not even herself. *There isn't any Emma anymore; she's gone. She went to dinner with Brix and she disappeared.*

She was terrified. *I'm here! I'm me! I'm Emma! I'm here!* But the words were trapped inside her. She heard her mother and the nurse talking, but her own voice was gone. She didn't have a voice; she didn't have anything. She was a hollow shell, brittle and heavy with weariness, so heavy she could not move; she could not even lift her hand.

Dinner with Brix. She remembered that: she and Brix had gone to dinner and he'd said some terrible things. She couldn't remember what they were, but she knew they were awful. She couldn't remember anything but Brix's cold face and the waiter looking worried as he pulled out the table.

Brix. Her lips formed the word.

"He's not here," Claire said briefly. "I don't know where he is. We found you in your room in the hotel, Emma, alone; no one was with you. You were very sick. Something happened to make you sick."

Emma closed her eyes. *I'm going to die, I'm going to die, I'm going to die.*

"Emma! Open your eyes! Please, Emma, you're going to be all right, you're going to get well; listen, I'm here, I'll help you, but you've got to open your eyes again—"

"Excuse me, Mrs. Goddard." The doctor stood beside Claire. "I'd appreciate it if you'd stay in the waiting room for a few minutes; it won't be long, and then you can come back."

"But I want to know if she's all right—"

"I'll talk to you after I examine her. I'm sorry, Mrs. Goddard, but I can't tell you anything until then."

Claire lingered, watching Emma's closed eyes, her face settling back into stillness. But the doctor stepped in front of her, bending over Emma, and after another moment she went back to the waiting room.

"Well?" Hannah demanded.

"She woke up. She can't seem to talk; I think she tries, but nothing happens. But then she went back to sleep." Suddenly Claire felt herself collapse. Alex jumped up and held her as her knees buckled and she began to fall.

"Here, sit down," he said, and brought her with him to the couch. "You've been in there almost three hours, and you haven't slept and you haven't eaten."

"I brought muffins," Hannah said. "Just in case." She opened her enormous purse and brought out a paper bag filled with muffins in cupcake papers. "We can get more coffee."

"I'm not hungry," Claire said. "I'm not tired."

"What did the doctor say?" Gina asked.

"Nothing, yet; she's with Emma now. She'll call me when she's examined her. The nurse said they don't know—even if she wakes up—they don't know if she'll be all right."

"Of course she'll be all right," Hannah said. "I've seen many people in comas in my time, and when they start responding, you know you're out of the woods."

Claire was too tired to ask Hannah when she had seen people in comas. She leaned against Alex, looking dully at the table in front of them. Hannah was clearing a space among the magazines and setting out muffins. "I'll go get us some coffee," she said.

"Did the doctor say how long it would be?" Gina asked.

Claire shook her head. "I guess a few minutes."

"Then I've got time to make a phone call. I'll be right back." She walked down the corridor to the pay phone and leaned against the wall, her lips close to the mouthpiece. "Hank, it's Gina, I wondered if you got the memos and test reports I faxed you."

"I called. I told your friend Roz I got them."

"Oh. Well, I haven't been home and haven't talked to her; I'm at the hospital with a friend. So? What's your office going to do about it?"

"We're going to check it out, Gina, but not the week before Christmas. Even the Connecticut State's Attorney gets a holiday, you know. We'll wait till next week, or maybe after the first of the year. Nothing's going to happen in the next couple of weeks."

"You mean you'll send people out to search Eiger Labs?"

"I mean one of us will go out there and talk to the pres-

POT OF GOLD

ident of the company. As long as a product sits in their warehouse, they haven't committed a crime. They'd be in trouble if they shipped a product they knew could cause health problems—"

"Or blindness."

"In one test, according to the stuff you sent me, and not proven to have been caused by the cosmetic, though it looks like a high probability. What I'm concerned about here is keeping possibly unsafe products off the shelves of stores in Connecticut, so I think it's likely that we'd compel them to hold up shipping until we check everything out. Isn't that what you wanted?"

"Sounds fine to me. I was just wondering . . ."

"Now what?"

"I thought it would be good for Quentin Eiger's board, his partners, to know what's going on in their company."

"How do you know they don't?"

"I'm guessing they don't. If you could call them, Hank . . ."

"That's not the job of the State's Attorney, and you know it. We've been friends for a long time, Gina, and I love you and think you're terrific, and I definitely think you did a good deed sending me that stuff, but I'm not playing whatever game you're into now."

"Then I guess I have to call them myself," Gina said, and as soon as she hung up, she dialed the first of the two numbers she had written in her pocket notebook and took a deep breath, so she could tell her story quickly and devastatingly, and then get back to the waiting room, to find out what was happening with Emma.

As soon as he was back in his office, Brix called the hospital in New York. He spoke to the operator and then someone in the emergency room and finally a nurse in intensive care. "I'd like to know how Emma Goddard is; she was brought in—"

"Are you a relative?" the nurse asked.

JUDITH MICHAEL

"I'm a friend, a good friend—"

"I'm sorry, we can only give out information to relatives."

"But is she dead?" he cried.

"No, sir," said the nurse, relenting as she heard the anguish in Brix's voice. "She isn't dead."

Brix hung up. Not dead. Christ, what was he supposed to do now? He slumped in his chair, looking at his feet. He'd probably made things worse. If he was worried about her talking when she was crazy about him, she'd sure as hell talk now, when she thought he'd ruined everything. And if she lived and told the doctors she hadn't taken any Halcion, the whole goddamn bunch of them would think about other ways she might have gotten it, and the first thing they'd think of was him. Unless she died before they could ask her, and he had no control over that. Christ, what a fucking mess, he thought.

His telephone rang. "I want you in my office," his father said.

It's too soon. She wasn't due at Hale's office until this afternoon, and Hale wouldn't call him when she didn't show up. Not right away, anyway. It's too soon. He doesn't know anything. "Should I bring something? Any reports or—"

"Just get the hell in here."

Shit. What's happened? He took two quick snorts of coke, then grabbed a stack of papers so his secretary would think he was on important business and walked down the corridor to his father's corner office. "Yes, sir, reporting for duty," he said, trying to make it a joke, but at the look on his father's face, his grin faded.

"What the hell is going on with you and Emma?"

"Me and Emma?" Brix repeated. "Nothing. I mean, I've been going out with her, you know that—"

"What does she know about the PK-20 line?"

Brix felt his stomach contract. "Nothing. I mean, she knows what it is; she's been in enough photographs with the stuff in her hand or whatever—"

POT OF GOLD

"She knows something about the tests, and you've known it, and you haven't told me. How did she know?"

"Where do you get this?" Brix demanded, thinking this was his only way out. Emma might still die; he could deny any rumors, he could bull his way through anything, as long as Emma wasn't around. "I mean, it sounds like some idiot's been making up crazy stories."

"Her mother knows. Her mother's boyfriend knows. For all I know, the whole fucking world knows. What the hell is wrong with you? You can't fuck a girl without telling her every goddamn thing that's in your head?"

"I didn't tell her anything," Brix said, but the words came out weakly. The tightness in his stomach came back. *Her mother knows. Her mother's boyfriend knows.* She'd told people and she'd kept it from him. The little bitch; all the time she'd been swearing she hadn't told anyone, all the time she'd looked at him with those incredible eyes and he'd believed her, she'd been lying to him. Lying to him! What the fuck kind of love was that? "I didn't tell her anything," he said again.

"Then how did she know? God damn it!" Quentin roared when Brix was silent. "How did she know? You're the only one she's been sleeping with; how did she—"

"Well, I'm not so sure about that." It was like a lifeline and Brix grabbed it. "I mean, I don't know who she's been screwing. It could have been anybody. Maybe Kurt. Maybe Hale, after Roz moved out. She gets around, you know; I've been pretty sure for a long time that I wasn't the only one."

Quentin looked at him with contempt. "She hasn't looked at another man since she met you, much less slept with one; she's been a lap dog, following you around, begging for anything you could give her, and if you were a man instead of a whimpering asshole, you wouldn't try to hide behind that kind of shit." He stood up and leaned over the desk, leaning on his hands, towering over Brix. His voice was colder than Brix had ever heard it. "I want to know what she knows and how she knows it. I'll ask her if I have to—"

"No! I mean, she's not here."

Quentin's eyes narrowed. "Where is she?"

"New York, at a photo session. I went in with her last night, but I wanted to get to work on time so I came back this morning. I don't know what she did after dinner last night; we had separate rooms. She didn't like it but I thought, you know, a big hotel, it would be better for her repu—" He stopped. He was talking too much.

"She didn't go to the photo session."

"What? I don't believe it! She's never missed one. Maybe she's sick. Did Hale check the hotel?"

"I told her mother to tell her we wouldn't be needing her anymore."

Brix stared at his father in bewilderment. "Her mother? You talked to her mother? How come? I mean, I thought you weren't seeing her anymore."

"Her mother was worried about her. Her mother's boyfriend was worried about her. They were afraid you'd think she was a threat because of whatever she'd found out about the PK-20 line, and they remembered what you'd done in college when you thought someone had done something you didn't like."

Brix sat frozen in his chair. He was ice-cold with fear. How did they know what had happened in college? Emma didn't know; she would have said something. How did her mother know? Anyway, his father took care of that mess a long time ago; why would anybody talk about it now? He shrank into himself, cold and alone. His father filled his entire field of vision; there was no one else in the world but that huge, commanding figure, leaning over him, but not with love.

"They came storming into my house last night, looking for her, asking for the names of hotels you usually stay in. They thought she was in danger. Was she?" Quentin waited. *"Was she?"*

Brix shook his head. Once he started, he could not stop.

468

POT OF GOLD

His head wagged back and forth while he tried to think of something to say.

"I assume they found her; her mother hasn't called again. Did they find her?"

"I don't know," Brix said, his voice barely a croak.

"You know damn well they found her; otherwise we would have heard from them. She's probably at home, unless you have some reason to think she's somewhere else." Quentin waited. "Then I'll call her at home, or you tell me what the hell is going on. All of it."

Brix stared helplessly at his father. He could not think of anything to say except the truth, and the truth terrified him.

"From the beginning," Quentin snapped. "All of it, from the beginning."

Brix gave up. "She was in my office one day when I wasn't there." He stared at the toe of Quentin's gleaming shoe, and his voice was a monotone. "I told her not to do that, but she did, sometimes, and she saw a couple of Kurt's memos on my desk. I told her a million times not to read anything on my desk, but she did, she opened the folder, in fact, and read them, and sometime, I don't remember when, she asked me about them and I told her they didn't mean anything, that we were doing new tests and everything was fine, but she shouldn't talk about it because it could hurt our reputation, you know, if it got out. Something like that; anyway, she believed it, she said she wouldn't talk. And she didn't, I know she didn't, I scared her, she knew I'd drop her if she talked, but then she found out we didn't do any new tests and . . . oh, shit, I don't know, I guess she told somebody." Brix looked up. "But I didn't know it. I mean, I didn't know she told anybody until just now, when you told me."

"So she wasn't in danger. Is that what you're saying?"

"How did her mother know about what happened in college?" Brix burst out.

"Lorraine told her."

"Oh, fuck Lorraine," Brix muttered. He looked up. "But then you told her mother I didn't have anything to do with it, right? I mean, that was what you told everybody. That was the line."

"Was she in danger?"

Brix was silent.

Quentin shoved the telephone toward him. "Call her at home."

Brix stretched out an arm. It felt heavy and reluctant. He picked up the telephone and slowly punched the numbers for Emma's home. He listened to the ringing at the other end; he let it ring for a long time. "She's not there." He hung up the telephone. "They're probably still in New York. Maybe they decided to stay another night."

"Where is she?"

Brix cast a swift glance around the room, as if there might be a way out, then looked back at the toe of his father's shoe. "I guess she might be in the hospital. She got sick at the restaurant. I mean, she felt lousy, she went to the bathroom and then she decided to go back to the hotel. I didn't see her, I didn't want to wake her up, but I called this morning, early, and they told me she'd been taken to the hospital. They said it was her parents; I guess that was the guy her mother was with."

"What was wrong with her?"

"I don't know; I told you, she didn't feel good—"

Quentin picked up the telephone. "Which hospital?"

"She took an overdose! That stuff she was taking, you know, to help her sleep, Halcion, she took too much of it and she was drinking a lot at dinner and then she wanted a cognac and I didn't know she'd taken so much of that stuff so I said she could have one. I guess I should've said no, but she didn't tell me exactly—"

"For Christ's sake." Quentin's body was rigid. "Did you see her take it?"

"No, she told me—"

"She told you she took an overdose?"

"No, not just that way, I mean, she said she'd taken a few, to help her sleep, you know—"

"And you let her drink at dinner?"

"I didn't know! I mean, I did know, but not how many. She didn't say how many."

"What else did she say?"

"That was it! That's all I know! She took a few, she said. But they found the empty bottle in her room—"

"How do you know that?"

Brix stared at his father. Slowly, his body folded in on itself. He huddled in his chair.

"You stupid bastard." Quentin burst from behind his desk, and Brix shrank as he came close. But he kept going, passing his son with barely a glance, to pace the length of the room, his head down. A deep rage, like a serpent, coiled inside him, its venom in his blood and bones. His chest and head felt constricted; he wondered if this was how a heart attack felt. He breathed deeply, trying to get past the constriction, trying to clear his head so he could think. Trapped, he thought. Fools all around me, and I could be trapped.

But why should he be? He could manage events. He just had to think. The company first. He'd been thinking about the company since Claire left the night before, and it probably wasn't as bad as he'd thought then. Rumors were a fact of life in business, but they were ephemeral; the crucial thing was to counter them before they had a chance to take root. If a handful of insignificant people were talking about problems with PK-20, Eiger Labs would give a few interviews to carefully chosen reporters and get articles printed early in the new year, based on the test reports that Brix had altered. No one had seen the original reports; no one ever would. That would take care of the rumors, and it would still leave time to locate a new model, launch a second advertising campaign, heavier on TV than they'd planned, and make the scheduled release in March, or at the latest, early April. It would be tight, but it could be done.

But his half-assed son wouldn't be a part of it. He turned and walked back to his desk and sat in his chair, looking across the polished surface at the slumped figure of his son. "How sick is she?"

"I don't know," Brix muttered. "All the nurse said was, she's still alive."

"What did you put it in?"

His father's voice was relaxed, almost friendly. Brix looked up. His father knew, and he wasn't angry. He felt a burden begin to lift, just as he had felt it lift before, in college, when his father took over. Quentin had been like a whirlwind then, making telephone calls, talking to people, telling Brix what to say and when to stay out of sight. He'd been just like God, creating the world. "The cognac," he said. "She never liked the taste."

In the office, the air was very still. It seemed to settle around Brix like a shroud, and he shifted uncomfortably, as if trying to free himself. But it was too late; as soon as he said those words to his father, admitting everything, his father thought of him as dead.

"Her mother found her," Quentin said.

"I don't know how that happened. I mean, we've gone to New York a lot and nobody ever came . . . I don't know what made things different this time."

"You don't know very much, do you? You don't know how to keep the affairs of this company private, you don't know how to keep your girl quiet, you don't know enough to tell your father about something that could undermine the whole company, you don't even know that murder is a stupid waste of energy that only weaklings think of; it's a weapon of impotent people, and it can backfire. Well, maybe by now you know that much, at least."

"I was trying to help you!" Brix cried. "I was worried about the company!" Quentin was silent. "I wanted you to be proud of me!"

"Christ." For a brief moment Quentin felt a wave of helplessness. He had no one to talk to, no one to share his problems. He missed Claire; she had a quiet way of listening and a clear understanding that he had come to rely on, even though he told her very little of what was most important in his life. He might someday have trusted her with some of his secrets, he might even have loved her, if they had stayed together. But she would not wait. Impatient and shallow, he thought. Like all of them.

As for his son, he had never thought of Brix as anything but a weakling who took after his mother, neither a colleague nor a companion to his father. But he had thought Brix could have a niche in the company and be useful; after his graduation from college, when he had come meekly into his father's orbit, Quentin had been confident he would at least be useful.

Well, not anymore. "You'll have to get out." His voice had a strain of weariness in it that frightened Brix more than anger would have done. "You've gotten yourself out on a limb once too often; there's nothing more I can do for you."

"Wait a minute!" Brix cried. He leaped from his chair and leaned over his father's desk, in just the pose his father had held earlier. "Wait a minute, don't say that! We're partners, I'm your vice president, I'm the one you ask to do things nobody else can do, like those test reports—"

"You are not to mention those reports to anyone," Quentin snapped. "Is that clear? They don't exist, and if you say a word about them, I'll see to it that you never get another job, anywhere."

"Another job? I don't need another job! I work here! I'm vice president!"

"Not anymore. You don't have a title; you don't have a job. If you get out of here quietly, I'll write you a letter of reference that will get you a job somewhere, assuming you're not arrested for murder."

"Jesus Christ, Dad!" Brix leaned farther over the desk; he was almost lying on it. "You can't just drop me like this, it's not fair! I mean, I'm your son, you don't just kick out your son—"

"I kick out any stupid bastard who's a liability to me. I

moved heaven and earth to keep you out of jail once before, and now you expect me to do it again. Why should I?''

"Because you love me," Brix said, the words forced out in a sob.

"I don't love you. I have no reason to." Quentin walked to the door and stood beside it. "Clean out your office by this afternoon; I have a lot of work to do to clean up the mess you've made, and I have to hire somebody to do it."

I don't love you. The words were knives, cutting into his stomach, into his chest. He stood up. The son of a bitch, he thought. The fucking son of a bitch. But he could not afford to think of his father that way. *He doesn't mean it. He's mad at me, that's all. He'll get over it; he loves me and he can't get along without me. He'll get old and he won't have anybody. That's probably what the bastard deserves.* But once again Brix pulled his thoughts back. He could not be angry at his father, he had to make him love him again and he could not do that with anger.

He straightened and turned to walk toward his father, to face him, their eyes close and on a level, but nothing happened. His legs were like stones and everything inside him fought to stay where he was, at Quentin's desk, far away from the door. "I haven't got any place to go."

"You've got a place to live, and you'll find another job. I'll give you three months' salary. Plenty of time to figure something out. I suggest you stay in the neighborhood for a while. Whether she dies or not, moving to another state would look like running away."

"Dad, I mean I don't have any place besides this. Eiger Labs. There isn't any other place. It's like . . . I mean, it's like home."

"It's not your home anymore."

"Yes, it is! I mean, it doesn't just stop; I'm your son!" Brix looked at his father across the room and suddenly felt like a child, small and helpless. He began to cry. "You've got to take care of me. You always take care of me. I did everything I could for you, I wanted to help you and make you proud of me, and I did everything for you, not for me, and now you've got to take care of me—you've got to!—because I don't know where to go and . . . I'm in trouble, Dad, you know I am, and I need to be here, where you can protect me. That's what fathers do; *that's what they do.* Dad? You've got to take care of me!''

"I don't give people second chances," Quentin said, and opened the door.

Slowly, Brix stirred, moving like an old man, bent over, tears still running down his cheeks. "It's not fair," he said, and sidled past his father without looking at him.

Quentin closed the door behind him. *I don't give people second chances.* He had said those words to Claire. And to how many others over the years? None of them work out, he thought. No one stays. No one gives me what I need.

Once again he felt that wave of helplessness, and this time there was a small thread of fear in it. It shocked him. Christ, I'm letting that bitch get to me. It was ridiculous. There would be more women; there always were. Right now he had other things to think about. He had a company to run, a product to save, a future to guarantee. He sat at his desk and began to make a plan of action. And as he wrote, he gained strength. This was what he was best at: creating his own life, without worrying about other, weaker people. This was where he was king: Quentin Eiger, forging his own future.

"It's our best guess that she took somewhere around three milligrams of Halcion on top of a considerable amount of alcohol," the doctor, Claudia Marks, said to the others in the waiting room. "If her prescription was for a one-quarter-milligram tablet, which is the most it should have been—did you ever see it? It would be pale blue."

"No," said Claire. She looked at Gina and Hannah. They shook their heads.

"But there was an empty bottle in her room," Alex said. "I gave it to the paramedics last night."

The doctor nodded. "I saw it. It was for ten one-quarters.

But sometimes patients use the same bottle for other pills. Do you know if she had more than one prescription? Were there more pills in her purse, for instance?"

"Not when I picked it up at the restaurant," Alex said. "She'd left it there when she ran out, after dinner, and I can't imagine anyone in the restaurant taking anything from it."

"What about the dose?" Claire asked the doctor.

"Three milligrams of Halcion is twelve times the dose that was prescribed, and it could be fatal, especially when combined with alcohol." She looked at Claire. "There have been cases of suicidal tendencies being exaggerated in patients taking Halcion; have you seen signs of that in Emma?"

"No," said Claire. "I know she didn't try to kill herself. I know Emma. It was an accident."

"Or someone gave it to her," Alex said. "Could someone do that, without her tasting it or being put off by a change in the taste of something she was eating or drinking?"

The doctor looked at him gravely. "You're saying someone tried to kill her."

"It's something we have to think about. Could it be done? In a glass of water, for example?"

"Halcion is poorly soluble in water, so the answer to that is no. But it is highly soluble in alcohol."

Alex looked at Claire. "They had three bottles of wine for dinner, and then cognac. I talked to the waiter on the telephone today. He saw Emma drink her cognac all at once; he said it was as if on a bet. Or as if she didn't like the taste."

"She doesn't," Claire said, trembling. She folded her arms, holding herself in.

"He also said she went to the bathroom around the time he brought the cognac, as if she were ill. He was worried about her, he said."

"So she left the table and the cognac was there and so was Brix," said Gina. There was a silence in the waiting room. "But wouldn't it take a long time for twelve tablets to dissolve?" she asked.

"Not if they'd been crushed to a powder," Claudia Marks

replied. She turned to Alex. "Do you know with whom she had dinner?"

"Yes."

"And you suspect him of trying to kill her?"

"It's something we have to think about," he said again.

"Do you know where to find him?"

"Yes."

"Then you must pursue it."

"There's no question of that," Alex said. "I've called a friend who knows someone in the Norwalk Police Department. I imagine they'll be talking to him today."

"Fast work," said Gina, thinking of her own telephone call. They had both felt they had to do something, as if going after Brix and his father would help keep Emma alive.

"We can't tell Emma," Claire said.

"She'll know," said Gina. "Either she took an overdose or somebody gave it to her; how else could she have swallowed it?"

"She didn't take an overdose," Hannah insisted.

"I don't think she did," Gina agreed. "So she'll know that somehow she swallowed a hell of a lot of Halcion at dinner."

"I wouldn't worry about telling her now," said the doctor. "When she wakes up, you won't want to bring it up, so you have a while to think about what you're going to say. If she asks, I'd change the subject. I don't think she'll be concentrating on anything for a while."

"But she's fine," Hannah said, not asking a question. "She's just sleeping now; she's not in a coma."

"She's sleeping, but we don't know yet if any damage has been done to the central nervous system. We'll know better tomorrow."

"Thank you," Claire said, and held out her hand to the doctor even as she took a step to go back to Emma.

"Mrs. Goddard," the doctor said, "she'll sleep for several hours; why don't you get some rest?"

"I'm fine," Claire said, and walked down the corridor.

Alex thought she looked small and defenseless beneath the bright fluorescent lights, a slender figure in a dark blue suit. She walked with heavy steps amid the bustling nurses and doctors, who moved purposefully about their tasks while Emma's family could only wait.

"Is there any reason why I can't sit with Emma and her mother?" Alex asked.

The doctor looked at him consideringly, knowing he was not a family member, but liking his quiet stability and the deeply sustaining way he and Claire looked at each other, the sureness of affection between them more pronounced than in many married couples. "Don't broadcast it," she said, "but go ahead."

"Thanks." Alex grinned. He turned to Gina and Hannah. "Do you want to go home and wait to hear from us?"

"No way," Gina said. "We'll go to a hotel. Is that all right, Hannah?"

Hannah nodded. "But I think I'll stay here for a while longer. It's better to be close. I don't feel so helpless."

"How long do you think we'll be here?" Alex asked Claudia Marks.

"I'm not thinking about sending Emma home yet. I wouldn't even guess. You go ahead; I'll stop in again before I leave tonight."

Alex found a plastic chair and placed it close to Claire's. He took her hand and they sat together, watching Emma. Claudia Marks came back and was with Emma a few minutes and then left. "Call me anytime; the nurses have my home number. And I'll be back at six-thirty tomorrow morning."

"I like her," Alex said when she left.

Claire nodded. "But she wouldn't say anything definite about Emma."

"It's her job not to say anything definite unless she's definitely definite."

A small smile played on Claire's lips. "I'm so glad you're here."

Alex moved closer and put his arm around her, and Claire

let her head rest against his. So it was the two of them, drooping with weariness but still there, that Emma saw when, beyond the windowless hospital room, dawn was brightening the sky and she opened her eyes.

"Who's that?" she asked, her voice thin but clear.

Claire started. *She can talk; oh, thank God, she can talk. But why doesn't she—?* She leaned forward. "It's Alex, darling, you know who he—" She stopped at the confusion in Emma's eyes. "His name is Alex Jarrell," she said quietly, masking her fear. "He's a good friend."

Emma looked at him without curiosity; then she looked at her mother. "I was thinking how you used to sing to me when I was sick," she said, as if continuing a conversation. "All those songs. 'It's a Long Way to Tipperary.' That was my favorite. It made me happy."

Claire had sung that song the afternoon before, when Emma was in a coma. Now she sang it again, leaning forward. Alex held one of her hands; with the other, she took Emma's and held it tightly, as if she could send through it her love and all her energy, enough to make Emma stay awake, enough to make her well. Her voice was small but true, and it flowed sweetly through the room.

Emma sighed. "Remember when you'd make pies, and I'd sit on the counter and watch you? You'd put the top crust on and pinch it all around in little ruffles, and then you'd hold it up with one hand underneath it and cut with a knife around the edge, and the extra dough would be like a long ribbon, falling, falling onto the counter, and I'd squeeze it all together so you could roll it out again and make little jelly tarts— remember?—because there wasn't enough left for another pie. Little squares with raspberry jam or orange marmalade in the middle, and you'd fold them into triangles and press the edges with a fork so they'd stay together, but some jam always leaked out anyway, and it would burn in the oven and make an awful smell and we'd have to clean it. But you'd always let me have one of the tarts as soon as they were cool, sometimes two, and they were so good."

Her eyes were wide, but she was not looking at Claire; she was looking up, at something only she could see. "We made a snowman once, I remember, it was bigger than me, and it was cloudy outside, but the sun came out, just a little bit, poking through the clouds, and you were in the sunshine and I wasn't and neither was the snowman, just you, so bright, like gold, and you looked so beautiful and you were laughing. You looked happy, too."

"I remember," Claire said softly. She was terrified because Emma seemed farther away than ever, but she kept her voice even and spoke almost lightly. "You were five. Almost six. You made his mouth out of grapes, and his eyes were two prunes, and he had red yarn for hair, and we put a book in his hand and a straw hat on his head."

"The professor," Emma said with a little giggle. "He melted awfully fast."

"We made another one the next year. Even bigger."

"Oh," Emma said incuriously. She was silent. "I liked it when you put the sewing machine on the table in the living room—remember? There were pieces of fabric and pattern pieces, too, all over, sleeves, and a front and back, and parts of the skirt, and one day you made soup, it was cooking on the stove, and it was freezing outside, a really cold winter day, and all the windows steamed up, and it was so cozy, like being in a warm cave, just the two of us. That was a happy day."

"And you came over and hugged me." Claire's eyes were filled with tears. "And you said, 'I love you, Mommy.'"

"I'm sorry," Emma said, still looking at whatever she saw beyond the ceiling. "I'm sorry I wasn't nice to you, Mommy. I'm sorry, I'm sorry." Her voice was fading away.

"Emma," Claire said urgently. "Don't go away. Tell me, when weren't you nice to me?"

"All those things I said when you ... when you didn't want me to ..." She sighed.

"Didn't want you to what? Emma, come back, come back; you're talking about the last few months, aren't you?

It's all right, Emma; it's better to talk about the present than the past. Because then we can talk about the future. Emma, do you hear me?"

"Didn't want me to see . . . didn't want me to go out with . . . didn't want me to be a . . . the . . . girl. Can't remember . . . The Older Girl. Other. Awful. Dead. The Dead Girl. Magazines, you know, photo sessions. You know."

"Not the dead girl, Emma; it wasn't anything like that; it was something much different. You'll think of it later. And you were always nice to me, Emma. We've always loved each other. I remember that."

Emma turned her head and looked at her mother. Their eyes held for a long moment. Then Emma began to cry. "He said bad things to me."

Claire gave a swift glance at Alex, who was watching her and Emma with complete absorption. "Should I force her to remember?"

"I think it's all right," he murmured, and Claire turned back to Emma. "Who said bad things?"

Emma's head rolled back and forth. "Said I wasn't his girl. Said he hated me. *Didn't love me.*"

"Who said that?" Claire asked again.

"I'm finished," Emma said clearly. "I told the waiter. I'm finished."

No, no, no, Claire thought. I don't believe it. "Emma, what did you mean? What did 'finished' mean?"

"Dinner. And . . . everything else."

"What else? *What else?*" When Emma was silent, Claire put her hand on Emma's head and turned it until their eyes met again. "Emma, did you try to kill yourself because of what he said to you?"

Emma looked bewildered. "What?"

"Did you want to die? Did you try to kill yourself?"

"Why?" Emma frowned. "Can't remember."

"What can't you remember?"

"Ran away. Everybody was watching."

"You ran away from dinner?"

"Through the restaurant. Everybody watching. You ruined everything."

"That's what you said to him?"

"You ruined everything. I ran away."

"And then what? What happened in the hotel, Emma?"

"Can't remember."

"You went through the lobby. Did you talk to anyone?"

"Can't remember. Oh, yes, somebody told me what room."

"Told you your room number? Why didn't you remember?"

"Too sleepy. So sleepy. Heavy and sleepy and I fell down."

"Then how did you get to your room?"

"Can't remember. Oh, somebody. Red uniform. He took off my shoes. Put me on the bed. The quilt was warm."

"And then what? Did you get up after he left?"

"Get up where?"

"Get out of bed. Go to the bathroom. Take any pills to help you sleep."

"*Already* asleep," Emma said with a touch of impatience. It was the first note of animation they had heard in her voice. "Couldn't move; too heavy, sleepy, I felt so sick." She lay still, the tears running silently down her face. "I'm dying."

"No, darling, you're not. You're not." Claire paused. "You didn't want to, did you? Last night?"

Emma looked at her, wide-eyed. "Why?" she asked clearly. "I only wanted to love."

"The best answer," Dr. Marks said. She had come in quietly and was standing behind Claire. "Excuse me," she said, and moved forward. "Hello, Emma, I'm Claudia Marks and I'm your doctor while you're here, and I need to take your temperature and a few other things. It won't take long, and then you'll have your mother back again. Please," she added to Claire and Alex.

Claire kissed Emma's forehead. "We'll be right back," she said, and she and Alex returned to the waiting room.

POT OF GOLD

Hannah and Gina were there, playing word games on pads of paper.

"I brought some more food," said Hannah, gesturing toward the coffee table. Alex told them briefly about Emma while Claire sat on the edge of the couch, her hands clasped in her lap. It was twenty minutes before Claudia Marks came to them. Her face was radiant. "She's going to be fine," she said.

20

THE police called on Brix on Christmas night. He had been at a party in one of the town houses a block from his own. It had not been a great evening; most of the time he had sat in a corner, drinking Scotch and water and looking at girls, trying to get interested enough to take one of them home with him. It was not like him: everyone commented on it and tried to get him to lighten up. But he couldn't; he couldn't even concentrate on the girls—he was having trouble concentrating these days, and, anyway, he was drinking steadily and he'd done coke all day—and after a while he stopped looking and wandered off, forgetting to say good-bye to his host. Outside, he pulled on his coat and walked a little unsteadily on the winding walk that followed the undulating line of town houses to his own door, identical to every other door in the complex. From the corner of his eye he saw a police car parked at the curb. Somebody's making too much noise, he thought vaguely. Disturbing the neighbors; shame on them. He walked up the front steps and stared at the door, making sure it was his. "Thirty-eight," he muttered. That was his address, so this must be his door. He reached into his pocket to pull out his keys.

"Mr. Brix Eiger?"

POT OF GOLD

He swung around. A policeman was there, standing a little too close to him. Another policeman sat in the car. "Got the wrong guy," Brix said. "I haven't made any noise; haven't made a sound. I've been somewhere else. Very quiet."

"We want to ask you some questions about Emma Goddard," said the policeman, and Brix felt the earth slide out from under him.

He stopped himself from falling, turning it into a stumble. He was trying to think, to get his leaden mind working. "Whoops," he said as he straightened up. "Had a little too much Christmas cheer, looks like. Emma? I haven't seen her. I know she's been in the hospital, but I didn't go; we had a fight, you know, lovers' fight, whatever, and I thought, better stay away. I sent her flowers, though; I hope she got them. She didn't call, so I guess she's really mad at me." He paused. "So, that's all," he added lamely. "I can't tell you anything about her."

"We'd like you to come with us, Mr. Eiger."

"What? Where? Oh. You mean—" He was sounding stupid, Brix thought. He couldn't afford to sound stupid. They wanted to take him to the police station for questioning. Maybe he should say no. If he didn't know anything about Emma, would he say no? Probably not; the smart thing was to cooperate. They were always easier on people who cooperated. "Sure," he said cheerfully. He looked at the badge on the policeman's uniform. "Janowski. Well, let's go meet your friend."

"Sergeant Janowski," the policeman said in a neutral voice, and stood aside to follow Brix to the car.

"Detective Fasching," Sergeant Janowski said to Brix, introducing the man in the driver's seat, who was not in uniform.

"Detective," Brix said, trying to be friendly as he got into the backseat with the sergeant. "Like an Agatha Christie novel, isn't it? Well, I'll be glad to help you and your friend, but this can't take too long; I've got a date in half an hour." He had nowhere to go and nothing to do for the rest of the night, but his mind was working now and he figured he could handle these two guys without any trouble, but if he didn't give them a deadline, they'd never stop asking questions because that was how they got their kicks.

In fact, he had rehearsed this meeting. The only difference was, when he'd practiced it the first few times, he'd been sure Emma would be dead. Now, from persistent phone calls, he knew she was alive and she'd be fine. Christ, he thought, she had the constitution of a horse; only two days since their dinner and already she was on her way to being fine. So he wasn't sure exactly how this would go, but he knew he was ready, and he knew he was smarter than a couple of cops off the street.

In a small room at the police station, Detective Fasching sat on the corner of a metal desk and Sergeant Janowski leaned on a windowsill. In a corner, hidden by a folding screen, a young woman sat at a computer terminal. Brix sat between the two policemen; he had been nudged into a straight chair near the desk, and he turned his head as he talked to them, as if he were at a tennis match. "We need to know everything you can tell us about the night you had dinner with Miss Goddard at the Luberon Restaurant. That would be last Tuesday night."

"Everything? That's kind of tough." They knew where he and Emma had had dinner. They'd been talking to people, looking for things. If they knew that much, why didn't they know she'd tried to commit suicide?

Because she'd told people she hadn't. And like a bunch of idiots, they believed her. An overemotional teenager, an empty bottle, despondency over a lovers' quarrel—they must have heard about that from the maître d' and the clerk at the hotel—and still they believed her. Well, then, he had to try something else.

He shook his head. "I can't tell you everything; it wouldn't be fair to Emma. She was upset and said things she wouldn't want repeated, you know, things that showed she was really out of control."

POT OF GOLD

"For instance," said Detective Fasching.

"Look, I told you, she wouldn't want—"

"But *we* want, Mr. Eiger, and it would be best if you just told us what happened and stopped telling us what Miss Goddard would or wouldn't like. What made you think she was out of control?"

Brix shrugged. "Well, like, one minute she was telling me these crazy stories about how she used to talk to her dog, you know, have conversations with it, and then she started in on how she knows what men want and she's the only one who does, you know, like maybe the dog told her. It didn't make a lot of sense." He paused. "And then, a little later, she almost fought with the waiter when he tried to pull the table out for her, you know, when she wanted to go to the bathroom; she was shoving it, like it was in her way, but he was trying to help her, except that she really couldn't control herself. She really ran to the bathroom, too; everybody was looking at her. In fact, when she got back, I told her to stop drinking because it would only make things worse, but she said I'd gone to all that trouble to plan the dinner and she was going to do it the way I'd planned it, the whole thing. I think she was trying, even though we weren't getting along very well right then, she was trying to, you know, get me to say that everything was all right."

"Why weren't you getting along very well right then?"

"Because she wanted to get married and I didn't. I mean, someday I probably will, but not now, and anyway, she's too young. I told her that; I guess I shouldn't have. It's not just her age, it's that she doesn't know anything. She's like a little kid, happy when things go her way and then having a tantrum when they don't. That's what she did at the restaurant: she had a tantrum and she ran out. She even left her coat, she was in such a hurry."

"Was she sick when she left the restaurant?"

"Sick? Of course not; I told you: she ran out. She'd had too much to drink—I guess maybe I did, too, but it was supposed to be a Christmas dinner just for the two of us, so

I ordered some really fine wines—anyway, she drank more than she should have, but she wasn't sick, just out of control, that's all."

"What does that mean: 'out of control'?"

"Just what it says. She couldn't control what she said—lots of really nasty things came out of that pretty little mouth—and I don't think she could control what she did, which is why I told her she should stop drinking. But it was like she didn't even know what she was drinking. Like she didn't have any idea what she was doing about anything. And I thought, she takes pills and if she doesn't know what she's doing, she could take too many of them. In fact, when she was in the bathroom, I looked in her purse so I could take her pills out and keep them for her until she was in better shape, but they weren't there."

Brix stopped, pleased with himself, and waited for the next question. When it did not come immediately, he made a show of looking at his watch.

"You didn't go with her when she left the restaurant?" Sergeant Janowski asked.

"Well, no, and I'm sorry about that. A gentleman shouldn't let a lady wander around New York alone. But, you know, like I said, she'd spouted some pretty nasty things at me and I wasn't feeling too mellow about her, so I let her go. I asked if she was all right, though, when I got to the hotel, and they told me she'd gone to her room. I thought she was sleeping it off, which was what she needed, so I went to my room and I didn't call her. Until the next morning, that is."

"When was that?" the sergeant asked.

"Around seven. I thought we'd have breakfast and try to patch things up; we had to work together, after all; she was—she is—the model, you know, for one of the cosmetics lines we make in the company my father and I own. But the clerk told me she was gone, she was in the hospital; her mother had come to get her."

The two men gazed at him in silence.

"Of course I called the hospital," Brix said, conscious of

POT OF GOLD

the gaps in his story. "They said she was alive, but no one could see her. And then today they told me she'd be fine, so I guess my prayers were answered. And that's all I know. Cross my heart."

He wished he could take back those last, flippant words, but they hung in the air, and the officers let the silence stretch out while they gazed steadily at him. "Miss Goddard had almost three milligrams of Halcion in her stomach," Detective Fasching said at last. "Do you know what Halcion is, Mr. Eiger?"

Brix nodded sadly. "Emma told me she took it; that's what I meant when I talked about the pills she took. It's a powerful drug and I told her so, but she said she needed it to sleep. I don't know how often she took it, but I always told her a glass of warm milk was better for her." He smiled, but neither of the policemen returned his smile. "Is three milligrams a lot?" Brix asked, thinking he should have asked that first.

"Enough to kill her if she hadn't been found as early as she was. The bottle that was found by her bed—"

"There was a bottle?" Brix cried.

The officer's mouth tightened in a quick flash of contempt. "The bottle was labeled for ten pills. There's no reason to assume she still had them all; she probably had taken some at other times, but even if she did, and even if she took them all, they wouldn't add up to three milligrams. The only conclusion we can reach is that someone gave her enough additional Halcion to make it a fatal dose."

Brix frowned. "I don't think she knows anyone in New York who would do that for her."

"We have an idea that you did it for her, Mr. Eiger," said Sergeant Janowski casually.

It took Brix a minute, but then he realized how perfect it was . . . and this idiot cop had just handed it to him. "Well, you're too smart for me," he said. "I guess you know what it is not to be able to turn a lady down." He smiled at them man to man. "I wouldn't have said anything if you hadn't

JUDITH MICHAEL

brought it up, but Emma did ask me for more of that stuff—she was always asking, as if she was stockpiling it. Well, I mean, I didn't think that at the time, but now, looking back ..." Once again he shook his head sadly. "I should have watched out for her more; she really was—is—a child, those tantrums and everything ..."

"So you provided her with Halcion," Sergeant Janowski said. "How much?"

"Oh, I don't know, over the last couple of months maybe ten, twenty pills."

"What color were they?"

"What?"

"What color were they?"

"I didn't really look. Aren't all pills white?"

"And I seem to have missed something here. Where did you get them?"

"You mean ... oh, well, a friend of mine gave them to me."

"Without a prescription?"

"Well, yes, he knew he could trust me."

"You told him they were for you?"

"Well, I ..."

"You said they were for you? You lied to him? You obtained a prescription drug by lying?"

Brix wondered if there was a penalty for that. He was feeling dizzy; bubbles of Scotch were scooting through his brain, bursting on the edges of his thoughts, making them skitter away. "I didn't lie. I never lie. I told him they were for a friend."

"I don't believe it," Detective Fasching said flatly. "Lenny, you believe this?" he asked Sergeant Janowski. "No pharmacist would give drugs for somebody he's never met. Of course it's illegal either way, but even the ones who sometimes give drugs to friends, when they're caught they say they don't give them for third parties. No way they'd do that is what they say."

POT OF GOLD

"You're right; he's lying," Sergeant Janowski said. "Maybe he stole them."

"Oh, for Christ's sake," Brix burst out, "I told him they were for a friend and he didn't have to worry because there was no way she'd ever take too—"

When he broke off his sentence, there was a long silence.

Finally Detective Fasching sighed. "Because you knew she wasn't the kind who'd do that."

"Well, I was wrong about her," Brix said a little wildly. "Women are hard to figure out; we all know that. And in a lot of ways she wasn't really honest, you know, she had her little games, little ways to pretend, to . . . to seem like one person when, really, you know, she was . . . another . . ."

As Brix's voice ran down, Sergeant Janowski stood up and moved close to him, looking down at him. "What we think is, you didn't do a damn thing for Miss Goddard, Brix; we think you did it *to* her."

Brix gave a little jump, hearing the officer use his first name. It frightened him; it changed everything in the room. He felt smaller, more at risk. They weren't treating him with respect anymore. Without thinking, he reached into his pocket for his coke, then, terrified, he yanked his hand out. But his fingers were twitching. God, I really need it, he thought.

"Now, what we want you to tell us," Detective Fasching said, "is how you got Emma Goddard to take three milligrams of Halcion without knowing it. It's not likely that you could force her to swallow twelve or more pills at once, so what else could you do? You could have gone to that pharmacist friend—we'll get to his name a little later—and built up your own supply. And then you could have crushed them and dissolved them in something. In what, Brix?"

Brix was shaking his head; his dizziness was worse and he was having trouble thinking straight. "No," he said, and hated the weak sound of it. He forced himself to speak more loudly and his voice came out like a bark. "I don't know what you're talking about."

"What did you dissolve the Halcion in? It doesn't dissolve well in water, so we probably can rule out the coffee, but it dissolves very well in alcohol. Which means the wine. Or the cognac."

"No. This is stupid. You don't know what you're—"

"The waiter saw you doing something with the cognac, you know. He told us about it."

"He did not! He didn't see a goddamn thing!"

"How do you know?" Detective Fasching said. He looked at Brix without expression, and Brix had no idea whether he was bluffing or not.

"You're accusing me of murder!" Brix cried, finally putting it all together in his mind.

"Attempted murder, Mr. Eiger, unless the young lady dies; then it would be murder. Of course you don't have to talk any more, without an attorney; you know that, don't you? Hold on." Sergeant Janowski took a small card from his pocket and read it aloud, rapidly and tonelessly. "You have the right to remain silent. Anything you say can and will be used against you in a court of law. You have the right to an attorney, and to consult with an attorney before questioning . . ."

Brix heard the reading of his rights, all six of them, as if they came from far off. He was breathing in short bursts. *Don't say anything.* The waiter hadn't seen him doing anything with the cognac; how could he? There was no way . . . *Don't say anything.* They were bluffing. But they seemed to know so much. Halcion didn't dissolve in water? Brix hadn't known that. It dissolved well in alcohol? He hadn't known that either. *But you're still smarter than they are; they're a couple of clods. Don't say anything.*

The silence went on and on. There was a roaring inside Brix's head, like the ocean surf, or an approaching storm. I'm afraid, Brix thought, and that scared him most of all: that these bozos could make him afraid. Somebody's got to help me, he thought. I'm all alone here. "I'm calling my father," he cried.

Sergeant Janowski pushed the telephone across the desk

POT OF GOLD

so Brix could reach it. No one spoke. "Dad," Brix said when Quentin answered. He could hear sounds of a party in the background; women laughing, ice cubes in glasses, a man and woman singing a song from some Broadway musical. "Dad, you've got to help me! I'm at the police station in Westport. I'm all alone here and they're accusing me of mur—attempted murder. I'm all alone here, Dad! You've got to come down and help me!"

The man and woman finished their song and the party guests applauded. The couple began another song. "Dad? Dad!"

"I'm not coming down," Quentin said tonelessly. "You got yourself into this; you'll have to get yourself out. You can't come running to me like a college kid; you're a grown man. You're on your own; you're not my son anymore."

The music was cut off as Quentin hung up. Brix started shivering. He held the telephone to his ear for another moment, trying to think.

"How soon will he be here?" one of the officers asked.

Brix hung up and turned around. "He won't. Fucking son of a bitch!" he burst out. Suddenly he realized he was about to cry. Christ, he couldn't cry! He sat with his head down, fighting back the tears that rose in his throat.

He couldn't let them think he was weak. He couldn't let them think he was stupid. He was smarter than all of them put together, and that included his father. He'd take care of himself. He didn't need anyone.

"We didn't finish with those rights I read you," Sergeant Janowski said. "Do you want me to read them again?"

"What for?" Brix growled. He was still pushing back tears and getting himself together.

"We have to know if you understand them. Did you understand them?"

"For Christ's sake, a baby could understand them!"

"Then"—he was reading from the card again—"keeping your rights in mind, do you wish to waive your right to remain silent and answer our questions?"

Brix gave an angry bark of laughter. "I've been answering your questions for half an hour."

"But you can stop anytime," Detective Fasching said. "You can remain silent."

Brix shrugged.

"Then sign here." Sergeant Janowski placed a form in front of Brix printed with the six rights and a space at the bottom for his signature and the names of witnesses.

Brix looked at it. He shouldn't sign anything, he thought. But then he glanced at the list of six rights, and thought, what the hell, they didn't have anything to do with him. They were for criminals. They were for people who didn't know anything. They were for people who weren't as smart as he was.

He scrawled his signature at the bottom and made a slashing check mark beside the "Yes" below the question about waiving his rights. "Now what?"

"You can still call a lawyer," Detective Fasching said.

Brix shook his head.

"You're sure?" Sergeant Janowski asked. "Even though you signed this, you could still—"

"I don't want a goddamn lawyer," Brix shouted. "Stop dragging it out. Get it over with!"

"Mr. Eiger does not want a lawyer," Detective Fasching said, and then the two officers began taking turns, like a vaudeville team tossing a ball back and forth. "He has refused to call one. That's right, Mr. Eiger?"

"Right, right, right. Why the fuck can't you just leave it alone?"

"Because we're not through. You haven't told us what you dissolved the Halcion in."

"I didn't dissolve it in anything, for Christ's sake; I didn't do anything!"

"Then how did she get three milligrams of Halcion in her stomach?"

"I told you, I—" Brix stopped as a thought came to him. He wondered why he hadn't thought of it earlier. "How do you know it was three milligrams? If Emma told you, then you ought to know that she took it. Nobody could know how much she took."

"The doctors know; they've had experience at this. It's an estimate, Brix, but it's probably pretty close, based on the estimated time since she took it, her symptoms, and the recovery time. What we still don't know is how you got her to take it."

"She did it herself! I told you I gave her—"

"You said she'd never take an overdose. You told the pharmacist that. Did you tell the pharmacist that?"

Brix was silent.

"Was there a pharmacist?"

Brix was silent.

"Well, there was somebody, wasn't there, Brix? Somebody gave you the pills and then you crushed them or ground them up. What did you do, go to this company you and your daddy own and use somebody's mortar and pestle? Do they still use mortars and pestles, like in the old days? Or did you go home and put it in your coffee grinder? Or your spice grinder? Or your Cuisinart? Probably wouldn't work in a Cuisinart, would it? I never tried to grind up pills in a food processor; can you tell us anything about that, Brix?"

"I don't know what you're talking about."

"How you ground up the Halcion before you put it in Miss Goddard's cognac or wine or whatever."

"I didn't do it. I didn't do anything."

"The waiter saw you."

"Nobody saw me!"

"He saw you. He wondered what you were up to, but he figured it wasn't his business. He thought it might be to help her sleep. He was right, wasn't he? Wasn't he, Brix?"

"I didn't do anything. Nobody saw me."

"We'll call him; he can be here in twenty minutes." Sergeant Janowski reached for the telephone. "A lot faster than your daddy. Does your daddy think you tried to kill Miss Goddard? Is that why he isn't coming down to hold your hand? Maybe we should talk to him, too." He was punching numbers on the telephone, very slowly. "We could go to his house if he doesn't want to come here. I think we should do that, talk to your daddy."

"Keep away from him!" Brix screamed. He grabbed the telephone from the officer. "I did it to help her sleep. That's what the waiter said, right? He was right; it was to help her sleep. That's all it was. I was always taking care of her; she couldn't take care of herself; she was a mess. And at dinner she was all worked up, screaming and yelling and I thought she had to get out of there and go to sleep and then she'd be fine."

Sergeant Janowski pried the telephone from Brix's grasp and put it on the desk. "Fine," he repeated. "Fine. Fine. Fine. What does that mean, Brix? Does it mean not able to talk about what you did at this company you and your daddy own?"

Brix jerked backward in his chair. "I don't know what you're—"

"Oh, sure you do, Brix, come on, we all know what's going on here. Miss Goddard found out you were involved in a crime and you had to kill her to shut her—"

"I wasn't! I wasn't involved in a crime! What the fuck is going on here? First you accuse me of putting stuff in her cognac and then you start talking about my company; you're so mixed up you don't know what the fuck you're doing."

"But you admitted you put the stuff in her . . . was it the cognac? I guess it was. You just said it was. And the test reports on PK-20—"

"You don't know anything about PK-20! Nobody outside the company does! That's all confidential!"

"We do, Brix. We know everything. And so does the State's Attorney. The test reports, the first ones, are in his office. So are those memos from your friend Kurt. Everybody but you knows everything, Brix. How does that make you feel? Left out? You won't be, if you just tell us the truth. Then we'll be together on this thing. Everybody knows, Brix. Everybody knows."

POT OF GOLD

"Does my dad know?" It came out in a whisper.

"The State's Attorney called him tonight."

Brix crumpled in his chair. It did not occur to him to doubt that the State's Attorney would call his father on Christmas night; it did not occur to him to doubt anything. He was alone and everybody knew why.

The roaring in his ears was louder; it sounded like a train coming through the room, aimed at him. Slouched in the chair, he looked up, to see what was happening. Nothing was happening. Sergeant Janowski sat on the windowsill; Detective Fasching sat on the desk. They were watching him with interest, and all the patience in the world. No one else was in the room. Nothing was in the room that would make a sound like the roaring inside his head. He was alone, with that awful noise. Alone, alone, alone, alone. Because of his fucking father.

"I did it because he told me to." The words were out and Brix shrank a little from them, but then he thought, the hell with it; it's true—it's goddamn truth—and he wouldn't come down and help me and why the fuck should I protect him anymore? I risked everything to protect him and the company, and he threw me out anyway. I don't owe him a goddamn thing anymore.

"You did what because he told you to?" Sergeant Janowski asked.

"Oh, you know, fixed the test reports. He wanted me to change the percentages of women who'd had problems, and up the ones who liked the stuff, it was an eye cream, and take out the one who went blind in one eye—I mean, nobody could really blame that on us, but my dad wanted it out anyway so nobody'd have anything to talk about. So I did all that; I did everything he told me. I always did what he told me, you know; whatever he wanted, so he'd be proud of me."

There was a pause. Detective Fasching stood up. "And you didn't want him to know that Emma had found out about it, is that it? You thought he'd be mad at you."

JUDITH MICHAEL

Brix nodded. The roaring in his ears had gone. He sat in absolute silence, slumped over in exhaustion.

"Okay, Brix, we'll want you to sign a statement," said Sergeant Janowski. "We'll have it in a minute."

Brix looked at him dully. What was he talking about?

"And here it is," the sergeant said as the young woman behind the screen handed him a sheaf of papers. "Wonderful things, computers; like instant replay in a football game. You'll want to read this before you sign it."

Brix looked at the pages in his hand. He ignored the first ones and went to the end, reading what he had said about his father. *I did everything he told me. I always did what he told me, you know, whatever he wanted, so he'd be proud of me.* Well, if anything did in the old man, it would be that. Brix didn't give a damn what happened to him as long as his old man got it, too. Lost the company. Went to jail. Went broke. Whatever. He'd see what happens when a man kicks out his son. He leaned forward and put the last page on the desk and signed it.

"You didn't read all of it," Detective Fasching said.

"I don't need to."

"You don't want to read the other pages?"

Brix shrugged.

"Then would you please initial each page at the bottom."

"For Christ's sake," Brix mumbled, but he went through them, scrawling his initials in the bottom corner of each page. Slowly he sat up, then stood, stretching his stiff muscles. "I'm going home now."

"I'm afraid you can't do that," Sergeant Janowski said. "We've charged you with attempted murder. Until a judge sets bail, you'll have to stay here."

"You can't do that! Who the hell do you think—You can't keep me here; I don't even have a lawyer!"

"I'm sure you will tomorrow," Detective Fasching said. "I'm sure you know many lawyers and they'll be glad to come down when you call. You could have called earlier, but

POT OF GOLD

you weren't interested." He took hold of Brix's arm. "So, at least until tomorrow, you'll stay here."

Brix stared at him. Slowly, through the bubbles of Scotch that still shot like little missiles through his brain, he understood that he was under arrest for the attempted murder of Emma Goddard, and that he would be spending Christmas night—*and how many other nights; Jesus Christ, how the hell did this happen?*—in jail.

Quentin sat in his study, working on strategy. His window looked out on Long Island Sound, gray and as still as glass this time of year, the sailboats put away, the swimmers gone. The beach was windswept and abandoned. Lonely, Quentin thought, and then wondered why that had occurred to him; he seldom had fanciful thoughts. March, he said to himself, to bring his mind back to his work; he wanted to have everything organized by January 2, when everyone was back at work, and that only gave him three days. "March," he said aloud. "Release the PK-20 line with extra advertising, with two models instead of one, about ten years difference in age, to reach different targets. We should have thought of that earlier. But first the series of memos for the company, maybe a newsletter, undermining the rumors without referring to them directly, since to repeat them would be, in a way, to legitimize them. . . ."

His ideas came swiftly. Occasionally he thought of Claire, of Emma, of Gina, of Brix, but not for long: he had a job to do. When the telephone rang, he reached for it absently, finishing a sentence, thinking of the next one.

"Quentin Eiger," he said, still writing.

"Mr. Eiger, my name is Hank McClore; I'm with the Connecticut State's Attorney's office."

Quentin's head came up. "And?"

"And I'm calling to tell you that, because of information received, we are going to court tomorrow morning to get an injunction enjoining you from making any shipments within Connecticut of a line of cosmetics containing a proprietary

JUDITH MICHAEL

ingredient known as PK-20, pending an investigation of the safety of that ingredient. I also have sent copies of our information to the FDA, and I would anticipate that they will enjoin you from interstate shipment of those cosmetics. The Connecticut Department of Health will join in our investigation, the purpose of which will be to look for evidence of fraud, criminal intent, and criminal conspiracy."

Quentin stared at bare trees, black slashes against a steel gray sky. "Our products are safe and always have been. You may have heard rumors—there are always rumors in any business—but you have nothing else." His voice barely contained his fury. "If you know what's good for you, you'll call off this witch-hunt before it goes a step farther. You may be able to terrorize small businesses, if that's what gives you kicks, but not Quentin Eiger; if you don't stop this, I warn you, I'll see to it that you're out of a job, and no one else will look at you."

"Mr. Eiger," McClore said, his voice oddly gentle, "we are in possession of memos reporting moderate to severe reactions, including a case of blindness in one eye, in test populations using PK-20 Eye Restorative Cream. Those memos reflect the findings of test reports that were collated within one week of the date on the memos. We also have a second set of test reports in which the damaging percentages were altered, and the case of blindness omitted entire—"

Quentin slammed down the telephone and burst from his chair, through the door of his study to the terrace facing the water and then onto the windswept beach. He strode on the hard-packed sand, his thoughts in tumult. His carefully constructed strategy, lying neatly on his desk, was worthless, a ruin. And he could think of nothing with which to replace it. How the hell had they gotten the test reports? He had assumed Brix had destroyed them; he should have made sure. But that should not have made any difference. Someone had gone into the files and found them and given them to the State's Attorney. Someone in his company, perhaps more

POT OF GOLD

than one, was a traitor. The son of a bitch; he'd find out who it was and—

But it didn't matter anymore. He walked along the water's edge, kicking small stones and twigs out of his way. He'd have to start again, with a new line of products, or, more likely, give PK-20 a new name, give the whole line a new name and a new image. Maybe he'd get away from the whole perpetual-youth gambit; try something completely new. Health, maybe. Everybody was a nut on health these days, and if they were convinced that certain creams and ointments would keep their skin, their hair, their nails, what the hell, all the cells in their body healthy, they could draw their own conclusions about youth. It was a whole new approach. Quentin slowed his steps. Nobody else was doing it. If he used the PK-20 line under some sexy name that implied perpetual health and got a couple of new models, he could do it in less than a year. Excitement filled him. He would save it all and end up with a better product than the first one, end up bigger than he'd ever anticipated.

Slowing, he became aware of how cold he was. He was wearing only lightweight pants and a sweater over an open-necked shirt, and the air was bitter. Shivering, he turned and jogged toward his house. He had a lot of work to do; he'd cancel his date for tonight and get to work. He glanced up to see how far his house was, and his steps slowed. Two men stood in the doorway of his study, watching him, and as he came closer, he recognized them: his partners, the two men who, with himself, made up his board of directors. What the hell were they doing here? They were never here in the winter.

"I thought you'd be in Florida," he said as he came up to them. "Or was it fishing in the Caribbean this year?" He shook their hands. "Sam, Thor; how are you?"

"We just got in," said Sam. The two of them backed into the study and Quentin went in and closed the door. He had sand in his shoes; it felt like stones, cutting into his feet. But to take off his shoes in front of the two men was impossible; to be in stocking feet would put him at a disadvantage.

"Well, sit down," he said, standing beside his desk. "What's going on?"

They remained standing. "We're sure you know by now," Thor said. "We heard some things about the company that bothered us and we called the State's Attorney; he said he'd be talking to you today. We assume by now he's called."

"You heard some things?" Quentin repeated. "From whom?"

"It doesn't matter. A lot of people are in on this by now. Has he called?"

Quentin nodded stiffly. "He doesn't have anything; he's fishing. But to save a lot of trouble, I've decided to rework the PK-20 line, modify it, rename it, bring it out with a whole new approach, a whole new message. I can do it within a year. I'll have some losses to make up, but that's nothing to worry about. There's nothing to slow me down—"

"It's always interested me, Quentin," said Thor thoughtfully, "that you never say 'we' when you talk about Eiger Labs. It's always 'I,' as if you do everything yourself."

Puzzled, Quentin frowned. "That's a peculiar thing to say. Of course I don't do everything myself. Though I must say there are days when it feels like that." He smiled, but the two men did not return his smile.

"We're asking you to resign as president of Eiger Labs," Sam said. "More accurately, we're removing you. We'll try to save the company; at the moment, it seems there isn't much to save. But whatever happens from now on will happen without you."

"You can't do that." Quentin's voice sounded desperate, and he stopped to take a breath. He felt the edge of the desk digging into his thighs; he had backed into it and was leaning against it for support. Sand dug into his feet like pieces of glass. He was still cold; even the jogging had not warmed him up. "It's illegal. We have an agreement, ninety days' notice of any change in corporate structure—"

"That agreement is null and void. We've talked to our lawyers and there's no question about our rights and responsibilities here, as trustees. You've imperiled this company by staking its financial well-being on a product that could make us liable for a criminal investigation five minutes after you ship it. Given that information, there's no way we'd allow you to remain as president and chief executive. You can ask your lawyers about this if you care to divulge all the details of why it happened. Or they'll read about it in the papers; we've been trying to think of a way to keep it quiet, but once the State's Attorney's office has it, it's probably impossible."

The papers. He hadn't thought of the papers. Or television, radio, magazines. He'd lose the company, and the media would gobble it up; there was nothing those bastards loved better than bringing down anyone with power and influence. He felt himself sink into the desk. A couple of half-assed memos, that was all. He'd lose the company. All his plans, his timetables, his scenarios for using the right people at the right times to increase his sphere of influence beyond the state . . . swept out, gone. He'd lose the company. No. He'd lost the company.

Jesus Christ, how the hell did this happen?

"Too bad you didn't consult us at the beginning," Sam said as he opened the study door. "We could have avoided this. Thor and I don't have a lot of sympathy with fraud; in fact, we've got zilch. You knew that, of course; that's why you never told us what was going on. Too bad." The two of them walked out; Quentin watched them walk along the terrace and disappear around the corner of the house, to the front walk, to the street, to their car, to their ownership of Eiger Labs.

Sons of bitches, he thought, but the thought was weak, like a tendril of smoke from a dying fire. It hung in the air for a moment, and then it was gone.

The Christmas tree was still up, its ornaments dusted by Hannah that afternoon, the floor beneath it swept clean of the needles that had dropped, strings of pear-shaped lights circling its branches like glowing stars. Emma sat in an armchair beside it, looking through the arch into the dining room as everyone cleared the table and carried dishes to the dishwashers in the kitchen. "I can help," she had said, but no one would let her. "Absolutely not," Hannah said. "Another time, but not tonight. This New Year's Eve is in your honor and you're not going to do a speck of work."

And so she was seated at the dinner table, between Claire and Alex, when all the cooking was done, and she was served all four courses—"like royalty," she said with a giggle—and then David, who had been looking at her with awe all through the meal, staggered by her beauty and romanticizing her brush with death, led her into the living room to sit beside the tree "and we'll do all the chores," he said, holding her hand as if it were made of glass.

And that was how she looked, Alex thought, watching his son stand beside her for a moment before returning reluctantly to the dining room. Whatever Emma did, her movements were tentative and fluid, with the slow grace of a dancer. She was thin, but in a way more beautiful than ever, with a kind of fragile translucence, almost as if one could see through her. Like an angel, Alex thought fancifully, if ever there were angels. But the sadness that had been in her eyes for so many weeks was gone, and when she smiled, it was the smile of a young woman who had thought she was lost and had now found her way home.

Emma saw him watching her and she smiled at him, remembering how she had liked his face from the first time she saw him, and thinking how nice it was to have him with them now, at ease and at home, with a look on his face when he watched her mother that brought the only pang to Emma's heart that she felt that whole New Year's Eve. She sat quietly in her chair, not thinking about very much, letting the warmth and love around her gather her in. Her mind felt washed clean, almost shiny, too smooth and slippery for anything to take hold. Thoughts and images swirled in and out, nothing lasting for more than a minute. The doctor had said she should not worry about that, she'd be back to normal in a little while, but it had been Claire who was worried; Emma had not minded at all. Emma felt fine. She could think about everything, but she could not think about anything long enough for it to hurt.

She watched everyone come in to sit near her and she smiled at them, loving them all. They didn't care whether she talked or not—and most of the time she didn't feel much like talking—they just loved her and treated her like royalty, and she loved them so much she thought she couldn't keep it all inside her: it was like the fire in the fireplace, dancing and lifting, curling all through her, warm and shining, filling her up, leaving no room for anything else.

Now, the dinner table cleared, the dishwashers humming, the fire leaping as Alex put on another log, they all came to the living room. Hannah sat in an armchair, Claire and Alex sat on one couch, Gina and Roz on the other. David sat on the floor, at Emma's feet. In the background, the "Ode to Joy" from Beethoven's Ninth Symphony was playing on the radio.

"Let me do the coffee," Roz said, and filled delicate china cups from a silver coffee service.

"My turn," Gina said, stopping Hannah from getting up, and she cut Hannah's cake. It was decorated with *Happy New Year* in curlicues of icing, and the inside was swirls of chocolate and white—"because it's been a year of both joy and sadness," Hannah said. Gina cut the slices with a silver and ivory cake cutter, putting them on French dessert plates that Claire had found in a tiny, exclusive shop on Madison Avenue in New York.

Claire looked at the exquisite china and silver, and then she looked at her beautiful, fragile daughter. The only thing that matters, she thought, and wondered how that could ever have been something that had to be demonstrated. For nine days she had been at Emma's side; Hannah had brought meals and the three of them had eaten together, and the rest of the time Claire stayed in Emma's room, sleeping at night on a cot she had ordered even before they came home from the hospital. During the day, when Emma slept, Claire worked on designs for a job her new company had gotten after she finished the Eiger contract; as soon as Emma woke, she put them aside, and they talked. They talked about everything that was in the past: all the years of Emma's growing up, her schools, her friends, the evenings and weekends at home when she and Claire had cooked together, played word games, listened to music, entertained friends. And they talked about Alex. "He's really in love with you," Emma said. "He keeps sort of leaning toward you, wherever you are. Are you in love with him?"

"Yes," Claire said.

Emma looked at her closely. They were sitting together, Claire on the edge of the bed, Emma propped against the pillows, wearing a silk bedjacket, content to sit perfectly still; she could sit for an hour or more without making a move. But now she leaned forward and covered her mother's hand with her own thin one. "You really are. You look different. Sort of . . . shiny."

"Shiny?"

"Like there's a light inside you. You know . . . happy."

"I am," said Claire simply. "But a lot of that is because you're here and getting well."

But that brought the conversation too close to what was wrong with Emma, and Emma would not talk about that or ask about it. If anyone began to talk about why she was sick, Emma turned her head away or talked about something else. "Are you going to marry him?"

"We haven't talked about it." Claire paused. "But we've talked about his coming to live here, and bringing David. How would you feel about that?"

"Oh. Everything would be different. *Everything's changing.* I said that once, a long time ago, didn't I?"

"Yes, you did, and good and bad things happened after that. But I think this will be wonderful, Emma. Different and wonderful."

"You haven't loved anybody, have you? Since my father."

"No. I thought I did, a couple of times, but it wasn't like this."

"So you really want them to live with us?"

"I want to live with Alex, and it's important to him that he and David live together. So, the answer is yes. I really want this. More than anything except your getting well."

"I might not be here anyway. I might go to college. So this way you and Hannah wouldn't be alone."

"Hannah won't be here, either. She's going to be a sort of housemother in a poetry center her friend is building."

"She can't! She lives with us!"

"You mean she's ours," Claire said with a smile. "It felt like that, didn't it, ever since she came? But she isn't, you know; she has her own life. And she wants to go where people need her."

Emma shook her head. "I don't like things to change."

"I'll always be here for you," Claire said gently. "This house will be here, and the door will always be open for you. And Alex will be part of the welcoming committee."

"And David. How old is he, anyway?"

"Fourteen."

"Oh, Mother, boys are such a pain at fourteen. Couldn't it just be Alex? I like him. I've never even met David."

"You will, on New Year's Eve. I think you'll like him. I think we'll all get along fine. He's a very nice fourteen."

Emma thought about it. "Whose room is he going to sleep in?"

"We haven't talked about it. I guess Hannah's. He certainly isn't going to be in here; your room stays just like this, for whenever you want to be here."

"Well." After a moment, Emma sat back against the pillows. "I guess. But I wish Hannah wouldn't go."

On other days, they talked about Gina and Roz, and about Roz's farm and Emma going there to ride the horses, and about what Emma wanted in the gardens around their house when it came time to plant, in the spring. They talked about college, beginning next fall; Emma wanted a place that was small, and not too far away, where she could take different courses without having to settle on any specialty right away. The idea of making decisions frightened her, although the doctor told her that would pass, too, after a while.

Some evenings, Alex joined them for dinner in Emma's room, and they talked about his writing and the theater group in the Village, and about David, and Alex told stories of places he and David went on weekend excursions around New York. Emma listened, and talked briefly, in small spurts of energy, about whatever Alex or Hannah or Claire wanted to talk about, anything except Brix and Eiger Labs and the Eiger Girl. The others waited for her to bring them up, but she did not.

"Give her plenty of time," the doctor had said. "And space. Don't crowd her. She'll deal with things in her own way, at her own pace. If she can't, she can get help from a psychologist, but I'd give her a chance to handle it herself."

Sitting in the chair beside the Christmas tree, Emma ate her piece of New Year's Eve cake and asked for a second helping, as she had at dinner. "I'm so hungry all the time," she said, holding out her plate.

"Well, don't apologize," said Hannah as she cut another slice. "It's about time you started appreciating my cooking."

"Now that you're leaving," Emma said.

"Well, you'll come and visit, and I'll cook for you."

"But I don't want you to go," Emma said. "It's nice, the three of us; I want it to stay that way. I want you to stay."

"It would change anyway," Alex said quietly. "We talked about that."

Emma looked at him sideways and said nothing.

"You remember," David said urgently. "I'm coming to live here, with you and your mom. Dad said he told you. You didn't forget. Did you? Or . . . don't you want me to?"

"No, it's all right," Emma said. "I do remember. You're a nice fourteen."

POT OF GOLD

"What does that mean?" David asked.

"It means we're going to get along fine," Claire said.

"And I won't be far away," Hannah said. "You can come for visits all the time. Things will be different, but not as different as they would be if I went really far away, to Singapore or some place like that. I did go away once, almost as far as Singapore, in fact, and my daughter was staying with my mother, and she said just what you said—'I don't want you to go; it's nice, the three of us; I want you to stay'—but I had to go, and then when I was gone, she missed me so much she carried on every night on the telephone. So what I did was, I sent her special packages of food and presents, lovely little dolls, lace-trimmed blouses, exotic earrings, wonderful presents, and I wrote a poem or a story to go in each package, so it was as if I were there every day, talking to her, and she wasn't so unhappy that I had to be somewhere else. You see, Emma, we can always find ways to be with people we love."

"That's nice," Emma said dreamily. "You could write stories for me, too."

"Well, I will. But you're coming to visit, too. As often as you want."

As Hannah talked on about visits to New York, Claire watched her with narrowed eyes. She glanced at Alex and saw her doubts mirrored on his face. "When did that happen?" he murmured, leaning close to her.

"I don't know," Claire replied; it was what she had been asking herself. When, in the long series of adventures Hannah had told them about—a love affair on a cruise, and another, long one with a real estate magnate, and being a caterer and a bouncer, and losing her daughter, and traveling in Africa and teaching in St. Louis—did she go somewhere almost as far as Singapore, long enough to send her daughter special packages of food and presents, stories and poems?

"I don't think it happened," Claire murmured to Alex. "I think she made it up to make Emma feel better about her leaving us. She always tries to make us happy if we're unhappy."

"Then what about the other stories?" Alex asked.

"I don't know. She told them with such vivid detail and such passion . . . and the death of her daughter! No one could make that up, not the way she did."

A small smile was on Alex's lips. "But all of them had a reason."

Slowly, Claire nodded. "She gave them to us, like special gifts, and we used them in our own ways, to help ourselves." She was still watching Hannah, whose lively, crinkled face was looking at Emma with love and laughter as she spun tales of the adventures they would have in New York.

After a moment, Claire looked at Alex and smiled. "It doesn't matter whether they're true or not. I'd never ask her. Fairy godmothers do what they have to do, any way they can, and we shouldn't question them. And when their job is done, they leave, to go someplace else where they're needed. Just like Hannah."

Alex chuckled. "I remember when you told me she was your fairy godmother. I thought it was a charming fantasy. But if anyone fits the fantasy, she does. Did you ever tell Hannah that's what you think she is?"

"Yes. I think it amused her. You know, when she first came to us, she said she was my cousin, and we—" Claire stopped, a small frown between her eyes.

"Do you think she really is?"

"I don't know. It doesn't matter. But if it ever became an issue, I'd adopt her."

Alex laughed. Hannah looked their way. Her bright eyes met theirs in a long look. "I love you all," she said. "There's no one in the world I love as much as I love this family. And when you come down to it, that's the only thing that counts, isn't it?"

"Love and health," Gina said.

"And money," Roz added dryly. "If love and health are first, money has to be second."

POT OF GOLD

"I don't know," Claire said. "There's such a thing as too much money, I think."

"Only when people become careless," Alex said. "The trouble with having a lot of money is that it becomes too easy to forget how tough life can be."

"You mean that there are hungry people in the world?" Hannah asked. "But we never forgot that; we give money to all kinds of groups and organizations and people. Like the Mortons; I'm sure Claire told you about them. We've kept in touch with them, and their little boy's leukemia is in remission, he's getting better, and they've even paid back some of the money."

"I think Alex meant that it's easy to forget how people can hurt each other," said Claire.

Her hand was in his, and Alex tightened his clasp. "They forget how hard we have to work at relationships, protecting the ones that are good for us and recognizing the ones that aren't. Given enough money, too many people begin to operate on the principle that money, by its weight and abundance and importance, can cure everything. If they're in a bad relationship, they can buy their way out of it. If they're in a good one, they don't have to work at it because money keeps it going."

"But a lot of the time that's true," Roz said.

"It didn't keep your marriage going," said Hannah.

"Well, it doesn't always work, but you can't just say that money isn't important, because it is."

"But important for what?" Alex asked. "What money does best is pile up possessions. It's a little like bribing the gods; give them enough and they'll make your life rosy again."

Roz shook her head. "Money buys freedom. You're not free if you have to spend all your time making enough money to get from one day to the next."

"It's just a lot more fun having it than not having it," Gina said. "And I don't believe Claire ever forgot about people or relationships or anything else. I don't think she ever thought she could bribe the gods with her lottery money, either."

"I thought our worries were over," Claire said. "I thought we weren't vulnerable. I thought we couldn't be touched."

"Well, we know that's wrong," Hannah said. "But you wouldn't want to give all the money back, would you? And go back to work?"

"Well, you couldn't, not for the same guy," David said. "I heard about him on the news, on TV, it was in the paper, too, that guy you used to work for. Eiger? There was this story that he said his son—his name is Brix; it's really a creepy name, isn't it?—he covered up some tests they did, some cream that people use on their eyes, or anyway, women do, and they were getting sick and somebody went blind, well, anyway, in one eye, I guess, and his son covered it up, and he doesn't work there anymore." He looked up from his position at Emma's feet and noted the intense interest on the faces of everyone and went on, enjoying the attention. "And then they said his *son* blamed *him,* you know, his father, for the whole thing; he said his father was the one who covered it up, or anyway, told him to do it for him. And his father isn't head of the company anymore, and it looks like there's no more company, either. And everybody's fighting with everybody else on TV, and I guess in the newspaper, too, which is really weird."

"What did Brix do?" Emma asked.

"Well, like I said, he—" David looked up and realized she was not speaking to him. She was looking at her mother. The vague, wandering look in her eyes was gone; she was focusing on Claire, waiting for what she would say.

"He tried to make you sick," Claire said immediately. She had thought about this moment and had decided what she would say. "So you'd be frightened and not tell anyone about the memos you'd seen."

"But what did he *do?*"

"He put a quantity of Halcion in something you drank at dinner. Enough to make you sick."

512

"But you thought I was going to die."

"I didn't know, Emma—"

"He didn't want me to be sick. He wanted me to die."

David looked at Alex. "You told me not to talk about it. When I showed you that story in the paper—"

"It was in the newspaper?" Emma asked. "What did it say?"

"That it was attempted murder and he was trying to get out on bail."

"That's enough, David," Alex said.

Claire sat on the arm of Emma's chair. She put her arm around her and held her close. "He said it was to help you sleep."

"But you don't believe that. You think he tried to kill me. You never liked him."

"That doesn't mean I'm sure he tried to kill you. I think he may have tried to frighten you."

"You never liked him. You *knew* him, better than I did. He wanted me to die. He told me he hated me. And I said . . . something . . . I told him . . . oh, why can't I remember? Something about ruin." She was looking into the distance. "That he'd ruined everything. And the waiter was there; I told him I was finished. And I ran away. I fell, outside, and somebody helped me up."

"You told us you hadn't taken any pills that night," Claire said. "We asked you, in the hospital, and you always gave the same answer. That you hadn't taken any pills."

"I didn't. Why would I? They were only to help me sleep and we were going to dinner. And I was happy. Brix loved me . . ." Tears ran down her cheeks. David yanked out a handkerchief and put it in her hand, closing her fingers around it. She held it, but she did not try to wipe the tears away. She snuggled against her mother, nestling into the curve of her body. She looked up and met Claire's eyes. "He wanted me to die. Why does that happen?"

Claire shook her head. "I don't know. Some people are capable of evil acts. Others aren't. It has nothing to do with how much you love a person, or how much you try to please him; there are things inside him that you can't touch. And if someone is capable of evil and can't control his furies, he's beyond the reach of people who care for him, even when he's behaving in a quiet way; maybe even a loving way."

"I didn't know he was like that," Emma whispered.

"Maybe he didn't know it himself."

"Where is he?"

"He was arrested; he admitted putting the Halcion in your drink, so he was refused bail. I don't know what will happen next."

"He's in jail?"

"Yes."

"He'd hate that."

"I'm sure he does."

Emma's tears had stopped. "Maybe he couldn't love anybody. I mean, it's like he couldn't walk by himself if he was missing a leg, or pick up things if he didn't have his fingers, so maybe he's missing something inside him, so he can't love people. He just can't. He's sort of a cripple."

"I think that could be right," Claire said, her heart aching for Emma's pain, that she had not been able to bring out in Brix the loving person she offered to him, the person she imagined him to be.

Emma nodded. "He was so nice . . . sometimes."

And that, Alex thought, was Emma's epitaph for Brix Eiger.

The room was quiet for a long time. Then Hannah stood and began to clear the dishes. "I'm going to make more coffee. And we have champagne. Do you know what time it is?"

"Time for Emma to be in bed," Gina said.

"Oh, no, it's New Year's," Emma said. "I want to stay. I'm getting better, Gina. I'm almost well. And I'm happy."

There was a sigh in the room, like a soft breeze, of relief and gladness. Oh, thank you, thank you, thank you, Claire said silently, sending up her own inchoate prayer for all that was good, for the people in that room, and for all that they had together.

"Claire, *would* you give the money back?" Roz asked.

"No," Claire said. "There are so many things I want to do, people I want to help, Emma's college, my own company ... I don't want to give that all up. I like having money; I'll just have more respect for it from now on. I always knew it couldn't do everything; now I'll believe it."

"Well, *that's* a good way to begin the new year," Hannah said. She stood beside the fireplace, holding the silver coffeepot. "Quentin never learned that, did he, and I'd say that's his real tragedy. Not that he can't sell a bunch of cosmetics; not that he's lost his company. What's really tragic is that he doesn't love his son, and he doesn't think that matters. He has no family, no nothing. Dear me. He reminds me of a man I once worked with who didn't care about anything but his own importance. He—"

"Claire and I will clean up," Alex said, standing up, and while Hannah talked, he and Claire put cups and saucers and dessert plates on trays and carried them into the kitchen. The room was warm and quiet, the only light a small lamp in the breakfast room. They set the trays down and came together in the shadowy darkness, holding each other. "This has been an amazingly chaste courtship," Claire murmured.

Alex chuckled. "Between my son and your daughter, we never got near a bed. I think we should get out of here and see what we can do on our own."

Claire laughed. "I'd like that."

"What about Emma? You don't want to leave her alone."

"She'll stay with Roz and Gina. She loves them and there's no better place for her right now than the farm."

"And Hannah will go off to her Forrest. And you and I will go ... where would you like to go?"

"Your apartment in New York."

"Really? I was thinking of Hawaii. Kauai in January can be glorious. Or Puerto Vallarta. Also warm and beautiful. Choose one."

"Either one. I just want to be with you."

They kissed, a long kiss that contained within it the friendship of those weeks when they had worked together in Claire's studio, and the closeness of the past terrible and joyful days when they had clung to each other and to the awareness of each other, always close by: a new wonder for Claire and a discovery, for Alex, that the love he had known and lost could be created anew, in a new way, and once again give him a home.

Claire pulled back just enough to look at him, to feel the wonder of his closeness, and of tomorrow and the next day and the next, a future shared after so many years alone. *The birthday of my life is come, my love is come to me.* A long time ago a woman named Christina Rossetti had written that line in a poem, and Claire had cut it out and tucked it into her wallet. "The birthday of my life," she murmured to Alex. "I never thought it would come to me. I never thought *you* would come to me."

"I love you," he said. "My heart's ease; my soul's delight. We are going to have such a wonderful time."

Claire thought of Emma and David, and the house that sheltered all of them. Her body was alive with the warmth of Alex's arms around her and his strong shoulders within her embrace, and she knew a sense of richness she had never known before. She thought of Forrest Exeter, standing by the fireplace in her study, his resonant voice filling the room. *We are surrounded by wonders and possibilities ... my God, what a blessing to be alive, to embrace the infinite wonders of this magnificent world.*

"A world of infinite wonders," she said to Alex. "Waiting for us. All the discoveries we haven't yet made ..." She kissed him and spoke with her lips brushing his. "Happy New Year, my love."